THE WIVES

Rosemary—The prim beauty known as "Mrs. President." A colorful array of pills keeps her going . . . until her husband invites a young woman into their bedroom. . . .

Joanna—She has money, talent, and Multimedia's sexiest man. But it all blows apart on the night she sees a shocking secret rendezvous. . . .

Lizabeth—Her appetite for men is insatiable—but her husband's got surprises of his own. . . .

Vanessa—Her bright chatter hides a poor, bitter past—and a driving, ferocious ambition. . . .

Maureen—Insecure and gauche, she drowns her fears in gin—and hopes that her husband *won't* be promoted. . . .

Janet—She knows how the game is played—and she'll play down and dirty to protect her husband's image. . . .

Books by Parley J. Cooper

Dark Desires
Devil Child
Golden Fever
Marianne's Kingdom
Moonblood
My Lady Evil
Reverend Mama
San Francisco
The Shuddering Fair One
The Wives

Published by POCKET BOOKS

THE WIVES

PARLEY J. COOPER

PUBLISHED BY POCKET BOOKS NEW YORK

Distributed in Canada by PaperJacks Ltd., a Licensee
of the trademarks of Simon & Schuster, Inc.

Another *Original* publication of POCKET BOOKS

POCKET BOOKS, a division of Simon & Schuster, Inc.
1230 Avenue of the Americas, New York, N.Y. 10020
In Canada distributed by PaperJacks Ltd.,
330 Steelcase Road, Markham, Ontario

ISBN: 0-671-81627-6

First Pocket Books printing March 1987

10 9 8 7 6 5 4 3 2 1

POCKET and colophon are registered trademarks
of Simon & Schuster, Inc.

Printed in Canada

For Jack Osterritter
and Eve Wengler,
with appreciation.

PART 1

Chapter One

HOPE THE MID-DAY FOG had rolled in under the Golden Gate and created a spiraling mushroom over Alcatraz. By early evening it had enshrouded the entire city. With the fog came an accompanying chill and a temperature that was remarkably low for San Francisco in October. The hills, with their winding brick streets, were dangerously wet, and the gutters gurgled as if from the residue of a storm. The cable car traveling up Powell Street, usually crowded until well past nine, was nearly empty, the few passengers huddled inside the glass cage for the little warmth to be found there.

Hope Ingress sat in a front corner of the glass cage, her collar pulled up about her neck and her arms folded across her body as if to squeeze off the chills that shook her. She was a tall woman with grey eyes and high cheekbones. Her cheeks were flushed from the cold, and tiny beads of moisture glistened on her dark brows and eyelashes. Her blue evening gown had been moderately expensive—though not extravagant, considering her salary as executive secretary for Multimedia. That afternoon her hairdresser had talked her into a more fashionable style, but the weather was already causing it to lose its body. No matter, she thought. She hadn't liked it anyway; it emphasized her height and made her face appear gaunt. Tilting her head, she glanced down at her shoes and discovered the dampness had darkened the blue satin.

The cable car lurched and began its steep climb of Nob Hill. High above, seemingly suspended in midair, the lighted glass elevator of the Fairmont Hotel rose eerily into the fog.

Hope felt a sense of dread.

At the intersection of Powell and California she would leave the cable car and walk to the banquet hall to mingle with the other Multimedia employees at their annual party. Justin Wade would be there—and Justin's wife. Hope would smile, would dance with every man except Justin. She would chatter with the other secretaries and laughingly thwart any advances made by the men.

It would be sheer hell.

This would be her second annual party since coming to Multimedia. Last year's still haunted her.

Closing her eyes, she thought, I've been his mistress for thirteen months and eleven days. It surprised her that she could no longer remember the hours, and told herself with bitter humor that her efficiency was waning.

The clanging of the cable car bells brought her from her thoughts.

"California Street," the conductor bellowed.

Hope opened the door of the glass cage and fought the wind whipping about her skirt. Damned miserable weather for a party, especially a party she did not wish to attend.

But Justin had made her promise, saying her absence would be questioned. True, it might have been, but she had set about manufacturing excuses months in advance. Why should she submit herself willingly to

4

being trapped in the same room with her lover's wife. Last year she had been less involved with him and yet the casual glances and dancing embraces between Justin and Joanna had filled her with envy. And Justin—he had remained so oblivious to her presence. He had perfected the images of successful executive and devoted husband.

She stepped to the wet street and dashed to the curb to avoid being splashed by a passing car. Hesitating, she stared down the hill at the fog swirling about the buildings; they looked ghostlike. She breathed deeply and could smell the dampness and the aroma of Chinese food from a nearby restaurant. She imagined she could also smell her own dread.

Steadying herself, she hurried on to the banquet hall and entered before she could change her mind.

In contrast to the outside gloom, the interior of the banquet room could have been the end of the rainbow. Even that magical kingdom would have been dulled by the glitter of the gowns and jewelry of Multimedia's executive wives. They held court, as they had last year, from a long table in the center of the room. The awesome six—or reigning royalty—they were called by the employees.

Hope stepped to the side of the doorway out of the mainstream of arrivals and stared at the center table. She was struck by the theatricality of the setting. The lighting had to have been carefully arranged. It could be no accident that the tiny spots from the ceiling fell at spaced intervals only in front of the wives. The husbands in their dark tuxedos were lost in the shadows while their spouses were glorified in illuminated splendor.

But, Hope decided, it was as it should be. It was the wives the employees wanted to see, not the bosses they saw every working day. The wives—almost legendary because of society page coverage and company gossip—most of them wealthy, all of them oddly regal. They had come to be seen and to lend a somewhat detached humanization to the cold, businesslike auras of their husbands. The wives—they stared out from their spotlighted cones with meaningless smiles. Their movements always seemed to be made with deliberate thought, their words carefully chosen. It was a well-known fact that the wives had power. They could make or break an up-and-coming employee with a whispered word to their husbands. The hopeful and the ambitious ringed the darker area about the center table like court jesters vying for recognition.

Hope, herself, found the wives a curiosity.

Justin had told her they had formed close-knit friendships and met frequently. Sounding almost paranoid, he had told her the wives—Joanna included—had devised something of a social chain of command similar to that at Multimedia. Mrs. Marston was called *Mrs. President* and the others had taken titles corresponding to the positions their husbands held with the corporation. Hope thought it ludicrous, perhaps a neglected wife's way of chiding her husband. Yet, remembering this, Hope likened the arrangement at the center table to that of the conference room at Multimedia. The wives were seated almost as their husbands would be there. The only thing missing was herself, or some male counterpart, sitting at left center taking shorthand.

The orchestra began playing a slow version of a Beatles tune. Couples were moving onto the dance floor.

Forcing the corners of her mouth into a smile, Hope came down the stairs of the mezzanine and, as she thought of it, into the court of the executive wives.

ROSEMARY

BEHIND THE MASK of self-assurance Rosemary Marston presented to the world lurked a woman of nagging insecurities.

It was inbred, she thought.

Her mother had suffered from the same malady, and at thirty-two, after a morning-long visit to Elizabeth Arden, returned home to snuff out her misery with an overdose of barbiturates. She had made a beautiful, serene corpse, and Rosemary, then thirteen, had stood beside her mother's coffin and vowed to be like her in as many ways as possible. She had succeeded beyond her expectations.

Although she had survived five years longer than her mother, at age thirty-seven Rosemary was addicted to pink and blue, green and orange capsules. They managed to push her from one day to the next.

She was vain, but even her vanity, as vanity must, had begun to crumble in the reality of her mirror. Her porcelain-like beauty had begun to fade and makeup would no longer conceal the tiny lines edging outward from the corners of her eyes. The flesh of her throat had begun to sag, and no cosmetic discovery would remove the discoloration which had appeared overnight on the once flushed points of her cheekbones. Her doctor had blamed the pills and she had blamed her doctor for supplying them. Still, she insisted on a new prescription before leaving his office.

Yet Rosemary remained a beauty. Her face, once seen, was seldom forgotten. Her eyes were large, dark, and expressive and hinted at an intelligence greater than she chose to reveal. They could chastise and then forgive in one quick flickering of the lashes.

It was her eyes that Keith had fallen in love with

first. He had told her his first wife had had dark eyes like hers, but even in the throes of passion they were no more expressive than those of a cow at her cud. She had winced, regretting that Keith so often reverted to his farm upbringing for analogies.

His first wife had brought him position and enough wealth for him to make a fortune five times her own. Rosemary had brought him only herself, a woman anxious to please and starving for a protector with the strength and understanding of her father. In the divorce settlement, his first wife had taken half of Keith's fortune, and his most prized possession, a vintage Rolls-Royce, which she had immediately had gutted and set in her garden as a planter for red and orange nasturtiums. Rosemary drained only his strength.

During her bad periods, days when even the pills failed to help, she demanded his consideration for the slightest action. She never planned a meal or bought an article of clothing or arranged a bouquet of flowers without his approval. She hated Multimedia because it excluded her. She would quiz him about the most intricate details of his business until she understood them. She would give him advice, unasked, and then be shattered if he did not follow it. When she was angry with him she was incapacitated. If he should return her anger, she became hysterical.

Her greatest fear was losing him, and yet she knew she was driving him away.

Should he leave her, she swore she would follow her mother's avenue of escape.

Tonight she was miserable and considering the number of pills left in her bottles.

Her misery had nothing to do with Multimedia's annual party. She enjoyed parties and liked being surrounded by nameless, faceless people. Unsure of herself in small groups, she was at ease in crowds, where serious conversation was an impossibility and she had only to look the part of the wealthy San Francisco socialite. Her frequent meetings with the other executive wives were an exception. She never felt uncomfortable in their presence. To them, she was *Mrs. President.* They sought her favors and dared not offend her. She had a surface understanding of the workings of her husband's corporation (and was capable of pretending a broader knowledge). She could listen to the wives prattle about their husbands' successes and dilemmas, and sense their ambitions. She knew they were using her to further their husbands' careers, but she did not object. It gave her a sense of security. They would not abandon her so long as she remained *Mrs. President.*

Tonight, she was grateful to be among her friends. Even if their conversations were limited and spoken across their husbands, it took an edge off her misery. Had she been alone with them she might have sought their advice. At countless lunches and teas she had listened to them discuss sex. She had remained aloof, a verbal voyeur, and had never participated in those conversations. She knew that Lizabeth Williams's husband liked his sex in the mornings, Maureen Sterne's Jake liked it often, and Joanna Wade's not often enough. Justin Wade was extremely well-endowed and Merrill Williams had a wart in an unlikely place that Lizabeth refused to allow him to have removed. Janet Linquist had never had an orgasm and Vanessa Kirkman had had an affair with her analyst. Rosemary had never joined their "risqué" conversations, because there had been nothing unusual in her sex life to relate.

Lifting her eyes from the table, she glanced at Keith. He was fifty and looked forty. He was not, she imagined, as wildly handsome to her friends as he was to her. His eyes were deeply set, blue and alert, and his hair had greyed at the temples with distinction. Although he had developed a slight paunch, his body was solid and trim. He stood six feet tall and proudly weighed the same one hundred and seventy pounds he had weighed at twenty. His shoulders were broad, his waist narrow, and his buttocks slim. The sight of him naked excited her as much today as it had ten years ago on their wedding night. No, she told herself, she had to learn to be progressive—*before their wedding night*. She had never questioned their sexuality because she had thought there no reason to—she was pleased and had assumed he was also.

Until tonight.

Keith caught her eye and smiled, and she averted her gaze. She felt his knee brush her leg. Reassurance? She shifted her position to prevent him from touching her. She had been forced to surrender to his demands, but she need not let him feel she would accept the perversion graciously. If indeed, when it came to performance, she would be capable of accepting it at all.

"Many couples do it," he had told her. "It brings them closer together and makes their marriages more meaningful."

Never suspecting that he had become bored with her sexually, she had not felt their marriage needed more meaning. When he had talked to her before tonight's party she had been stunned. She now realized how careful his timing had been. He had understood the importance of the party to her and knew she would not allow herself her accustomed hysteria. If she had cried, it would have streaked her makeup. If she had fainted, it would have creased her gown. She had merely sat, stunned and dry-eyed, scarcely comprehending what he had told her.

After, she had taken a pill from her diamond-studded pillbox and washed it down with the dregs from a martini glass, not knowing or caring what she had taken, only that the action had forced her into movement. He had demanded an answer and had hovered above her, waiting. She had understood that if she refused, her marriage was doomed: *Mrs. President* would be reduced to nothing more than a frightened woman unable to cope with life by herself.

"Either that, or I take a mistress," he had said coldly.

She had closed her eyes and the image of her mother in her coffin had been stamped on the insides of the lids. Until he had snatched the pillbox from her hand she had been unaware that she had opened it again. The snap of the catch had been deafening. The French porcelain mantel clock had been wheezing like an old man struggling for breath. Outside, the foghorns blared as if they had been on the front lawn instead of far below on the bay.

The silence between them seemed to last an eternity before he said, "Which is it to be, Rosemary?"

"Not a mistress," she had answered weakly.

Then he had whisked her into her wrap and out the door to the waiting limousine before reaction had set in. Facing her friends and the guests in the banquet room, she had buried her misery beneath a sham of gaiety and charm. She chatted, she smiled, she laughed. It was expected of her; she was *Mrs. President,* the reigning queen of Multimedia's annual party. None of the wives noticed that she laughed a bit loudly, nor did they imagine the feat of sheer determination it required to prevent each laugh from turning into a piercing scream.

Rosemary let her gaze sweep the women at the table.

What would they say if she told them her husband would one night in the near future introduce a third person into their bedroom to bring them closer together, to make their marriage more meaningful, to prevent her from following her mother into an early grave?

Keith leaned toward her and touched her arm. "Shall we dance, my dear?"

The others had heard; she could not refuse.

He held her arm too firmly as he led her onto the dance floor. She thought his fingers might leave a bruise. Look at *Mrs. President!* She's wearing diamonds and emeralds and silks—and bruises! "You're hurting me," she told him. He loosened his grasp and she instantly wished he had not. The pain had been a stabilizer.

The orchestra was playing a waltz. Keith's arms left her for one brief, terrifying moment and then encircled her and drew her against the protective curve of his body. Remarkably, her feet began to move to the music without command from her brain. She stared at the gold studs on Keith's shirt. He smelled of his favorite shaving lotion and of gin. Always a poor dancer, he was humming to keep from losing the beat of the music.

Rosemary looked up into his face. "Have you . . . have you already found this woman? this savior of our marriage?"

"Yes, my dear."

Before she could say more he began whirling her about the floor to the crescendo of the waltz.

JOANNA

LEANING TOWARD JUSTIN, Joanna Wade asked, "Who is that woman who keeps staring at me?"

Justin followed her gaze, shrugged, and asked, "What woman?"

"The tall woman in the blue gown. The one taking a drink from the waiter."

"Oh, that woman. She's a secretary at Multimedia."

"Your secretary?"

"Mine, and Marston's, and Williams's. Her name is Ingers, or Ingress. She's the executive secretary. Very efficient."

"And you're not even certain of her name?"

"I always call her sweetheart."

Laughing, Joanna accepted a cigarette from him, puffed without inhaling and blew the smoke in the direction of Rosemary's empty chair. "Why do you suppose she keeps staring at me?"

"Probably trying to determine if you're good enough for me."

"From her expression, I'd say she's decided I'm not," Joanna murmured.

"She's probably envious because you're so beautiful," he murmured.

"She's very attractive. No reason for jealousy," Joanna mused.

"A bit too tall," Justin said critically. "Definitely not my type."

"And what type is that?"

"My type has to be the most beautiful woman in the room. She has to be wealthy and talented and fascinating. In other words, my wife." He leaned forward and brushed his lips against her cheek. "Come on, let's dance. I want to show you off to all these envious bastards."

13

"But the number's almost over," she protested.

"Then we'll make our own music."

As they made their way to the dance floor, Joanna noticed Justin glance in the secretary's direction. She made a mental note to bring the woman's name up at the next meeting of the wives. She wanted to know all there was to know about a woman who found her so intriguing she would pass up four invitations to dance.

MAUREEN OVERWEIGHT AND INCAPABLE of achieving a flair for dressing, Maureen Sterne always felt a misfit in the presence of the other wives. She liked them—all except Lizabeth—but she always felt inferior to them. She had gone so far as to hire a fashion consultant, but even he had difficulty draping her form with sophistication. Then there was her hair; it was graying rapidly, and she refused to dye it. She was forty-two, glad of it, and was not about to conceal the facts of age. Jake was always arguing with her, pleading with her to spend more time at the beauty salon, but she had three children to raise. The children were more important to her than her beauty or her social life. Only this evening Jake had accused her of trying to ruin his career by her refusal to look after herself properly.

Men's careers at Multimedia are made or broken by their wives, he had told her.

She had found that horrifying. She did not want to make or break any man's career, even her husband's. She only wanted to be left alone in her house in Atherton with her children, her cooking and cleaning. She considered herself a simple woman with simple tastes and concerns. The wives were much too sophisticated for her comfort, although she had developed friendships in the past three years since Jake had transferred from the Midwest to be a producer with Multimedia. Of the other executive wives, she was fondest of Rosemary Marston, sensing a bond that she could not explain.

Tonight, from her end of the table, she had sensed an urgency and a quiet desperation in Rosemary's laughter. It had been this observation that had kept her from drinking to excess—another of her faults, that sent Jake into fits of scolding when they were alone.

When most of the couples were dancing and Keith Marston had wandered away from the table, Maureen brought her half-empty cocktail glass to the middle of the table and slipped into the chair beside Rosemary. "Lovely party," she said. "Much better than last year."

Rosemary looked at her hazily. "Yes, lovely," she said without enthusiasm. Her pupils were slightly dilated.

"But you're not enjoying it," Maureen observed.

"Of course I am," Rosemary objected. "I'm the hostess. That requires me to enjoy it, doesn't it?" She glanced about the crowded room. "Or does anyone really give a damn?"

Maureen felt something bordering on panic. She had never known Rosemary to be in such a mood. It was obvious she had either had too much to drink or had taken one of the many pills she carried about in her purse. Maureen saw Jake watching them from across the room where he was talking with two men from the company. She felt a conflict of responsibilities; she did not want to leave Rosemary alone and yet if she remained and Rosemary's strangeness erupted into a scene, Jake would never forgive her. *The old man will never forget you were with his wife when she made an ass of herself at the annual party.* He would again accuse her of attempting to ruin his career, of trying to drag him back to the days when he had been a small-time producer at a local television station . . . *because she had deluded herself into thinking they had been happier before his advancement.*

Screw him, Maureen thought. She had been happier!

"I give a damn," she said quietly to Rosemary.

Rosemary looked at her again, still having difficulty focusing. "Yes, you would, Maureen," she murmured. "You give a damn about people—all people. If I were not supposed to be such a grand and proper lady I'd swear that of all these sonofabitches you're the only one with a functioning heart." Fortunately, her voice had been kept low enough not to be over-heard above the music and chatter.

"I'm certain all your friends care very much about you," Maureen told her.

"Do you really believe that?" Rosemary pressed.

Maureen nodded.

"Then you're extremely naive," Rosemary said. "My friends—better known as The Wives—and you're an exception to this—are interested in them-selves and what I might do for their husbands. None of them think or care about me as an individual." Rose-mary lowered her heavily mascaraed lashes and stared at the diamond rings on her fingers. "But then why should they?"

Maureen reached for her drink and realized her hand was trembling.

Rosemary must have noticed also because she said, "I'm not going to embarrass you by creating a scene." She laughed softly. "I only lost control for a moment. So unlike me. At least in public. Do you have a cigarette?"

Maureen lit a cigarette and placed it between Rosemary's slender fingers. "Do you want to talk about it?" she asked quietly. "We could lunch tomorrow."

"Talk about what?" Rosemary asked.

"About what's upsetting you."

Rosemary flinched. "Call me," she said after a moment's thought. She straightened herself and visibly fought to change her mood. "But it's not so important, not really. Don't you have moments when you give yourself up to depression or self-pity?"

"Often," Maureen admitted.

"That's all this has been, a momentary depression," Rosemary said, the statement belied by the expression behind her dark eyes. "Strange that it should happen in the midst of this lovely party. As you said, much better than last year's." She was suddenly nervous and wanted the incident forgotten. "That's what comes of being deserted by all the males," she said gaily. "Where have they gone to? Where's your Jake?"

Maureen nodded in Jake's general direction. "Talking shop with some of the men," she answered. She felt her tension ebbing. Reaching for her glass, she drained the contents and felt the need for another.

"How long have you and Jake been happily married?" Rosemary asked absently.

"Eighteen years," Maureen answered without hesitation. She thought, *The first thirteen were the happy years, the struggling years. The disintegration had started with Jake's transfer to the home office.*

"Of course he's good to you?" Rosemary went on.

Maureen nodded.

"And you have three children." It was a statement, not a question. "I wanted a child, but Keith didn't. He has a son by his first marriage. He felt he was too old to have others, said he would be retired by the time a child would begin college, maybe even dead . . . and he didn't want to leave me with the responsibility of raising a child on my own. Don't you find that ridiculous reasoning?"

Maureen said nothing.

"If I lost him now . . . if he died of a heart attack or was killed in an accident . . . if perhaps something . . . I would have no one except my friends." She patted Maureen's hand. "That's why I appreciate them," she said, and laughed again, that strange laugh filled with gallows humor. "See what I mean by giving in to one's depressions? Look at your face. I've infected you. And at such a lovely party. I'm ashamed of myself."

"I'm the only one with children," Maureen said absently.

"That's true," Rosemary murmured, as if just being made aware of the fact. "But Joanna has her art. Vanessa has her charities and worthy causes. And Lizabeth—well, we all know what Lizabeth has, don't we?"

Maureen flushed. She had never known Rosemary to speak so freely, especially about one of the group. Lizabeth's activities were always discreetly avoided.

"Now I've embarrassed you," Rosemary observed. "We're a lot alike in one respect, Maureen. We're both rather old-fashioned." She sighed helplessly. "I believe I'm the product of the innocent romantic novels and movies of the forties and fifties. I never understood the freedom of the sixties I guess. I think no matter how I try I'd never be capable of changing my ideals."

"Why would you want to?" Maureen asked, puzzled by the turn of conversation.

"Oh, no reason," Rosemary replied. "It was just a thought."

*   *   *

Rosemary was relieved when the orchestra ended its number and people began to flitter back to the tables. They drove Maureen back to her own chair and ended the conversation. She had, she thought, revealed more than was discreet. She never-never-never wanted any of the wives to learn of the humiliation Keith was forcing upon her.

Everyone had returned to the executives' table except Keith. His chair remained vacant and she glanced at it with a sinking sensation. God, what would her life be without him? The insecurity she felt when he was away from her was terrifying. To avoid sinking back into depression she turned her attention to Janet and Larry Linquist. They were the oldest couple among the group; both now breathing heavily from the exertion of the dance.

Just as she was about to speak, there was a drum roll from the stage. The lights were raised and Keith stepped onto the platform. It was unusual—there were never speeches at the company party.

Rosemary felt the eyes of the executive wives turn to her. If there was to be some sort of announcement, she should have told them. She smiled at no one in particular and focused her attention on Keith. He had told her nothing of an announcement. Or, had he, and had she been too stricken and dazed to comprehend? She dared not concentrate on her earlier conversation with Keith for fear her expression would reveal her ignorance. She was expected to know everything—or nearly everything—that her husband did or considered doing at Multimedia. She was *Mrs. President!* She was the pipeline, the final authority for the other wives.

The microphone sputtered and hummed, and then Keith's voice filled the banquet room. "Fellow Multimedia employees. The executive wives, mine more adamantly than the others, have forbidden speeches at our annual party. It's a good rule and one I regret breaking, but this afternoon one of our most respected executives requested his retirement."

Rosemary felt the heads of the wives turn again in her direction, but she kept her attention riveted on Keith. She vowed she'd prevent any of them from learning she had been ignorant of a retirement among their ranks. They would lose confidence in her—and she would lose their friendships.

"In his twenty-three years with Multimedia, Larry Linquist has made contributions too numerous to mention," Keith continued. "We regret losing this respected member of our family and I know we'll all want to take the opportunity of wishing him well."

Rosemary glanced at Larry and smiled knowingly.

Keith's speech continued after a spattering of applause, but Rosemary ceased to listen. She was glancing from one wife to another. She was considering, calculating. Her personal life was momentarily forgotten. The surprise announcement had called her to duty. Larry Linquist's position at Multimedia was second only to Keith's. His position would be filled from within the ranks. All the men—and their wives— would be vying for the advancement. Rosemary's gaze swept the group. Joanna showed no expression. Maureen had gone pale. Lizabeth's eyes were sparking with excitement and Vanessa, always optimistic, had clutched her husband's arm as if already congratulating him. But it was on Janet Linquist's face that Rosemary's gaze settled. In that face she saw relief, an expression that said Janet had done her turn, that she was tired and, thank God, was getting out.

Rosemary knew the wives would most certainly want to meet tomorrow. They would discuss and vote among themselves as to which of the candidates should be pushed into Larry Linquist's position. They would plan a campaign and then go to work on their husbands to see that their decision reached fruition. Of course, the greatest responsibility would fall to Rosemary. Only *Mrs.* President could reach *Mr.* President's ear. Whatever candidate the group decided upon, she would be expected to support and convince Keith of his merit.

But her heart would not be in it. She was being forced to share the one thing she had guarded so selfishly—her husband. It would require every ounce of her strength and all her cunning to survive that ordeal. Humiliation kept her from confiding in or seeking advice from the other wives. She had made Keith her world and had left only a narrow corner free to be filled by the wives and their challenge of controlling Multimedia through their husbands. In the beginning, when they had formed the club, she had agreed only because it had tied her into that part of Keith's life that had been denied her.

Lizabeth touched her arm and drew her out of her thoughts. "You should have told us," the blonde whispered. "You held out on us."

"I thought you might appreciate the surprise," Rosemary answered calmly. She noted with relief that Keith had returned the microphone to its stand and was leaving the stage. Polite applause rang about him as he made his way toward the table. Rosemary thought again of being forced to share him and a sharp pain stabbed at her heart.

"Any other surprises?" Lizabeth whispered.

"Liz, please!" Merrill coaxed from across the table. Turning to Rosemary, he asked, "Would you care to dance, Mrs. Marston?"

Politeness kept Rosemary from declining. As she danced with Lizabeth's husband she saw the men approaching Larry Linquist with regrets and good wishes while the wives huddled at the far end of the table to chatter among themselves.

Rosemary closed her eyes.

Merrill was an excellent dancer and she didn't have to concentrate to follow him. Her thoughts strayed. She wondered how many nights it would be before Keith produced the woman who was to share their bed. Did enough drugs exist to lull her into submission that first night? Any night? She felt a shudder pass through her body, and heard Merrill ask with concern,

"Did I step on you?"

"No," she answered. "Not you."

LIZABETH

LIZABETH WILLIAMS WAS forty. To her friends she was thirty-seven and to her acquaintances thirty-four. For some of her younger lovers, and there had been many, she had even dared dip down the liars' scale to thirty. Although she doubted that any believed her, none had disputed her claim to a few years that had slipped by too quickly. Real dears, some of those young lovers. She always made it perfectly clear in the beginning of such relationships that it would be a no-deposit, no-return affair. For stability, she had Merrill.

Merrill was in many ways an ideal husband—if she discounted his jealousy and inability to satisfy her sexual needs. Even with these faults he had been a good catch. Of course, with her background—San Francisco elite, and the wealth she had inherited from her father—she could have had most any husband who had taken her fancy. She had chosen Merrill because she knew she had not bought him. When they had met and begun to date she convinced him that she was only a servant in her parents' great Sea Cliff house. At the time Merrill had been a minor executive with Multimedia, a company in which Lizabeth's widowed Aunt Thelma was, unknown to the other wives, a major stockholder. Merrill had proposed marriage to Lizabeth, the servant. He had promised devotion and a small house on the Avenues. Only then, when she decided to accept, did Lizabeth confess the truth to him. His reaction had been surprisingly bland. He had repeated his proposal of marriage and a house on the Avenues. She had accepted his proposal of marriage, but had firmly rejected any house other than the one in which she had been raised. After all, she had argued, her father was dead and her mother spent most of her time traveling. Why should a grand old house stand empty while she was confined to five rooms without the accustomed conveniences of servants' quarters, swimming pool and a terrace with a view of the bay? Merrill had objected but had eventually accepted her reasoning. They had, she thought, begun marriage under the best of circumstances. How much more difficult it would have been for her to adjust to poverty than for Merrill to adjust to wealth. She had lavished him with gifts, a Mercedes-Benz, a yacht, and three racehorses. His gift to her had been far more precious. He had awakened her sleeping sexuality. Her appetite had proven almost insatiable. Morning and evening and the middle of the night, she had had him between her thighs at any moment he could rise to the occasion.

Then, as with the Mercedes and yacht and racing horses, Merrill's interest had begun to wane. He began to avoid her whenever possible, hiding himself in various rooms of the rambling old house with stacks of books and journals; studying, he told her, the craft of the cinema. Multimedia was looking for a bright young producer, a position he had been determined to attain. Lizabeth had arranged for the promotion through Aunt Thelma without his knowledge.

The quality of their sex did not diminish, only the quantity. When he began working late she had threatened in a rage to have him dismissed. He told her he would leave her and that had horrified her. She had gone to physicians and psychiatrists to curtail her obsessive sex drive. Neither had proven successful. After a period of almost utter madness, she had taken her first lover. She had kept him in an apartment hidden away on Russian Hill. Eventually, she kept another in a fashionable downtown hotel and a third in North Beach in a small house under the shadow of the phallic Coit Tower.

Over the years she had retained the apartment and hotel suite and house. Only the occupants had changed through whim and necessity. Her greatest fear was of being discovered for the tramp she was by Merrill. She never feared his jealous rages, only that she might lose him. He was the only decent thing in her life. Without him she would feel no better than a common streetwalker.

Then had come her reform period.

She had gone to additional physicians and numerous psychiatrists and had jokingly told herself she would be cured when she kept as many analysts as she had lovers. Results became evident. She had managed to go for days without sexual frustration. Merrill was again capable of pleasing her totally. She had emptied the apartment and hotel suite but had retained the occupant of the house, as a reformed smoker carries a package of cigarettes to prevent the panic of not being able to obtain what he is overcoming. She took up minor charity work—and became involved with the wives. She devoted herself to Merrill's career.

Her "absent period" lasted almost two years before she gradually began to slip back into her old ways. This time it was more from boredom than an insatiable desire for sex. Although her love had not waned, her passion for Merrill had gone out of their relationship. She searched for lovers, who were young, or a challenge. Once she proved herself victorious she lost interest quickly and came quietly back to Merrill's bed to wait for the next conquest.

She had recently set her sights on Justin Wade.

He was extremely handsome, rumored to be well-endowed and apparently devoted to Joanna—a sufficient challenge. Still, she had never risked a lover who knew Merrill. Nor one whose wife was an acquaintance. Additional challenges.

It wasn't until the annual Multimedia party that Lizabeth decided to carry through on the seduction of Justin Wade.

The fact that Keith Marston had announced Larry Linquist's retirement and that Merrill and Justin would now be competing for that position sparked her decision. Since the years of their marriage she had come to despise Merrill's devotion to his work. This new promotion was important to him. She could have her revenge by convincing the other wives they should support Justin Wade. As her reward she'd seduce Justin.

As Merrill and Rosemary returned to the table after their dance, Lizabeth leaned toward Joanna, deliberately brushing Justin's thigh.

Smiling, she said, "Joanna, you look particularly lovely tonight."

She was certain she felt a response from Justin.

VANESSA

VANESSA KIRKMAN, AT twenty-five, was the youngest of the executive wives. Redheaded, with violet eyes and a pale complexion, she was petite, charming, always friendly, never depressed, always ready with a laugh or a word of encouragement when needed. She constantly repeated herself with such phrases as, "Isn't it great to be alive?" or "Isn't the world a beautiful place?"—although sometimes people felt as if she were seeking confirmation. She was thoughtful, always there with a gift of flowers or a cheery telephone call or a compliment. She always remembered birthdays and had messengers deliver astrological charts with the unfavorable aspects crossed out in heavy black pencil. She was a perfect hostess and a perfect guest. There was no dinner that was not a culinary delight. There was no book or movie that didn't have merit and make some contribution. There was no acquaintance in whom she could not find favorable traits. There was no disaster that didn't have its brighter side. Vanessa, at funerals, was the type to corner the bereaved and expound on the glory of the hereafter.

Vanessa was exasperating.

But the Vanessa that everyone knew was not the real Vanessa.

Only Mark Kirkman knew his wife for herself. A frightened, conniving, bitter young woman who had never forgotten the horrors of Hell's Kitchen poverty. When they had met, Vanessa had been an actress. Her major role had been as a Doris Day-type character in a movie that had gone from its first week's run directly to the late show on television. She had given up her career "by popular demand." Mark often thought she carried that movie role into real life. But he loved her, forgave her her weaknesses, and understood that her fantasy personality had been created for his benefit as well as her own. He knew her machinations with the other executive wives were to further his career and insure her own security.

Now, after the announcement of Larry Linquist's retirement, he could feel the workings of her mind. Her violet eyes were sparkling, she moved her head so that her red hair spilled about her naked white shoulders, she smiled, she chatted with Lizabeth, she purposely ignored the possibilities—Mark's possibilities of replacing Linquist—and therefore made her interest all the more obvious.

"Then we'll definitely have a meeting tomorrow?" she whispered to Lizabeth.

Lizabeth turned to Rosemary for confirmation.

Rosemary nodded.

She's distant tonight, Vanessa thought. Why? She hadn't told them about Linquist's retirement. Maybe she was holding out on them. Maybe she had taken it upon herself to decide already who his replacement should be. She had been chatting with Maureen earlier. Perhaps they had conspired to push Maureen's husband into the position.

Vanessa bit her lower lip and tasted her lipstick. Her stomach was churning. She glanced at Mark, but he was occupied talking production expenses with Keith Marston. Damn! Little he cared about his career. If it wasn't for her he'd still be sitting behind an assistant production manager's desk in Manhattan. They'd be returning home nights to a fourth floor walkup in Greenwich Village and counting their loose change for evenings at The Five Oaks or The Downtown Club. She had pushed him into applying for the San Francisco assignment at Multimedia's home office; she had made careful plans to be drawn into the exclusive club of the wives, had won them over and dragged Mark through three advancements since his transfer. Now, when he should be discussing his possibility of replacing Linquist with Keith Marston, he was discussing production costs.

She wanted this promotion for Mark.

She wanted a better apartment in Pacific Heights. And new antique furniture from The Corinthian in Saratoga. She wanted a new wardrobe designed for her—as Lizabeth and Joanna did each season. She was in the group, and she wanted to live like them. This promotion for Mark could do that for her.

She leaned back in her chair and surveyed the other wives carefully. This was an important promotion. All the husbands would be eligible, all the wives anxious, greedy. As their rules stated, it would take three votes to select the candidate. Vanessa's gaze settled on Rosemary Marston. Rosemary would be the most important vote because the promotion would not affect her. Rosemary, she thought she could handle. Her gaze swept from Lizabeth to Joanna to Maureen. Which one? she asked herself. Which one did she try to convince first to cast her vote for Mark?

Lizabeth had an eye for Mark, Vanessa was aware of that. It had never occurred to her to worry. Mark was the monogamous type. She was confident of and secure with Mark. The mere idea that he would indulge himself in an affair was almost amusing. Frightening, too, if she let herself dwell on it. Still, there would be no harm in coaxing him to flirt with Lizabeth when it could further their cause. Lizabeth could be the third vote they needed. After she voted. . . .

Hope, clinging to the shadows at the opposite end of the ballroom, watched with interest as the wives prepared to depart. The last dance had been played and the wives, in their expensive evening gowns, had twirled about the floor in their husbands' arms.

Hope sighed.

Another annual party was behind her.

The orchestra was packing away their instruments. Her fellow employees were arranging further festivities at various nightspots. She would have declined if anyone had bothered to ask her. It was an advantage, she thought, to be aloof and unpopular with the staff. She could go home to her tiny apartment, kick off her shoes and sit in front of the television set—waiting, hoping Justin would find an opportunity to telephone.

If he didn't—there was always tomorrow. An afternoon in a downtown hotel, a stolen moment in the deserted conference room. Only now things would be different between them. She would be comparing herself to his wife Joanna. With all Joanna's beauty and talent and wealth, what did Justin see in her? She couldn't bear it if she discovered she was a mere sexual diversion. If she lost Justin. . . .

Grabbing her wrap from the cloak room, she swept quickly up the stairs and out into the night ahead of the executives and their wives.

Chapter
Two

As was typical of San Francisco weather, the heavy fog of the night before had vanished by early morning. The sky was clear and blue, and the wind, although chilly, was slight and scarcely rustled the branches of the elm trees beyond the Marstons' study windows.

Rosemary, perched at the writing desk, sipped her third cup of coffee and waited for her morning uppers to counteract the effect of last night's sleeping pills. Last night remained somewhat vague beyond the point of their leaving the party.

They had come directly home. She remembered standing outside the door waiting for Keith to select the proper key from his ring instead of ringing for the servants. She had turned her face up into the fog hoping the dampness would clear her senses. Had she really expected the fog to do what her pills would not? In the entryway, Keith had shed his topcoat and had gone directly into the study. She had stood in her sable wrap, watching him through the open door and feeling like a guest in her own home. That was when the idea of seduction had occurred to her—*introduce him to a new Rosemary and prove to him she could excite him without a third, unwanted party.*

Now in the light of morning, she saw such thoughts

for the fantasies they were. There was no new Rosemary, no depths she was aware of into which she could reach and extract a novel personality as a magician might a rabbit from his hat. Rosemary, the seductress, was a myth. Still, last night it had been a consideration, a desperate attempt at bringing Keith back to her and persuading him to abandon the idea of a third party in their bed.

If only the telegram from his first wife had not arrived.

She had watched him open the telegram and had then gone to him and peered over his shoulder.

Teddy will be arriving on Pan Am flight #102 Friday the 13th. Meet him! The poor dear always finds these trips traumatic. This time be certain to return him in exactly three months. The message was signed *Christina.*

Keith had turned to her and said with enthusiasm, "Teddy is coming Friday."

Rosemary had turned away to conceal her response.

The fact of Teddy had never failed to amaze her.

Teddy was an Alaskan husky over fourteen years old, blind in one eye and scarcely capable of maneuvering himself about the marble floors. He growled at the servants and lost control of his natural functions in places not easily discovered except by scent. In their divorce settlement, Keith had met Christina's financial demands; he had surrendered custody of their son, even his vintage Rolls-Royce, but he had refused to relinquish his rights to Teddy. Teddy, by court order, spent three months of each year with Keith, the remainder of his time with Christina in New Orleans. His arrivals and departures were always events with much planning and many telegrams.

Rosemary called the dog Teddy Bear because she felt both Keith and Christina looked on him as something cuddly and warm, a toy and the symbol of the only good that came from their marriage. Teddy took preference over their son, a slight, frightened-looking young man with eyes forever cast downward and a voice scarcely above a whisper. Rosemary hated Teddy. She never vented her hatred—she had never dared—but last night when Keith had informed her of the dog's arrival she had been almost consumed by jealousy and hatred. The dog's arrival had made him so happy. The event had given him an excuse to linger below with a cognac long after she had gone to their room. *Teddy took preference over her.*

Upstairs, she had bathed and perfumed herself with Keith's favorite fragrance. She had worn his favorite gown, black and sheer and shimmering, and had sunk into the yielding softness of their bed to wait for him. She had left three sleeping pills and a glass of water on the nightstand—for afterward. But the afterward never came. Her wait had stretched into hours. When, angry and hurt, she had gone below she had found the study dark and had known that Keith had gone to one of the guest rooms to avoid her. She considered it the cruelest imaginable punishment. Sleeping alone terrified her. Even in drugged sleeps, she would dream nightmarish dreams. The shadows crept toward her bed, terrifying in their shapelessness. When she slept alone she drifted from reality into a fearful hell. There was no one to reach out to, no Keith to touch for solidarity, protection and comfort.

Last night had been such a night.

Today promised to be little better.

She still had a sense of weightlessness, of drifting, of being suspended in a netherworld from which she could not escape. She sipped her coffee and told herself she was becoming immune to her pills. She

reminded herself to call for a stronger prescription.
Calling her doctor seemed to be the one task she could
perform without encouragement or mental aggrava-
tion. That, she thought with sudden insight, was because the pills he prescribed supported her weaknesses. Now more than at any time she wished she had
been created a stronger woman. If only strength were
a commodity that could be purchased, she would buy
enough to fight for Keith and their marriage.

The thought of using Keith's wealth for such a
purpose intrigued her. She pushed her coffee cup aside
and sat back in the desk chair, eyes closed.

She visualized a gigantic scale like the statues of
Justice hold. She saw herself sitting on one tray, the
opposite tray empty and so high above her that she
could see only the blinding light reflected off its under-
side. Her heart skipped a beat and she fought to break
the image, fearing it, but her fascination caused it to
hold. Keith appeared far above the scales, so minute
he was almost unrecognizable. He began dropping—
what?—gold coins into the empty tray. *Christina's
settlement so I might marry you*, he called. She felt the
tray beneath her jerk and lift. *Your extravagant ward-
robes*. She rose higher. *Your jewelry*. Still higher. *The
gifts you lavish on your friends*. The trays of the scale
were almost level now. I'm dreaming, she thought,
and attempted to awaken herself. But the money continued to strike the sinking tray opposite with deafening clarity. *Teddy!* Teddy? She laughed with gallows
humor as she saw the aged dog crash into a pyramid of
money and was immediately buried. She rose beyond
sight of the sinking tray and began to cry out with
terror for Keith to stop. *Now you want to buy
strength*, he shouted. She saw him fling something
downward that had no distinct form. It struck with a

33

loud ringing sound. She was drawn swiftly upward . . . up, up, up toward the brass points at the underarm of the scales.

She awoke with a start, trembling.

The ringing belonged to the reality of the telephone. She reached for the receiver as if in a panic. The plastic was cold, solid. Someone was breathing on the other end of the line. She heard a click, then Matty, her maid, said, "Marston residence."

Rosemary felt her trembling subside.

She heard, Lizabeth's voice. "Matty, this is Mrs. Williams. Is Mrs. Marston in?"

"I have it, Matty," Rosemary said, amazed at the calmness of her voice. "Good morning, Lizabeth."

"Rosemary, it was simply wicked of you to hold out on us last night," Lizabeth said with indignation.

"What?" Rosemary quickly reflected. "Oh, you mean about the Linquist retirement." She had forgotten.

"I've called the other wives," Lizabeth went on. "We have agreed to meet at my house this afternoon." She paused as if waiting for Rosemary to voice an objection. "At two o'clock." Silence forced her to add, "Is the arrangement all right with you, Rosemary?"

Rosemary answered quietly, "Two o'clock will be fine."

"Have you decided which man you'll back for the promotion?" Lizabeth asked directly.

"No, no, I haven't."

Lizabeth laughed softly. "You just won't tell me," she accused. "I know you, Rosemary. You play the game by the rules." She laughed again and then added seriously, "I think only Maureen considers our little club an alleviation to boredom for the executive wives.

She confessed she almost told her husband about our game of paralleling them among ourselves."

Rosemary, remembering Maureen's concern for her the night before, said, "Maureen is a simple woman—and a good woman. She'd not tell her husband. If our husbands knew, they'd stop us."

"If they could," Lizabeth said quietly. "How do you stop the wind from whispering in your ear? Or a wife with a purpose?"

"You are somewhat of a poetess, Lizabeth," Rosemary said. "But not all men listen to either."

"But they do, Rosemary, dear. Haven't we had successes in the past?"

"Yes, but we've never tried anything so important as the selection of a top executive," Rosemary reminded her. Thinking aloud, she added, "If the man we select gets the promotion, how will we know we've actually done it? There are only four possibilities for the promotion. It might be mere chance."

"Why must we select only from our husbands?" Lizabeth asked.

"I don't understand."

"Why," Lizabeth said slowly, "don't we select a man from the lower ranks? We've been playing this game for several years. Why don't we test our power?"

Rosemary stared at the telephone mouthpiece. *Power? Strength? Rosemary Marston?*

She had never really thought of their amusements as an expression of power over their husbands. What degree of power did the wives possess by influencing small procedures at Multimedia? As a combined force they had altered and modernized the corporate logo. They—mostly Lizabeth—had had a corporation attorney dismissed because they had not liked his attitude.

35

They had, Rosemary supposed, managed to influence many other Multimedia business dealings that had been their husbands' responsibilities. Yes, she decided, that *was* power. But she somehow felt outside it. She had been *Mrs. President,* the leader of the wives, but she had never considered herself more than a figurehead. If she had power and influence over her husband, why did she consider herself so weak? Why did she feel incapable of coping with the slightest problem? She had never been secure enough to place a painting on a wall without calling her decorator, or to buy a gown without Keith's approval, or to tell the cook, "This is the weekly menu." When she made decisions—and they were few—they were never definite, always subject to alteration or complete change. An acquaintance had once referred to a statement she had made as dogmatic, and she had been joyous for days.

Now Lizabeth wanted them to test their power.

Not her. Not now, not ever. "I think not," she said softly.

"We'll discuss it at two o'clock," Lizabeth said flatly. "Goodbye until then."

Rising, Rosemary moved to the windows and stood staring out at the sunlight on the Marina and the bay. She told herself she was glad the wives were meeting this afternoon. Even if she were incapable of sharing their excitement over the selection of an executive replacement, the meeting would get her out of the house and possibly dull her concentration on her situation with Keith. Playing *Mrs. President* had always required thought and energy.

Sighing wearily, Rosemary left the study and returned to her room. She rang for Matty, threw open her closet doors, and then sat down to wait for the maid to climb the stairs.

She never dressed without at least one person's approval. That person was often Matty. She never found any incongruity here. If she had asked, she would have found that Matty was color blind. If she had noticed, she would have realized that the confused maid always nodded in response to her questions about the selection of clothes and accessories—and always affirmatively. If she had not been so confirmed in her insecurity, she would have comprehended that she at least managed to dress herself.

And Rosemary Marston had twice made the country's best dressed list.

Chapter
Three

LIZABETH PARKED HER Mercedes at the Union Square
parking lot and hailed a taxi at the corner of Powell
and Geary streets. She gave the driver the address on
Telegraph Hill and sat back to wait out the ride with
growing impatience. Her strange route to reach the
address was, she supposed, ridiculous—who would be
paying attention to her comings and goings?—but she
enjoyed the intrigue. It heightened her sense of enjoyment, and there was that fear that Merrill might discover her escapades and leave her.

She glanced at her watch and estimated that she had
an hour to spend with Karl. Then she'd have to retrace
her steps and rush home to receive the wives at two
o'clock. Rosemary had seemed strange on the telephone earlier; last night she had also been distant. She
made a note to discreetly question her if she got her
alone. She dismissed Rosemary from her thoughts and
turned her attention to Karl.

He was twenty-four, her latest paramour, not handsome but striking, with his dark eyes and well-kept,
black beard. His body was solid, muscular, and he
kept it deeply tanned with daily visits to Aquatic Park.
For his availability she paid his expenses and provided
the apartment. It wasn't the money that interested

him—he was narcissistic enough to imagine most women would keep him—but rather her position as wife of an executive with Multimedia. Karl was an aspiring actor and Multimedia was the pot of gold at the end of his rainbow. The corporation produced numerous movies and television shows and only a word from Lizabeth. . . .

Lizabeth secretly laughed at his ambitions. She promised introductions, later, and knew that when she tired of him she would dismiss him without complicating her life by linking him to her by introducing him to anyone of importance. Actually, with her new infatuation with Justin Wade, she had decided to make quick work of Karl.

She left the taxi and walked up the long flight of wooden steps to the hillside apartment. She felt a dash of excitement as she inserted her key into the lock. She threw open the door and halted in complete surprise.

Crossing from the kitchen toward the bedroom, from which a television blared, was a young woman. Her hair was damp from a recent shower and she wore a towel about her middle. She clutched at the towel with one hand and carried a dish of pickles in the other. Her surprise matched Lizabeth's. She froze in mid-step, her doe-eyes widening as she attempted to decide whether she should be frightened, outraged, or indignant. She settled for a direct approach.

"Are you Karl's mother? He didn't tell me he came from . . . from money? But I should have known by his apartment."

Lizabeth placed the accent as New York Bronx. "Actually," she said icily, "he comes from the gutter. I'm his social worker."

The girl laughed. "You're putting me on."

Lizabeth came inside and closed the door. "You

have a remarkable grasp of the obvious," she said. She glanced toward the bedroom and expected Karl to materialize at the sound of their voices, but he was apparently caught in the simpleton excitement of his television western, perhaps imagining himself on the screen as the hero. Lizabeth was choking with indignation. Her apartment, and the bastard was using it to shelter his own little diversion. Unknowingly she had been keeping two for the price of one. Astounded by her jealousy, she realized she would have somehow felt less put upon if she had suddenly learned that Merrill had been having an affair. One's husband, expected—but one's lover!!! She turned her attention to the girl.

She looked as if she were struggling with adolescence and losing. Puberty had left her with babyish fat and a marked complexion. Maturity had hardened the lines about her mouth and, when she wasn't playing coy, the expression in her eyes. She seemed to be running the gamut of emotions, searching for the proper one to fit the occasion. She seemed at one moment a young teenager, and at the next a fully grown woman. Lizabeth found both dismal.

"I guess you want to know who I am," she said with a giggle. "I'm Sylvia. Karl and I study drama together."

"Drama, is it?" Lizabeth murmured.

"We've been having this thing for about a week," Sylvia continued. "Karl's a real sweetheart." She abandoned the plate of pickles to a corner of the cluttered end table and used both hands to secure her towel. "I hope you're not one of those mothers who moralizes," she said. "I've heard enough of that in-my-generation crap from my own mother." She tilted her chin defiantly.

"I'm not anyone's mother," Lizabeth announced

severely. "Especially not Karl's," she shouted above the noise of the television. She slipped out of her mink coat in one quick movement and flung it onto a chair back. She felt her face flush with outrage. "Now get that real sweetheart out here!"

Sylvia decided at last upon the proper emotion. It was fright. Without taking her eyes from the intruder, she shouted, "Karl! Come out here, baby! There's some broad . . ."

Lizabeth heard Karl's feet strike the floor. He was in the open doorway in an instant. Shirtless and barefooted, he wore only a pair of low-slung denims. The zipper was down, the fly gaping. Lizabeth, even through her rage, was aware of his sexiness. She stared at the developed biceps, the solid chest and narrow, boyish waist. Her eyes followed the pattern of his body hair, the kite-like triangle of his chest and the narrower ribbon that edged its way down over his abdomen to join the second wider growth that was evident above the waistband of his trousers. She remembered what she had imagined to be waiting for her inside his gaping fly and saw the bulge of its thickness pressed against his thigh. She lifted her gaze back to his face and a fury swept over her because she knew if she took him this afternoon she would have him secondhand.

"Your girlfriend thinks I'm your mother," she said.

Karl glanced at the girl and his dark eyes told her to leave quickly and without question.

The girl obediently fled into the bathroom, returned pulling a caftan over her head, and vanished through the door without a word or backward glance.

Karl crossed to the refrigerator and removed a beer. He snapped open the lid and drank, his back to Lizabeth. She stared at the way his back muscles rippled with the movement and knew he was aware of the action and her interest. "You haven't been here in days," he said, pretending hurt. "Do you want a beer?"

"No. You know what I want," she answered. She turned and walked into the bedroom, stopping to snap off the television set. Knowing that he had followed and was standing in the doorway, she began to shed her clothes with the lazy sensuality of a stripper, teasing him as she knew he enjoyed, although her compulsion was to literally shred her clothes from her body. Her fury had aroused her sexuality. She did not glance at him until she stood only in her brassiere and panties.

The window shades were drawn and his face was lost in shadows, but she could clearly see his body. It was his body she wanted this final time.

"What are you waiting for, my pet?" she asked.

He unfastened the catch of his waistband. "We never just talk," he complained.

"Talk about what?"

"About what you promised," he told her. "About introducing me to talent scouts from Multimedia."

"Oh, that," she murmured.

"*That* is very important to me," he said with veiled anger. "It was part of our agreement."

"Were strange little pieces of fluff also part of our agreement?" she countered.

"She had no place to stay," he said defensively. He pushed his trousers down over his thighs and stepped out of them. He moved forward and then stopped. "Are you going to keep your promise?" he asked.

"Yes, my pet."

"And stop calling me my pet."

"I promise." She stepped backward to the bed and sank onto the soiled sheets. From the pillows, she stared at his chiseled features and deep-set, brooding eyes. Damn striking, she thought. Too bad he's lost his appeal for me. Maybe she should keep him around for a rainy day. No, not allowed. No loose ends. When she began a new conquest she hadn't the energy to cling to the old. She twisted about on the bed, unfastened her brassiere and pulled it off. "I'm in a hurry," she murmured.

He came to her then, bending over the bed and removing her panties. She reached for him and urged him onto the bed beside her.

He was an obedient, if savage, lover. He was pressing, thrusting, causing her to cry out with pleasure. She stared up at his furrowed brow and the lust-tensed muscles of his neck. She inhaled deeply of the maleness of him, and with her body arching, her hands raking his back, urged him on to even more brutal abandon. Clutching at his hair, she guided his mouth to her breasts, and groaned and whimpered as he took them eagerly, his hot mouth going from one to the other and making her dizzy with excitement. Would Justin Wade be as good? she asked herself. Then pushed that thought from her mind.

Karl's greedy mouth stopped working at her breasts. His breathing became quicker, louder, until animal-like grunts came from within his throat. His buttocks lifted, he stabbed into her and his body went rigid.

"Not yet!" she cried.

But she felt the spasms shake his body. Then he became a heavy burden, a crushing weight on top of her. Damn him! That bitch of a girl had taken his real power. She had been secondhand and he second-rate.

"I'm sorry," he murmured hoarsely.

"So am I." She pushed at him, and he rolled off her.

"Give me a couple of minutes," he suggested. "Then . . ."

"I haven't time," she interrupted. She rose and dressed quickly, ignoring him as he watched her. Dressed, she moved to the bed and stood staring down at him. "You said we never just talk. Well, this is going to be a first, my pet. I have something to say to you. I'm no longer going to be your landlady."

He stared at her for several moments before the implication struck him. Then he sat upright in bed, the expression in his dark eyes going cold. "You're saying it's over?" he asked incredulously.

"Your mental agility is as great as your little friend's," she said.

"Is it because of her?"

"No. Although if I hadn't come here with the intention of ending it, discovering your roommate might have convinced me to do so." She reached for her purse, opened it and tossed an envelope onto the table. "Enough to keep you out of the parks until you find another sponsor," she told him.

Karl was on his feet, his fists clenched at his sides. "And your promise of introductions?" he demanded.

Lizabeth started for the door. "If it hadn't ended so soon," she said. "But then, you'll find someone else to introduce you to . . . to someone else," she murmured. She raised her arm and, without turning, waved her fingers in a gesture of goodbye. "You and your girlfriend be out by the weekend. I'll need the apartment." She opened the door and turned in the frame.

Karl was standing naked in the middle of the room, his face gone pale with rage. "Fuck you!" he cried.

"You just did, my pet," Lizabeth said with sweetness, "and not very adequately either, I might add." She closed the door and something shattered against the inside as she went down the stairs.

On the outside landing, Sylvia was sitting in the sun picking at her toenails. She looked up, startled, and seemed about to flee for the protection of the nearest doorway.

"Go in and help your real sweetheart pack," Lizabeth said without interrupting her stride.

Chapter
Four

HOPE HAD ALTERED her appearance, and the alteration was not an enhancement.

Her auburn hair, usually stylishly coiffured, had been pulled straight back from her face and clamped at the nape of her neck. The style gave her face a pained expression and her lips a thinner, harder line. She wore no makeup except a pale, ghostly shade of lipstick, and her dress, a drab grey, drained that color away. Add to this appearance the dark-rimmed glasses she had banished several months before in favor of contact lenses and you had the cartoonist's concept of every wife's favorite secretary. Her attitude, always businesslike, was tinged with icy coldness; that, however, went unnoticed because of the startling change in her appearance.

The executive offices were arranged in a horseshoe, with the private offices along the outside perimeter and the secretaries in the center. Hope's desk was located on a raised platform so she might oversee her charges. She had drawn considerable attention since her arrival, the least of which did not come from Justin Wade.

Hope, ignoring the interest, had kept herself remarkably busy since nine o'clock. She had quickly distributed the morning mail, taken several calls concerning scheduling for a new production, and had arranged luncheon dates between Keith Marston and two stars vying for the lead in the new series. When the other secretaries attempted to draw her into conversation concerning last night's annual party she had sent them back to their duties.

It was quarter past ten when the buzzer on her desk called her into Justin's office. She entered with her steno book, crossed to the customary chair and sat down, poising her pencil rigidly between her fingers. Although she kept her gaze averted, she felt his unfaltering stare.

Finally, he said, "Hope, for Christ's sake! What's with you today?"

Hope glanced at him with a blank expression. "The door is open, Mr. Wade," she reminded him, having deliberately neglected to close it. "Unless you want all of Multimedia to hear you, I suggest you lower your voice." She crossed her legs and returned her attention to her steno pad. "Did you wish to dictate a letter?"

"Damn you!" he whispered. Rising, he crossed the office and pushed the door closed. Leaning against the mahogany panel, he stared back at her. "I couldn't call last night," he said. "It was impossible. I'm sorry. Forgive me."

"To whom are you writing this apology?" she asked coolly.

Justin pushed away from the door and returned to his desk. "This is a side of you I've never seen," he said.

Hope remained silent.

"Do you want me on my knee to beg forgiveness?" he demanded.

"The question I have been asking myself," she

answered, "is if I want you at all." She closed her pad and stuck the pencil into the wire spine. The sting of her words had reached him, but she curiously felt no satisfaction. She had planned retribution through a long and sleepless night. Now when it should have come, it was evading her. Her words had stung her more than him. Want him at all! How absurd. She wanted him more than life, could not imagine life without him—and yet last night, waiting for him to call, remembering how he had laughed and cooed with his wife at the party had been more than she could bear.

How like a little boy he sometimes appeared. Now he was looking hurt, wounded, on the verge of tears. How moist his eyes became when he wanted them to. You should have been an actor instead of an executive in charge of productions, she wanted to say to him. "Have you really asked yourself that question, Hope?" he asked quietly. "How could you?"

Last night in her fury it had been easy.

"I watched you and Joanna together last night," she said. "I watched and I felt like . . ."

"It was a performance."

"Then it was a convincing performance," she blurted, and told herself she must not lose control.

"It was you I wanted to be with," he told her.

"Was it part of your performance of the perfect husband to kiss her hand? To hold her so close when you danced? To laugh and make jokes? I felt you were laughing . . . at me. Every moment I watched you I was in agony."

Justin pushed away from his desk. He stood erect, conscious of his height. Turning away from her, he drummed the pads of his fingers on the desktop. "It was because of your watching that I was forced to carry it so far," he told her. "Joanna saw you and questioned your interest. I had no alternative but to be the amusing, devoted husband." He glanced at her over his shoulder. "Did you think I enjoyed it knowing you were there? Knowing how it must hurt you? I only did what I had to do, what you forced me to do by your obvious fascination."

Hope strongly felt the turn of the defensive. Of course, what he said was the truth. She had been blatant in her interest. She blamed her behavior on too many scotch and sodas downed too quickly.

"You placed me in a precarious position last night," Justin went on.

Hope's head fell over her chest. "I didn't want to go to the damned party," she whimpered. "I knew what it would be like seeing the two of you together for the first time since we . . . since you and I . . ." She fumbled in the pocket of her grey dress and withdrew a handkerchief to dab at her eyes. Damnit! It was happening again! How easily he manipulated her emotions—turned her anger and hurt into guilt.

"If you hadn't gone it would have only fed the rumors," he said.

Her head shot up. "Rumors? I've heard no rumors. No one suspects." She stood and moved to the desk, her hand creeping over to covering his drumming fingers. "Why don't you leave her, Justin? You said you don't love her. You said you loved me."

"And I do," he assured her. "But I can't leave Joanna now." He pulled his hand from beneath hers and sat down, turning the swivel chair so that he stared out the window at the San Francisco skyline. "Joanna's powerful," he said. "She'd have my job, everything. She's a woman to be reckoned with."

Hope dropped to her knees beside his chair.

"You're an excellent businessman," she assured him. "You have a commercial understanding of what the public wants in entertainment. You'd find another job, probably a better one. Away from San Francisco. Perhaps Hollywood or New York. You always said it was ludicrous for the home office of Multimedia to be located in Northern California. I can go on working until you find a better position. I've enough saved to support us until . . ."

"I won't come to you like that," Justin said firmly. He turned his chair and took both her hands in his, brushing them against his lips. "Time," he said quietly. "Give me time, Hope. Don't throw me aside because of impatience. I'm impatient also, but if I threw everything aside to be with you I'd only end up destroying what we have."

Hope leaned her cheek against his neck. "I told you in the beginning I would be no good as the other woman in your life," she murmured. Tears were stinging her eyes. "It's just that I love you so, Justin. It's almost like an obsession. You ask for time, but it's time that's killing me. Time alone, thinking about you and wanting to be with you. I spend sleepless nights asking myself, *What's he doing now? Is he in bed? Is he with her? Is he thinking about me?*"

"I usually am," he murmured.

"Are you? I try to convince myself you are, but last night looking at Joanna I doubted it." She wedged her arm behind his neck and clung to him. "Joanna's everything I'm not," she whispered. "She's beautiful and sophisticated and talented. Maybe I'm having difficulty understanding why you chose me to love."

"But it is you I love, Hope," he assured her almost angrily. "You, not Joanna." Cupping her chin in the curve of his hand, he tilted her face and kissed her gently on the lips. His eyes met hers, and they held a pleading expression. "It may not be much more time," he said. "Promise me six more months before you cross me off."

"Justin, I . . ."

"Give me five, then?"

She knew when he looked at her that way she would have given him her lifetime.

And he understood it.

The intercom caused them to part abruptly. Hope returned to the straight-back chair, and Justin, straightening his tie, depressed the button and was reminded by Keith Marston that they had an eleven thirty appointment before his luncheon.

Hope gathered up her steno pad and pencil from the floor where they had fallen. With as much calm as she could muster, she asked, "Do you have dictation?"

Justin stared at her quietly for a moment. Then he asked, "What do you know about Linquist's functions with Multimedia?"

The question startled her. "I . . . I keep his files," she finally answered.

"Would it be possible for you to take some of those files home without being caught?"

She marveled at his quick transition from lover to questioning employer. "Yes, it's possible."

A smile hovered about the corners of Justin's mouth. "Then beginning tonight I want you to take a few files each day," he told her. "I'll give you a list of the important subjects. I'll come by, go through them, and you can return them the next morning. No one will be the wiser." He scribbled notations on a slip of paper and handed them to her. "We'll start with these. Take the complete files home with you."

Hope did not accept his instructions with unquestioning alacrity as he anticipated. She was forced by nature to ask, "Why, Justin?"

The smile playing about the corners of Justin's mouth broadened into a mischievous grin. "Because, Hope, my darling, if I should be promoted into Linquist's position with Multimedia, it might well mean a narrowing of that time we spend apart."

Hope asked no further questions.

Chapter
Five

JOANNA WADE WAS not blind to Justin's failings.

There were merely more than she recognized.

They had been married for four years. Justin, an Australian, had been working for the Australian Consulate when a shakeup had reduced the staff by forty percent. Having the least senority, Justin had been one of the first to be dismissed. He had been given six months to leave the United States. They had dated a few times prior to his dismissal; after, he had actively pursued her.

In the beginning, she had been fond of him. He had a little-boy quality that brought out her maternal instincts—and, having known many men, she found him sexually superior. He was handsome, to her, standing over six feet tall, with broad shoulders and trim waist and buttocks. He was charming, interested in her career, and easy to talk to. He mixed well with her friends; most were taken by his accent and that quality about him that so appealed to her and yet equally troubled her—the sexuality he seemed to exude without effort or awareness. He was extremely well-endowed, a fact that could not be hidden regardless of his tailor's efforts. He unconsciously flirted with women and men, which was the reason her mother had taken him for a hustler and warned her against him. Yet, she watched him closely and noted that he made no advances; in fact, he appeared naive when advances were made toward him. His romantic and sexual attentions were reserved for her only.

During this rush of his attentions, Joanna had been busy preparing for a one-woman showing at a Union Street gallery. She was behind in her deadline, two more canvases needed to meet the gallery's requirements, and still she would not send Justin away when he appeared at her door with flowers or candy (which she didn't eat) or a recording of a concert they had listened to on the radio the night before. She would silently cover her canvas, put her brushes away, and they would spend the day in Muir Woods or tramping along the beach at Stenson.

It was Justin who first mentioned love.

They had found a secluded spot in the dunes away from the beach. Like teenagers, they had undressed and made love. It had been glorious, with the cool wind against their bodies, the sounds of the surf and the blue sky above. After they had dressed, she had sat with her knees up and her head buried in the crooks of her arms.

"You know," she had finally said, "you've awakened something inside me. You've brought my sexuality to life again." She had meant to say it differently, to explain how after her divorce she had turned away from the physical because her husband had only been interested in her sexually.

Justin had gently placed his face against her head and wrapped his arms around her shoulders. "I've fallen in love with you, Joanna," he had told her quietly.

Love! She had not even considered the possibility. Her career had taken most of her time. Love, if she thought of it at all, was something she did not expect to experience. She could honestly say she had never really loved anyone, parents, friends, or her ex-husband. The emotion had always eluded her, and she thought herself incapable of it. Was this strong feeling she had for Justin love? Or merely sexuality? When she looked at him there was a strange stirring inside her. When he was away from her she thought of no one else. She had drawn away from him, risen and walked to the crest of the highest dune. When she had looked back at him he had stretched out, hands behind his head, and was watching her. He seemed to be waiting for something, something from her. She almost crumbled with the impact when it came. She was in love with him! She wasn't incapable! Her attraction wasn't merely sexual—the sexuality was an important part of it, but it wasn't the whole. She felt her heart would burst. Rushing down the dune, she flung herself on him, shouting, "I love you, too, Justin! God, how I love you!"

When she had quieted, he had said sadly, "It's going to kill me to leave you."

She had whimpered with the horror of losing him. To have found him and lost him so quickly. "Couldn't you appeal to the embassy?" she had cried in her panic.

"I've appealed to everyone." He had shrugged his shoulders to emphasize his failure to gain residence in the United States. "I've a few short months, and then it's back to Australia."

"For how long?"

"I don't know." His eyes were moist; she thought he was going to cry.

Good God, she thought. A man's who's not afraid to cry. "There must be something, Justin. Some way. I have powerful friends. One of them must be able to help *us*." She felt her stomach churn, her chest ache.

Tears were stinging her own cheeks. A goddamned stupid law was going to separate them.

After several moments of silence, Justin said, "Marriage. It's the only way I can remain here. Marriage to a U.S. citizen. Then a green card to allow me to work until I can apply for citizenship."

"Then we'll marry," Joanna said without hesitation. "I love you, so why shouldn't I marry you?"

They drove to Reno that afternoon and were married in a small chapel next to a gambling casino.

Love and marriage had come to Joanna on the same day.

Four years had passed since that eventful day on the dunes. Justin had received his green card and, through Joanna's friends, his position with Multimedia, where he had proved to have an uncanny knack for selecting television shows that were popular with the public. In less than four years he had managed three important advancements and was moved onto executive row. That was when Joanna had become a member of the wives.

The first year of their marriage had been perfection.

Two important events occurred during that year; she had all but abandoned her career, and her mother had died, leaving her a considerable income. Her father remarried, and her stepmother, half her father's age, became extremely fond of Justin.

Joanna began to understand her husband.

Justin had a streak of deceit. He often lied to her, not lies that were important, but small unnecessary untruths that she found unsettling. Facts he had told her about his family and childhood surfaced as fantasies. When questioned, Justin confessed that the fantasies were more acceptable to him than the truths; his father had not disowned him, his mother had not been a prostitute, his family had not lost its fortune—there had never been a fortune. He had not left Australia because of a desire to travel, but because he had become involved in an unfortunate incident while in the service and had fled because of embarrassment. His confessions were always made after too many gins, tears followed, and pleading for understanding. Joanna did not understand, but she pretended to. She loved Justin, and so long as she believed his love for her was not also a lie she would do battle against that part of him that was in conflict with himself.

Justin was moody, a chameleon. A happy conversation could turn morose without notice. Talented in his job with Multimedia, he was forever pushing forward, manipulating and using anyone possible for advancement. It was almost as if he were competing with her for fame and fortune. That was the reason she had let her career slide. When she eventually picked it up again, Justin began to have anxieties concerning his masculinity. Her success threatened him, forced him to work harder and longer hours to prove himself. Their sex life suffered, but not so that she complained. When they did make love it was as exciting and as fulfilling as the first time.

Marriage, to Joanna, was sacrosanct.

It held a higher priority than her career. But still she was unable to deny her art, even for Justin's benefit. So when she did complete a canvas she refrained from showing it to Justin; it was clear to her that if he never saw another Joanna Wade painting he would be happier.

Justin never dared attack her career. Instead he criticized another of her loves—her Sausalito home. In his angry moods, he would complain about the house, its distance from the city, the narrow streets, the constant weekend traffic of out-of-towners. Sausalito had turned into a drug paradise, and except for

Joanna, a stick-it-out-to-the-end personality, the artists had all abandoned the place long ago.

His arguments had some validity.

She knew it would be an important victory for him should she sell the house and move back into San Francisco. Still, she refrained from putting the house on the market. She had grown up in San Francisco. Her father and stepmother still occupied a great Victorian Mansion high atop fashionable Pacific Heights, with Keith and Rosemary Marston as neighbors. They lived in a parquet mold of life that she considered detestable. She disliked the city's social life. Had it not been for Justin, she would never have become involved with the other executive wives. She refused to live in a fishbowl because of her wealth and fame.

After last week, a particularly bad time with Justin, she had decided to rent out the Sausalito house and take an apartment in the city. Now, however, it might prove unnecessary.

If Justin succeeded in obtaining the promotion into Linquist's position, the advancement might elevate him to the point where he no longer felt the need to compete with her, and his demands might lessen.

As she drove across the Golden Gate Bridge toward the city, she realized that for the first time she really needed the wives. If she could gain their support for Justin, her life might change for the better. She and Justin could be as happy as they had been the first year of their marriage. She would do anything to have those old times back. *The way we were together,* she thought. *God, how good we had been for one another.* She rolled down the car window and let the wind whip at her hair.

Of course, she did not discount the fact that Justin was the least deserving of the promotion. Merrill Williams and Jake Sterne were better qualified. She pushed that thought from her mind as she took the exit toward Sea Cliff. She slowed the automobile and glanced out at the bay and the rolling green hills beyond. She saw the beauty with an artist's eye, and realized she was in the mood for creating today. Curtail it, she told herself. For Justin's benefit, the meeting with the wives came first.

Far out at sea, she saw a bank of fog creeping toward the mainland and hoped it would not reach the bay before Justin returned home. If it did, he would find an excuse for complaining about the drive to Sausalito and the winding drive to the house, always difficult in the fog.

Joanna smiled to herself. If only Justin could be as loving every night as he had been last night after the annual party. Then his failings would be easier to ignore. She wondered what had turned him on to such an extent. The champagne? The dancing? It had almost been as if he had been playing some strange new game with her. Stimulating, whatever it had been. Carrying her naked onto the terrace and taking her in the foggy dampness as he had taken her that first day on the beach at Stenson.

Only later before they had drifted to sleep in one another's arms had they spoken. Then, just as sleep was claiming her, Justin had whispered, "Do what you can for me with the wives."

Joanna was not blind to Justin's failings.

All things considered, his failings went into making him the man she loved.

There were merely more failings than she recognized.

Infidelity was one of them.

Chapter
Six

MAUREEN STERNE PARKED her station wagon in front of Merrill and Lizabeth Williams's Sea Cliff home, turned off the ignition, and then sat staring at the crowded driveway. She was the last to arrive. Rosemary's chauffeur was leaning against the side of her limousine, smoking, his hat pushed onto the back of his head, his legs crossed at the knees and his highly polished shoes glistening in the sunlight. Joanna's shiny red sportscar was parked behind the limousine, and Vanessa's classic Mercedes stood with the rear dangerously protruding into the street.

Only Janet Linquist's car was missing.

Good for Janet, Maureen thought. Janet no longer belonged to the group. The umbilical cord of ambition had been severed. Her husband's retirement had also been her retirement; she was free.

Maureen marveled at the envy that suddenly rose up inside her. She wanted her own freedom. She wanted never again to feel obligated to attend a meeting of the executive wives. She knew she was a misfit, that she was acceptable not because of herself but because of Jake's position with Multimedia. If Jake had not occupied one of the offices on executive row, none of the wives would have given her a second glance.

They had nothing in common. She was not as wealthy as Rosemary, Joanna, or Lizabeth. She was not worldly or a good conversationalist. She had never been good at "girl talk." And she was older than the others; not by many years—but older. Sometimes she felt as if she had never been young. Those memories that sometimes plagued her of a young girl or a young woman seemed to belong to someone else; memories she had stolen.

As companions she would have preferred a group of middle-class housewives, mothers like herself who were concerned with their children's growth and development. She had been friends with such women before Jake's promotion at Multimedia. Those had been her happy days. Jake had been busy with his career, but he had had time for her and the children then. Now he was a weekend father and husband. Their children scarcely knew him. Robbie, their youngest, was having serious problems in school; the teachers were constantly sending home notes about his disruptive behavior, but the boy would not listen to Jake: she knew Robbie thought of his father as a stranger, a house guest who arrived on Friday evenings and departed on Monday morning. A rivalry had developed between them for her attention.

Maureen took the keys from the ignition and dropped them into her purse. She reached for the door handle, but hesitated, thinking, *she wanted things back the way they were.*

If Jake knew of the decision she had made that morning he would have killed her. But she was determined to go through with it. She would plead if necessary to convince the other wives that she did not want her husband considered for the promotion into Linquist's position. Another promotion for Jake would draw them deeper into their web of unhappiness.

Perhaps she was an optimist, but she still felt there was hope for them to recapture themselves as the couple they had been.

Biting her lower lip with worry, Maureen opened the door and stepped out of the station wagon. Rosemary's chauffeur nodded and touched his hat in greeting as she passed up the walkway, but she failed to notice and respond.

She worried about what the wives would think of her for her decision. The critical glances she anticipated had already driven her to have three stiff drinks before leaving home for the meeting. Ringing Lizabeth's doorbell, she had a compulsion to turn and flee back down the walkway to her station wagon and drive away.

Before she could react, the door swung open and Lizabeth said crossly, "Maureen, you're late again. Well, come in, come in. I need your support. Everyone else is against me."

Chapter
Seven

LIZABETH'S EYES FLASHED beneath an anger-furrowed brow. Walking to the window, she stood with her back to the group, staring out across the windswept bay. "Damnit!" she murmured. "You're all so unreasonable. I think my suggestion is pure genius."

The other wives ignored her statement.

Maureen, settling in a chair with a martini, looked from one woman to another trying to determine exactly what had transpired before her late arrival. She detected anger in Joanna's face, in Vanessa's, but Rosemary appeared quite unmoved, even detached.

"And what is Lizabeth's suggestion?" Maureen asked quietly.

Joanna, not Rosemary, answered. "Lizabeth is suggesting we select a man from the outside to support for the promotion," she said. She glanced at Vanessa. "We think it's ludicrous!"

Lizabeth spun around from the window. "It's not ludicrous!" she snapped. "If we select an outsider for the position and succeed in getting him in, we'll be proving our power. Doesn't that intrigue you? We've been playing at running Multimedia for long enough. Let's really establish our leadership."

Joanna rose from the sofa and moved to the bar, her

movements revealing her tension and anger. She poured a generous helping of scotch into a glass and splashed water on top. "The promotion should go to a man already with Multimedia," she said firmly. She pulled the scarf from her head with an impatient gesture and her dark red hair cascaded about her shoulders. Her violet eyes fixed themselves on Lizabeth. "Granted, your power play is intriguing," she said, "but you're wasting our efforts on a stranger. Why not Jake or Merrill or Mark—or Justin?"

"Especially why not Justin?" Lizabeth murmured so quietly the sarcasm was almost lost.

"I agree with Joanna," Vanessa said weakly. The statement prevented Joanna from returning Lizabeth's sarcasm. "Why should so important a promotion go to a stranger? I know my Mark is the newest employee among our husbands, but I also know he's qualified for the position. I couldn't live with myself if I supported an outsider over . . . over any of our husbands."

"Over Mark you mean," Lizabeth said pointedly. "So it becomes a question of greed among ourselves? Joanna wants Justin promoted. Vanessa wants Mark in the position. Maureen's looking out for Jake's welfare. Rosemary, of course, remains neutral. Am I not the only one who can remain objective?" She turned back to the window, folding her arms across her stomach as if to hold in her anger. "Then we are nothing but meddling wives. Our club is nothing more than a game."

"Are you truly objective, Lizabeth?" Joanna asked. "Or do you have a particular outsider in mind? One you'd rather give your support to at the moment than Merrill?"

As soon as the insinuation had been voiced, Maureen stiffened. She set her martini glass aside and looked to Rosemary to prevent a more serious argument, but Rosemary was staring into space, lost in her own private thoughts.

Lizabeth, spinning around from the window once again, flushed with color. Her arms fell to her sides and her hands closed into fists, causing one of her long, perfectly shaped fingernails to snap. "Goddamn it!" she cried.

Joanna, about to resettle on the sofa, whirled around thinking the curse had been directed at her. Maureen had never seen Joanna so angry; she started to reach out to touch Rosemary's arm and draw her mentally back to the meeting so she might prevent the conversation from going further, but before she could react, Joanna said, "Do you expect us to seriously believe your interest is objective, Lizabeth? We all know one another too well to masquerade our intentions." She lit a cigarette with trembling hands, and from behind a cloud of smoke, added, "I don't believe you're suggesting this merely to test our power. You've a particular outsider in mind, one you're attempting to buy with a promise of the position with Multimedia."

Lizabeth's eyes narrowed to mere slits. "I'm the only one who buys men with money or favors," she shouted. "You, my dear Joanna, are equally familiar with the practice. Isn't that how you got your husband? Wasn't Justin's citizenship the price of your marriage?"

Maureen sprang to her feet. "Stop this!" she cried. "Both of you! Stop it this instant! Rosemary, tell them to stop!"

Rosemary pulled herself back to reality. She stared from Maureen to the smoldering Joanna and Lizabeth. "Yes, do stop arguing," she said distantly. "You're getting nowhere. I'm certain the board meetings at

Multimedia are held with less emotionalism." She pulled herself up in her chair as if awakening from a dream. "Now, where do we stand?"

"At odds with one another," Joanna mumbled as she reseated herself beside Vanessa.

Lizabeth was more direct. "If you had been listening, Rosemary, we wouldn't have to cover the same ground again." The anger she felt with Joanna was quickly transferring itself to all the wives.

Maureen tossed Lizabeth a glance meant to silence her. To everyone in general, she said, "There is one thing I would like to clarify." She felt the muscles in her stomach contracting. Be honest, she told herself. She took a healthy sip of her martini before saying, "I don't want Jake considered for this promotion."

"For heaven's sake, why not?" Rosemary asked. "He's qualified."

"Probably more qualified than any of the others," Maureen said honestly, "but if Jake becomes more involved with Multimedia than he is already . . . well, I feel it will end our marriage." She saw the shock on Rosemary's face and added, "Jake is a demon when it comes to his work. He's already giving more of himself to Multimedia than any wife should have to tolerate." She glanced longingly at her half-empty martini, but restrained herself from reaching for it again. "Jake's become a weekend father and even less of a husband. I know all of you will think it selfish of me, but I truly don't want him to have this promotion. If he gets it, we'll end up in a divorce court." She leaned back in her chair and sighed. "There," she said, "I've been honest with you. As for doing my part to support any other man, I'll go along with the majority."

"So much for Jake," Lizabeth said with satisfaction. "Let's also cross off Merrill." She turned to Joanna, her anger waning. "No, I'm not sacrificing my husband's chances for a new lover," she said. "If we're all going to fly the banner of truth, then I'll say that my situation isn't too different from Maureen's. I want more of Merrill's time than he's willing to give me and I don't want him to have the excuse of additional responsibilities at work. I also want to test our power. I want to know if we're the great manipulators we've pretended to be all this time. Does our interference really produce results? Or are we being ridiculous?"

Rosemary, in the silence that followed, glanced from one to the other of her friends. She did not much feel the part of *Mrs. President* today. She wanted the meeting over and done with. "And you, Joanna? Do you want Justin considered?"

Joanna nodded affirmatively.

"And Vanessa?"

"Yes," Vanessa answered quickly. "I know Mark's the youngest executive with the company, but he's quick and intelligent. Multimedia can use young blood in a position of authority." She glanced from Maureen to Lizabeth. "And there's no problem with the time he's kept away from me. It's a sacrifice I'd make for his career because I understand we'd be happier in the long run."

You'd be happier with the extra money, Lizabeth thought, but held her tongue. She didn't want to be at odds with Vanessa, not now that she had alienated Joanna. "Commendable," she said. "But I don't think Mark is ready for such an important promotion. I still vote for an outsider."

Rosemary felt herself again drifting away from the meeting. An afternoon with the wives had not been the diversion she had expected it to be. She shook herself and tried to concentrate on the meeting. "Then," she said quietly, "it's to be between Justin, Mark or an outsider. I suggest we vote in private ballot. I understand that's the method used at Multimedia when it's a matter personally involving the board members."

Lizabeth left the room and returned with paper and pencils. A secret ballot amused her. Only Rosemary's and Maureen's votes would not be obvious; Joanna would vote for Justin, Vanessa for Mark, she for an outsider.

The votes were cast and passed to Rosemary who opened them on her lap.

Apparently Rosemary had also expected different results. It was with obvious surprise that she announced, "Two votes for Justin, two for the outsider, and one undecided."

Both Joanna and Lizabeth cried, "Undecided!"

Rosemary repeated the results. "Which means," she concluded, "that we still do not have our candidate."

Vanessa's eyes were cast down. She had anticipated the votes better than the others. Maureen, she had concluded, would vote for Justin because her loyalty lay with Joanna—they had been friends longer. Rosemary had voted for the outsider—Vanessa had seen the interest in her eyes at the suggestion of proving their power. She had known that if she voted for Mark it would have concluded the voting in favor of Justin; therefore, to prolong the outcome she had cast her vote as undecided. As she had anticipated, the undecided vote had tied the selection between Justin and an outsider. One of their rules was that they never repeated a vote on the same day. Time would allow her the opportunity of swaying either Maureen or Rosemary to her side. Possibly even Lizabeth, if she could lead Mark, a lamb to the slaughter, into Lizabeth's clutches.

Rosemary, sighing wearily, rose from her chair. "Then we meet again tomorrow," she said. "In the meantime, I suggest our undecided voter come to some firm conclusion."

Lizabeth was glaring at Vanessa; yet a smile played about her lips. "Never underestimate a clever or desperate woman," she half-whispered. *So, my darling Vanessa, don't underestimate me either.* "I think our undecided member should be forced to make her decision now," she said. "Why prolong the inevitable?"

"It's against our rules," Rosemary said. "We'll meet at my house tomorrow. Another day to reach our decision on a candidate will not hinder us."

Maureen rose also. "I must be going," she said hurriedly. "The children are already home from school. I can see myself out." With a quick goodbye, she hurried from the house.

Lizabeth saw her other guests to the door. She watched from the porch as Joanna drove quickly away; she waved to Rosemary, a mass of dark fur and blonde hair huddled in the back seat of her limousine, and ignored Vanessa's wave altogether. When they had gone she went inside and hurried to the telephone. She waited impatiently until there was an answer on the other end of the line; then, forcing herself to smile, she said, "Hello, Aunt Thelma. It's Lizabeth. I know I've been a neglectful niece, but . . ."

When Lizabeth hung up the receiver she was pleased with herself. Aunt Thelma had forgiven her neglect. Aunt Thelma would be delighted to join her for dinner. Aunt Thelma had been lonely and had missed her. Aunt Thelma still held controlling interest in Multimedia.

With Aunt Thelma's support, Lizabeth would be

able to get Justin into the open position. Justin would be extremely grateful. Grateful enough, she imagined, to become her lover.

Maureen, halfway to Atherton, suddenly turned off the highway and stopped at a cocktail lounge. She had used the children as an excuse again. It didn't matter if she was home when they returned from school. They had their friends and after-school activities. As long as she returned in time for dinner no one would notice her absence—or care where she had gone. If she told Jake about the meeting with the wives he would give her more attention than he had in weeks, but, of course, she could not tell him. How did a woman confess to her husband that she did not support his drive for success? That she had voted in favor of another man? She felt enough of a traitor without seeing it reflected in Jake's eyes. Choosing a stool in the corner of the lounge, she ordered a double martini and drank greedily.

Joanna, driving back across the Golden Gate Bridge toward Sausalito, saw that the heavy fog bank had crawled in as far as Land's End. It would reach the city in another hour. Justin would be forced to drive through the fog and it would give him another excuse to complain about the Sausalito house. She told herself to prepare for another of his dark moods. Tonight, her mood would come close to matching his. Damn Lizabeth! And Vanessa! Damn all the wives! Justin should have been chosen as their candidate for the promotion.

Rosemary's eyes stared out from a pale, troubled face at the passing scenery beyond the limousine windows. She had cast her vote for the outsider, not to support Lizabeth, but because the idea of proving their power had intrigued her. She had felt as if she had suddenly confronted Keith and defied his authority. Lizabeth had somehow understood and had winked knowingly at her. Was she so transparent? She pushed the question from her mind. Her thoughts were at floodtide. Strange, she remembered her mother had always used that expression. Leaning her head against the leather seat back, she closed her eyes.

The game of paralleling their husbands was losing its importance to her. She had only done it to claim a part of Keith's life that was denied her. Even with him unaware of their game, she had felt a part of his business life. She had helped make decisions, or had thought she had, and was responsible for them to him as he was responsible to the corporation. If it seemed incongruous to her that she could make decisions concerning Multimedia, and yet was incapable of even small decisions in her personal life, she had not explored it. But now she knew she was forced to make decisions concerning her personal life—if she was to save her marriage.

Rest, she thought. I'll think more clearly after a nap. When she reached home she would take two sleeping pills and have Matty or one of the other maids sit with her while she slept. She would leave instructions to be awakened an hour before Keith was due home. She would dress her best, wear the clothes he appreciated most, and they would have a quiet dinner. After dinner, they would talk sensibly. Once Keith realized how strongly she felt about this third person he wanted to introduce into their sex life he would surely abandon the idea.

Even as she thought this she was shaken by doubts.

He would probably give more consideration to his goddamned dog Teddy than to her. Unconsciously aloud, she said, "If I'd been a four-legged bitch instead of his wife he'd make me suffer less."

The chauffeur was watching her in the rearview mirror.

Embarrassed, she tapped on the dividing glass and instructed him to stop the car. She climbed out, walked to the edge of the cliff overlooking the bay, and drew cool, deep breaths of air into her lungs. Then, with the limousine slowly following, she walked to the bottom of the hill. Somewhat less tense, she motioned the limousine forward and climbed back inside.

At home, Matty met her in the entryway. "There's a young woman waiting in the drawing room," the maid said as she helped Rosemary off with her fur coat. "I'm sorry, but I don't remember her name."

Rosemary suddenly turned cold. She had been expecting no one. Her first instinct was to have Matty get rid of the visitor. What a coward Keith was if he had arranged for her to meet the young woman he had selected without being present himself. If he had dared—! She turned to tell Matty to send the young woman away, but the maid had already walked to the drawing room doors and thrown them open.

The young woman, sitting in a chair near the window, sprang to her feet. She was in her mid-twenties, attractive, although not strikingly so, not the sort Rosemary would have thought would appeal to Keith. Her hair was dark and straight and framed a full, pale face with blue eyes and thin lips tinted an unbecoming shade of red. She held her chin at a slight upward tilt which emphasized her long slender neck. Her clothes were inexpensive but stylish and well-chosen for her slender figure. She kept brushing her hair away from her face in a tell-tale nervous gesture, then turning her head so that it fell freely across her face again. She took a few steps toward the center of the room. Then she stopped and waited until Rosemary had entered through the double doors. "Your husband sent me," she said softly. "He said we were to become acquainted."

The bastard! Rosemary stopped herself from screaming.

"I . . . I imagine this is as awkward for you as . . . as it is for me," the young woman continued in the same soft, almost inaudible voice.

Rosemary stared at the intruder without speaking. Her eyes were taking in every detail of the young woman's appearance. She clung to each half-whispered word, weighing and analyzing, trying to place the hint of an accent, searching for any possible tones of hostility or mockery.

The accent was English, possibly Canadian. As for hostility or mockery, she found none. The young woman feared her confronter as much as Rosemary feared her. Her nervousness was almost pathetic; it would have been to Rosemary if the situation had been different. To keep her hands away from her hair, the young woman finally laced her fingers together in front of her body.

"My name," she said, "is Patricia Eliott. You may call me Pattie."

"And you may call me Mrs. Marston," Rosemary said crossly.

Turning, she swept out into the entryway and up the spiral staircase to lock herself inside her room.

Chapter
Eight

"I FELT LIKE some sort of international spy stealing those files," Hope said from the bedroom. Belting her robe, she appeared in the doorway and stood watching Justin.

Justin sat in a corner of the sofa, the files open on his lap. He had been reading for over an hour, speaking only when she pressed him to do so.

In the meantime, Hope had started a simple dinner and had gone to shower while the swiss steaks steamed in their sauce. "Are they what you expected?" she asked from the doorway.

Justin looked up and nodded. "Linquist was very thorough," he murmured. "He didn't neglect making notes on the smallest details, even the restaurants, foods, and drinks preferred by station representatives. Look at this." He held up a sheet from one of the files and read, *"James Freedkin, likes North Beach area. Food unimportant except for quantity, good-looking waitresses a must. Best place for discussing business—a nudie Broadway club."* Justin laughed as he dropped the sheet back into its file folder.

"Is that ethical?" Hope asked. "Keeping such records on a man because he does business with you?"

"Damn the ethics," Justin said. "I'm only glad

Linquist's memory was becoming so bad he was forced to write everything down. These files are a gold mine to the man who replaces him." He thumbed through another file and pulled out a sheet. "Jackson Sutter," he read aloud, "takes his accounts seriously. Possibly gay. Favorite restaurant—Ernie's. Impressed by the upper classes. Constantly refers to the Multimedia executive wives like a movie fan ogling his favorite actresses." He placed the sheet carefully back into Jackson Sutter's file. "I didn't realize Linquist was such a clever bastard," he said with obvious admiration.

"A dirty old man would be more apt," Hope said strongly. "I didn't realize he kept such notes in those files." She came into the room and crossed to the cocktail table where she took a cigarette from Justin's pack. "Which wives do you think Sutter ogled? Mrs. Marston? Lizabeth Williams? Joanna?"

Justin glanced up at her. "You're jealous," he accused. He reached for her, but she stepped away from his grasp.

"I'll finish dinner," she said coolly. "It's rare that I have you here for so long at one time."

"Oh, I can't stay, darling." He closed the file folders and dropped them onto the cocktail table. "With this goddamned fog it's going to take an hour to get to Sausalito."

Hope's countenance changed, her face paled. "Please stay, Justin. Let me play wife for tonight." When he didn't answer, she came back to the sofa and sat beside him, her eyes pleading. "Just tonight?"

"Darling, I'm sorry. There's nothing I'd like better." He reached for her, drew her to him and kissed her firmly on the mouth. His hands sought the fold of her robe; parting it, his fingers traced the nipples of her breasts.

Hope, angry, struggled against his advances. "Not if you're going to take me and then run," she protested. She pushed his hands away.

Justin stared at her in surprise.

"I would like just once to have you make love to me and then to fall asleep in your arms," Hope told him. "I'd like just once not to be made to feel like . . . like . . ."

Justin, unaccustomed to rejection, brushed her objections aside. He pushed her back against the pillows. Her robe parted and his mouth came to rest on her breast; undoing the belt of her robe he parted the fabric and caressed the soft flesh of her thighs and abdomen. His breathing was becoming heavy and irregular, his mouth working greedily at her breasts.

Hope shuddered beneath the urgency of his hands and mouth. She told herself she did not want him like this, not again, not tonight. She needed the reassurance of his lovemaking, but—for once—she'd like it on her terms. She did not want him to make love to her, then leave her to lie alone listening to foghorns until morning. Besides, she somehow felt that he had been turned on by what he had read in Linquist's files, and that disgusted her. She freed herself from his embrace and rose quickly from the sofa. She paused on her way to the bedroom to stare back at him with anger and hurt. *Damn him to hell!* But she knew she was the one who was damned. She pushed her robe from her shoulders and it settled in a heap about her feet. "If you want me, it won't be on the sofa," she told him. "Come to bed."

Without waiting for him to reply, she turned and went into the bedroom. She dimmed the lamp, removed the bedspread, and stretched out on the sheets to wait for him.

He was removing his tie as he entered.

Hope watched him undress through partially lowered lashes and could not prevent herself from thinking that Joanna watched his systematic disrobing every night while it was only a once or twice a week experience for her. She knew his procedure by heart—first the tie, then the shoes and socks, the shirt, the trousers—each item carefully draped over the back of the chair. Hooking his fingers under either side of the elastic band of his undershorts, he pulled them out and down off his legs.

"You're so damned desirable it's almost criminal," she murmured. "If I thought most Australians were like you, I'd emigrate." She stretched out her arms toward him.

Justin held back; his expression told her he was in the mood for teasing her—or for punishing her for objecting to his not spending the night with her. "Sometimes," he said, "I think your attraction to me is strictly physical." He ran his hands down over his hard abdomen and cupped the weighty bulge of his maleness. "If another man came along with the same equipment you'd turn me out." He laughed at her, but there was no laughter in his eyes.

"Damn you! I wouldn't steal company files for anyone but you. I wouldn't put up with our arrangement with any other man. Beneath this sham of a modern woman lurks a puritanical heart." She motioned him forward with her hands. "Make love to me *now*, Justin."

Still, he hung back. "Tell me how much you want me, Hope."

"More than I ever wanted anything in my life." The truth of the statement stunned her. "And you, Justin? How much do you want me?"

Without answering, he crossed to the bed and lowered himself into her outstretched arms.

77

Hope groaned with the heaviness of him. She could smell the nicotine and alcohol on his breath, the maleness of his body. She could feel the heat of his flesh, the throbbing of his penis as it pressed against her thigh. His mouth hungrily sought hers, and his tongue pressed between her teeth. She felt him lift, reach and position himself to enter her.

"Slowly, Justin," she murmured. "Make it last. At least give me that tonight."

Ignoring her, he forced her legs apart with his knees and drove himself into her with such fury that she screamed with pain. She dug her fingernails into his back as he encased himself.

Let him explain those scratches to Joanna, she thought.

"Justin, you're hurting me!"

"I slipped," he lied without even a tone of apology in his voice. He pulled back and drove into her again with the same brutality.

As Hope's pain ebbed she found the harmony of movement. Her urgency soon matched his, and he knew there would be no further demand to make it last. His mouth came back to her breasts, his teeth unsheathed by his passion.

When his body suddenly went rigid, Hope cried, "Not yet, Justin! Please, not yet!"

But he lifted his buttocks until he had almost extracted himself from her, drove himself down to the hilt, and froze. She felt the spasms shake his body. Then he became a lifeless weight on top of her, crushing her, making breathing almost impossible. She whimpered and struggled to turn, and Justin, moaning, rolled off her and lay quietly at her side. Smothering her frustration, she turned and kissed him gently on the lips.

"I love you," she whispered.

After a long moment of silence, his eyes fluttered open. "And I love you." He returned her kiss, his lips parched and unlingering. Rising from the bed, he said, "But I can't spend the night so don't ask again."

Hope said nothing. She felt suddenly embarrassed by her nakedness and pulled the sheet over her body. She watched him go into the bathroom, heard the water turned on, then the spray springing from his body and striking the plastic shower curtain. He was humming that damnable "Waltzing Matilda," and for some unexplainable reason it irritated her and made her want to cry out to silence him.

When he came out of the bathroom she was sitting up in bed smoking one of his long, brown cigarettes. She hated the taste of the damned things, but she felt they made her look sophisticated. Besides, Joanna smoked them. They were even pretentious enough to have *WADE* stamped in gold above the filter.

As Justin crossed to his clothes, he said, "Next week I'll arrange to spend the night. I'll tell her I'm going to stay at the club to get some work done." He dressed quickly, almost carelessly, which was unlike him. "Our time will come, darling. And soon, if I get the promotion into Linquist's position."

Hope crushed out the finished cigarette. "Justin, am I better than she is?" she asked sharply. "Is it better with me than it is with her?"

"There's no comparison," he answered without looking up from the shoes he was lacing.

"That wasn't my question."

He didn't answer until he had finished lacing his shoes. Then he stood and looked down at her, his expression intense. "Yes, it's better between us," he said. He crossed to the bed and bent down and kissed her cheek. "You're the best, Hope Ingress." He straightened before becoming entangled in the arms

79

she attempted to slip about his neck. "Don't forget to return those files tomorrow."

"I won't. If I did and they were missed, I'd lose my job. I'd see you even less." *Because I would be of less use to you,* she thought. As always when he was preparing to leave her, she had a sinking sensation, an unspoken panic that she would not see him again. "Must you leave immediately? It's early. Dinner must be ready. It would mean so much to me, Justin. A quiet dinner, just the two of us, with candlelight and soft music."

"Next week," he said impatiently. From the outer room, he called, "Good night, darling."

When the door had closed behind him, Hope got out of bed, went into the kitchen and turned off the flame beneath the swiss steak. She returned to bed without eating and lay listening to the foghorns, Justin's promise of "next week" echoing inside her head.

Chapter
Nine

LIGHTS WERE ABLAZE in the Marston house on Pacific Heights.

Three people were seated at the massive dining table—Keith and Rosemary Marston at either end, and in the middle, looking extremely uncomfortable and not eating, Patricia Eliott.

The use of the formal dining room had been Rosemary's idea. The room was seldom used for less than twelve guests; more intimate dinner parties were held in the smaller dining room with windows overlooking the bay.

Rosemary had counted on the discomfort the young intruder would feel, but she had not anticipated her own. The great distance between Keith and herself and the young woman between them appeared symbolic of their situation. She wished now she had not been insistent on the formal room with its cold crystal chandelier and glaring ancestral paintings. In the smaller dining room the fog-shrouded lights of the Marina would have afforded her something on which to focus her attention. As it was, she had only her plate with its uninteresting veal cordon bleu, the Tiffany centerpiece, the accusing eyes of the paintings, or

Keith, his eyes as accusingly damning—or the young woman.

Rosemary would not have come down to dinner at all if Keith had not insisted so vehemently. Afraid of angering him and driving him into the arms of their guest for companionship, she had unwillingly complied. She wished now she had not; better to have fitfully paced her room than to sit in the midst of this oppressive silence. She laid her fork aside, and staring past the young woman, watched Keith.

The silence did not seem to concern him. He ate with his usual appetite. The young woman, in his mind, had apparently passed from the position of guest to that of resident; he felt no obligation to entertain her with table talk. *The bastard! Patricia Eliott was young enough to be his daughter!*

Rosemary felt obliged to break the silence. "What of Larry Linquist's successor?" she asked. "Have you settled on anyone?" To avoid the more important topics of which she had not felt capable of dealing with, she had spent the better part of the afternoon thinking of nothing else.

Keith, dabbing the corners of his mouth with his napkin, leaned back in his chair and fixed his gaze on her over the expanse of the table. "Is Larry's successor of interest to you, my dear?" he asked, smiling.

Rosemary mumbled, "Of course. Everything concerning Multimedia is of interest to me."

"But not, I think, to Miss Eliott," Keith said. "We cannot bore her with such trivia on her first night."

Rosemary felt herself pale. "I certainly would not wish to bore Miss Eliott," she said stiffly. "Nor to be bored by her." She turned her gaze to the younger woman. "Perhaps Miss Eliott could suggest a topic of conversation," she said, "that would be agreeable to all of us."

Patricia Eliott's head was lowered over her plate. She was making an effort to eat, but a futile one; she had already pushed her food about on her plate until it had begun to resemble a goulash. Her head shot up at Rosemary's remark as if she had been struck. "I . . . I don't . . ."

"Patricia is here to size us up, so to speak," Keith said, coming to her rescue. Keith met Rosemary's questioning stare, explaining, "She insists on becoming acquainted with us before—"

"I understand," Rosemary interrupted, before he could verbalize their situation. Her tension snapped like a wire under too much stress with the realization of what Keith had said. She had expected the worst tonight, to retire to her room and undress beneath a third pair of eyes, to crawl into bed, her bed, not knowing if she had been designated the right side, the left side, or the middle. How did such arrangements work? What was she expected to do? But she had had a reprieve! The relief almost made her burst into tears. "I understand," she repeated, and even managed a weak, senseless smile.

"Since you do, my dear, I shall leave you and Patricia to do just that, to become acquainted," Keith said. "I have some pressing business matters to attend to." He pushed back his chair and rose. "Perhaps you will both join me for a cognac in the study later."

Neither woman answered.

After Keith had left them, the silence settled back in, heavier and not now even broken by the younger woman's silver tapping against her plate; she sat with her head lowered and her hands folded in her lap.

After what seemed an eternity, Rosemary drew in her breath and asked, "Do you find my husband attractive, Miss Eliott?"

"Not very."

The bluntness shocked Rosemary. "Are you always so truthful?"

"I try to be." The younger woman's voice was low pitched; her nervousness evident, and, to Rosemary, suddenly sympathetic.

"If you don't find him attractive, why have you agreed to this . . . this arrangement?"

The younger woman lifted her head, her blue eyes probing Rosemary's. "Why have you?"

Rosemary, shaken, reached for her wine glass. Twisting the stem between her fingers, her gaze didn't leave Patricia's. Even if she could, she wondered if she would answer the question the younger woman asked of her?

"I had not realized until I met you this afternoon that you had not agreed to . . . to this arrangement," Patricia told her with her same straightforward honesty. "Mrs. Marston, if you prefer, I'll leave. Immediately."

"No!" Rosemary almost shouted. The stem of the wine glass snapped between her fingers. The bowl of the glass toppled and the wine spilled and began to spread like blood across the lace tablecloth. "Leave it," Rosemary said when Patricia leaped to her feet to attend the mess." Please sit down, Miss Eliott. Let me explain why I do not wish you to leave us. Or, let me attempt to explain. I'm no good at such things, at explaining motives, especially my own. Of course, I do not wish you here." A faint smile crossed her face. "You see, even I can sometimes be quite honest. I don't wish this type of arrangement. I find it loathsome. But my husband does. He finds something lacking in our relationship. It was to be either this arrangement or he would take a mistress. Frankly, I can't decide which I'd find more devastating."

."But then why not leave him?" Patricia asked incredulously.

Rosemary sighed. "Why not indeed?" She took her napkin and lay it over the spilled wine. "The point is I can't leave him," she confessed. "I can't imagine life without him. But should you go away, should I send you away now, there would only be another young woman to take your place. I'd merely be buying a few days' time. I know my husband, and he's quite determined. Since above all else I don't want to lose Keith, I'll simply have to adjust to the situation. But it won't be easy for me, Miss Eliott. I'm what you would call a prude. I don't believe in casual sex or extramarital affairs. Before Keith Marston, I knew only one other man. I never expected to know another after Keith." Covering her face with her hand, Rosemary suddenly laughed bitterly. "You see how much of a prude I am? Now it seems I am to submit to an . . . an unnatural act merely to keep my husband. I am expected to do this to give my marriage meaning—those are my husband's words, not mine." Removing her hand from her face she looked at the younger woman. "And you, Miss Eliott? You're an attractive young woman. Why did *you* agree?"

"It's strictly financial," Patricia answered.

Rosemary knew that the younger woman had told her first obvious lie. "What I'm asking you for, Miss Eliott, is time," she said. "I don't know how much time, but enough to adjust. Only you can force my husband to give me that time. You can reason with him. I cannot. I am, I'm afraid, a very weak woman."

"Weak? Oh, no, Mrs. Marston. I find you remarkably strong." The younger woman's gaze wavered; she pulled her eyes away from the surprised

Rosemary. "I'll help you in any way possible," she said.

Of course, after such an evening, Rosemary could not sleep.

She lay at the extreme edge of their king size bed, her eyes closed, while Keith went over some contracts for Multimedia. Occasionally she would stir as if disturbed and stare at him through her lashes.

He knew she was pretending sleep, and she knew he knew it.

"Tell me," he said without looking up from the contracts, "did you like Miss Eliott?"

She knew he expected her to voice objections, to cry out about the outrage of it all. "Yes," she answered. "I like her."

Surprise made him look away from the contracts. "You did?"

"Don't take that for easy acceptance of the arrangement," she told him. "You merely asked if I liked her, and I do." She pulled herself up against the headboard and half-turned to face him. "Could it be, Keith Marston, that you, yourself, are having second thoughts about your little arranged *ménage à trois?*"

"None whatsoever," he said blandly.

"Then what makes you bring work to bed? You've never done it before."

"A pressing matter," he answered.

"Surely with a company as large as Multimedia you've had *pressing matters* before. You've never brought them home in the past, especially into the bedroom."

"Are you fishing for some information?"

"Just to satisfy my curiosity," she said.

"You know what that did to the cat."

"No clichés, please. They're beneath you."

With a sigh, he closed the folder that lay against his legs. "You're trying to force me to say I'm disturbed about 'our' arrangement."

"*Your* arrangement," she corrected.

"As you will. But it's not the arrangement that's keeping me from sleeping. Larry Linquist's sudden retirement leaves a major gap in operations. I have to decide on his replacement."

Rosemary glanced at the closed file. "Who are you considering?"

"Does it truly interest you? That is, beyond who the new wife will be to join your group?"

"I've always taken an interest in your company."

Keith was silent for a moment, thinking, then said, "Yes, that's always intrigued me. It's so unlike you to take interest in matters of business. You're the most feminine of women, and business is a man's world."

Rosemary laughed softly. "You'll always remain a riddle to me, Keith. In some things you are so progressive and in others you're so old-world. To bring you up to present times, the business world is no longer exclusively the man's domain."

"Well, you won't have to suffer through that *change* with me for a while yet, my dear. I'm not considering a female replacement for Linquist."

"Of course, the position should go to Merrill Williams or Jake Sterne."

"Why of course?"

"Because they're the most qualified."

"But they're both doing well in their present positions. Should I promote one of them then I'll not only have to train them in Linquist's duties, but someone in theirs as well."

"Then you're considering someone from the lower ranks?" Rosemary pressed.

Keith smiled. "Yes, my dear. And now you'll have something to report to the other wives."

Ignoring his remark, Rosemary said, "You're not even considering Justin Wade or Mark Kirkman?"

"Have Joanna and Vanessa approached you to make that inquiry?"

"No."

"Then I'll tell you I am considering both men. But frankly I don't feel either is qualified. Mark suffers from lack of a business drive and Justin is perhaps driven by personal devils. But I don't wish this information passed along at one of your afternoon teas with the wives."

"Of course not," Rosemary said, offended. Then Lizabeth was right, she thought, if even Keith thought an outsider better qualified than the men presently on executive row. Perhaps it would be a challenge for the wives to select the candidate most unlikely for the promotion and test their power by pushing him into the position. "Who are you considering?" she asked casually.

Keith took the folder from his legs and laid it on the bedside stand. "Several men," he answered evasively. "None you would have met who would have made an impression."

"Then that's what you were doing tonight? Grading them according to their possibilities?"

"Precisely. And now, my dear, if you don't want to question me further, I'll get some sleep." Without waiting for her to speak, he reached for the lamp and switched it off.

Rosemary lay in the darkened room listening to the foghorns outside and Keith's heavy breathing inside. She had pushed thoughts of Patricia Eliott from her mind until she heard muffled sounds from the room across the hallway. What, she asked herself, was the woman doing at this late hour? Had their meeting upset the younger woman to the point of sleeplessness? No, she mustn't think of Patricia Eliott tonight! She had been given a reprieve. For that she was grateful. Like Scarlett O'Hara, she would think about Miss Eliott—and the arrangement—*tomorrow*.

Tonight her thoughts belonged to the selection of Larry Linquist's replacement. She must function as *Mrs. President*. That would help her to maintain her sanity.

She lay for over an hour until Keith's breathing told her that he had drifted into a deep sleep. Rising carefully so as not to awaken him, she took the folder from his bedside table and carried it into the bathroom.

There were sheets on six men. A covering page listing their names had been marked in red pencil by Keith before she had interrupted him. Two names were lined out. Of the four that remained, numbers had been placed beside each—one, two, three and four. Possibly, she thought, the order of preference Keith had decided upon. What did the selection depend on now? Interviews? Employment records? Then she saw a small notation in the right-hand corner. *Check out wives!*

She supposed it was customary for the wives of future executives to be scrutinized. The executive whose wife objected to his career would have outside problems to deal with that would reduce his commitment to business. But didn't all of them, those in her little group, object in one way or another to their husbands' careers?

Keith stirred in the other room; she heard the mattress creak as he turned over. Fearing he would reach for her and awaken if he did not find her beside him, she quickly jotted down the names of the four candidates on tissue paper with her eyebrow pencil.

She slipped quietly back into the bedroom, returned the file, and crawled back into bed.

Still, sleep would not come.

She continued to hear Miss Eliott moving about across the hallway. She shut her eyes tightly and tried to make a blank of her mind.

PART 2

PART 2

Chapter
Ten

ERICA ABBOTT STOOD on Montgomery Street in the heart of the Financial District and watched the pedestrians with acute interest. She drew—or attempted to draw—the excitement into herself to make her, no matter how slightly, a part of the business world to which her husband was committed.

It was ten o'clock. Her appointment at Multimedia was scheduled for eleven.

She faced the appointment with both excitement and dread.

Today, she would be scrutinized by Keith Marston, the company's president. The appointment had been made yesterday by telephone. But she had been expecting the call—the wives of the executives had warned her.

How odd that had been—visiting them! Even now, two days later, the visit seemed more like a dream than a reality.

It had been Lizabeth Williams who had explained the visit.

Christopher was being considered for an important promotion with Multimedia. Out of four candidates, the wives had selected Christopher to back. "A little game of ours," Lizabeth had told her, "to parallel our husbands." And she had told Erica about the exclusive club the wives had formed. "All very secret, of course," the blonde-haired Lizabeth had told her, "but we're determined for you to join us."

Why her? She hadn't even questioned their choice of a candidate, assuming that they found Christopher the most highly qualified for the promotion.

Strange, they were—the wives. She had been in such awe of them that she had not reacted to them individually except in retrospect. Two, Joanna and Vanessa, had seemed to resent her. Maureen Sterne had been pleasant, motherly, but rather distant, and Rosemary Marston, whose husband was to interview her today, had seemed preoccupied. Only Lizabeth had been friendly, outgoing, and excited about the prospect of welcoming her into their group.

Erica drew the chilled air deep into her lungs.

So much had happened to them since Christopher's transfer from the Detroit office. At first she had resented being uprooted and relocated at Multimedia's command, and expense. Their Russian Hill apartment did not compare to the small suburban house they had been forced to sell. She had never lived in an apartment in her life, and had never had to contend with clanking steam radiators, noisy neighbors, and hallways that constantly smelled of mildewed carpets. Her life had been comparatively simple, if a little dull. But she had wanted Christopher's transfer; he had not. Where he had been content in Multimedia's Detroit office, she had felt herself being stifled, locked into a boring existence as her parents had been. San Francisco had sounded so sophisticated. To push him into accepting the transfer, she had accused Christopher of surrendering to the mundane, of lacking ambition, of actually becoming dull and dreary. How long since the transfer—one and a half years? Christopher had ceased to grumble and had applied himself.

And now this! An important promotion that would change both their lives! Hers possibly more than Christopher's. She could easily imagine herself as one of *The Wives*.

When Erica had first met Christopher Abbott she had looked upon The Company—as Christopher always referred to Multimedia—with mixed feelings of jealousy. It had stolen too much of his attention away from her. As a young bride, she had found it difficult to adjust to sharing the man she loved with an organization. But then, when she had settled into the routine of being the wife of a company man and their lifestyle had depended on Christopher's advances and raises, she had developed toward Multimedia a sense of awe and apprehension along with respect. They lived, she felt, at the mercy of The Company. She had then begun to encourage her husband's late night working hours and his devotion to the monster that supported them. She had feared, and still feared, that Christopher did not do enough to insure their future. She wanted, like Vanessa, the finer things in life and knew no way of obtaining them aside from pushing her husband into obtaining them for her. The visit of the wives had reawakened and fed her dream. She wanted to be surrounded by friends like the wives; she wanted their aura of wealth and sophistication.

Christopher's promotion, if it came through, could be an important step toward obtaining her goal. If he were made an executive, she would automatically take her place among the wives—Lizabeth had promised her as much.

Lifting her head, Erica stared up at the skyscraper

whose top five floors housed Multimedia. From high above, less than a thousand employees ran the great corporation—and in some way, the lives of the multitudes through their movies and television shows. She remembered a graph Christopher had once showed her; a map, it had been, with tiny lines spreading out from San Francisco like a gigantic spider web to the television stations and production companies located across the United States. She had been impressed, but she had also wondered if Christopher possessed the ability to make himself significant in the leadership of so complex a corporation.

There was a gold-framed tile on the door with his name: *Keith Marston*.

The man behind the desk was not what she expected.

He looked to be in his late forties, young for the president of so great a corporation, with deep-set blue eyes and hair greying at the temples. When he stood to greet her she had noted he was over six feet tall, with a trim, muscular body that could not be concealed beneath his clothes. His blue eyes were alert, intelligent, and seemed to study her intently. His suit was expensive, impeccably tailored, and she told herself that she would have to look more carefully to Christopher's wardrobe.

Erica knew that Keith Marston was examining her clothing also, but she did not find that disconcerting. Lizabeth had told her how to dress; a simple brown suit and hat, no jewelry except her wedding rings. Her blonde hair was worn simply; the eye shadow that usually accentuated her grey eyes had been forgone to achieve a freshly scrubbed look. The collar of the white silk blouse she had purchased at Saks framed her face and gave her, she thought, a pure, if not virginal, look. Christopher would protest when he received the bill for the blouse, but she would be able to justify the expense if he got the promotion.

Reflecting, she thought it inconceivable that an employee should be judged on his wife's merits in addition to his own. Christopher, although possibly lacking in the exhaustive ambition she thought he should have, had always been an asset to Multimedia. He had discovered and produced two very successful series for the corporation. Personally, she had detested both of them, but the public had been less demanding of plot and character development. *Steiner,* a detective show, had even popped up twice in first place in the Nielsen ratings.

She wondered what questions Keith Marston would ask her.

As it turned out, he only chatted with her briefly.

Then, giving her a questionnaire to complete, he left her alone in his office.

He did not return until she opened the door and informed the secretary that she had completed the form.

Moments later, she was wondering why Keith Marston was scrutinizing her questionnaire so thoroughly. It had been simple, almost juvenile. She compared it to a test for her driver's license which she had taken a few weeks before; anyone with reasoning power could determine the expected answers.

If your husband promised to take you out for your birthday and then called at the last minute to say he would be detained on company business, would you:

    ___ *(a) Create a scene over the telephone*
    ___ *(b) Threaten to divorce him*
    ___ *(c) Tell him you understand*

She had, of course, checked "c" and she suddenly wondered if the simplicity of the questionnaire had somehow been a deliberate trap. She had a moment of panic; then reasoned that she had answered truthfully. She would have (c) told him she understood. Then she would have (a) created a scene over the telephone by (b) threatening to divorce him if the company meant more to him than his wife.

Erica expected the most from Christopher where his advancement with the company was concerned, but she firmly believed that a man could be multi-faceted enough to devote himself to his wife and his company—in that order.

Keith Marston was pulled away from her questionnaire by the telephone. He answered in a deep, practiced business voice. While he talked Erica craned her neck to examine the markings he had placed on her questionnaire, but could decipher none of the notations in their upside down position. The markings, in red ink, reminded her of school.

She stared past Keith Marston's shoulders at the San Francisco skyline. It was a clear, windy day after last night's fog, and the glass and steel of the buildings glistened in the weak afternoon sun. Even from high above the streets, she could sense the pulse of the city. She told herself she would never allow Christopher to take her away from the city. If he failed in this promotion, there would be others. She had accepted the challenge of becoming a member of The Wives. Nothing would make her fail.

Keith Marston mumbled an almost incoherent goodbye and returned the telephone receiver to its cradle. "Forgive me," he said. He smiled at her, his eyes confirming the fact that he was attracted to her.

Men make allowances for women who appeal to them. She returned his smile flirtatiously.

"There's no need to keep you longer, Mrs. Abbott. We just wanted to have a look at you. Under the stress of an interview, you might say."

Erica found his use of the pronoun "we" gave her a strange sensation. She felt as if eyes other than Keith Marston's had been watching her since her arrival, some Board of Inquisitors hidden away behind a see-through mirror to observe Mrs. Christopher Abbott's merits as a possible executive wife.

Keith leaned back in his chair and made a pyramid of his hands, his long, slender fingers resting against the tip of his chin. "Thank you for coming in, Mrs. Abbott."

"You mean that's all?" Erica asked.

"Were you expecting more?" He seemed amused.

"Frankly, yes," she admitted. She suddenly felt as if she had failed Christopher and herself. Wouldn't Keith Marston have questioned her further if he had truly been considering Christopher for the promotion?

"Multimedia places an importance on the wives of their executives," Keith said quietly, "but we have no way of testing their skills. We must content ourselves with brief meetings and little chats."

What had he meant by "testing their skills"? Erica wondered. There was something decidedly sexual in the way he stared at her.

"I've heard of corporations going much further," she said, remembering an article she had read in one of the women's magazines. In that case a woman had suffered a nervous breakdown because detectives employed by her husband's company had uncovered her private, rather sordid life. Her husband had lost his promotion, but he had sued her for divorce and taken custody of their children. Of course that woman *had* something to hide—she, Erica, didn't.

"Yes, I've heard of extreme cases myself," Keith

admitted, "but that isn't true of Multimedia. Meeting you and having you complete our questionnaire was sufficient." He rose behind his desk. "Now, I mustn't take up more of your time," he said, which, of course, meant he wanted no more of *his* time taken by the interview. "Have a good afternoon, Mrs. Abbott."

Outside Keith Marston's office, Erica paused to gather her thoughts. She really had no way of determining the impression she had made. Had she helped or hindered Christopher's chances? Perhaps Lizabeth Williams, who had invited her to lunch after the interview, could explain the enigmatic Keith Marston.

Erica started to move away from Marston's door when she stopped, caught by sight of a familiar figure. The center of the horseshoe shaped offices occupied the desks of the secretaries. Now, at lunchtime, the desks were mostly unoccupied. But one woman was stooped before a large section of filing cabinets. Erica recognized her as Hope Ingress, the secretary Christopher had introduced her to at the annual party.

"Miss Ingress?"

The startled secretary turned so abruptly the files she had been returning to the cabinets slipped from her hands and fluttered to the floor. She had turned remarkably pale.

Erica hurried forward. Stooping, she began gathering the dislocated sheets from the folders. "Do forgive me for startling you," she apologized.

The secretary's composure began to return. She accepted the file sheets from Erica, and managed a weak smile. "How are you, Mrs. Abbott? If you're looking for your husband, I'm afraid you're on the wrong floor. His office is located on the floor below."

"Yes, I know," Erica said, laughing nervously. She glanced back at Keith Marston's closed door. "I just had an interview with Mr. Marston."

Hope's question was asked by a slight arching of her eyebrows.

"As a prospective executive wife," Erica explained. "Isn't it exciting? Christopher is being considered for Mr. Linquist's position."

"Oh?" Hope began returning the dislocated sheets into the proper files. "Your husband's future with Multimedia seems to be advancing quite rapidly," she said. "I must congratulate him."

Erica imagined something of a criticism in the secretary's remark. She thought to question it, then decided it was best to ignore such encounters. What did she care for a secretary's opinion of Christopher's success? If Christopher got this promotion, then she would have to learn to rise above such pettiness. Hope Ingress was undoubtedly an embittered woman with no life of her own. Perhaps she favored some other man for the position and considered Christopher a usurper.

Erica bid Hope a good afternoon with emphasis on *Miss* Ingress.

By the time she reached the sidewalk and turned toward California Street to meet Lizabeth Williams she had forgotten about the secretary entirely.

Chapter
Eleven

When Erica Abbott entered the restaurant where Lizabeth was waiting, Lizabeth noticed two men giving the younger woman approving glances, and she felt a tinge of jealousy.

She is pretty, Lizabeth thought. *And so damned young.*

"I'm sorry I'm late, Lizabeth," Erica said as she reached the table.

Before Erica could slip into the chair across from Lizabeth, Lizabeth asked, "How did it go with Keith Marston?"

"Fine, I think," Erica answered uncertainly. She leaned her purse against her leg and shook her napkin out on her lap. "He's kind of cute."

"Who?"

"Mr. Marston," Erica answered.

Lizabeth laughed, hoping the gin had not flavored her voice after three martinis. Keith Marston—*cute!* She supposed her luncheon companion would consider Paul Newman cute. Dumb little bitch! "What did you mean by, Fine, I think?"

"I really don't know," Erica confessed. "We talked a little and I filled out a ridiculous questionnaire." She lifted her hands in an expression of confusion and then dropped them back into her lap. "It certainly was nothing like I expected. Did you fill out one of those questionnaires when Merrill got his position with Multimedia?"

"No, dear," Lizabeth answered dryly. "The circumstances were quite different."

Erica understood the implication. "If Christopher doesn't get this promotion, I don't know what I'll do. He hates San Francisco and I know he's considering asking to return to the Detroit office."

"Why does he hate San Francisco?" Lizabeth asked with mild interest.

"He says the people are cold and uncaring."

"People are cold everywhere," Lizabeth murmured. "I hope Christopher hasn't expressed his discontent to his fellow employees. If he's not felt to be completely brainwashed into the company, it might affect his chances of promotion. The Multimedia executives have as much pride in our fair city as they do in that damned company. And you as the wife of a potential executive mustn't mention his discontent to the other wives."

"Perhaps I'm not as equipped to be an executive wife as I thought," Erica said with frustration.

"You'll learn, my dear. With my help."

"Perhaps I should stop dreaming and hoping and let fate do what it will."

"That, my dear, is definitely not the statement of an executive wife," Lizabeth said with a laugh.

Erica felt a sudden insight into Lizabeth. "You hate it, don't you?" she asked. "Being the wife of a business executive?"

Lizabeth shrugged. "I've learned to live with it," she said. "I suppose it's preferable to being the wife of a ditch digger or an undertaker." She drained her martini glass. "Why do you look at me that way? I'm not nearly so miserable as you're imagining." She ran her index finger absently about the rim of her empty glass. "Actually, my life is quite orderly. I do occasionally become bored, but I've found a way of alleviating that." She glanced about for the waiter to refill her glass. *Your husband might be the next,* she thought. He was handsome, Christopher Abbott, with his unruly dark hair and innocent brown eyes.

The waiter approached, took their order, and vanished.

"Let's not talk about me," Lizabeth said. "Tell me about you. And your Christopher."

"Christopher?" Erica said. She looked thoughtfully at her luncheon companion. "I wouldn't know how to explain my husband, except that he's good to me and that we're happy."

"Ah, yes, happiness," Lizabeth remarked. "Tell me why you're happy then. To what magical ingredient in your relationship do you attribute this happiness?"

"I haven't really thought about it," Erica answered. She felt Lizabeth was being rather flippant, perhaps laughing at her.

"Perhaps you're soulmates," Lizabeth said. "Mythical lovers. One is supposed to experience the epitome of happiness with one's soulmate. Of course I've never met anyone who's actually met their spiritual partner. I thought maybe you and Christopher would be the first."

"Are you making fun of me?" Erica asked bluntly.

"Gracious, no," Lizabeth assured her. "Is Christopher a good lover? Is he fantastic in bed?"

Erica's cheeks flushed with color.

"I see he is," Elizabeth observed. "That's good. A woman should always have a man who's good in bed." She paused before continuing, "Does Christopher take tranquilizers?'' Lizabeth was becoming quite personal and Erica began to feel nervous.

"No, he doesn't," Erica answered coolly.

"Well, don't let him start no matter how difficult things become at Multimedia."

"You make it sound as if he already has the promotion," Erica said.

"Oh, but he will have," Lizabeth said with assurance.

Erica leaned across the table. In a half-whisper, she asked, "How can you be so sure?"

"There you go again, staring at me with those wide innocent eyes. Sometimes you remind me of a Keene painting, Erica. Of course, I'm not entirely certain about the promotion, but I'm reasonably convinced we wives can pull it off."

"The other wives didn't seem as devoted to Christopher's advancement as you," Erica said.

"That's because Joanna and Vanessa wanted the promotion for their own husbands," Lizabeth told her. "We had difficulty deciding on a candidate, but when Rosemary . . . oh, but why bore you with details?"

"I'm far from bored," Erica confessed. "I find all the wives fascinating."

"Really? You must fascinate easily."

"Naturally I feel closer to you. You've taken such an interest. Shall I anticipate difficulties with Joanna and Vanessa? After all, if they wanted the promotion for their husbands . . ."

Lizabeth shrugged. "Little good it would do them to object now. With Rosemary and Maureen and I voting for your husband, they'll have to accept the majority rule." Lizabeth reached across the table and patted Erica's hand. "Trust me to do all I can for your husband," she said.

"I do," Erica assured her. "And I'm so grateful."

Lizabeth's eyebrows arched with a sudden thought. "I wonder if your Christopher will be as grateful," she said softly. Before Erica could comment, she said hurriedly, "It's going to be refreshing having you in our little group, Erica. You'll be a welcome replacement for Janet Linquist. Fresh blood, so to speak."

"You make it sound absolutely ghoulish," Erica said with a nervous laugh.

"A good description, I suppose," Lizabeth said thoughtfully. "You'll be the first new wife in our group since Kathleen Barrett's husband threw himself out of the thirty-first floor window."

"How awful!" Erica cried.

Ignoring her, Lizabeth went on, "Then we got Vanessa Kirkman and her husband Mark. Dear Vanessa, dear Mark. You've much in common with Vanessa, Erica. It shouldn't surprise me if you become the closest of friends."

"I'd like to be friends with all the wives," Erica said.

"Perhaps you shall. But we're a strange group. Joanna, as I've told you, is a famous painter. She isn't very social. Maureen is even less social. She has her home on the Peninsula with a brood of growing brats. She nips a bit, and will probably end up an alcoholic within another three years. Rosemary is quite social, but distant. In the years I've known her I can't tell you much about her personal life. She's been going through something lately, but pry as I may I can't get a word out of her. Vanessa is always ready for a cocktail party, a dinner, or any other engagement that she feels might push her husband's career. Then there's yours truly. Aside from Joanna, I'm the only one in our group who belongs to what people refer to as Old San Franciscans. My family reaches back to the gold rush days when some enterprising relative bought up land from the miners who went broke. There was a lot of graft involved, but time has washed the money clean. I think the bastard was hanged, but that tidbit of family history has been locked away in one of our closets." Lizabeth stopped talking and stared at Erica. "Now you'll be in the group. I wonder what you'll be like in a year, two years."

"Oh, I'll never change. I'll always be me," Erica said with assurance.

"Will you?" Lizabeth said dubiously. "And your Christopher? How will a promotion and more responsibility affect him? Maybe it'll make him less of a lover. Have you thought of that? Perhaps the brass ring will make you miserable."

"A company could never change Christopher," Erica said.

Lizabeth smiled knowingly. "I don't know if your naviete is refreshing or not," she said bluntly, "but it will be interesting. By the next annual Multimedia party you and Christopher will be quite different people. Now, I'm simply starving. Where is our lunch?"

As if on cue, the waiter arrived and served their lunches.

Erica stared at the food and realized she had lost her appetite. There was a tightness in the pit of her stomach.

"We'll have to get together with our husbands," Lizabeth said. "Does Christopher like to gamble?"

"We haven't had time to go to Lake Tahoe or Reno," Erica answered.

"Well, with the right connections you can gamble in the Chinatown casinos," Lizabeth said. "I have those connections, so perhaps one evening . . ."

"Oh, but on Christopher's salary we can't afford . . ."

"My treat," Lizabeth interrupted. "Since I'll be working for your husband's promotion, I might as well get to know him."

"You'll like him," Erica told her.

"I'm sure I shall," Lizabeth murmured.

"Gambling sounds fascinating," Erica said as she pushed the food around in her plate. "I've never gambled."

Yes, you have, my dear, Lizabeth refrained from saying. *You've bet on your ambition and the ante was your husband.* "You're fond of the word fascinating, aren't you, Erica?"

Erica make a mental note to use the word less. "I'm so glad we became friends, Lizabeth."

Lizabeth averted her gaze. "Tell me that at the next annual party," she said. "If we succeed in getting your husband promoted. If you feel the same. And if you remember."

"I'll remember," Erica assured her. "If Christopher is promoted, I'll thank you at the next annual party. And every day in between for what you and the other wives have done for us."

Smiling, Lizabeth began to nibble at her lunch.

Chapter
Twelve

LEARNING THAT CHRISTOPHER ABBOTT was being
considered for the position coveted by Justin drove
Hope into a near panic.

For several days she had been stealing Linquist's
files and taking them home for Justin to read at night.
Each night she had thought their time apart was growing shorter. Justin's promotion meant a divorce from
Joanna and marriage to her. Now, this. Neither of
them had considered that Keith Marston might look
outside executive row for Linquist's replacement. If
Christopher Abbott was being considered, how many
others were? Just what were Justin's chances?

After Erica Abbott had walked out of the office,
Hope returned to her desk and sat staring numbly at
the telephone. She saw all her hopes and dreams of
being with Justin withering.

Hope was so lost in her thoughts that she failed to
see Keith Marston's signal light flashing. He was
forced to press the buzzer to attract her attention.
Rising, she rushed into his office.

Marston glanced up as she entered; he retrieved a
file from the clutter of his desk and handed it to her.
"Give these to personnel," he instructed. "Then drop
this memo off on Larry Linquist's desk."

"Yes, sir." Her voice quavered and she found herself fighting to restrain herself from screaming at Marston that Justin was the man for the promotion, not Abbott, not any other employee. Head held high, she turned and left Marston's office without another word.

The file she was to deliver to personnel was marked: *Christopher Abbott*. On her way down the hallway she flipped open the cover and read Abbott's personnel covering sheet. The questionnaire Erica Abbott had completed had been inserted sideways to call it to the attention of the personnel director. Hope memorized as much of the file as possible so she might inform Justin of his competition's merits. Nothing, she concluded, that made Abbott's record outstanding other than the selection of two hit series. His last personnel evaluation sheet had not been spectacular. He had not even been given a salary increase aside from the customary cost of living upgrading. There were two formal complaints against him made by people working under his supervision. One accused him of openly plagiarizing another series, the complainant denying all responsibility should legal action be taken. The second was petty, accusing Abbott of a personal vendetta against an employee because of his homosexuality. Abbott must have seen the second letter, because he had written *"Bullshit"* across the page in red ink, underlined it, and signed his initials.

Hope left the file with the personnel clerk and returned to executive row to deliver the memo to Larry Linquist's office.

Linquist had not been in that morning. His mail had been opened and placed in order of importance beside his telephone.

Hope had never cared for Linquist. He had always been too secretive and had preferred another secretary to her. She had taken few of his letters and cared for none of his files except to log them in and out as requested. She liked him even less now that she had read the comments he had made on most of his clients. It did not seem ethical to her that he should list a man's personal data so blatantly in his files. *Hawkes, possibly gay. Masters likes masculine women, possibly S & M oriented. Greenberg isn't beyond payola! Calvert is more cooperative when getting a massage; ten percent kickback a must! Linn will back any production his kids can watch, a possible Lewis Carroll complex.* How many such reports had she read in the files she carried home for Justin? And Justin had relished them! Had seen those disgusting reports on Multimedia clients as his passport to promotion. She had understood with a shudder that he had intended to continue Linquist's style of doing business by using the reports to his advantage. Even though she had considered it wrong, she had gone along with it. After all, it meant that they could be together sooner.

But now!

She paused in Linquist's office to regain her composure.

Except for Marston and Williams, the executives were all out to lunch; she would not be needed. She helped herself to a glass of water from Linquist's private bar. The clear liquid did not satisfy her; she craved something stronger. When she opened the lower cupboard in search of liquor she saw the hidden file cabinet. There were only two drawers, both locked, both marked PRIVATE in heavy black lettering. This then, she realized, were Linquist's files that he did not trust to be handled by the secretaries. God, could he have made even more disgusting notes on clients than those in the files she had carried home to Justin? No wonder she had heard him referred to as the J. Edgar Hoover of Multimedia.

It suddenly struck her that something in these private files might assist Justin in gaining the promotion. If Linquist had remained second in command only to Marston, then why not pass the source of his power along to Justin now that he was retiring? Properly equipped, Justin could *demand* the promotion.

Hope went quickly to Linquist's door and closed it.

She attacked the file drawers with her set of keys to the outer office files, but none would budge the locks. The longer she struggled to open the files the greater her determination became. She was convinced there was something inside that would give Justin an edge over any other man considered for the promotion.

When one of her keys slipped and scratched the painted surface of the file drawers she drew back in alarm. If Linquist recognized the fresh scratch—! Proceed with caution, she told herself. She sat back on her haunches and studied the file drawers like someone contemplating a puzzle. Then, remembering how she had once watched an antique dealer making a key for a locked armoire, she went to Linquist's desk and searched through the drawers until she found a book of matches. She held a flame under a key from her ring until it had been blackened, then inserted it carefully into the lock. When she withdrew the key an imprint had been made on the blackened metal. She then closed the cupboard, left Linquist's office and returned to her desk. When she left for lunch she went directly to a locksmith, showed him the key and told him she had lost the key to an important file drawer and would lose her job if he couldn't make a key to open it. He was sympathetic and ground the key along the markings on the blackened metal.

"If it fits, bring it back and I'll make a duplicate," the locksmith told her. "You wouldn't want this happening again."

Fighting her impatience, Hope forced herself to stop at a coffee shop for lunch. If she returned to the office too soon after leaving, one of the secretaries might think it suspicious. She ordered a sandwich and coffee, but found that her throat was too constricted to swallow the food. She sipped the coffee and sat staring out the window at the noonday crowd.

Perhaps, she told herself, she had jumped to conclusions. Maybe the files in Linquist's office were merely his personal home accounts; bank statements, mortgages, department store bills. She often did personal accounts for the other executives, but never for Linquist.

When she returned to the office the secretarial desks were again occupied, business proceeding as usual, with the tap, tap, tapping of typewriters, muffled chatter and ringing telephones. Her senses seemed acutely alert and the customary noise seemed to make a drum of her skull. She removed her coat and checked the messages left on her desk for the executives. Nothing that couldn't wait. Justin hadn't returned from lunch. Only Merrill Williams's door stood open. There was a message for Keith Marston to call his wife *immediately*.

Taking a deep breath to steady her nerves, Hope picked up several file folders, moved across the open horseshoe of the secretarial office and entered Larry Linquist's office. She closed the door and locked it.

The locksmith's makeshift key stubbornly would not budge the file drawer locks; then, with a grinding sound, the key turned and the drawer literally popped out of the frame.

As she had feared, there were files marked *Mortgage, Bank Statements, Investments*—all carefully written in Linquist's familiar scrawl. There was a grey metal cashbox, an expense ledger, a small box gift

113

wrapped with a Gump's sticker and a card reading, *To Janet With Love,* possibly meant for some future occasion.

Behind all this Hope found the files.

When she saw the names carefully printed on the file tabs she caught her breath and felt her pulse begin to race. Linquist was definitely a bastard, the J. Edgar Hoover of the company. He not only kept files on clients, but also on company employees. She thumbed through the files, reading, *Marston, Williams, Wade, Sterne, Kirkman, Barrett.*

Hope's fingers paused on Howard Barrett's file, feeling a strange sensation.

Barrett had always been a favorite of hers. Of all the executives, he had been the most considerate, so unassuming and thoughtful of all the secretaries. He had never missed giving her a small gift on her birthdays and Christmas; he and his wife Kathleen had even had her to their home for dinner the first summer after she had come to Multimedia. How shaken she had been the day he had flung himself through the thirty-first floor window to the pavement far below. No one had known the reason for his suicide. It had finally been determined that his depression over losing his only son at the hands of terrorist fanatics had driven him to the act. But Hope had never believed that. Barrett had talked to her about his son. In the two years since the youth's death, he had adjusted to the loss.

Hope opened the Barrett file and began to read.

Her reading was interrupted as someone tried the handle of Linquist's door.

She panicked as she watched the handle turning, thinking Linquist had come into the office after all.

Then she heard one of the secretaries say, "Mr. Linquist isn't in today, Mr. Wade."

She didn't hear Justin's mumbled reply, only his footsteps retreating down the tiled corridor.

Taking Linquist's files from the drawer, she stacked them with the files she had carried into his office. She locked the drawers, closed the cabinet and checked to see if everything had been left in order.

She hesitated at the closed door, listening.

If one of the secretaries or executives questioned her coming from Linquist's office, she would plead a migraine and say she had gone into the empty office to compose herself. Why should they doubt her? Even if they did, who would miss the files except Linquist himself—and she would return them tomorrow morning long before he arrived at the office.

Chapter
Thirteen

JOANNA WALKED INTO the Sausalito Gallery, and Max Whitely walked abruptly away from a customer, his face lighting up at sight of her.

"Good God! A ghost of times past!" He took her hands, and being shorter than she, raised himself on tiptoes to kiss her cheek. "Joanna, Joanna! Friend estranged from me! To what do I owe this visit? Don't tell me you've divorced that objectionable beast you called husband?"

"No, no divorce, Max." She had stopped seeing Max because Justin had objected to him so vehemently. She had not realized how much she had missed the little man until she had entered the gallery. "How are you, Max?"

"Fair to middling. And you, precious? You look like hell. What's that beast doing to you? I know, he's draining your youth away like some modern day Dorian Gray. I knew there was something about him." The gallery owner's jesting was belied by the seriousness behind his eyes.

Max and Justin had developed an instant dislike for one another. Joanna had never understood it, but she had gone along with Justin's insistence that she change galleries and end her friendship with "that dreadful fairy." She removed her hands from Max's, and ignoring his remarks about Justin, turned and examined the new painters displayed on the gallery walls. "A totally new group," she observed.

"Yes, but with you went my finest artist," Max said with sincerity. "I still get requests for your paintings. Although it's bad business, I send them to your new gallery. You may have abandoned me, but I still worship you. In a sisterly fashion, of course. But tell me truthfully, why are you here? Has that husband of yours finally found enough security in his masculinity to allow you to associate with gays?"

"Don't, Max, please."

"All right, precious. A truce. I'll not dish hubby if you'll have a drink with me."

"Agreed," Joanna said.

"It'll be like old times. Wait a second." Max turned, spoke briefly to his irritated customer, and summoned his assistant from the office to complete the sale he had begun. "And no bargaining," Joanna heard him whisper to the assistant. "She either pays full price or tell her to pick up something for her walls at the Salvation Army Thrift Shop." He threw a suede jacket over his shoulders, took Joanna's arm, and led her out to the street.

At the Sausalito Inn, Max left her at a table and went to the bar to order their drinks. Joanna sat watching him, thinking how good it was to be in Max's company again. He had always made her feel at ease, had been the first of the Sausalito crowd to accept her when she had moved from the city. He had aged since she had last seen him; his struggle to retain youth was pathetically obvious—the dyed hair worn fashionably over the collar, the youthful clothes. "The gay world is youth oriented," Max had once told her. "I know I'll have to be an Old Auntie someday, but, Precious, I'll fight it until the wrinkles can't be stretched from my face and the body's so bent I can't walk without a cane." Max, she observed sadly, was losing his battle. She felt guilty for having abandoned him in his hour of need.

"Here you are, Precious. A margarita without salt." Max set the drink in front of her and perched on the edge of his chair. "All right, let's skip the girl talk. What's the problem? Why have you sought out Ole Max after so many months?" He held up a beringed hand to silence her when she started to speak. "No, I promise not to say I-told-you-so if it concerns what's-his-name. I've had husband trouble myself. God, how often I've had husband trouble! Mostly trying to keep them." Seriousness flickered behind his faded blue eyes. "Is that it, Precious? Have you found rust in your knight's shiny armor?"

"You promised not to dish Justin," Joanna reminded him.

"God, let me roast in Queen's hell! All right, I repeat my promise. Is it your art? Trouble there?"

"Well, I'm not producing as I'd like to," Joanna admitted.

"Because I'm not around to keep your butt in front of a canvas," Max told her. "I thought Justin would give you inspiration. If not for the sake of art, then for the sake of money. All right, all right! But I told you, you can't be an executive's wife and an artist. There's greatness in you, Joanna, and greatness can't be dissected. It has to take precedence. Over everything and everyone." He reached across the table and covered her hand with his. "I love you, Joanna, as much as I can love any woman. For you I'd even try to go straight. But what would we do in bed? Bump pussies?"

"Max, you're outrageous!"

"It's my image. I have to uphold it. I'm now known as a Sausalito landmark, along with Juanita and Sally Stanford. It wouldn't surprise me if Grey Line Tours put my gallery on their list of shops. Would you like to know what it's like to be a character? It's the pits. I hate it. But it brings in business. You saw my walls. There's not a decent artist hanging there, hasn't been since you left me. I might as well be selling number paintings."

"Don't make me feel any more guilty than I already do," Joanna said. "You know I didn't want to leave you, Max."

"I know, Precious. I understand. You aren't the first friend who deserted me because of a man. You only meant more than the others. But I say, 'Max, she's got to open her eyes one of these days. She'll come back to you.' And here you are." He lifted her hands and kissed them. "What's Justin done, Precious? Is it another woman?"

"No, nothing like that!"

"Oh, then it's more serious. Another woman you could handle because I doubt that there's any who could compare to you. After all, you've got everything, looks, talent, breeding, and money. What more could a man ask for in a woman?"

"Max, I'm going to sell the Sausalito house," Joanna blurted.

"What? You love that house! It has everything. Good lighting, privacy. Why would you sell it?"

"I'm moving back into the city."

"I thought you hated living in the city. You came here to escape what you called the Society Zoo."

"I've . . . I've changed my mind."

"You changed your mind, or Justin changed it for you?"

"Whichever," Joanna said. "I wanted to tell you before I put the house on the market. You always said you wished you had bought it and made me promise to offer it to you if I decided to sell."

Max's eyes bored into hers. "He's still making you prove yourself to him, is that it?"

"I don't know what you mean."

"Of course you do. What is it with you, Joanna, that you can't open your eyes where Justin is concerned? Justin's like a wicked little boy that you've played mother to since you met him. He made you give up your friends, change your gallery, hindered your painting. I thought the days of mother love and sacrifice ended with Stella Dallas."

"You don't know what you're saying!"

"Yes, I do. And you know I do! You've given him everything he's demanded. You married him, got him his green card, his job, introduced him into a social group he aspired to, now you're going to give up a house you love in a community you love. Where is it all going to end? Are you going to become a San Francisco matron giving special little dinner parties for your executive husband? With no career of your own? No life outside his? Then what? When he succeeds in changing you, you'll bore him and he'll turn to other women. Of course they won't be whores. When you're wealthy enough they're called mistresses, and it's acceptable, something to joke about with the boys at the club."

"I shouldn't have seen you!" Joanna said. "You obviously resent me as well as Justin. You're striking back at me for leaving your gallery."

"You know better than that! But ease yourself with that if you will. Precious, I've known hustlers, gay and straight, for most of my life. I've supported the best of them, but I've never let them drag me down to their level. A roll in the hay here and a night of ecstasy there. A short, fat fairy can't expect much more. But you I don't understand. What is it, an obsession? Justin's no more than a cheap hustler. If you were a man you'd be called a john. You've gone beyond—"

"Stop it!" Joanna cried. She knew people in the bar had turned and were watching them, but she didn't care. Max had gone beyond the limits she would allow him. "You little bastard!" she hissed. "Justin was right about you!"

"No! I'm right about Justin. I only hope you realize it before it's too late. You're destroying yourself under a banner called love. But, Precious, the banner's tattered, the crest doesn't show on both sides. Pack it in, pick up the pieces and do something with your career—and your life."

Joanna sprang to her feet. She still held her drink; for a brief instant she considered flinging it into Max's face. But even as she considered it, she knew she could not. Max *had been* her friend. Max didn't mean to hurt her—he just didn't understand. She had decided to sell her house to compensate for her inability to gain Justin's promotion with Multimedia; it would lessen the blow of his failure. After all, what did a house mean in comparison with the man she loved?

Calmly, she set her drink back on the table. "You're wrong about Justin, Max," she said evenly. "As much as I remember you reciting poetry about love, I don't believe you know the meaning of the word. I love Justin and Justin loves me. There's no sacrifice too great to lay at that altar."

Max shook his head sadly. "You're as great a fool as you are an artist, Joanna. Your sacrifices are going to slip right off that altar into your lap."

"Goodbye, Max."

"Goodbye, Precious. And good luck."

Joanna walked calmly from the inn. When she was out of sight of the windows, she ran for her car.

Chapter
Fourteen

WHEN ROSEMARY CAME down the spiral staircase to the entryway, she saw Teddy, newly arrived that afternoon, curled up near the outer door. The Alaskan husky glanced up lazily, saw her, and whimpering, rose and ambled across the entryway and through the partially opened door of the drawing room.

Rosemary could hear Keith's muffled voice from inside the drawing room, but could not discern his words. She crossed the marble floor and stood for a moment outside the door.

"And you prefer the west coast to New York?" Keith asked.

"Definitely," Patricia answered. "It's more relaxed here. The pace of New York is hectic. It was exciting also, but after my husband died . . ."

Rosemary flinched. Patricia was a widow; she hadn't known. Somehow it seems to explain things about the younger woman that she had thought to question. Steadying herself, Rosemary pushed the door open further and walked into the room.

There was a fire blazing in the fireplace, soft music coming from the hidden speakers.

Keith and Patricia stopped talking when she entered.

Keith, wearing a navy blue dinner jacket and gray slacks, rose. She thought that he looked particularly handsome tonight. "Rosemary," he said, "you look lovely." He stepped toward her and would have kissed her had she not side-stepped him. As she seated herself on the sofa opposite Patricia, he sat back into the wing-backed chair, looking confused by her obvious rejection of affection.

Rosemary glanced from her husband to Patricia; both, she thought with satisfaction, looked uncomfortable and ill at ease. Her gaze turned to Teddy who had curled up at the legs of Keith's chair. "I see you've met Teddy," she said to Patricia. "Poor Teddy is an offspring of my husband's first marriage. He spends three months with us and nine with his mother. The human offspring of the union, however, visits less frequently, being, I suspect, aware that the dog takes precedence with his parents."

Keith laughed. Rising, he went to the silver tray of crystal decanters and began mixing martinis. "Rosemary has always resented Teddy," he said quietly.

The dog, hearing Keith mention his name, got painfully to his feet and, trodding across the room, put two paws on his master's legs.

Rosemary laughed as Keith petted the dog's head. "Doesn't it remind you of a Gainsborough painting?" she asked Patricia. "Master and man's best friend captured in a tender moment?"

Keith's eyebrows arched above his deep-set blue eyes. "Is there something troubling you tonight, my dear?" His eyes seemed to mock her, and she became momentarily silenced. He brought her a martini and her hands trembled as she reached for it.

Patricia declined a cocktail. "I'm not a drinker, Mr. Marston."

It was still Mr. Marston, Rosemary thought. That

was good. In the hour they had spent alone before she had come down they hadn't broken the barrier of host and guest. "Drinking is a vice one should avoid," she said, "but I find myself depending on alcohol more and more, in addition to my pills." She raised her glass in a mock salute. "Cheers, both of you." Damn you, she told herself. She had sworn to be on her best behavior, not to be a bitch.

They sat in silence for several moments, the crackling of the fire and the soft, background music the only sounds. She knew Keith was angry with her by the arch of his brows, the steady fix of his gaze, the abrupt strokes of his hand as he comforted the disgusting dog. But there was more than anger in his eyes. He hadn't stared at her in that manner since the first days of their courtship.

She settled back against the down sofa cushions and tried to compose herself. "Did anything happen today in regard to Linquist's replacement?" she asked, her voice somewhat constrained.

"Nothing yet. But I just don't understand why you seem to be so interested in this particular promotion," he said.

"I think it only proper for a wife to display interest in her husband's business, don't you, Patricia?"

"My husband was in accounting," the younger woman answered. "It was difficult to muster interest in ledger sheets and debits and credits."

"Yes, I see your point. Fortunately Keith's business is one of the most exciting in the world. Movies, television, even an occasional investment in a Broadway play or publishing venture. He hobnobs with some of the great actors and actresses of our time. It would be difficult not to be interested." She smiled at Keith and tried to make it appear genuine, tried to convey her apologies for her earlier bitchiness.

The smile must have been a success, because he visibly relaxed. "As for Larry's replacement, after I've narrowed it down to three men, I'll bring it before the board of directors."

"And if you disagree with their selection?" Rosemary pressed.

"I doubt that I would disagree. You naturally want to know what wife you'll be welcoming into your group?"

"It's crossed my mind, to wonder," Rosemary said. "We were lucky with Mark Kirkman's wife Vanessa."

"Why? She had none of the status common among the rest of you."

"We, too, are democratic," Rosemary answered. "Vanessa may not be wealthy or from an old San Francisco family but she's . . . well, she's acceptable."

"Very democratic," Keith said with a smile.

Ignoring his sarcasm, Rosemary said, "I have met some charming Multimedia wives. One in particular comes to mind: Erica. Let's see, I believe it was Abbott."

Keith's eyebrows shot up once again. "How did you meet Christopher Abbott's wife?"

"Oh, I think it was at one of Lizabeth's afternoon teas," Rosemary lied, hoping he would not question her about Erica. The younger woman's visit had revealed little of her personality. She had, to Rosemary's best recollection, been pleasant; but lately Rosemary had moved through the days like one functioning through habit, without grasping much of what went on about her. She could not even remember the color of Erica Abbott's hair or eyes. "Is her husband being considered then?"

"He may be," Keith said evasively.

"Well, for my part, I hope he's selected. Erica will be most welcome to our cult of executive wives."

"An employee's wife has little to do with her husband's advancement," Keith said quietly. "As much as I'd like to oblige you, I can't guarantee Christopher Abbott's selection for the position, my dear." Rising, he returned to the martini pitcher, found it and the decanter empty, and sighed. "We may as well go in to dinner," he announced. "Ladies?"

Dinner was a quiet affair, with Keith and Rosemary speaking little, Patricia hardly at all. When the ritual was finished, Rosemary pushed her chair back and rose from the table. "I've a dreadful headache," she announced. "If you'll both excuse me?" But she caught Keith's gaze and was temporarily held by it. Why was he staring at her as he was, as he had been all evening?

As if reading the question in her eyes, Keith said, "Your dress is lovely, my dear. Is it new?"

Rosemary was aware of all her insecurities emerging with the question of her dress. She glanced down at the emerald green wool, feeling herself begin to choke with panic. He had said the dress was lovely, but had he really meant it was unbecoming to her? "It is new," she managed. "Do you think it wrong for me?"

"No. I said it was lovely. It's just that I've never known you to select a dress without soliciting my opinion."

"Actually, Patricia helped me," Rosemary told him. She glanced at the younger woman for support.

"Rosemary flatters me," Patricia said. "The dress is lovely. But I only gave my approval. She selected it herself."

They were both sincere, Rosemary decided. But had she selected the dress herself? She couldn't remember. And Keith? Wasn't that an expression of disappointment on his face? Hurt? "Good night, then," she said, and left the dining room still puzzling his attitude.

She had undressed and was combing her hair in front of her vanity mirror when there was a knock on her door. Before she could call out, the door opened and Patricia stuck her head inside.

Rosemary panicked, thinking Keith was behind Patricia, that tonight was to be the night of her initiation into the disgusting world of their *ménage à trois*.

"May I come in?" Patricia asked.

Rosemary nodded uncertainly; then sighed with relief when Keith did not enter the room behind the woman.

Patricia came up behind her, Rosemary watching in the mirror. She took the brush from Rosemary's hand and began to quietly stroke her auburn hair. "I used to do this for my sister," Patricia said. "She had beautiful hair also, the same color as yours."

Rosemary said nothing. When they had been shopping that afternoon she had felt an unexpected closeness to Patricia. The younger woman had obviously not been accustomed to shopping in the stores Rosemary frequented, and she had been like a child mesmerized by the expensive clothing and accessories. Riding home in the limousine, Patricia had expressed her delight, and Rosemary had reached across the seat and patted her hand. The action had been spontaneous and as soon as she had felt contact she had drawn her hand away as if their touch had violated some unspoken agreement between them. Then tonight, seeing Keith and Patricia together in the drawing room, her sense of closeness had vanished and her old fear had returned. *Don't let yourself like her,* she had told herself. *Don't let her like you.* And so she had given in to her bitchiness.

When Rosemary drew herself away from her thoughts she glanced at Patricia's reflection. Her lips were moving; she was still talking about the auburn hair she was brushing. "I inherited my hair from my mother," Rosemary murmured. She reached back suddenly and clasped Patricia's hands. "Tell me, did he send you to my room?" She could not erase the panic in her voice. "Did he send you here to prepare me for . . . ?" She couldn't complete the sentence; her voice cracked, and she released her grasp of Patricia's hands.

"No, he didn't send me," Patricia answered. "He's in the study. He doesn't even know I came to your room." Reaching past Rosemary's shoulders, she laid the brush on the vanity. Then she stepped back, resting her weight against the bed post. She had worn a dull brown skirt and jacket to dinner. The jacket was now unbuttoned, exposing a blue blouse, the top three buttons unfastened to expose the flesh of her cleavage. Her breasts were small, her figure almost boyish, a trait accented by her straight, short hair. "Are you still afraid of me, Rosemary?"

"Afraid?" Rosemary echoed. She turned from the mirror and faced Patricia directly.

"Yes, afraid," Patricia repeated. "Are you afraid of the situation your husband proposes, or of me?"

Rosemary's hands fluttered in confusion. "I'm not the sort who indulges in self-analysis," she said. "I pay a psychiatrist for answers to such questions."

Smiling, Patricia shook her head from side to side, her dark short hair swinging back and forth across her thin face. "Don't be afraid of me, Rosemary," she said. "I would never hurt you, never do anything that would offend you." She pushed away from the bed post and stepped back to the vanity stool where Rosemary sat.

Trembling, Rosemary averted her gaze and sat staring at the floor.

Patricia lifted her chin with a gentle hand until their eyes again met. "I'd like to be your friend, Rosemary," she said scarcely above a whisper. "How long since you've had a real friend? Someone you could trust without question?" Her eyes boring into Rosemary's, she knelt in front of her.

For one moment of panic, Rosemary thought she was going to be kissed.

But then Patricia released her chin. She straightened, smiled, and said, "We could be that kind of friends, Rosemary. As for your husband, I'll do whatever you ask. I'll submit to what he wants. I'll sleep with him alone. I'll go away. It's entirely up to you, to what you ask me to do."

"I . . . I don't know what . . . what I want you to do," Rosemary murmured. "Just give me time as you promised."

"Yes, time," Patricia said, and turned to leave.

Rosemary, suddenly wanting to detain her, cried, "Yes, I am afraid! But I'm really not certain of what—of losing Keith, of complying with his demands, of you! Of myself! Of life in general! I'm such a miserably weak person!" She turned back to the mirror and buried her face in her hands.

"You're not weak!" Patricia insisted firmly. "You underestimate yourself!" She took Rosemary's hands and squeezed them gently. "Good night, now," Patricia said. "We'll talk tomorrow."

Again, Rosemary stopped her before she opened the door.

"Tell me, Patricia, how did Keith find you?"

The younger woman opened the door, turned in the frame, and said, "He placed a very cleverly worded ad. I was interviewed by a secretary at Multimedia. A Miss Ingress. I don't believe she understood the position she was interviewing me for, but I passed inspection and was shown in to be given approval or rejection by your husband. It was all very businesslike, almost comical, really, when you consider all the innuendos that passed between us before he could tell me exactly what he had in mind."

"I don't see the comedy in it," Rosemary admitted. "I suppose if I sent you away this Miss Ingress would only begin further interviews?"

"I suppose," Patricia answered. "But don't send me away, Rosemary. Remember what I told you. We can be friends, close friends. Good night."

Rosemary stared at the door long after it had closed behind Patricia.

She had just turned the lamp off when Keith came to bed.

She kept her eyes closed and pretended to be fast asleep.

Chapter
Fifteen

LIZABETH SNUGGLED BESIDE Merrill after he had turned off his reading lamp. She wanted him to make love to her, but he had been silent and moody most of the evening and she knew she had no hope of his meeting her need. Even the way he held her displayed his lack of interest, a limp arm under her neck, his hand scarcely putting pressure on hers.

She knew she should go to sleep, let him sleep. But she lay listening to his heartbeat, his breathing, and she felt her sexual need being replaced by frustration and anger. "You should stop smoking," she said. "You're breathing like a horse."

He snorted. "As long as I'm hung like one I'm certain you'll put up with the breathing," he said.

Lizabeth raised herself onto her elbow and stared down at the darkened shadow of his head against the white linen. He was angry with her—that's why he had been moody and silent. She had thought something from the office had been bothering him. "Actually it's that unlikely wart on your penis that binds me to you." She reached for him under the blankets, but he intercepted her hand and pushed it away. "Why are you angry with me?"

"I didn't say I was angry with you," he answered.

"But you damned well are," she said. "I have the right to know why. I have the right to defend myself."

"This isn't a court of law, Lizabeth. We're not defendant and plaintiff. We're man and wife, in bed. To sleep."

"You would stress that."

"You would ignore it."

"You're a bastard!"

"I've never denied it. Neither did my mother. Now go to sleep. Let me sleep."

"Not until you tell me why you're angry at me," she persisted.

"It's not anything you've done."

"Then it's something I haven't done?"

"Perhaps."

"Oh, Christ! Don't play games with me, Merrill!" She fell back off her elbow onto the pillows.

"Are you happy in our marriage, Lizabeth?"

The tone of his voice caused her to catch her breath. God! Had he discovered her extramarital affairs? "Yes, I'm happy in our marriage."

"It took you a moment to consider," he said.

"It was a strange question. Why the hell did you ask me such a thing? Have I done anything to make you believe I'm unhappy with you? With our marriage?"

"As I said, perhaps it's something you haven't done."

Lizabeth sat up in bed and reached for a cigarette. She fumbled in the darkness, found the cigarette lighter, and her face was suddenly bathed in its harsh glare. She inhaled deeply and blew the smoke into the darkness of their bedroom. "You're exasperating tonight," she said. "What *haven't* I done?"

"You haven't shown any interest as to whether I get

the promotion into Larry Linquist's position," he answered. "None. It's as if you don't realize how important it is to me. Or that you don't give a damn."

Lizabeth immediately felt her tension waning; he hadn't discovered her affairs. Anything else she could deal with. As for the promotion— "I thought you wouldn't want me to interfere."

"It never stopped you before."

Ignoring this, she said, "It's crazy, your world of business. I don't understand it. I don't understand why you'd want the additional responsibility."

"Well, I do," he said. "I do very much."

"Why? For Christ's sake, why? It isn't as if you need the money that goes with the promotion. You have everything a man could want." Uncertainly, she asked, "Don't you?"

"I have everything your money can buy me," Merrill answered.

"Oh, that again," Lizabeth murmured.

"Don't make it sound unimportant."

"It is to me. My money, your money—what difference does it make?"

"It's a question of self-respect."

Oh, shit! Lizabeth wanted to scream. Was it self-respect that kept him from refusing the Mercedes she had bought him? the race horses? the yacht? Why did he always accept the gifts she lavished on him and then make her feel guilty for giving them? Now this! Good God! What would he say if he learned she was instrumental in getting the wives to support someone other than him? Or her reason for doing it? She had convinced the wives it would be a test of their power. How gullible they had been. With her Aunt Thelma's Multimedia shares as a trump card she intended to switch loyalty at the last minute in favor of Justin Wade. With his knowledge, of course, so that he might gratefully reward her. How eagerly she had used the pending promotion to plot and plan the seduction of Justin Wade.

"It's that you don't want me to spend more time away from you, isn't it, Lizabeth? That's why you've never mentioned the promotion? Why you've chosen to ignore it entirely?"

"Yes," she answered, "that's it, Merrill." It wasn't entirely a lie. She crushed out her cigarette, turned and kissed him.

"But now that you understand how important it is to me, you'll support me in my bid for the promotion?"

The question surprised her. The implication was that he knew about Aunt Thelma's shares in Multimedia or about the power game practiced by the wives, that she actually could help him achieve the promotion—had she been so inclined. "I'll do what any wife can," she told him. "Which isn't much."

"In your case, it's considerable," he said quietly. "Just knowing you're with me gives me confidence."

"Then you're no longer angry?"

"No. I won't even scold you for sending that young man to me."

"Young man? What young man?"

"I think his name was Karl. A handsome youth."

Lizabeth caught her breath and hoped Merrill didn't recognize her panic. *That bastard!*

"He said you sent him to me about a part in one of our upcoming television series," Merrill said. "But you know, Lizabeth, that's not my bailiwick, giving young hopefuls a start toward stardom. Where did you meet him?"

"I really don't remember," Lizabeth answered. "I don't even remember the young man. Perhaps it was at some party. I'm often approached when they discover my husband is an executive with Multimedia."

135

"Then you didn't tell him to come around and see me?"

"No, of course not!"

"Funny, he was so definite," Merrill recalled. "I thought perhaps he was the son of one of your friends."

"I told you I don't even remember him."

"Then he was bluffing, I suppose." Merrill chuckled softly. "Anyway, it worked for him. I got him an audition with Chris Abbott, who's in charge of the series."

"How generous of you," Lizabeth murmured. "When it gets around you'll have every hopeful in San Francisco pounding at your office door." She slid down in bed and pulled the sheets about her neck. *Goddamn Karl! She'd kill him.*

"Oh, Miss Ingress will protect me. She's one hell of an executive secretary."

"Good for Miss Ingress. Good night, Merrill."

But Merrill reached for her and pulled her back against his body. "You meant it, didn't you? About supporting me in my bid for Larry Linquist's position?"

"Yes," she murmured. "If that's what you want, I'll be behind you." She lay her cheek against his chest. "Behind every great man," she mumbled.

Long after Merrill was asleep she lay, eyes open and staring at the dim light behind the window shade, wondering about their conversation and the implications of the things that had remained unsaid, only hinted at.

Chapter Sixteen

ALTHOUGH SHE HAD promised herself to remain calm and collected, Erica's nervousness had come pushing through. She sat on the sofa, her hands in her lap, but her fingers fidgeted and her eyes wandered about the enormous room from person to person as if expecting to catch them staring back at her with an expression that accused her of being a usurper.

And Christopher, he was also out of place. Although he worked with Keith Marston and Merrill Williams, Jake Sterne and Mark Kirkman and Justin Wade, he had never before been invited to their homes, and it was almost as if they were all strangers. Erica saw the muscle at the corner of his mouth twitching, saw the way he kept shifting his weight from one leg to the other, and she understood. He had wanted to decline the sudden invitation, but she had insisted they attend Rosemary's dinner. It was, she had argued, advantageous to his career.

Perhaps, Erica thought, Christopher, like herself, was awed by the splendor of the Marston mansion. She had never seen anything like it, except in movies or museums. Every piece of furniture was antique, the upholstered pieces covered in silk damask; the accessories silver and gold and crystal. One of the paintings that hung to the right of the fireplace she was certain was a Rembrandt.

She sighed quietly. She had wanted the advancement for Christopher so he might be able to afford such a lifestyle. But this world into which they had suddenly been invited was beyond all expectation. She wished she could feel more comfortable, that Maureen, who sat beside her, would engage her in conversation. Instead, the older woman was contenting herself by sipping a martini and staring into the space of the room.

"There's a rumor," she heard Christopher say, "that Multimedia may become the fourth network. That would be . . ."

She turned her hearing away: just like Christopher to discuss business instead of being more social and relaxed.

"You'll get used to it," Maureen suddenly said.

Erica turned and studied Maureen. Maureen was the least glamorous of the executive wives. She was slightly overweight, and her gown was ill-chosen, accentuating her excessive pounds. Unlike the other wives, her hair did not look as if she had just stepped from the hairdresser's chair; she wore streaks of grey almost proudly as if defying youth. She had a kind face, but there was a strange sadness in her eyes.

"The men always discuss business," she went on, "unless we continually maneuver them away from it. They'll humor us during dinner, but immediately afterward they'll retire to the study, for more business talk, I suppose, and we'll be left in the drawing room. I think that's why we formed our club. We became bored with discussing fashions and theater and other gossips. We had nothing in common except that our husbands were all executives with Multimedia. Stuck together so often we either had to drive one another mad with our personal interests or come up with something we could mutually relate to."

"And who came up with the idea of the executive wives' club?" Erica inquired.

"Lizabeth, I think. I don't really recall. Lizabeth is a very clever woman. I don't say that critically. But I sometimes wonder if our club wasn't a mistake." Emptying her martini glass, Maureen set it on the side table, and looked as if she were about to lapse back into her thoughtful silence.

"I think the idea was genius," Erica said. "It gives the wife a sense of belonging in her husband's career. Just since the afternoon when the four of you visited me, I've taken more interest in what Christopher does at Multimedia. It's fascinating. I never realized there was so much involved in putting together a television show."

"By the few I've had time to watch, it would appear very little is involved," Maureen said. "But why would you want to feel a part of your husband's career?"

"A sense of closeness, I guess," Erica answered uncertainly.

Maureen raised an eyebrow. "Are you and your husband planning a family?"

"Oh, eventually. But there's no rush. Maybe after Christopher is better situated."

"I had my first child at twenty-four," Maureen told her. "Jake was far worse situated then than your husband. Our eldest is now seventeen and a senior in high school."

"That's nice. But you don't look old enough to have a seventeen-year-old son."

Maureen smiled. "You don't need to flatter me, Erica. I look every day of forty-two and proud of it. As you can tell at a glance, I'm not a vain woman. If I was vain earlier in life, three children cured me. I haven't time for bi-weekly visits to a hairdresser or gown fittings or sessions at Elizabeth Arden's. As for wanting to feel a part of Jake's career, it isn't his career that interests me to any great extent. It's how it affects him, and therefore me and the children. Things were better before Jake became an executive at Multimedia's home office. San Francisco isn't a place to raise . . ."

Maureen was cut off by the chiming of the doorbell, and Erica breathed a sigh of relief. She didn't want a discourse on the raising of children in the big, wicked city. She thought this the proper time to escape Maureen, and rose and went to join Lizabeth and Justin Wade, who were standing nearby. She was about to speak to Lizabeth when she noticed the woman staring questioningly through the open drawing room doors, into the entryway.

"Most unusual," Lizabeth said to Justin. "Rosemary never invites outsiders when we get together for these dinners." She became aware of Erica, smiled, and added, "A clever move for her to have invited you and Christopher. I think she wants to show Keith how well the two of you fit into our group."

Rosemary was also looking questioningly through the open doors.

When the maid answered and Larry and Janet Linquist entered the foyer, it was Keith Marston who went forward to greet them. Those who remained inside the drawing room exchanged glances.

"It looks like Keith invited surprise guests also," Lizabeth said with a low laugh. "But I thought the Linquists had stopped socializing. The last two times I invited them to dinner they had previous engagements."

"You don't suppose Larry's changed his mind about . . . about retiring?" Justin murmured, his face drained of color.

Laughing, Lizabeth patted his hand in a familiar manner. "Don't fret, my dear. Janet would have told one of us if he had. There will still be that position for you competitive males to do battle over."

After greeting the new arrivals and allowing time for Erica and Christopher to be introduced to the Linquists, Lizabeth took Erica's arm and lead her to one side as if to impart a female secret. "Be especially nice to Janet Linquist," she said in a low voice. "It occurred to me when she arrived that it would help our cause if she would whisper a few well-chosen words in her husband's ear on Christopher's behalf."

"But how would I solicit such a favor?" Erica whispered.

"You be nice," Lizabeth answered. "I'll do the rest."

As they joined Rosemary and Janet Linquist, Erica saw Joanna watching them with a strange expression in her blue eyes.

No sooner had Lizabeth seated herself than she excused herself and moved away to speak to Vanessa and Justin, leaving a frightened Erica with Rosemary and Janet. What, Erica asked herself, did Lizabeth mean by being nice? Was she to flatter Janet Linquist? No, she had tried that on Maureen without success. Janet was talking about her plans to visit Rome the following month, and Rosemary was inserting reminiscences about her past visits to that grand and beautiful city. Erica found herself merely sitting and listening and smiling and thinking how difficult it was going to be to become one of the wives.

When Justin and Lizabeth were again alone, Justin

asked, "What did you mean when the Linquists arrived by referring to them as surprise guests *also?*"

"Why, the Abbots, of course," she answered. "Couldn't you tell by Keith's expression when they arrived that Rosemary hadn't told him she had invited them?"

Justin looked confused. "Why would Rosemary do such a thing?"

"Isn't it obvious? She's supporting Christopher Abbott for promotion into Larry's position."

"Rosemary!" Justin had raised his voice. He glanced up, found only his wife Joanna glancing in their direction, and turned back to Lizabeth. "Why would Rosemary care who was promoted into Larry's position? And why Abbott?" he asked quietly.

"Who knows?" Lizabeth murmured with a shrug. "Maybe she's just bored and wants to test her power over Keith by influencing his decision."

"But it isn't his decision alone."

"No, but he's the one who will propose the candidate," Lizabeth said knowingly.

"But surely he won't be influenced by a meddling wife," Justin said.

"Don't be too sure," Lizabeth said. "Behind every man is a great wife. Or, have I distorted that cliché?"

"This is no time for humor," Justin told her.

"Humor is for any time," Lizabeth laughed. "For example, the way Joanna is watching us. Don't you find humor in that? She looks like the typical jealous wife."

"You're mistaken," Justin said. "Joanna's not the jealous type. Besides, she has no cause, does she? I thought it was Merrill who suffered from jealousy."

"Anyone's the type for jealousy. As for Merrill, he has no cause either, darling, despite what you might have heard. But he could have, so could Joanna—if you understand me."

"Are you trying to seduce me?"

"Would that be possible?"

"You seem to have a penchant for answering a question with a question, Lizabeth."

"And you have a penchant for evasion," she retorted. "Are you or are you not susceptible to seduction?"

"After all these years. I didn't know you were interested." He stared at her closely. "Are you drunk, Lizabeth? Or is this another facet of your humor?"

"Would you understand how serious I am if I told you I want you to be selected for Larry's position?"

"But Merrill wants that position as much as I do, or Jake, or Mark," Justin told her. "Why me over your husband?"

Lizabeth merely lifted an eyebrow.

"You're also implying that wanting me to get the position is going to assist me in doing so," Justin went on. "How?"

"I have ways."

"Now who's being evasive. Don't fence with me, Lizabeth."

"It isn't fencing that interests me." Lizabeth glanced away from him, nodding and smiling at Joanna who was talking to Maureen but still keeping a watchful eye on them. "I have more power to help you than Rosemary has to help Christopher Abbott. Rosemary must have coached the wife. The little twit told me she was supposed to charm Janet Linquist so she would put in a good word with Larry. That was so beneath Rosemary. But I suppose Larry's recommendation for his replacement would carry weight." Smiling, Lizabeth raised her martini glass and stared at Justin over the brim. "This is going to prove an interesting year at Multimedia. All of you vying for Larry's position. Everyone taking sides. Vanessa pressing for Mark, Maureen for Jake, Rosemary for Abbott. What about Joanna? She got you the job with Multimedia in the first place. Is she making bids for your promotion?"

"You seem to place a lot of importance on who the wives support," Justin said. "Joanna may have gotten me the job through her friends, but she hasn't the power to go any further. I intend to get this promotion, but on my own merit."

Lizabeth laughed. "What bravado," she murmured. "But, darling, why struggle on your own when you have me offering support? Think about it. I do have a few trump cards that might just push the others out of the running. Can you afford to refuse such an offer? Especially at such a low cost? What's a short affair? We're both sophisticated people."

"And Joanna and Merrill? Are they sophisticated enough to ignore a short affair if they find out about it?"

"Darling, they'll never suspect. Joanna's busy dabbling with her paints and Merrill's so dedicated to his work he'd never find time to consider the possibility. Oh, oh, here comes Lady Picasso. Call me, darling. Joanna, Justin was telling me about your coming show. I can hardly wait to add another Joanna Wade canvas to my collection."

Joanna, smiling, said, "You have two already, Lizabeth."

"I know, darling, but they're not only beautiful, they're an investment."

"For Justin to talk about my paintings it would have to concern investments," Joanna said. She continued to smile, but her voice was serious.

Justin opened his mouth to speak, but Lizabeth

stopped him by saying, "We're about to be summoned to dinner. I do hope Rosemary isn't serving veal again. Since she got that Italian chef her menus have been very limited."

As Justin and Joanna followed Lizabeth and Merrill into the dining room, Joanna mumbled, "Another entertaining evening on Nob Hill."

Chapter
Seventeen

JANET LINQUIST HAD always presented a cool exterior, but Rosemary had suspected the tempest brewing inside her.

After the other guests had departed and Keith and Larry remained sequestered in the study, Janet's charade of composure began to crumble. She paced the expensive Marston drawing room, her brow furrowed, her face contorted by anxiety.

Rosemary sat on the sofa and watched her longtime friend with concern. She was exhausted, the evening had been most trying, especially since Keith had been so upset over her invitation to the Abbotts. It had been, she supposed, a foolhardy action, trying to force Christopher Abbott on him in such a blatant manner; she should never have listened to Lizabeth, whose idea it had been. If anything, the inclusion at her dinner party had hurt Christopher Abbott's chances of being promoted. The young man and his wife had been awkwardly ill at ease and lacking in social graces.

But Christopher Abbott's problems were not as important as Janet's. She had known Janet since marrying Keith. They had never become intimates, but they were friends. It distressed her to see Janet so troubled. "Janet, do come and sit down," she said.

"You're wearing out the carpet to no avail. At least we can talk about what's upsetting you."

Janet's pacing came to an abrupt halt. She turned and stared at Rosemary as if seeing her for the first time. "I'm sorry," she said weakly. Moving to the sofa, she sat down beside Rosemary. "Do you know why Larry's retiring?" she asked.

Rosemary could not conceal her surprise.

"Oh, he told me he was just too tired to go on pushing himself from day to day," Janet said, "but I know that isn't true. I thought perhaps he had told Keith and Keith had mentioned it to you."

"No, Keith has said nothing," Rosemary told her. "But why does it distress you so? I thought you'd be pleased. You've always wanted to travel, always talked about what you'd do when Larry *did* retire, the places you'd see, the tours, the quiet life you two would live in the country when you weren't traveling."

"Yes, yes, I know. His retirement was my dream."

"Then why does it upset you?"

"Because . . . because I know there's something he isn't telling me," Janet stammered. "His decision was so sudden. Larry's only sixty-two. I expected him to retire at Multimedia's mandatory retirement age of sixty-five."

"Have you questioned him?"

"Repeatedly. But I know he's lying to me. Don't ask me how I know, but I know. He's not bored with his daily routine. As for pushing himself from day to day, that's ridiculous. Larry's always been a dynamo of energy. He's lived for that damned job for over twenty years. He can't even take a Sunday off without spending the afternoon working at home." Leaning forward, Janet clasped her hands together, wringing them nervously. "I've considered every possibility," she said.

"I even imagined that he had discovered he was dying of some dreadful disease and decided to retire to spend more time with me before . . . !"

"It's unlike you to let your imagination run away with you, Janet," Rosemary said.

"I called our family doctor. Larry hadn't had an appointment with him in over eighteen months."

"But the company requires its executives to take annual physicals."

"Yes, I know. I called the personnel department and asked if Larry's annual physical report had been received from the doctor. The executive secretary, a Miss Ingress, returned my call. She told me there must have been an oversight, that Larry had not taken his physical and she would call it to his attention. There was something strange about her voice, too. As if she was a part of a conspiracy to keep the truth from me."

Rosemary rose, poured two cognacs, and handed one to Janet. "You're beginning to sound paranoid," she said. "I'm certain Larry isn't ill or dying. Even if he had wanted to keep such news from you, he would have told Keith, and Keith would have mentioned it to me."

Janet's gaze found Rosemary's and her expression was one of doubt. "And you swear he didn't?" she asked.

"I swear," Rosemary assured her.

Janet sipped the cognac. The strong liquor burned her throat and she pulled a face. "How can men drink this?" She set the glass aside. "Then why, Rosemary? Why would he retire so suddenly? He's worked so hard to get where he is. When you're King of the Mountain you don't abdicate without reason."

"I don't know," Rosemary admitted. She hadn't even considered the reason for Larry's retirement; she had assumed Janet had somehow talked him into it.

After all, he was sixty-two, and thousands of men took early retirements to enjoy their later years free of job responsibilities. It wasn't as if Larry needed the money an early retirement cut from his pension; Keith had told her that Larry had invested well and had, miraculously, tripled his financial worth during the past ten years. "I hate seeing you like this, Janet." Rosemary returned to the sofa beside her and took her hands. "I'll question Keith," she said. "If Larry's given him a reason for his retirement, then he'll tell me."

"And you'll tell me, no matter what the reason?"

"Yes, I promise," Rosemary told her.

Janet relaxed visibly. "Perhaps I am just being paranoid," she said. "I hope to God I am. I love my husband, Rosemary. He's a difficult and sometimes secretive man, but he's my life. He's twelve years older than I and chances are I'll outlive him, but the possibility of becoming a widow so soon devastates me. Even though I've considered it, I haven't prepared myself."

"I'm certain you're not going to lose Larry," Rosemary told her. "Now push that from your mind. There's probably a very simple explanation for his early retirement. You'll laugh at your anxieties when it's proven he has no dark ulterior motive."

"You're very reassuring, Rosemary," Janet said. "I feel better just having expressed my fears." She reached for the cognac again, sipped it as if testing her first reaction, and pushed it away. "Could I trouble you for an Irish Mist?"

"No trouble," Rosemary said.

While Rosemary poured the Irish Mist, Janet, watching her, said, "What are the wives up to these days? I suspected from seeing the Abbotts here that you've all decided on pushing a candidate for Larry's

149

position. That wasn't very subtle of you, Rosemary, having them to dinner."

"I realize that now. It was Lizabeth's suggestion." She brought Janet her Irish Mist, and then it was her turn to pace. "We agreed to test our power by supporting an unlikely candidate."

"Was that also Lizabeth's suggestion?" Janet asked.

"It was."

"I never trusted Lizabeth," Janet admitted. "Her relationship with Merrill is so complex. It's almost as if they're locked into some sort of psychological struggle and she does what she does to defy him."

Rosemary had stopped before the fireplace and had extended her hands as if to warm herself from a sudden chill. None of the wives had ever discussed Lizabeth privately. It almost felt like a betrayal doing so. "I'm sure Lizabeth loves Merrill very much," she murmured without turning.

"Of course she does. Too much, perhaps! But she can't believe that he returns her love. I think she's always meant for him to discover her affairs. She wants to awaken his jealousy and also prove his devotion to her by forgiving her. This test of power . . . I wonder what she has up her sleeve."

"Oh, Lizabeth wouldn't use us to . . ."

The opening of the study door caused Rosemary to hold her thought. She turned and saw Keith and Larry come out into the entryway. Their faces were very serious; Keith even looked perplexed. She wondered what conversation had been going on behind the closed doors.

Janet rose from the sofa, came forward and kissed Rosemary's cheek. "Do call me tomorrow," she whispered. "I have to know why Larry's retiring."

Rosemary nodded her understanding. She followed

Janet into the entryway and she and Keith said good night to their guests at the door. As they turned back from the door, Rosemary said, "I know it's been a long night, but I'd like to speak to . . ."

Her gaze had been caught by movement on the second floor landing.

Patricia stood there watching them.

Keith followed Rosemary's gaze. "Ah, Patricia. Come down and join us for a nightcap."

Rosemary sighed and swept back into the drawing room as Patricia's heels echoed on the staircase.

Chapter
Eighteen

JUSTIN GLANCED MOMENTARILY away from the highway.

Joanna sat huddled against the opposite car door, the collar of her mink coat turned up about her slender neck. The harsh lights from the dashboard bathed her face unflatteringly and made her appear older than her thirty-four years. Her countenance appeared frozen, chiseled from marble, and only the fogging of her breath spoke of life.

"I told you to have the heater fixed," Justin murmured. "It's your own fault if you're freezing."

"I'm not freezing," she answered evenly.

"Well, you could have frozen everyone at the dinner party tonight. Joanna Wade, the modern Medusa. I know you wanted to beg off, but since we went . . ."

"Since you insisted we go."

"Since we went you could have been your usual charming self," Justin finished. "Is that too much for a husband to ask? That his wife act civilized at important dinner parties?"

Joanna turned and stared at him. If the dashboard lights were unflattering to her, they were especially cruel to Justin. The harsh glare gave him the appearance of a demented satyr. The comparison gave her a sudden chill, and she wrapped her mink coat tighter about herself. "You've begged off on several of Rosemary's dinner parties," she said. "Now they're suddenly important?"

"Damned important with me being considered for promotion. Or had you considered that and deliberately set out to destroy my chances?"

"And why would I do that?" Joanna asked coldly. "I'm proud of what you've achieved at Multimedia. I hope you do get the promotion. But how do you know you're even being considered?"

"It's only logical," Justin answered. "It'll be Merrill, Jake, Mark, or me. Although your friend Rosemary may be campaigning for Abbott, it'll be to no avail. He hasn't a chance in hell despite her meddling."

Joanna said nothing. She wanted to tell him about the list Rosemary had taken from Keith's bedside table, about Christopher Abbott being on that list as a potential replacement for Larry Linquist, but the confession would have been a betrayal of her friends. And to what purpose?

They rode on in silence until the entrance of the Golden Gate Bridge came into view. The fog was turning thick and Justin cursed beneath his breath. He slowed the car, fumbled for the fog lights, and found they weren't working. "Goddamn!" he said. "A fucking new car, and nothing works! If you'd sell that house and move back into the city where we belong we wouldn't have to go through this every time we went out."

"I'm putting the house on the market," Joanna said quietly.

"You are?" he said, surprised.

"If only to silence your complaining," Joanna murmured. "I saw Max Whitely today."

"That faggot!"

"I promised him I'd give him first option on the house if I decided to sell."

"And?"

"And I really don't know. We got sidetracked."

"On what? Your art, I suppose. Does he want you back with his gallery?"

"Yes." Joanna turned in her seat and looked at Justin again. "He says you're a hustler, that I'm letting you destroy my life."

Justin laughed. "He hates me because I wouldn't let him have his way with me. The slimy bastard! If I had, he'd be singing my praises in that falsetto voice of his." Justin glanced at her briefly, then back to the road. If it hadn't been for the lights glowing eerily he'd never have known he was now driving across the bridge. "You're not still angry at me because of Max, are you?"

"No, just disappointed that you couldn't get along."

"Oh, I get it. The old transfer of guilt routine," Justin said. "I'm to feel guilty because I destroyed your friendship with Queen Max and I'll forget my anger at the way you acted at the dinner party tonight."

"That's not it at all," Joanna insisted. "Besides, you were being charming enough for the both of us. Especially with Lizabeth."

"Oh, jealous?"

"Not that either. What were you talking about? And don't say my art. Lizabeth wouldn't know an impressionist from an old master."

"We talked about Multimedia, mostly," Justin told her.

"Mostly," Joanna echoed. "That's an ambiguous word!"

"All right, then! We were discussing her sex life! Does that make you happier?"

"No, but it sounds more like Lizabeth." Suddenly, Joanna threw her head back and laughed. "This is a ridiculous exchange," she said. She scooted across the seat beside Justin and laced her arm through his. "Let's not fight," she told him, and lay her head against his arm. "Forgive me for being less than charming tonight. It wasn't jealousy, or Max, or selling the house. It was just a mood."

"Then I'm glad you're not given to frequent fits of mood," Justin said. "Two moody people. Our relationship would be explosive." He took one hand from the wheel and squeezed hers.

"I love you, Justin."

"And I love you, baby."

"I'll do something to make up for tonight. Tomorrow night I'll prepare your favorite dinner, even the crepes. We'll put on soft music and have candlelight and after we'll . . ."

"I'm sorry, Joanna. But I can't tomorrow night. I have some important work at the office."

"But it's Sunday!"

"I know, but I'm trying to make a good showing because of this promotion," he explained. He took his hand from the wheel again and patted hers. "You understand, don't you? As for tonight, forget it, baby. We all have a right to our moods."

"Yes, we do," Joanna mumbled as she felt her own mood turning again.

Chapter
Nineteen

SUNDAY WAS THE worst day of the week for Hope.

She often spent the entire day in bed reading the *Chronicle* or a novel, and only got up to snack or pour herself a toddy. Saturdays were more hopeful; she often worked because Justin came into the office for an hour or more. But Sundays—he was lost to her, spending his time with his wife in Sausalito or boating down to Carmel or playing tennis in Belvedere.

This Sunday, however, was different—if indeed her entire life had not been different since discovering Larry Linquist's private files. When she had taken the files home, read them, and discovered the contents, she had gone into the office early the next morning, photostated them and returned the originals to Linquist's file drawers. The photostats now lay in the bottom of her bureau drawer under her nylons and underwear. Justin didn't know of their existence and she hadn't decided if she would tell him. There was too much power there for him to use; too much power and she would surely lose him.

Justin called late Saturday night. She knew by his whispering that he was calling from home and did not want Joanna to overhear him. "I'll be in tomorrow," he said. "Did you bring files home last night?"

Hope hesitated before saying, "Yes. But, Justin, I . . . I want you to take me to lunch."

"Lunch! Christ, Hope! We can't risk it!"

"Even if it's an out-of-the-way place," she persisted. "On Sunday, who'll see us? If you refuse . . ."

"You'll what?" he demanded, and she could imagine the look of anger on his handsome face, the vein that stood out on his forehead, the swelling of his neck, the way he clinched his fists threateningly.

"If you refuse I'll stop stealing the files," she blurted.

There was a long silence, with only his breathing coming over the line. Then she heard Joanna calling his name in the background.

"All right," he said. "Lunch tomorrow."

He arrived promptly at noon on Sunday wearing the Pierre Cardin suit she had helped him pick out at Grodin's and a pastel sports shirt open at the throat.

She was already dressed, smartly but simply, and put her coat on as soon as she saw his car pull up and park at the curb in front of the building. She met him at the door, purse in hand.

He stared at her with a dark expression and she understood he had intended to talk her out of her demand to be taken to lunch. "This is a mistake," he said sharply. "Do you realize what could happen if we're seen?"

"We won't be seen," she said firmly. She stepped into the hallway and locked her door. "I have to get out of the apartment. It's becoming oppressive. I'll go mad if I'm locked inside another Sunday."

"Then how about a ride?"

"No, lunch!"

Justin drove to highway 101 and turned south toward San Jose. She knew he was seething with anger. He was silent, moody, and turned the radio so loud that conversation was impossible. The heater wasn't working and her legs became chilled, but she refrained from complaining. She was convinced his anger would pass; he was often like a spoiled child, pouting when things did not go as he wanted. A child, she thought; that's what Justin was, a child trapped in a man's body. Perhaps that was one reason she loved him so; he brought out all her instincts, including the maternal.

At Milbrae, Justin turned off the freeway and drove into the town. He turned the radio down then. The muscles of his face were relaxing, losing their stressed tone. He glanced at her and attempted a weak, little-boy smile. "I'm sorry," he said. "It's just that it's been such a hell of a week. Then last night Joanna pulled one of her scenes at the Marston dinner party. When she's snippety and aloof it grates on my nerves under the best of circumstances." He slowed the car and came to a stop at a traffic light. "It was wrong of me to object to taking you to lunch." He reached over and squeezed her hand. "Am I forgiven?"

"Yes, for that," Hope murmured. Before he could question her statement, she pointed to a restaurant on the next corner. "That place looks inconspicuous enough," she said.

Justin pulled into the parking lot. She noticed as they crossed to the restaurant that he glanced in all directions like some thief about to be caught committing a crime.

"If you'll feel better," she told him, "you go in first and make certain there's no one we know. No office boy or secretary or maintenance man who'll carry the story of our illicit lunch back to the office."

Instead of answering, Justin took her arm rather roughly and lead her through the glass doors.

The restaurant was no more than a coffee shop with bright neon lights and vinyl-covered seats. There was a bar at one end with tinted windows through which candles could be seen flickering in their red bowls. The music from the juke box blared out into the dining room, a country and western tune with a twanging guitar and sobbing-voice female singer.

After they had slipped into a booth, Justin glanced around. "Christ!" he said. "I haven't eaten in a place like this since . . ."

"Since you met Joanna," Hope finished for him when he let the sentence trail off. She averted her gaze in the event she had brought the anger back to his face. She didn't want that; didn't want him angry with her for the entire day. She opened the plastic menu the waitress had dropped onto the table and pretended to examine it with relish. Actually, she thought if she attempted to force anything down her throat she would vomit. Her stomach had been in knots since Friday when she had read Linquist's files. "I think I'll have the diet plate," she said pleasantly.

Justin was examining the menu with as much pretended interest as she had displayed. "That sounds fine," he said, and closed the menu with a snap. "Now, tell me, Hope, why did you insist on this lunch? It wasn't because you wanted to be taken out for a diet plate special. A hamburger patty and cottage cheese could have been sent up by the deli."

"I just wanted you to take me out," she answered. "You haven't, you know, since that first day when you decided to put the make on me. You weren't worried then about who saw us together. You took me to the Starlight Room at the St. Francis. I remember Jake Sterne was entertaining clients across the dining room. You waved at him."

"That was different."

"Was it? Why? Because you had nothing to feel guilty about? The other executives take me out to lunch occasionally—and without ulterior motives. They think I'm a good secretary. They appreciate me."

"I appreciate you. As a secretary and as the woman I love," he said. "Why is it suddenly so important we be seen together in public? You haven't insisted since our affair began until now."

"Howard Barrett used to take me to lunch frequently," Hope said, ignoring his question. "He was a wonderful man. You remember Howard, don't you?"

"Yes, of course. Who could forget a man who swan dives through a thirty-first floor window?"

"They said he did it because his son was killed so tragically."

"Yes, I know." Justin was becoming impatient with her.

"Actually it was because Howard was also having an affair," Hope told him.

Justin's head shot up. "How do you know that?" His eyes were asking if the affair had been with her.

"You wouldn't think Howard was the type to have an affair, would you? I didn't. He was so happy, he loved his wife so. No, darling. It wasn't me. The young lady was in the steno pool. She turned in her resignation right after Howard's suicide."

"If you knew this, why didn't you come forward when the police were questioning the employees?"

"Because I didn't know then," Hope answered. "I'm not so certain I would have come forward anyway. What good would it have done? It would only have hurt Mrs. Barrett, and I think that's why Howard killed himself, so she wouldn't be told about his affair. It cost him his life to spare her. Why should I make his suicide meaningless?"

"You mean he was being threatened with exposure?

By whom? The young woman?" Justin's dark brows arched above cold eyes.

"No, I think not," Hope said.

"Why are you telling me this, Hope? You're not suddenly threatening me? If you are . . ."

"No, darling, I'm not threatening you," she assured him. She found that her hands were trembling despite her efforts to control herself. "It's just that I had to tell someone. I think it's so awful. His death was such a waste. He was perhaps the company's most efficient and intelligent executive."

"Thank you for rating him above me."

"You hadn't been with the company that long then," Hope explained.

"I know. Barrett's suicide caused all the executives to move up a notch. Linquist took his position. Now the position's going to be open again. And with your help, I'll be the one who fills it."

"Have you ever considered that perhaps the position is jinxed?"

Justin laughed. "You're not serious? That's superstitious bunk."

"Perhaps. But why is Larry Linquist retiring? Aside from Keith Marston, he holds the number one position with the company. He has three years to go before mandatory retirement. And don't say it's because he's unhappy with Multimedia. He gloats on his position and power. He's filled with self-importance and an inflated ego. He swells up like a bantam rooster when he gets to lord it over the producers and directors. And the ad agencies, you know by his files he has them where he wants them. Not ethically, but he has them. Why would he give all that up before he had to?"

"I don't know. Maybe he's found religion and can't correlate it with the world of business. What do I care why he's retiring? I only care that he *is* retiring and that I have a chance to step into his shoes."

"Would you conduct business in the same manner? Using his files? Those disgusting files?"

"Is that what has you so worked up?" he said with an amused chuckle. "You think Linquist is an unethical bastard and you're afraid I'll be the same?"

"If you wouldn't be, why are you reading his files?" Hope asked bluntly.

"To get in, darling! I'll use them to show Marston I can handle the accounts and the agencies, but once I'm in the goddamned files can be shredded. I won't need to know a man's sexual preference or his perversions to sell him on a television series. Hell, I'm a natural born promoter. You've told me that yourself. Maybe it's my personality or just my Australian accent, but I know I could sell bat guano to a chicken farmer."

Hope nodded, thinking, *You sold me on yourself. And I bought it all right down the line.* "Yes, your personality and accent," she murmured. "I sometimes wonder if you realize just how far you could go with those attributes." *If you didn't find it necessary to be deceitful in the bargain?*

"Linquist's position will just be the beginning," he said. "Who knows? Marston has to retire one of these days. The charter clearly states no exceptions on mandatory retirements. I might find myself running the entire company."

"On your personality and accent?"

Justin touched his temple with his index finger. "On the knowledge I'm going to store here," he said. "I'm going to study Marston's position just as I'm studying Linquist's. I'll make myself indispensable to him. I've got what it takes, Hope. I only need the chance to prove it."

"And us?" she asked.

"We've already discussed that. As soon as I'm promoted, I'll leave Joanna."

"And marry me?"

"Isn't that what you want?"

"I only wonder if it would hurt an executive's chance of promotion if he married his secretary. I don't want to be a burden to you, or hold you back. After all, you've set your sights at the top. President of a company as large as Multimedia is . . ." Hope stopped speaking when the waitress appeared to take their order.

After the waitress had gone Justin did not appear eager to continue the same line of conversation. Hope was in a strange mood today, and he didn't like it. He questioned her about the files she had brought home for the weekend and was pleased at the usefulness of the latest information.

Their lunch arrived; Justin ate sparingly and Hope not at all. She didn't even make a pretense of an appetite. There had been so much more she had wanted to say, but she decided it could wait until they returned to her apartment. She still doubted the power of her convictions.

They returned to San Francisco by a different route, Highway 280 to Sixth Avenue and then up the hill to where her modern apartment building perched among the Victorians like an edifice from some future time.

She had left the heat turned up in her apartment and it was stifling. She opened the sliding glass doors to the small terrace and let the cool air inside. It wasn't yet dark, but she could see over the buildings that the fog had started to come in.

Justin settled on the sofa with the files. She mixed him a drink and then left him. She showered, the third time that day, put on her robe and stretched out on the bed to read until he had finished with the files. She stared at the pages, but the print blurred and she couldn't concentrate. She tossed the book to the floor and closed her eyes with a deliberate tightness, causing tiny explosions of lights against the insides of the lids. She felt her determination to continue her conversation with Justin ebbing and tried not to consider her doubts. Fortunately, because she had slept fitfully the night before, sleep claimed her before she could abandon her determination.

She awakened an hour later to find Justin on his knees beside the bed. He had parted her robe and was caressing her bare flesh. Her eyes met his, and she saw that he wanted to make love to her. Something inside her rebelled—but only momentarily. She submitted, all the while cursing herself for her weakness. If his touch could turn her into a spineless female, then what would his words do to her when she told him of her decision? Even without the appealing accent, Justin knew the right words to achieve a desired effect. He could turn her to putty, as he was doing now, his tongue tracing the mound of her abdomen and leaving a trail of warm saliva to cool in its downward path toward her loins.

She extended a hand to his neck. He was naked, his body warm, desirable to the touch. She whimpered his name with a moan as his tongue found the crevice it had been searching for. Her hand ran down his back, trailing along the vertebrae. In the area above his buttocks was a patch of downy hair; she grasped it between her fingers and pulled. The pain encouraged him; and his reaction, her. She urged him onto the bed beside her and buried her face between his legs. He was demanding, rejecting her hand for the preference of her mouth. At first she rejected him, but, as they both knew she would, she submitted.

When he rolled off her and rose there were tears in her eyes. She wiped them away with impatience, rose and disappeared into the bathroom. She gagged, gargled, and washed her face. Resting her hands on the sides of the basin, she stared at her reflection in the mirror. The grey eyes that stared back at her were red and swollen and ringed by dark circles. Her hair looked as if a beautician had abandoned her in the midst of a combout. There was a patch of his semen crystallizing on her neck. She grabbed the washcloth and wiped at it until her flesh reddened.

When she came back into the bedroom Justin was stuffing his shirttail into his trousers. "It's late," he said. "I have to go. I don't want Joanna calling the office and being told I wasn't in today."

Hope leaned against the door frame and watched him. He was so goddamned handsome, so suave, so sure of himself. He sat on the edge of the bed to put on his shoes and she absently wondered what size he wore. Large, that's all she understood of men's shoe sizes. *Big feet, big . . .* She forced the dirty cliché from her mind.

"Tomorrow I think I'll be ready to test myself with one of the agency representatives," Justin said, not looking up at her. "What a coup it would be to take one of Linquist's accounts away from him before his retirement. He hasn't had much luck selling that new series to the advertising boys. If I could succeed where he failed."

Hope pushed away from the door frame and moved to the bedside table for a cigarette. She lit it, exhaled, and stood staring down at him. "Who's Marsha Drury?" she asked.

His head didn't snap up as she suspected it would. But there was a reaction. The fingers tying his shoes froze in the process of knotting the laces. After a moment, he said, "Who?"

"Marsha Drury," she repeated slowly, accentuating each syllable.

"A girl I once knew," he answered, shaken.

"When?"

"A long while ago. Before I met Joanna."

"Oh? My sources say you knew her less than four months ago."

Justin lifted his head then; his eyes met hers, the lids half closed. "Your sources seem to have given you a wealth of information," he said. "The reason for Howard Barrett's suicide and now this tidbit on me."

"There's more," she said. "There were others. A nameless woman who spent the night with you in a seedy motel near the airport. You were supposed to be off to Los Angeles that night. Instead you arrived the next morning just in time for the conference. You didn't look rested."

Justin rose slowly from the bed. He was tall, over six foot, and towered above her, but, despite the expression in his eyes, she was not frightened. She was too angry, too incensed by his betrayal and her trusting gullibility to feel fear. Her determination took over once again. She wanted everything out in the open, done with—over.

Puffing on her cigarette as if she was doing a parody of Bette Davis, she turned away from him and walked to the window. She snapped open the blinds and stared out at the apartment building lights across the street, eerie dots in the fog. "Then there was a Laverne Helms. She has a bit part in the company's new series. A brunette with a large bosom and small mind. Oh, dear God, Justin! Why couldn't you have been honest? Why did you make me go on thinking I was the only one? Why did you keep me hoping? Dreaming? I would have gone on seeing you, stealing moments here and there! Only I wouldn't have turned the affair into a fantasy with marriage and fidelity at the end of the rainbow. I would have accepted it for what it was! I might have hated myself for doing it, but I would have accepted it!" She spun around to face him, her vision blurred by the tears she swore she would not shed. "God, how you must have laughed at me! Was I a shared joke with men in the locker room at your club?"

"I never laughed at you, Hope," he said, his voice none too calm. "No one knows about us."

"Oh, yes they do!" she cried, remembering her shock when she'd discovered the page detailing her affair with Justin. In a fit of rage she had burned that particular page. "The same person who knows about Marsha Drury and the nameless whore and Laverne Helms! And, do you know something, I don't give a damn! Let them know! I'm only a statistic, one affair among many! Christ, how cheap and tawdry you've made me! I've showered three times today and I still don't feel clean!" She moved to the side table and crushed out her cigarette.

"What are you going to do?" Justin demanded.

"What do you expect me to do?"

"Do the same to me as you did to Howard Barrett," he said. "Blackmail!"

"Me! God! What do you think I am? The Barretts were like parents to me."

"Then that would make it parricide. If you didn't drive him through that window, who did? Who is this source?"

"Oh, no, Justin! Putting me on the defensive isn't going to get you that information! Not that, not any of the rest of it!"

"The rest of it?" His eyes narrowed to mere slits. "What Pandora's box have you uncovered, Hope? The rest of it on whom? What? How? Personnel? Does Multimedia employ a detective agency to keep tabs on its executives? Come on, tell me, goddamn it!" He was no longer handsome, his face contorted with rage and fear.

"You suddenly see your plans for promotion crumbling, don't you?" Hope cried. "If someone knows about your secret life, they could hold you where you are. All they would have to do is threaten you with going to Joanna. You never intended to divorce her. You not only want position, you need her wealth and social connections. Why should you divorce her? You have the best of two worlds. A beautiful, wealthy, socialite wife and your whores. Is that where I fit in? Just another of your whores? Someone to use? It was all there in your file, how you arranged the introduction to Joanna, your courtship, your need of her to retain residence in this country, a respectable position. To think I was jealous of her! I pity her more now that I do myself!"

Justin stepped toward her. Before she could escape him, he grabbed her roughly by the shoulders and shook her. "What file? Who has it?" he shouted. "Tell me, goddamn it, or I'll beat it out of you!"

Hope was frightened now, but with a last effort at bravado, she cried, "Is that what you resort to when your personality and charming accent fail you? You're nothing but a crude . . ." His slap across her cheek silenced her. Whimpering, she cowered and tried to pull away from him.

But Justin held her firmly, still shaking her, still

demanding to know who possessed the file that could destroy him. He struck her again and would have continued if a pounding on the neighbor's wall had not brought him up short. Cursing, he flung Hope onto the bed as if she were a weightless rag doll. "Tell me," he said through clenched teeth, "or I'll . . ."

"Or you'll what?" she cried. "Go on beating me? I'll never tell you, Justin! That'll be your punishment! Not knowing who has the file, who knows about you besides me, who can destroy your marriage and career on a mere whim!" She sprang off the opposite side of the bed, putting it between them should he be incapable of controlling his violence. "Now get out, you bastard! Go home and tremble in your shoes, Mr. Would-Be-President!"

"You fucking bitch!" he shouted.

For a moment, Hope thought he was going to leap over the bed and beat her again. She glanced around in panic, judging her chances of reaching the bathroom and locking herself inside before he could grab her.

The pounding on the wall began again. A man's voice shouted incoherent warnings through the plaster.

Justin hesitated, looking like an animal indecisive as to whether he should or should not spring, but then, as Hope cowered against the wall, his countenance underwent a sudden change. His arms fell to his sides, the anger on his face vanished. "Dear God!" he moaned as if in pain. "Everything I've worked for . . . !" His chin fell down against his chest as his eyes began to fill.

Justin's sudden metamorphosis from angry man to beaten little boy affected Hope. Her fear and sense of betrayal began to ebb and she was flooded by emotions. The love she felt for Justin surfaced and took precedence. His anguished moaning went through her like an electrical current. She pushed away from the wall and staggered to the foot of the bed. One side of her robe had been torn and hung in shreds; she pulled the material over her breast and held it in place. She started to speak but hesitated, and sank down onto the bottom edge of the mattress, unable to pull her gaze away from Justin. Had he not suddenly straightened and visibly tried to gain control of himself she would have gone to him, held him and forgiven him.

But he snatched his suit coat from the chair back and, glaring at her, his eyes filled with hatred, he turned and hurried from the bedroom.

Hope remained on the edge of the bed. She heard the door slam behind him with finality, and the sound seemed to tear something precious from inside her body. Pain centered in her chest and she cried out from the agony of it. "Justin, Justin!" she moaned and fell back on the bed, hands covering her face.

She lay crying for several minutes until her mind adjusted to the fact that Justin was now permanently lost to her. Her stolen moments with him, their secret affair and exchanged glances at the office suddenly seemed more cherished than before she had lost them. She cursed Larry Linquist's files, thinking it would have been better to have gone on in her blind ignorance than to have learned the truth. So Justin was a philanderer—he could have changed; she could have changed him!

"Too late now," she mumbled.

She pushed herself off the bed. The reflection looking back from the vanity mirror showed her an eye that was quickly blackening from Justin's slap. How would she explain that at the office? Could she bear to go into the office again? seeing Justin daily? knowing what she knew about him? and Howard Barrett's death? and Merrill Williams and Keith Marston and the rest of the executives she so efficiently cared for? She pushed the torn robe from her shoulders and left it on the floor where it settled.

She took a kimono Justin had given her from the closet and slipped into it. Emotions had drained her; she was exhausted but knew sleep would be impossible. She would only lie in bed reliving the scene she had had with Justin, hating herself for not handling it differently, for not having let her compassion and understanding outweigh her sense of his betrayal.

A noise from the living room brought her up short. Had he come back? Had he felt as lost as she and returned to beg forgiveness? She knew instantly she would forgive him. She hurried into the living room.

The room was dark; he had turned off the lamp before coming into the bedroom. She peered into the shadows; then saw that the sliding doors remained open. The draperies were billowing into the room, the weights in the hem striking the window frame. Her expectation of finding Justin there faded and her despair was heavier to bear. She returned to the bedroom for a cigarette and came back into the darkened living room to smoke it. She felt his presence with her in the darkness, as if a ghost of him remained to taunt her. Her thoughts went back to the first time she had brought him home with her; she had felt like a teenager then, having been so attracted to him for months. How utterly charming he had been, attentive, not rushing her into the sex they had both wanted. She had loved him from that afternoon. Now he was gone, and the loneliness she had never accustomed herself to before Justin would return. She would go back to her routine single existence, only now it would be even more difficult. She would be haunted by him, by memories, by what could have been.

Despite the cold draft from the open sliding doors,

she felt feverish. Like someone walking in a dream, she moved out onto the narrow terrace and stood staring absently into the swirling fog. From the streets below came the sound of traffic, unseen through the blanket of greyness; from the bay the foghorns blared warnings, forlorn, a dirge for the lonely.

Hope did not turn immediately at the sound in the room behind her, knowing this time it was not the drapery weights striking the window frame. She took time to wipe the tears from her eyes and erase the anguish from her face. When she turned it was with a smile and outstretched arms. "Justin!"

The shadow in the doorway moved forward too quickly for her to identify it. The arms were also outstretched, but they did not reach forward to embrace her. Instead they slammed into her chest and sent her reeling backward. Her thighs struck the terrace railing. Her arms flailed at emptiness. She screamed with terror as her body was hurled into space and sank into the fog.

PART 3

Chapter
Twenty

BRYCE COCHRAN WAS a man whom few of his fellow cops in the San Francisco Police Department knew. He was a loner, an enigmatic detective who did not invite closeness from his comrades. He was a large man, standing six foot three inches in his stocking feet, with broad shoulders and chest and a thick neck. His features, however, were refined, so refined and sensitive in appearance that the combination of his face with his great frame seemed a jest of God. His eyes were deep-set, grey, and capable of staring down an opponent. He had high cheekbones that always carried a tint of color and a chiseled jaw that squared off at the chin, which housed a deep cleft. His dark hair was streaked with grey, as was his moustache. He wore the moustache not because he felt it added to his appearance, but because it concealed the scar from an operation performed in his youth to correct a faulty palate. Because of this corrected defect, he spoke slowly, measuring the pronunciation of his words, something he had learned to do as a youth because the other children had teased him mercilessly until he had conquered his speech impediment.

He was a native San Franciscan, born in the Mission

District, and had left the city only once, to do his part in the U.S. Navy during the Vietnam War. When discharged, he had joined the S.F.P.D. and worked his way up through the ranks. He loved the city of his birth and had no desire to travel again. A marriage had ended in divorce after two unmemorable years. He had been devoted to his work and unwilling to give his wife and his private life precedence. He did his work well and enjoyed it.

It was Bryce Cochran who was assigned to investigate the death of Hope Ingress.

On Monday, after a sleepless night, Bryce entered the Multimedia offices. It was not his first time there; he had also investigated the suicide of one of the company's executives, a man who had oddly chosen to fling himself through a plate glass window to the street thirty-one floors below. Most leapers took an easier route, the Golden Gate Bridge, a rooftop, at least an *opened* window. The case had left Bryce uneasy. That uneasiness had grown when Hope Ingress's name had struck a familiar chord; having found her to be an employee of Multimedia, he connected her to the suicide. He vaguely remembered her distress when he had interviewed her.

Bryce stood just inside the carved oak doors separating executive row from more lowly departments. It was, he determined, apparently business as usual at Multimedia. But he noted that although the typewriters continued tapping and file drawers opened and closed with a bang, there was no chatter from the secretaries. Even the telephone conversations sounded restrained.

A long-legged secretary who introduced herself as Margaret Lynch escorted him down the carpeted hallway to the president's office. She tapped lightly and opened the door.

Keith Marston rose from behind a massive desk and extended his hand. "Inspector Cochran, isn't it?"

Bryce nodded, noting that Marston's handshake was firm, his palm dry. He seated himself in the chair motioned to across the desk and lifted one leg over the other. He hoped he would be offered coffee; after twenty-eight hours he was functioning on caffeine and willpower.

Marston sank back into his leather chair. "I assume this is about Miss Ingress," he said. "It's dreadful. She was an exceptional executive secretary. She appeared so self-possessed. It's difficult to imagine a woman like Hope Ingress leaping from her balcony."

Bryce's eyebrows shot up. "Who told you she leaped from her balcony, Mr. Marston?"

"Well, of course I only assumed," Keith answered. "When she didn't report to work one of the secretaries telephoned and when she couldn't reach Hope she called her building manager." There was no discernible change of expression as he asked, "I take it, then, that it wasn't suicide?"

Bryce did not mean to be evasive, but he was exhausted; he had come to ask questions, not answer them. "How well did you know Miss Ingress?" he asked.

"I knew nothing about her personal life," Keith answered. "Only, as I said, that she was an exceptional secretary. She had complete charge of the other secretaries, assignments, hiring and firing. She took care of the executives' needs and kept the office running smoothly. It will be difficult replacing her."

"But surely in the time she's worked for you you've picked up some personal information," Bryce suggested.

"Well—" Keith ran a hand through his greying hair and stared thoughtfully at the inspector—"I remember someone saying she was single. I don't remember who, but they said it was no mystery why she'd never married. You see, she was rather standoffish and cool to anyone who attempted to get to know her. She was respected, I think, but not especially liked by her fellow employees."

Something Miss Ingress and I had in common, Bryce thought. "Anything else you remember, Mr. Marston?"

"Well, no, nothing that comes immediately to . . ."

There was a gentle tapping on the door. It opened and the secretary who had shown Bryce into the office entered with a tray containing a steaming pitcher of coffee. It was obvious that the secretary was nervous with her new assignment. She set the tray on the edge of the desk and left without offering to pour the coffee.

Bryce stared at Keith Marston and wondered what sort of man he was to work for. Had Hope Ingress found him difficult? Had she had a crush on him? He was handsome, Bryce supposed, distinguished in his expensive blue suit and striped tie, his greying hair neatly trimmed, his fingernails expertly manicured. His blue eyes mirrored intelligence and a disguised softness.

"Coffee, inspector?"

"Please." Bryce rose and stood leaning against the side of the desk while he added three spoons of sugar and a dash of cream. He could smell Marston's after-shave lotion and wondered why a man, obviously so well-off, would wear anything as inexpensive as Old Spice. He returned to his chair and balanced the coffee cup on his right knee. "Miss Ingress had been with your company for a little over two and a half years," he said. "She must have formed a few friendships during that time."

"None that I'm aware of," Keith told him. Then,

"Oh, there was Howard Barrett and his wife. Howard and Kathleen were fond of Miss Ingress and she of them. I think they had her to dinner several times, and Howard often took her to lunch. Poor Howard always spoiled his favorite secretaries by taking them to lunch and remembering their birthdays with small gifts. It created some petty jealousies in the office."

"Yes, I remember Miss Ingress was quite shaken by his suicide," Bryce recalled.

Keith sat with his hands laced around his coffee cup as if to draw from its warmth. "Weren't we all? Howard was not only a friend, but second in command. His death left more than one void. But tell me, inspector. About Miss Ingress. A woman is found on the sidewalk beneath her balcony. What's to tell if it's suicide or murder?"

Bryce was enjoying his coffee, hoping it would take effect quickly and help him fight his exhaustion. Exhaustion always put him in the worst of moods. He had an inclination to tell Marston to stop questioning him, to let him get on with his own questions, but he fought his urge to be rude. There was nothing incorrect in his giving the victim's employer information; it would all be in the newspapers by afternoon. He heaved a sigh and said, "A neighbor heard Miss Ingress fighting with a man shortly before her death, says he pounded on the wall to quiet them down because they were disturbing his favorite television show."

"One of ours, I hope," Keith said. "But surely that isn't enough . . ."

"Then there was her torn robe," Bryce continued. "She'd left it on the bedroom floor and changed into a fresh one. That substantiates the neighbor's report. There were two brands of cigarettes in the bedroom and living room ashtrays, a popular filtered brand and a less common type rolled in brown paper and favored by gentlemen, according to the company's ads. The doorman also reported that Miss Ingress had gone out and returned earlier in the afternoon with a gentleman who called frequently."

"And did the doorman give a description of this gentleman?" Keith inquired.

"Yes, but it would fit some thousand San Franciscans. If fifteen people saw Miss Ingress and her gentleman, there would be fifteen different descriptions." Bryce finished his coffee and helped himself to a second cup. He noted that Marston had not touched his. "Then there was the evidence on the balcony," he said as he sat down once again. "The balcony ledge isn't very high. A ten-inch metal framework had been added to meet building specifications. It's decorative, doesn't hide the view, and prevents tenants from keeping potted plants on the ledge. Pieces of Miss Ingress's silk robe were found clinging to the metal. Miss Ingress also kept pots of geraniums on her balcony. Several stalks were found clutched in her hand. She apparently grasped them in her effort to keep herself from going over the ledge."

"Christ!" Keith murmured. He had gone pale. "How dreadful!"

"It would seem even more dreadful if I described what a fall from seven stories does to the human body," Bryce said. "But then there's no necessity for that."

"No, none," Keith agreed. He gulped coffee, his expression making it obvious he wished the liquid had been something stronger. His color returned and he managed to compose himself. "But since I cannot give you any personal information about Miss Ingress, what more can I do for you, inspector?"

"I'd like photostats of Miss Ingress's personnel file," Bryce answered, "and your permission to question some of your employees, the other executives she worked for and the secretaries who worked under her. Even someone as secretive as Miss Ingress apparently was can't work closely with people for over two and a half years and not reveal some information about her personal life." When he made this statement Bryce was watching Marston closely. It was obvious Hope Ingress had been having an affair, and who more likely to be her lover than a man with whom she came into daily contact?

But Keith's expression revealed nothing. "I'll instruct Personnel to make the photostats," he said, "and Miss Lynch will introduce you to the other executives." He reached for a panel of buttons and signaled the secretary replacing Hope Ingress to enter. "If I can be of any further assistance, inspector, please call on me." Then, almost making it sound like an afterthought, he said, "I hope this won't bring too much adverse press coverage to the company."

Bryce leaned forward and set his empty coffee cup on Marston's desk. "I don't pander to the press, Mr. Marston, but neither do I have control over what they print. My job is to find out who pushed Hope Ingress off her balcony."

"Yes, of course. I was only thinking aloud." Keith turned as his office door opened and began giving Miss Lynch instructions to assist Inspector Cochran.

Bryce rose and, nodding at Marston, started to follow Miss Lynch from the elegant office. At the door, he hesitated, turned, and said, "Is there any reason Miss Ingress would have for taking company files home with her?"

For the first time since entering the office, Bryce saw Keith Marston's calm pierced. His deep-set blue eyes were startled, his broad shoulders slumped, and the hand he ran nervously through his graying hair was trembling. "I take it you found some of our files," he murmured.

Bryce nodded. "Not the sort of files I would expect a company to keep on its employees," he said. "They were, shall we say, extremely personal."

Keith was gaining control of himself. He rose from his desk and came forward as if to confront the inspector, but then turned and leaned against the front edge of his desk. The color had returned to his cheeks and his hands no longer shook. "Our personnel files are no different than those of other companies," he said. "When an employee is investigated for employment purposes we use the standard investigatory agencies. We are even lax in some of our requirements. We deal primarily with the arts, and artistic people are known for their deviation from the norm."

"Ah, yes, the norm," Bryce murmured. "But tell me, Mr. Marston, would one of your executives . . ." Bryce turned and saw Miss Lynch waiting for him. Smiling an apology, he closed the door on her and walked back to the chair he had occupied. "First," he said, "who would compile personal files on your executives? And second, what would Miss Ingress be doing with them?"

"I can't answer either question," Keith admitted. "I've authorized no investigations other than those used for employment purposes. How Miss Ingress would come by such files is beyond my comprehension. But see here, Cochran, if the files relate to Multimedia employees then they should be returned. If Miss Ingress had files at home, it was without authorization. In short, theft."

"Regardless, the files are now in my hands, Mr. Marston. They have a direct bearing on her death." Bryce, resting his elbows on the chair arms, made a pyramid of his hands, the fingertips pressed thoughtfully against the cleft of his chin. Averting his gaze from the executive, he stared at the sun reflecting on the plate glass window. "As best I can remember her, Miss Ingress did not seem the type, but it would appear she was blackmailing Multimedia employees."

"Impossible!" Keith cried.

"I have long since removed that word from my vocabulary," Bryce said, looking away from the window. "Ah, well, we shall see, Mr. Marston. We shall see." He rose again and started for the door.

This time it was Keith who stopped him. "Tell me, was there a file on me, inspector?"

Bryce glanced back over his shoulder without turning. "Yes, there was."

"Well, then, it wasn't blackmail," Keith said with certainty. "Miss Ingress wasn't blackmailing me."

"Perhaps your time just hadn't come," Bryce said. "Good day, Mr. Marston." He opened the door and went out without glancing back again.

Keith returned to his chair, dropped into it, and spun it about so that his office was behind him. He could see just over the window ledge. Although the sun was shining on the thirty-first floor, the streets below were still shrouded in fog. Rising, he stood, forehead pressed against the cool glass, remembering how he had stood in the same manner once before, staring down into the street when he had heard Howard Barrett had plunged through a window. That day had been clear. He had seen people the size of pinpoints running toward the sidewalk beneath the skyscraper. God forgive him, but he had known his friend Howard had been splattered down there on the concrete and his first thoughts had been on how to prevent unfavorable publicity from touching the company. That was exactly what concerned him now. A multimedia secretary had been murdered, there was talk of executives being blackmailed—and all he could think about was how to protect the company. Christ! Perhaps he had been in business too long!

"Yes, of course I knew Hope Ingress," Miss Lynch answered. "She hired me for the secretarial pool."

"How long ago was that?" Bryce asked.

"Six months. The 22nd of June to be exact. I remember distinctly because it was her birthday. I do astrological charts, you see. Since she was born on the cusp between Gemini and Cancer, I was hoping her Cancerian traits would be minimal. I've never gotten along well with Cancerians and I wasn't looking forward to having a boss born under that sign."

"Did you get along well with Miss Ingress?"

"Oh, no problem there," Miss Lynch assured him. "One never got to know Miss Ingress well enough not to get along with her. If you arrived on time, didn't take longer than an hour for lunch, and did your work well, there was no communication beyond a good morning and a good night."

"Then I take it she was more Cancerian than Gemini?"

Miss Lynch raised a perfectly shaped eyebrow.

"Communication being a Gemini trait," Bryce explained.

"Oh, yes!" The secretary was obviously impressed that he had a grasp of astrology.

Before he could be questioned and exposed for a lack of further knowledge, Bryce said, "Did Miss Ingress have any enemies at Multimedia? Anyone who obviously disliked her?"

Miss Lynch looked reflective. After a moment of silence, she said, "No. Everyone respected Miss Ingress even if they didn't particularly like her. The executives thought she was the queen of secretaries.

They all used her for major assignments. All except Mr. Linquist. He never uses any particular secretary, just asks for whoever's available at the time."

"Do you know if Miss Ingress had a boyfriend?"

Miss Lynch shrugged her shoulders. "I'm certain she did, but I could not tell you anything about him."

"Why are you certain she had a boyfriend? Was there office gossip?"

"About Miss Ingress?" Miss Lynch laughed. "Heavens, no! She wouldn't glance at a male employee twice. That's why I assumed she had a boyfriend. A few of the men have tried to take her out, but she wouldn't have any of it. She even came alone to our annual party."

"Perhaps she was . . ." Bryce raised one hand and turned it slightly back and forward.

"A lesbian? No, she wasn't!"

"You have a way of sounding so certain of things you say about Miss Ingress, and yet you confessed to hardly knowing her," Bryce observed.

Miss Lynch laughed again. "I'm a Libra," she said. "That means my lesson in life is to learn balance. I tend to be a bit dogmatic. But take it from me, Inspector, Miss Ingress wasn't a lesbian." She brushed her long dark hair away from her face, a beautiful face, Bryce had decided, with her high cheekbones and wide, dark eyes. "How can I be so certain? It's simple. I'm a lesbian. If she had been a sister I'd have known it."

Bryce tried to conceal his shock, but obviously without success.

"Oh, come on, inspector," Miss Lynch said. "This is San Francisco. Surely an honest, open declaration of one's sexual preferences doesn't shock you?"

"I didn't think it would," Bryce told her. "About Miss Ingress . . ."

"There really isn't much more I can tell you," Miss Lynch interrupted. "I know she had a boyfriend because once in a while she'd wear something into the office. A brooch or a necklace, and I'd see her fingering it with that 'God-it-came-from-him' expression."

"I see," Bryce said, although he didn't see at all.

"Oh, there's Mr. Williams," Miss Lynch said.

They had been sitting in the employee lounge, the door open. Bryce glanced up and saw a distinguished looking man in a pin-striped suit enter one of the side offices. He took out a key, unlocked the door, and disappeared inside.

"Do all the executives lock their offices?" he asked.

Miss Lynch nodded affirmatively. "The inner sanctum, we call that row," she said. "Or the unholy five."

"Unholy five?"

"The top five executives," Miss Lynch explained. "Their doors are locked when they're out. Only Miss Ingress had a passkey. If we had to take something in or out she would have to unlock the doors for us. Strictly top secret stuff kept inside those offices. Proposals for new shows, private ratings, that sort of thing. There's a lot of thievery in this business, even before the shows get on the air. Anything truly original is kept under wraps until it's previewed. Show-biz espionage."

"You'd never know originality was a consideration from what you see on the screen," Bryce murmured.

"Isn't that the truth?" Miss Lynch laughed. "Would you like to meet Mr. Williams now?"

Bryce found Merrill Williams an affable man, but he could shed little light on Hope Ingress. He knew only that she was an exceptional secretary, one who would be extremely difficult to replace in today's market. Like the three executives Bryce met after Williams, Sterne and Wade and Linquist, Williams had no knowledge whatsoever of the dead secretary's private life. It would appear from the information he carried away from Multimedia that Hope Ingress had been little more than a robot that typed, took dictation, and kept the office staff operating smoothly. For all that was known of her private life she could have crawled into a box at night and disconnected the electrodes that caused her to function so efficiently during the daylight hours.

But he suspected one of them of lying.

Bryce carried Hope Ingress's personnel file back to his office. The forms inside told him about the woman. She had been born in Medford, Oregon, educated at the University of Oregon at Ashland, some twenty miles from her birthplace, and had previously been a secretary with the Oregon school system and a local television station. Under nearest living relative, she had written, *NONE*. Her address at the time of employment had been different, an apartment building on Mission Street that Bryce knew well—a far cry from the modern glass and steel structure perched on the side of the hill where she had lived until yesterday evening. There were three evaluation reports, all listing her performance as exceptional, all recommending an increase in salary, but none so spectacular as to allow her to afford her apartment and the expensive clothes that had filled her closets. She had obviously had an additional income. But from where? From whom? Had a well-off gentleman called her mistress? Or had she been blackmailing Multimedia executives? It could have been both.

Bryce closed Hope Ingress's personnel file and pushed it to one side.

The other files he had taken from the bottom drawer of her bureau lay at his elbow. Photostat copies of investigatory reports on the five executives he had interviewed that morning, plus Howard Barrett who had long since leaped to his death. If Hope Ingress had been blackmailing Barrett and driven him to plunge through his window, her display of grief had been a performance. Bryce wondered if a woman working around actors could develop enough of their talent to be so convincing? And why were the files only photostats? Where were the originals? If a blackmail victim had murdered her, why hadn't he searched for the files? Or had he found the originals and not suspected there would be copies? All questions he could not answer.

Exhausted now to the point of falling asleep in his chair, Bryce flipped casually through the photostat files. The murderer could have been any of the five, or none of them. It could have been a madman with no previous connection to the victim. God knew the streets of the city were filled with madmen. What had the mayor said, "San Francisco is a mecca for odd people"? A dumb statement to give to the press. True—but dumb.

Bryce tapped his fingers absently on top of the photostat files. He would learn nothing from what Miss Lynch had called the unholy five. Perhaps something could be learned from the past. He opened Howard Barrett's file and glanced through the pages. As he read, the case came back to him. He remembered Kathleen Barrett well; a small-boned woman who had carried her grief with dignity. She had received him in her parlor, served him tea, and sat with her hands folded in her lap, her chin tilted to defy the tears that had threatened to fill her eyes as she had answered questions about her husband.

Then Bryce remembered something else. He ran his index finger down the notes he had taken when interviewing Kathleen Barrett. He found what he sought near the bottom of the page.

Wives have a sort of club . . . parallel husbands . . . social structure with authority given among wives to match husbands' position with company . . . silly but amusing (her words).

That was it! Bryce thought. He'd get nothing from the husbands, but he might learn a considerable amount from their wives.

Satisfied, he left his office and drove home for a few hours' sleep.

Chapter
Twenty-One

IT HAD BEEN a strange weekend for Rosemary.

First there had been her Saturday night dinner party, a disaster because she had inflicted the Abbotts on Keith without warning him. Joanna had been distant, almost unpleasant. Maureen had gotten a bit tipsy. Lizabeth had blatantly made a play for Justin, and Vanessa had proceeded to bore everyone with her latest astrological predictions. Janet Linquist had been depressing, and Keith irritable.

But she could have survived that. It was not her first unsuccessful dinner party.

It had been Patricia's joining them in the drawing room for a cognac that truly upset Rosemary. She had watched Keith with the younger woman, the way he catered to her by introducing suitable topics for conversation, by pretending he cared for her opinions, enjoyed her humor. Still, she sensed he was not quite comfortable with Patricia, and possibly with the arrangement he had gotten them involved in. Again, the fear that it would be tonight had sent shivers along her spine. Revulsion at the prospect had risen up inside her like a bile that could not be swallowed or expelled. For the first time she had found herself considering her own feelings with no regard for Keith's. But you'll lose him, she had reminded herself. And that thought had not brought the accustomed pain. Pleading a headache, she had left them in the drawing room and gone upstairs.

As she had made a habit of doing, Patricia soon arrived at her door. She entered without knocking, and, saying nothing, had crossed to where Rosemary sat at her vanity, taken the hairbrush from her hand, and began brushing Rosemary's auburn hair with smooth, firm strokes.

Rosemary, fighting a compulsion to scream, had kept her eyes averted from the mirror. She had felt Patricia's gaze fixed on her reflection and it had unnerved her.

"I think he's frightened of us," the younger woman had suddenly said in her customary low tone.

Rosemary had looked up then, in surprise. "Who is frightened of us?" she had asked.

"Your husband."

"Why would he be frightened of us?"

"Because he thinks we're getting too close," Patricia had answered. "Didn't you see the jealousy in his face the other night when you told him I had helped you pick out your dress?"

"That's absurd!"

"Is it, Rosemary? Things aren't working out as he expected. I think he thought you'd fight me more than you have. I think he'd planned to prove his power over you by forcing this arrangement. If he'd only wanted another woman why hasn't he come to me alone? He's made no advances. Or, why didn't he just go to a call girl without threatening to take a mistress if you didn't agree to a *ménage à trois?* I think he sees the strength in you and . . ."

191

"Strength in me?"

"Yes, and he's trying to somehow feed on your strength by making you submissive to . . ."

"Oh, please stop this amateur analysis of my husband!" Rosemary cried. She had had a compulsion to tear the hairbrush from Patricia's hands, but had managed to control her temper.

The stroking of her hair had paused briefly, then resumed. After a moment of silence, Patricia had said, "I don't mean to upset you, Rosemary. I wouldn't upset you for anything. But you have to consider these things."

"Why? Why do I have to consider them?" Rosemary had demanded. "Because you tell me I must?" She was on the verge of tears. "Sometimes you remind me of that movie with Ingrid Bergman and Charles Boyer. *Gaslight*. You're trying to play tricks with my mind!"

"You don't believe that," the younger woman had said quietly.

"Yes. But in reverse. You're trying to convince me I have a strength I don't possess, have never possessed. You say that Keith is weak. He's not. He's strong. I'm the weak one. I've always been weak. I've never been capable of functioning without a man. First my father, then Keith. I've relied totally on both of them. Men and pills! A woman with the strength you claim I possess wouldn't rely on either."

"You don't need the pills, Rosemary."

"Like hell I don't!"

Patricia had taken her by the shoulders then and forced her to turn on the stool until they had been facing. She had bent until their faces had been in a direct line with one another, separated by only inches, their eyes meeting. "Do a favor for me," Patricia had said. "Prove to yourself that you don't need pills.

192

Don't take any tonight. Just one night without a sleeping pill."

Rosemary had tried to turn away, but Patricia had held her by the shoulders. "You can do it," she had insisted.

"Impossible! It's been a dreadful evening! I'd never sleep!" But Patricia had made it sound like a challenge and already her mind had been struggling to accept it. "Why would you care one way or another?" she had asked.

"Because I'm very fond of you," Patricia had answered. "Because I'm your friend and I want you to understand you're not the weak, helpless female you think. You don't need pills for survival. Nor do you need a man to lean on. Will you do it? No pills?"

If it had not been for the pleading in Patricia's eyes, Rosemary would have flatly refused. Instead, she had murmured a weak, "I'll try."

A strange thing had happened then; Patricia had leaned forward and had kissed her on the cheek. She had not understood why the contact had not repulsed her. But it hadn't. She had watched the younger woman leave her room and she had thought the kiss to have been pleasant, reassuring.

She had not taken her customary sleeping pills.

She had lain awake in bed beside Keith until the light had begun to grow brighter against the shades. But when she had slept she had slept soundly and had awakened without her usual grogginess. It had been unnecessary to take another pill to counteract the sleeping pill. Coffee alone had sufficed to ready her to meet the day.

But by noon on Sunday her body had been screaming for its accustomed medications. There had been so many aches and pains in her body that it had been impossible to pinpoint what had hurt the most, her head, stomach, chest, arms, or legs. She had retired to her bedroom and locked the door, telling herself that Patricia had known what she would suffer, that the bitch had been trying to kill her under the disguise of pretending to be her friend. But the challenge of surviving without pills had still been with her. She had succumbed in the end, but only to half her normal dosage, and that had lessened her pain.

When she had finally felt capable of leaving her room she had come downstairs to be told by the maid that both Keith and their houseguest had gone out, Mr. Marston to the office and the young lady to a movie. Rosemary had felt abandoned, angry and lonely, and had returned to her room to spend the balance of the afternoon. There had been several phone calls, two from Janet Linquist, but she had told the maid to say she was out. She had forgotten to broach the subject of Larry Linquist's reason for early retirement to Keith and had not wanted to listen again to Janet's fears.

Keith had returned in the early evening, in a strange mood. Since Patricia had not returned from the movie by dinnertime, they dined alone, and then Keith locked himself away in his study.

That night Rosemary again refused to take her sleeping pills. But she had also sent Patricia away when the younger woman arrived for her hairbrushing ritual. She had not wanted to rely on Patricia. Why exchange one crutch for another? Or, she had wondered, is that what Patricia had had in mind?

She had lain awake a second night until near dawn.

And that had been her weekend; upsetting, painful, sleepless, too many hours spent with her own thoughts—something with which she was not familiar.

The week had also begun badly.

This morning when she had come downstairs she had seen Teddy curled up outside the study door.

Usually the aged dog would awaken from a deep sleep when she appeared and slink off into another area of the house. This morning Teddy hadn't budged and that had drawn her closer attention. She had called his name and he had not responded. She had stamped her foot on the entryway tile; still no response. She had ventured closer and had seen the dog's fur alive with fleas. His eyes were open and lifeless. She had screamed and the maid had come running. "That dog is dead!" she had cried at the startled maid. "Get it out of my sight!" And she had watched Teddy being dragged away across the tiles by his stiff hind legs. She had never understood Keith's attachment to the dog he saw three months out of the year, but she sympathized with the effect his death would have on him. She had telephoned him at the office, but he had been in conference and had left instructions not to be disturbed.

When Keith had not returned her call by late afternoon she conditioned herself to delivering the news of Teddy's death in person, something she would rather have avoided. Keith knew she had always resented the dog and she didn't want him thinking she was gloating as she told him of Teddy's death.

Patricia, her friend, was not understanding. When she came down for breakfast she had been in a distant mood, possibly from the rejection of her hairbrushing ritual of the night before. She had taken the news of Teddy's demise with a shrug and laughed at Rosemary's concern for telling Keith.

"Why should he blame you because his dog died?" Patricia had asked. "The dog was ancient. It isn't your fault it chose to die in San Francisco instead of New Orleans."

"But the point is I don't want Keith thinking . . . oh, never mind!" she had cried in frustration.

She had gone into the drawing room to escape Patricia and was still there at four o'clock when the doorbell rang and the maid appeared to announce an Inspector Cochran.

Rosemary liked Bryce Cochran immediately. There was something about him that reminded her of her father; she could not decide if it was the contrast of his sensitive face to his brutish body or his deep-set grey eyes with their expression of having seen other worlds. She offered tea, and he accepted graciously. It wasn't until after tea had been served that Bryce began his questioning.

"You must know a great many employees of your husband's company," he said.

"Heavens, no!" Rosemary answered. "I've met many employees, but I don't know them. Other than the executives, their wives, and a few directors and producers, I know scarcely any."

"I was under the impression you took an intense interest in Multimedia," Bryce told her.

"Oh, I do," Rosemary admitted. "But the only person who could have told you that would be another executive wife. My interest is, shall we say, discreet? My husband is a strong-willed man. He wouldn't tolerate interference from me. If he realized I influenced any of his decisions—if I indeed do—he'd be most displeased."

"Then it's more or less a game?" Bryce suggested.

"You could call it that." Rosemary sipped her tea and stared at the inspector over the rim of the cup. "You've obviously heard rumors of our wives' club," she said.

Bryce admitted he had, evasively changing the subject so as not to be pressed for the source of his information. "Did you know a Miss Ingress, Multimedia's executive secretary?"

"Miss Ingress," Rosemary repeated the name, casting her memory back to the employees she had met on her infrequent visits to Keith's office. "Oh, yes. Hope Ingress. A tall woman with gray eyes and brown hair. Why do you ask?"

"Have you ever entertained Miss Ingress in your home?"

"No, certainly not."

"Then she's not one of the employees with whom you have more than a passing acquaintance?"

"We've spoken on the telephone frequently," Rosemary answered, "when Keith failed to answer on his private line. I met her once or twice in the office. I remember Keith telling me what an efficient secretary she is."

"How did you feel when your husband praised his secretary?"

"How did I feel? Oh, you mean was I jealous? No, not at all." Rosemary smiled. "I've read those articles that say a businessman's secretary is the second most important woman in his life. Often her contribution extends beyond their business relationship. Frankly, I think that's something of a fantasy of *Playboy*."

Bryce laughed. "You read *Playboy*, Mrs. Marston?"

"I have, yes. But I frankly find it revolting. I suppose there are men out there who subscribe to the magazine's philosophy, but I've never met any of them. Not that I discuss sexual philosophy with male acquaintances." It surprised Rosemary that she was speaking so freely with the inspector; she had never even participated in sexual discussions when that topic reared its head at meetings of the wives. Well, hardly ever. "But why these questions, inspector?" she asked. A thought suddenly crossed her mind and put her on guard. "What has Miss Ingress done?

Obviously something illegal. She hasn't accused my husband of . . ." She could not bring herself to complete the sentence.

"No," Bryce assured her. "It isn't what Miss Ingress has done. It's what's been done to her. I'm afraid the unfortunate woman is dead."

"Dead? What's been done to her? My God! You mean she's been murdered?"

"I'm afraid that's exactly what I mean," Bryce answered.

Rosemary sat forward on the sofa and set her teacup on the table between them. "But surely you don't suspect my husband! That's utterly ridiculous! If you think my husband was having an affair with this woman, you're badly mistaken. Keith isn't the sort for shabby affairs!" She thought of Patricia, and of Keith's arrangement—but then she pushed that quickly from her mind, afraid the inspector, now an adversary, would read something in her expression to fan his suspicions.

Bryce tried to keep himself from smiling. As much as Rosemary Marston had objected to *Playboy* philosophy, the first conclusion she had leaped to was an affair between her husband and Hope Ingress. "I'm not accusing your husband of an affair with Miss Ingress," he said. "I'm not actually accusing him of anything." He saw the woman visibly relax, and added, "I'm merely questioning people connected with Multimedia, people who might have known the unfortunate woman and be able to shed some light on who might have wanted her dead."

"I'm certain there's nothing I can tell you," Rosemary said guardedly. "As I said, I scarcely knew the woman."

"But you do know the other executive wives," Bryce said, "and women have a way of . . ."

"Of gossiping?" Rosemary finished when he hesitated.

"Yes, gossiping. Have any of the other executives' wives expressed a suspicion that their husband is having an affair?"

"No," Rosemary answered emphatically.

Bryce stared thoughtfully at the half-empty teacup in his hand. "Of course a woman might not tend to confess such suspicions even to her friends," he said. "It's something that would be difficult to confess."

Rosemary thought of Lizabeth's easy confessions, her actual gloating over her affairs.

"But then I'm not certain Miss Ingress was murdered because of an affair," Bryce said, watching Rosemary's expression closely.

"But you do feel it's somehow connected with the company?" Rosemary pressed.

Bryce nodded affirmatively.

"But you have no intention of explaining your suspicions?" Rosemary went on. "You're being exasperatingly evasive, inspector."

"Tell me, Mrs. Marston, have you noticed anything unusual in any of the executives' attitudes?"

"What do you mean by unusual? Moodiness, that sort of thing?" She stared at the inspector thoughtfully, as if trying to recall some incident trapped in the recesses of her mind. "No, nothing," she finally concluded. "The only thing happening out of the ordinary is the retirement of one of Multimedia's executives. Competition among the men to be chosen for his position is high."

"Which executive is retiring?"

"Larry Linquist," Rosemary answered.

Bryce recalled his interview with Linquist; the oldest of the executives, white-haired, sternly businesslike, the only executive who had not preferred Hope

Ingress's services to the other secretaries. "And who's favored for the promotion?"

"I wouldn't know," Rosemary replied.

Now who's being evasive? Bryce thought. He finished his tea, made a mental note that he still did not prefer it to coffee, and rose from the uncomfortable French chair. "Thank you for seeing me, Mrs. Marston. I hope I haven't taken too much of your time."

The seriousness that had clouded Rosemary's face since the mention of Hope Ingress's murder faded. "Time is something I've plenty of, Mr. Cochran. It was pleasant meeting you even if the reason for your visit was disturbing." She walked with him into the entryway, extending her hand as he opened the outer door. "Good luck with your investigation."

"You will call me if you think of something that might be pertinent?"

"Of course," she assured him as he removed a card from his wallet and handed it to her. She glanced at the name. "Bryce is an interesting name," she said. She didn't understand why, but she felt an impulse to delay his departure.

"A typographical error," Bryce told her. "It was meant to be Bruce, but some clerk in the department of birth registrations pressed the wrong typewriter key. My parents liked the name, so I was stuck with it. Human error. But I'm glad you like it. Good day, Mrs. Marston."

Rosemary closed the door behind the inspector and was walking thoughtfully back to the drawing room, mulling over what he had told her, when the cook emerged from the hallway in a state of loud anger.

"I can't take it any longer!" the excitable Italian cried. "That . . . that woman!" His eyes blazed with Latin fury. *"La donna! La bestia!* She's changed the menu after my wonderful sauces were made!"

"Who changed the menu?" Rosemary asked.

"La bestia!" the cook cried, waving his hands toward the upstairs balcony. "That . . . that Eliott beech! I quit! I cannot work for two mistresses! Two women running one house too much for one cook!"

Rosemary, following the direction of the cook's flailing hands, saw that Patricia had been drawn to the railing by the commotion. The two women's gazes locked. There was a smile on the younger woman's lips that was belied by the unfaltering expression in her eyes. Rosemary discerned the expression to be a challenge.

Without taking her gaze from Patricia's, Rosemary told the cook, "I authorized no change of menu, Roberto. So there will be none!"

Turning, she fled into the drawing room and slammed the double doors.

Chapter
Twenty-Two

"PERHAPS SHE WAS attempting to help you," Keith said. "After all, you've never taken a particular interest in the menu before. You usually left it up to Roberto himself. That's undoubtedly why he threatened to quit. He objected to losing total control over the kitchen."

"You're taking her side!" Rosemary cried in astonishment. "She meddles in the operation of this house, almost forces our cook to quit, and you're defending her!"

"I'm not taking sides," Keith said calmly. "I'm merely trying to make you see reason." He had just come home and had not even removed his coat and hat when Rosemary had called him into the study to complain about Patricia. "But if you want, I'll speak to her," he said.

"Damn right I want!" Rosemary told him. She saw the pained expression of his face, was suddenly smothered with guilt, and added, "I'm sorry to burden you with this. I should have handled it myself."

Keith paused in removing his coat and glanced at her, an odd expression on his face. When had she ever handled anything herself? "Yes, well, I don't object to your coming to me," he said. "Would you make me a drink? A martini, very dry."

Rosemary mixed the martinis while Keith went back into the entryway to dispose of his hat and coat. When he returned he dropped wearily into a chair and drank his first martini in one quick gulp.

"A bad day?" Rosemary inquired as she refilled his glass.

"A very bad day," he murmured.

"Then I'm even sorrier for attacking you like a fishwife when you came home," she told him. She took her own drink to the sofa and sat down in a corner. "Was it Hope Ingress's murder?"

"Partially," he said without thinking. Then, he glanced up at her. "Was it in the papers? Was Multimedia mentioned?"

"You know I don't read the newspapers. They depress me. An Inspector Cochran came around to see me this afternoon."

Keith's face went suddenly pale. The hand holding his martini jerked and the clear liquid splashed onto the chair arm. "Damn him!" he cried. "He had no right! What did he want with you? What did he ask you?"

Rosemary was startled by his violent reaction. She regarded him with concern. "He only wanted to know if I was acquainted with Miss Ingress," she said. "He was a pleasant man. More polite and dignified than the policemen on those television shows you produce. Why did his coming here upset you?"

"It's an invasion of my private life," Keith said, still shaken by anger. "A company employee is killed and Cochran comes to my home to question my wife! The bastard spent the entire morning questioning our employees."

"Well, she *was* murdered, Keith," Rosemary pointed out. "The inspector has the right to question anyone who might give him a lead."

"What did he expect to get from you? You scarcely knew Hope Ingress."

"I told him just that."

Keith set his drink aside and leaned forward, elbows resting on his knees. "Tell me exactly what he asked you, Rosemary, and what you told him. Exactly."

Rosemary related her conversation with Bryce Cochran as best she could remember it, eliminating any reference to the possibility that Keith might be having an affair with the unfortunate secretary, or to the executive wives' club.

Keith had calmed down during the time it took for her to relate the details or her meeting with the inspector. When she had finished the color had returned to his face and the vein that always stood out on his forehead when he was upset had lost its swollen appearance. "And that's all?" he asked.

"That's all," Rosemary assured him. "Did I say anything wrong?"

"No, nothing," he said. "But should he come back again I want you to refuse to see him."

"But why? Keith, what is it with this woman's death? You . . . you act so guilty. As if you were somehow involved."

"Cochran thinks someone at the company is responsible," he told her. "It's my responsibility to protect the company's reputation."

"The company's reputation? Good God! If someone at Multimedia is guilty of murder, it's your responsibility to see they're brought to justice. That's more important than a little bad publicity."

Keith rose from his chair. "Cochran's mistaken," he

said. "No one at Multimedia is involved in Miss Ingress's death."

"You don't sound very convinced," Rosemary observed.

"Well, I am convinced. Now, I'll dress for dinner."

He had reached the doors before a forgotten incident struck Rosemary. "By the way, Keith," she said, "I'm sorry, but Teddy died today."

Chapter
Twenty-Three

JOANNA TURNED FROM the canvas. She had been sitting in front of it for over half an hour without touching brush to paint. She had been so lost in thought she had no idea how many times the doorbell had rung before she had heard it.

She rose from her stool, irritated at being disturbed, and hurried down the stairs to the front door. She noted that the glass doors onto the terrace were open and the room was chilled; she would have to light a fire before Justin came home. He hated cold rooms, liked the temperature kept at an unfaltering seventy-two degrees.

She opened the door just as the bell rang again, and found herself confronting Max.

"Did you forget about me today, Precious?" he asked, and brushed past her into the room. "We had a bargain, remember? I do a favor for you and you in return give me one of your canvases for my gallery. I'll once again have a Joanna Wade hanging in my front window. If that doesn't bring the art collectors in, nothing will."

Joanna closed the door. "I'm sorry, Max. Forgive me. I did forget." She glanced at the grandfather clock in the foyer as she led Max into the living room. Justin would be home in another forty minutes if he was on time—which he seldom had been in the past few weeks; she'd have to get rid of Max before he arrived. "A quick drink, Max?"

Max laughed. "You're losing your subtlety, Precious," he said. "Yes, a very quick drink will do. Something straight—forgive the pun—scotch, whiskey, vodka, gin, tequila, sterno." He flopped onto the down cushions of the sofa and let his gaze sweep about the walls. "Artists!" he said with distaste. "You create beauty, but you never hang any in your own homes. What's that?" He indicated an abstract hanging above the fireplace.

"Something Justin did," she answered reluctantly.

"Ohhh! You didn't tell me he paints—or tries to. Tell me, did he dabble in painting before he married you, or is it just one of his little quirks to compete with you?"

"Don't be a bitch, Max," Joanna warned as she handed him a double shot of vodka.

"I thought you'd be the one who was a bitch on her broom today after what I found out last night," he said. "No? Well, you're probably still in shock, poor baby. It's not every day that the blind are made to see. Tell me, what was Romeo's reaction when you confronted him with the fact that you knew about the other woman? I suppose he denied it, told you it was his long, lost sister who was a prostitute and he just hadn't had the heart to introduce you to the poor creature. Shame! Shame! She hadn't conquered the family penchant for selling herself!" He placed the back of one hand against his forehead in a mock-theatrical gesture reminiscent of silent movies.

Joanna glared at him. Turning away, she moved to the fireplace, took a match from the holder, and lighted the gas. "I didn't confront him," she said without turning.

"What?" Max sat up straight. "You mean I followed him at your request and reported him picking up that woman and you didn't even confront him?"

"I . . . I couldn't," Joanna mumbled.

Max looked at her thoughtfully. "Joanna, you're not serious? A wife discovered her husband is cheating—and you waste a scene like that? You obviously didn't see enough movies when you were growing up."

"I don't have your sense of the dramatic," Joanna said, still standing with her back to him, staring into the blazing fire.

"Repression is not good for the soul." Max suddenly set his vodka aside, rose and came to her. He put his arms about her and leaned his head gently against her back. "You know, you're the only girl I've held since high school. Then I only did it because I was after her brother." He lifted the cascade of her red hair and kissed the nape of her neck. "All right, Precious," he said understandingly. "Tell Max all about it."

"There's nothing to tell, Max. I just didn't confront him." She wiggled out of his embrace, walked away from him, and stopped at the bar to pour herself a drink.

"Didn't, wouldn't, couldn't!" Max said, exasperated. "Oh, come on, Joanna! Don't tell me you're going to forgive him without even telling him you're aware of that little piece of fluff he's keeping in the city? I thought infidelity was supposed to be the final straw that ended straight marriages."

Joanna downed a straight shot of scotch, shuddered, and pushed the glass aside. "I meant to confront him, Max," she said. "After you called and told me where he went, who he was with, I paced the floor in a fury I've never known before. In my mind I formulated accusations that would devastate him. I would have done you proud. Even your favorite actresses couldn't have come up with better lines than those I planned to deliver when he walked through the door."

"So what happened? Stage fright? You weren't afraid he'd hit you? God! All the greats, Davis and Crawford and Dietrich—they all got banged around, but they didn't keep silent about injustices."

"Max, be serious!" Joanna cried. "This wasn't one of your forties movies! It was real life! It was me! By the time he came home my temper had cooled. I had my humiliation and jealousy under control. I still meant to confront him, but in a civilized manner."

"Now we go into Noel Coward. Very sophisticated. Oh, sorry, Precious. Go on."

Joanna crossed to the sofa, sat down, and stared out of the bank of windows at the lights of Sausalito and San Francisco beyond the bay. "He came home late," she went on. "He'd been drinking. I could smell it on his breath. Justin's most vulnerable when he's been drinking. He's like a little . . . I was already in bed. Not sleeping. I haven't slept all night or today. But I had my eyes closed, only the nightlight on, and I lay watching him through half-closed lashes. He undressed in the semidarkness so he wouldn't awaken me. I intended to sit up in bed at any moment and confront him, but there was something about the way he moved, the slump of his shoulders . . . I don't know, something that kept me silent, watching him."

"It isn't as if you haven't seen him drunk before," Max said.

"It wasn't because he had been drinking," Joanna told him. "It was different, much different. Have you ever watched a boxer leave the ring who's just lost the fight?"

"I don't go in for that sort of brutish sport."

"Their entire body seems to express their defeat. Justin was like that."

"Probably guilt," Max suggested.

Joanna ignored the remark. "When he came to bed, crawled in beside me, I still intended to confront him. I was trying to recall the marvelous lines I had invented to express my disgust when I suddenly realized he was . . . he was crying."

"Joanna, Joanna, Joanna!" Max cried. "It's the man who's supposed to be turned to putty by the woman's tears! What kind of role playing did your mother teach you?" Waving his arms in an expression of impatience, Max returned to the sofa and sipped his vodka. "As I said, darling, it was probably guilt. Combine guilt with alcohol and the most insensitive bastard can burst into tears. I know because I do it frequently."

"How can you be so . . . so flippant, Max? Anyway, I couldn't confront him. I lay listening to his crying and I was the one who felt guilty."

"Oh, Christ!"

"I felt like he had been with another woman because I had driven him to it. Now don't laugh at me, don't say anything!"

"You mean I can't even call you a natural born martyr?"

"If you do, I'll call you all those names we both find so offensive."

Max held up his hands in the gesture of surrender.

"This morning when Justin got up I pretended to still be asleep. He showered, dressed and left without attempting to awaken me."

"And you've spent the entire day stewing," Max said knowingly. "Well, Joanna, if you want my opinion I'd say you're as crazy as . . ."

Joanna turned and glanced at the grandfather clock through the doorway. "I don't want your opinion tonight," she cut in. "Justin's due home any minute, and I don't want you here when he arrives. Things are bad enough without the two of you having a go at one another."

"Well, I've been thrown out of worse places. God knows I've been thrown out of better ones too." Max threw down the remainder of his vodka and got to his feet. "So where's the Joanna Wade painting I earned for my useless cloak and dagger work? Do you know what I felt like following your husband like some second-rate paperback detective?"

"I'm sorry I put you through it, Max, but there was no one else to turn to. But you're partly responsible. It was our conversation the other day that planted the doubts in my mind about Justin and another woman. That's one weakness in him I never suspected."

"But now that you know you're not going to do anything, are you, Joanna?" Max asked seriously. "You're just going to swallow this as you have his other faults?"

Joanna, ignoring the question, said, "You can pick out any painting in my studio for your gallery, Max." Before he could say anything more, she led him into the foyer and up the stairs to the room she had converted into her studio.

The room was filled with paintings she had readied for her San Francisco showing. Max moved about the room studying each critically. Justin, even Joanna, were forgotten as he savored the paintings. Finally, stopping in the middle of the studio, one hand raised to his chin, he confronted Joanna. "These are your best works," he said. "I don't know what that bastard's given you, probably suffering, but there's a new depth to your paintings since you married him."

Joanna, still fearful Justin would return before Max

had departed, brushed off the compliment. "Which one do you want, Max?"

Max read the impatience in her voice. He quickly scanned the paintings a second time. "That one," he said, pointing to a large canvas of two shy lovers on the dunes at Stenson Beach.

"It's one of my favorites," Joanna told him. "Take it."

"If only I could handle them all," Max murmured. "It would be like the old days. We had a good thing going then, Joanna. Not only did we both make money, I understood your art. Those San Francisco galleries, what do they know? If it's called art by a few critics, they revere it for the price they can charge."

"I can't go over that again with you now, Max," Joanna said.

"Yes, yes! Out before Justin comes home!" He took the canvas from its place on the wall and followed Joanna back down the stairs. At the door, he said, "Listen, Precious. If you need me, if you want to talk more, you know where to reach me. If I'm not at the Sausalito Inn, I'll be home. If I thought it was you calling, I'd throw out the handsomest trick in the western hemisphere. Okay?"

"Thank you, Max."

"Oh, here! The fog's going to get your newspaper unless you take it inside." Max stooped, picked up the already damp newspaper, and was about to hand it to her when he stopped and held it closer to his failing eyes. The small photograph on the fold was familiar. He set the canvas against the wall, unfolded the newspaper, and opened it under the porch light.

Giving in to her impatience, Joanna asked sharply, "What is it, Max? For God's sake, if Justin drove up now . . ."

212

Max, his face paler than usual, handed her the open paper.

WOMAN FLUNG TO DEATH OFF BALCONY read the headline.

"No wonder Justin was crying," Max said. "That's the woman he was with."

Chapter
Twenty-Four

ROSEMARY KNOCKED LIGHTLY on Keith's study door, and then opened it and went inside without waiting for him to invite her.

She seldom invaded the privacy of the study. To her mind, it was Keith's room, his retreat, a place he could go to escape her—something she understood because she, too, had such a room, a small sitting room she had had redecorated on the third floor. Keith had never entered that room; she regretted the necessity of disturbing him in his study.

He was slumped in an overstuffed cordovan leather chair. He had changed into his lounging jacket, deep blue velvet with black piping; his slippers lay on the floor beside the footstool. The pipe he held between his teeth was unlit, but the room reeked of tobacco. A half-empty snifter of cognac sat on the table at his elbow. He looked up as she entered, but without any discernible expression.

"I'm sorry to disturb you," Rosemary told him. She stood just inside the door waiting for him to acknowledge that her presence in the study did not offend him.

"You're not disturbing me," he said. "Would you care to join me in a cognac?" There was a weariness in his voice, and she suspected he had consumed more alcohol than was customary.

"No, nothing." She came into the middle of the room and seated herself on the edge of his footstool. It was then that she noticed the sound of the clocks. Keith was a collector of antique French clocks. The room was filled with them and the sound was deafening to her sensitive hearing. She glanced around the study as if seeing the clock collection for the first time. All were ticking and precisely set—one of his obsessions. It was quarter past ten. She wanted to say what she had to say and leave before all the chimes and bells created their pandemonium at the half hour. "There's something we have to talk about," she said.

He stirred in the chair, shifted his position, and reached for the snifter. "Can't it wait?" he asked. "It's been one hell of a day."

"I'm sorry. It can't wait. I'd never get to sleep with or without sleeping pills." But then, how to begin? she asked herself. His feet rested on the stool beside her. He wore no socks. She stared at his pale flesh with the dark shading of hair reaching below his ankles. Curious, but she had never before noticed how old his feet looked, how thinly the skin covered the blue veins beneath. The flesh about his toes was wrinkled and the nails were miscolored and oddly shaped. It somehow destroyed the illusion she had carried that he represented male perfection. How could she have lived with him, slept with him, and not noticed how ugly his feet were?

"I suppose it's about Patricia Eliott," he said. "If it is, I warn you I'll not welcome the conversation."

"No, it's not about *her*," Rosemary told him. "It's about you."

"Me?" The weariness in his voice vanished and with the one word had taken on an inflection of mild interest. He paused with the snifter halfway to his lips.

Rosemary, because she could not say what she had to say and look up at him, rose from the footstool and reseated herself in the companion leather chair. It was beyond her comprehension why men preferred leather chairs; they were cold when you first sat in them and then clung to your clothing when heated by body temperature.

"All right," Keith said. "I'm willing to talk about me. What about me that can't wait until tomorrow?"

"You've had me in a state of upset all evening," she began. "When you came home you were in a strange mood. Then when I told you about the inspector's visit you became completely unlike yourself. You even forbade me to receive the man should he call again. Forbidding me anything is totally out of your character. It started me thinking."

Keith straightened up in his chair. "You sound like a woman about to accuse her husband of beginning the change of life," he said lightly.

Rosemary, ignoring his feeble attempt at humor, went on, "Then Teddy's death. I know how much you loved that dog, and yet the news scarcely affected you. I knew when you hardly reacted that whatever was troubling you was more serious than you wanted me to realize."

"Teddy was fourteen years old," Keith said quietly. "That would make him the equivalent of ninety-eight by the human measure. But what are you getting to, Rosemary?"

Rosemary swallowed and said quickly, "Hope Ingress!"

Perhaps it was only her imagination but the mention of the name seemed to create an unseen current in the room.

"Earlier you excused your strange reaction as responsibility for protecting your company from bad publicity," Rosemary reminded him, "but I think it was more than that."

"You have an overactive imagination, Rosemary. You always have had. It can be a curse."

"The inspector asked me whether I felt any of the executives might be having an affair with Miss Ingress. Since I didn't know the woman I didn't know if she was the sort for casual affairs, but I know you aren't, and I assured the inspector of that fact." She waited for him to speak, but when he did not, she went on, "Then I thought perhaps Mr. Cochran has leaped to the wrong conclusions. Perhaps Hope Ingress was killed for completely different reasons."

"And what reason did you come up with?" Keith asked quietly.

"I . . . I don't really know," she confessed. "But it was Miss Ingress who interviewed women for you for this arrangement you're so set on," she said.

"You didn't tell the inspector that!"

"No, of course not. But when that occurred to me it also crossed my mind that perhaps Miss Ingress knew why she was interviewing those women and decided to take advantage of it. You've always been a stickler for proper appearances. Was she . . . was she . . .?"

"Was she blackmailing me?" Keith finished for her. "No, dear Rosemary. Miss Ingress was not threatening to expose me as less than the gentleman I pretend to be. As for the arrangement, she was merely acting as an executive secretary interviewing women with specifications I had given her. One of those specifications was not a women willing to involve herself in a *ménage à trois*. Appearances being as important to you as they are to me, you can rest assured that Miss Ingress knew nothing of our arrangement with Miss Eliott."

But Rosemary was not convinced. "Keith, where were you yesterday evening?"

"Why, here with you! Don't tell me your overactive imagination is destroying your memory."

"Before you returned for dinner?" Rosemary persisted. "Both you and Patricia Eliott were out when . . . when Miss Ingress was killed."

Keith set his snifter aside and leaned forward in his chair. There was astonishment and anger in his eyes, but Rosemary also thought she discerned fear. "Are you accusing me of murdering Hope Ingress?"

"Oh, God, no!" she cried. "I'm pleading with you to assure me you didn't!"

Chapter
Twenty-Five

BRYCE WAS THANKFUL he wasn't driving today. Officer Martin, who was, was given to frequent outbursts of anger at the traffic tie-ups.

It was December 23rd, two days before Christmas, and the downtown traffic was at its peak. Bryce stared from the car window, his gaze taking in the Christmas decorations, the blinking lights, the scurrying pedestrians, but through the shoppers along Union Square he saw the prostitutes, the pickpockets, the male hustlers, the beggars. It wasn't only the shopkeepers who were prospering. It was a good season for the human dregs.

Beyond the square he could see the towering peak of the Multimedia building and his thoughts left the crowd and returned to his present case. He was on his way to Sea Cliff to interview Lizabeth Williams.

He recalled the details in her husband's file found in Hope Ingress's apartment. He also recalled meeting the sophisticated Merrill Williams on his visit to Multimedia; tall, handsome, suave, immaculately dressed in his pin-striped suit, affable, upset over the news of the executive secretary's death, apologetic because he could give so little information about her private life.

The man Bryce had met and the man profiled in the

photostats hidden in Hope Ingress's bureau drawer did not seem the same. The Merrill Williams of the Ingress files was noted to be a scoundrel, a parasite. As a younger man he had earned a living by escorting and being attentive to older ladies. Born and raised in Hollywood, he had had a stint as an actor, but failed. An escort service had turned him on to the financial gains to be made from widowed or divorced older women. Southern California had been filled with potential clients, and he had made a success of it. Young, handsome, attentive, and eager to please, he had been supported by a famous actress, an actress Bryce had admired since his boyhood days. Then the actress apparently found a replacement for Williams, and turned him out. He left, but not empty-handed. The actress had him arrested and charged with the theft of her jewelry. The scandal was hushed up by the actress's attorney; she had acted too hastily in charging her gigolo and decided later that the publicity would hurt her chances of a planned comeback. The jewelry in question was returned and the charges against Williams dropped. But she had her revenge by spreading rumors among her friends of Merrill's thievery and planting doubts about his virility.

Williams eventually fled Southern California and moved to San Francisco where he resumed his career of milking lonely, vulnerable old ladies. But his youth was abandoning him. He found his employers were becoming less and less responsive. He was forced to seek other employment. Since he understood something of the acting profession he took a job with Multimedia, dividing his time between accounting and the production of inconsequential programs on shoestring budgets. The salary was small and he had longed for the luxuries of his past life. Finally, in a last-ditch

effort, he had decided to find a woman of means and—
against his cardinal rule—marry her.

Lizabeth Manning had been the woman he had
selected. It had not been an easy task making that
decision, but he had done it by the process of elimina-
tion. Of the three women on his list of possible wives,
Lizabeth Manning had been the most vulnerable and
most likely to lavish her wealth on a husband. He had
access to Multimedia files and knew that Lizabeth's
Aunt Thelma was a major stockholder in the firm. He
also knew through the newspapers that Lizabeth's
father had died and left her a considerable fortune. He
began to follow her, and compiled a list of her friends,
habits and nightspots she frequented. Arranging an
introduction was not difficult; the flamboyant Lizabeth
liked meeting new men. But she, also, had been playing a game, pretending to be a servant in her own
house. She tried to take him to bed the first night, but
he knew her game and understood that quick submission would mean he would be discarded when the next
attractive man entered her life. He wanted his future
insured, and for that she would have to fall in love with
him. That, he soon discovered, was the easiest part of
his plan. Refusing to sleep with her immediately created a challenge; she fell for him as quickly as a naive
male would a girl pretending innocence. When he
proposed to her, it was to Lizabeth, the servant. He
acted as surprised as possible when she revealed the
truth, then again proposed to Lizabeth, the wealthy
socialite, and she accepted.

After their marriage she gave him a new Mercedes, a
yacht, and, when he expressed interest, three racehorses. She wanted him to quit his job with Multimedia and live exclusively on her money, but he refused.
Having once tasted poverty, he had no intention of

relying on one source of security; instead, he manipulated her discreetly into having Aunt Thelma back his promotions with the company.

Merrill had known that there was one way in which he might fail his wife—and that was sexually. With the older women the demands had not been exhaustive. He was bisexual, something he had hidden and struggled with since his youth, and the lack of sexual demands of the older women did not drain him beyond the point of sneaking out occasionally and finding satisfaction for that other facet of his sexual self. Lizabeth, however, was younger and extremely sexual. In less than a year of marriage, he had been aware that his lack of response had driven her to seek other men, but he had never felt threatened so long as the men she sought were younger and so long as she took great efforts to hide her indiscretions from him. To insure this, he had affected a jealous streak that was outside his nature.

Bryce Cochran did not read all this in the Ingress files, but what was not there he surmised. The files described Williams's conquest of his wife, and gave a detailed list of his nocturnal escapades with younger men. Both sufficient motive to push Hope Ingress from her balcony.

Officer Martin's sudden sigh of relief drew Bryce from his thoughts. The driver had turned the car into the side streets where the traffic was negligible. He relaxed behind the wheel and glanced at Bryce with a weary smile. "Damn, but I hate the Christmas season," he said.

"Don't tell me you're an atheist, Martin," Bryce said rather coolly. He knew Martin didn't like him, had objected to being assigned to him. He would have preferred it if the officer had not attempted to make conversation, had just done his driving and kept his

222

mouth closed. As long as Martin functioned efficiently, they would have no problems, unless they talked themselves into them.

"I considered being an atheist, but there were no holidays," the officer said with a feeble attempt at humor.

"Then you're a Christian," Bryce said, deliberately taking the officer's humor seriously.

"Oh, hell," Martin said, "I don't know what I am. Forget it." And he went back to his driving, his body resuming the tension it had displayed in the heavy traffic.

Sea Cliff had always been one of Bryce's favorite sections of San Francisco; the streets were always clean, the lawns manicured, the white houses outlined against the blue of the entrance of the bay and the red earth hills beyond. He often came here, parked his car, and just sat staring at the scene. At Sea Cliff it was possible to forget the crimes that plagued his beloved city. Of course crime did reach Sea Cliff, but it had left no visible scars.

The Williams house was a rambling old mansion in the Spanish style, perched on the bay side of the hill. There was an iron gate and inner courtyard. The porch was tiled and so crowded by potted plants it was almost impossible to make one's way to the carved arched door without stepping on a drooping frond or branch. Bryce pressed the bell and heard chimes echo inside.

Presently, he heard footsteps echoing across interior tiles and the door was opened by an Oriental woman in maid's uniform. Bryce presented his card and said, "Mrs. Lizabeth Williams, please."

The maid nodded, closed the door, and went away.

As he waited, Bryce glanced over his shoulder. He could see the car through the iron gate, see Martin slouched behind the wheel with his hat pulled down over his eyes and a cigarette dangling from his lips.

When the door opened again, he turned to find himself confronting a tall woman of about forty with blonde hair and brown eyes. She was wearing tailored slacks and a silk blouse, very expensive, and had a fur coat slung over her shoulders. She seemed disturbed by his being on her front porch. "I was just on my way out," she said—she glanced down at the card the maid had given her. "What can I do for you, Inspector Cochran?" She had no intention of inviting him inside.

"What I have to ask won't take long," he assured her.

"I suppose it's about the Ingress woman?" She saw the questioning arch of his eyebrows and explained, "Rosemary Marston called me this morning and told me to expect you. I can't really see that a conversation would do anything but delay me and take up your valuable time. I scarcely knew Miss Ingress. She was the executive secretary at Multimedia, which means she performed her functions for my husband and four other executives. Beyond that, I know nothing."

"Then you never met her?" Bryce pressed.

"Oh, a few times, I suppose, but she couldn't have made much of an impression because I can't remember what she looked like. I can't remember the color of her eyes, and I remember everyone by the color of their eyes."

"They were gray," Bryce told her. "Her hair was brown, and she was murdered."

His remark had the desired effect. Lizabeth Williams looked startled. The anger left her eyes—which were brown—and was replaced by a questioning curiosity. "What has that to do with me?" she demanded as she regained her composure.

"Possibly nothing," Bryce said. "But I would appreciate a few moments of your time to discuss it."

"Oh, very well." She turned and they went through an entryway that could have come straight out of *Architectural Digest*. Spanish tiles and rough stucco walls made a setting for fine French furniture, an oriental carpet, and gigantic crystal chandelier that hung suspended on a chain from the second story ceiling. "In here," she said with growing impatience, and led him into another impressively decorated room.

Bryce sank onto the edge of a chair without removing his coat. He knew that it would irritate her, and so he spent a moment glancing about.

"I won't offer you a drink," she said to draw his attention back to her, "because I'm in a hurry."

You'd cancel any appointment no matter how important if you suspected what I know about your husband, he thought. He removed a notebook from his breast pocket and opened it; that always got to them, their curiosity as to what was written there that might concern them. He glanced at the notebook; nothing written there except a reminder to himself to check the bank accounts of Multimedia executives for periodic withdrawals of any sizable amounts. He knew what Lizabeth Williams expected: Has your husband ever mentioned Hope Ingress? Have any of the other Multimedia employees with whom you associate? Possibly the same questions he had asked Rosemary Marston, because she most likely had conveyed them. Bryce glanced up quickly and met Lizabeth Williams's gaze. "Has your husband been acting oddly lately, Mrs. Williams?"

"Oddly? My husband?" The question had confused her and she was obviously fighting for composure. "Now, see here, inspector . . ."

"Will you please sit down, Mrs. Williams?" he interrupted.

Although she had determined to remain standing, Lizabeth crossed to a chair and sat down. He may have shaken her, but she was quick to reclaim her coolness. The expression in her eyes became more amused than hostile. "Is my husband a suspect in this secretary's murder?" she asked calmly, and he thought for a moment she was going to burst into laughter.

Bryce answered frankly, "Yes."

Then she did laugh. She threw her head against the chair back and burst into amused laughter. When the laughter had passed, she asked with the same calmness, "And what is the motive?"

Bryce didn't answer.

"I suppose you think he was having an affair with that little tart?"

"What do you think?" he countered.

"I don't think. I know," she answered. "I had her checked out. She was having an affair, but it wasn't with Merrill."

"Oh. Who then?"

"I didn't go that far," she said. "When I knew it wasn't Merrill I dropped it. As long as it didn't affect me, her sex life was her own business."

"Do you often have women who work around your husband checked out?"

Lizabeth's gaze faltered.

She was quite pretty, Bryce decided, and would be prettier if she would shed her shell.

"Well?" he asked.

"I've never been one for mutual trust," she answered after a moment's thought. "Call it one of my flaws."

Bryce smiled at her. "I won't call it anything. Would

you like to tell me why you find it necessary to spy on your husband?"

"Not particularly. But I will. I don't want you thinking Merrill is the type for shoddy affairs with his secretaries." She rose, paced for a few moments, and then became still before the windows overlooking the bay. She stood with her back to him, her hands laced together in front of her, her head tilted back as if lifting her chin to defy an attacker. "My husband and I have one problem," she said. "I wouldn't want him to know I said this, but, well, he's not very passionate. Periodically, it arouses my suspicions. I'm a suspicious person, you see." She spun about and faced him. "Devious people always are."

"Oh, come now, Mrs. Williams," Bryce said. "You're not going to try to build your husband up by pulling yourself down?"

She laughed with that curious form of gallows humor that seemed part of her nature. "All right, inspector. I'll level with you. I saw Miss Ingress in the offices. I'd heard Merrill bragging about her efficiency and I made a point of seeing what this Wonder Woman of secretaries looked like. She wasn't beautiful, but she was attractive and she obviously impressed my husband. Attractive, single, working with him all day—there was a possibility some little indiscretion had begun between them. As I said, my husband has never been very passionate. But during one of his especially unresponsive periods I suspected someone else was satisfying his sexual needs."

"And that's when you had your husband and Miss Ingress checked out by a private detective?" Bryce pressed when she had apparently said as much as she intended.

Lizabeth nodded. "And my husband came out squeakingly clean," she said. "So, you see, you have no reason to suspect Merrill of any shoddy affair with Miss Ingress. It just wasn't happening."

"I see," Bryce said slowly. "But actually, Mrs. Williams, it wasn't me that mentioned an affair. It was you." Bryce closed his notebook and returned it to his breast pocket. "But thank you for assuring me there was nothing between them," he said as he rose.

Lizabeth looked at him curiously. "Is that all? No further questions?"

"No further questions," he told her flatly. "Thank you for your time, Mrs. Williams. No need to see me out. I can find my way."

He hesitated as he opened the door and waved goodbye to her before closing it behind him.

He woke Officer Martin as he slammed the car door. The catnap had made the man even more irritable. He drove more aggressively as he turned the car into the mainstream of Christmas traffic, but thankfully he was silent and on the ride downtown Bryce was allowed to contemplate Lizabeth Williams.

The woman had definitely been lying.

If she had truly had her husband checked out by a private detective she would have discovered his weekly nocturnal visits to a bathhouse devoted exclusively to homosexual clients. If she had known that, or any other information about her husband in the Ingress files, she would have been less eager to protect him against suspicion.

Chapter
Twenty-Six

WHEN LIZABETH BREEZED into the Multimedia offices, she knew Merrill would be out to lunch; he had told her before leaving home that he could not have lunch with her because he was entertaining a client.

To the secretary who approached her, a Miss Lynch, she pretended that dropping by her husband's office was a last-minute decision, and she showed disappointment at having missed him. She glanced at her wristwatch, not seeing the time, and asked, "When is he expected back?"

"Not for an hour, I'm afraid," the secretary answered.

"Well, I'd like to wait." Her face expressed a sudden idea. "Perhaps there's something happening on one of the sound stages." It was both a statement and a question. She knew very well that the pilot for the new western series, *The Toilers,* was being shot on Sound Stage One, on the floor below the offices. "Something," she said to Miss Lynch, "I could watch to amuse myself while I wait for my husband."

Miss Lynch, excusing herself, stepped back to her desk and consulted a clipboard. "*The Toilers* is being shot on Sound Stage One," she read from the schedule, "but I'm afraid it's a closed set."

"A western a closed set?" Lizabeth said with mock surprise. She knew the set for the pilot was to be closed because the guest star, an English actor of great renown, was making his American television debut and was terrified of the medium; he had only agreed to the part if the set were closed and all scenes he disapproved of reshot. "But surely an executive's wife . . ."

Miss Lynch looked uncertain. During the days since she had stepped into Hope Ingress's position she had constantly wished the dead secretary had trained a replacement; none of them knew what was or was not proper, what was expected of them in dealing with problems such as a bored executive wife wanting to get onto a closed set. "The executives can issue passes," she said, "but they're all out to lunch."

"I can sign my husband's name, and who's to know?" Lizabeth laughed conspiratorily.

Although Merrill Williams's wife was smiling at her, Miss Lynch felt an uneasy stirring. She sensed that Lizabeth Williams's visit to Multimedia had not been a spur of the moment decision while doing her Christmas shopping. It had been planned. But for what purpose?

Lizabeth read her reluctance and pressed by saying, "Perhaps we could telephone the restaurant where my husband is lunching and have him paged. He could always give you permission, which, I'm certain, you agree he would do."

Miss Lynch opened her desk drawer and drew out a pad of passes. She scribbled Sound Stage One, Mrs. Merrill Williams, and the date on the appropriate lines. Instead of having Mrs. Williams forge her husband's name, she scribbled her own, hoping as she did so that there would be no repercussions. As she handed the pass to the smiling Lizabeth, she had a sense of power, vague though it was, and wondered if that had been how Hope Ingress felt when she used her authority.

Lizabeth waited outside the sound stage door until the red light above the frame went out. Then she stepped inside. A guard started to speak to her, but she held out her pass and moved on before he could examine it and question the secretary's signature.

She saw Karl instantly.

He was under the lights, wearing cowboy garb. During a break before reshooting a scene, a makeup girl was applying or reapplying a bruise to his right eye. Another man was spattering his Levis with dust from a paper bag. But the majority of the attention was going to the English actor. He stood rigidly, like a manikin, while his makeup and clothing and hair were readjusted. Only his eyes moved in their sockets, glancing about suspiciously, as if trying to determine whether his performance was being criticized by the crew. Like so many actors she had met, the greats, semi-greats and the hams, the Englishman appeared to be a raw bundle of nerves. What monkey, she wondered, drew them into a profession that terrified them and then remained on their backs between performances until they were again on stage or before the camera? As for Karl, she thought she knew what drew him to the profession, and it wasn't the love of acting. Aside from the young bastard's egotism, he saw great pots of gold at the end of the rainbow.

But one thing she had to hand him—he had guts. She never suspected he would approach Merrill. Imagine saying she had sent him! The nerve of the little bastard! If Merrill had suspected the truth, he would have killed both of them.

The word *killed* echoed inside her skull like a hand striking a drum. The inspector's visit had unnerved her. She knew he had read her like a book; she had seen it in his gray eyes. He knew she had hired no detective, that the story had been for the purpose of removing suspicion from Merrill. Silly fool that she was. Her little game had backfired; Merrill had probably become the number one suspect, and it was all her doing. Why couldn't she be honest just once? Why did she have a compulsion to play games with everyone, to be so damned devious?

Someone sounded, "Quiet on the set!" and that brought her out of her thoughts. She moved to one side, far enough back in the shadows so Karl couldn't glance up and see her, and watched.

It was a simple scene. Karl was to be knocked down by the enraged Englishman, the villain, scramble to his feet, and receive a slash across the cheek from the Englishman's riding crop. He was to glare at the villain, reach for his trusty six-shooter, and then be stopped from doing the man in by a little girl who ran from the mock-up of a cabin behind him. He had no lines, but from the card Lizabeth saw held up in front of the camera the scene had already been shot five times. She wondered if it was Karl or the English actor who was muffing the scene.

As it turned out it was Karl; it seemed he could not display what the director considered a reasonable expression of fear and anger.

The bastard would express fear when she finished with him. Anger, too, perhaps, but she could handle that. She only hoped he had a dressing room where they could talk privately. As soon as she stepped from the shadows, she would be recognized; most of the crewmen probably knew her from the annual parties.

She decided to hold back until after the scene had been completed and then follow Karl.

When Karl goofed rising from the ground and slipped back on his haunches the director yelled "Cut!" with no attempt at concealing his annoyance. "Dammit, Karl!" he shouted. "This is a sixty-second scene! Let's not take sixty hours to get it right!"

Karl flushed with embarrassment and Lizabeth suppressed a giggle. She decided that the only thing Karl was good at was what she had kept him for, and even in bed he could sometimes be boring and awkward. How he had gotten through Merrill and the casting director to get even a small role in the series was a mystery.

The scene was done again, this time without mishap, and the director yelled "Take" in a relieved voice. People, who had been standing around quietly, began moving about; the actors stepped from beneath the hot lights, all except Karl and the Englishman. The Englishman had drawn him aside and seemed to be explaining something to him, perhaps, Lizabeth thought, telling him to seek another profession.

She waited impatiently until the two parted. Karl stepped out of the mock-up western set and slapped the dust from the legs of his Levis. A sexy bastard, she thought, and handsome as hell; she almost regretted ridding herself of him. But then she remembered the little tart she had found in the apartment she had paid for, and she remembered his effrontery at coming to Merrill and using her name, and her anger replaced her sense of desire.

Karl started to amble to the right of the set where the dressing rooms lined the outer walls. She was afraid she would lose him in the maze of equipment and props and not see which dressing room he disappeared into. She started to move out of the shadows and follow him when something caught her attention out of the corner of her eye—a familiar pin-striped suit. She froze in midstep.

Merrill was emerging from the shadows on the opposite side of the set. He had been there all along, as she had been, hidden and watching. He was stepping over the cables and cords. There was an air of importance to his stride, and an urgency. He nodded to crewmen but did not stop when they spoke to him, and he kept his eyes riveted ahead as if he, too, was afraid of losing sight of someone. Then he called out a name, but Lizabeth, because of the noise the crewmen were making shifting scenery, couldn't hear.

But she saw Karl stop suddenly. He turned and his lips parted in a smile.

A chill went through Lizabeth.

Merrill came up to Karl; they spoke briefly; then, with his arm around the younger man's shoulders, Merrill led him away from the noisy set and into one of the dressing rooms. As if, Lizabeth thought, he had been there often in the past.

What the hell was going on?

Why had Merrill lied about having lunch with a client? Even to his secretary? What could he possibly have in common with a hustler like Karl?

Something she had seen in Merrill's eyes kept trying to surface in her mind, but she kept pushing it away.

Finally, when she was asked to move out of the way by one of the crewmen who was shifting the light cables, she turned and walked out of the sound stage.

In the hallway while she waited for an elevator, she continued to puzzle what she had seen. But then the elevator came to carry her down to the building's lobby. She glanced at her wristwatch and saw she would be late for a meeting of the wives at Rosemary's. She stored away the expression she had seen in Merrill's eyes for later consideration, but it still plagued her as she hurried from the lobby and flagged a taxi.

She had somewhere to go before the meeting of the wives.

Chapter
Twenty-Seven

BRYCE RETURNED TO his office and found a new file on his desk—information on Hope Ingress sent down by the Medford Police Department. His Oregon colleague had been efficient.

Bryce sank into his chair, lit his pipe, and opened the files.

Bryce, ole buddy, the covering note read. *I hope the enclosed information will be of assistance to you. I nosed around and uncovered folks who knew your Miss Ingress—no easy matter since we're quickly growing out of the small town we once were. Progress, ole buddy, has even come to Medford, Oregon. We even have a massage parlor now and a gay bar. Jesus, do you believe it! Roxanne, the mountain where we took our dates to make out in the backseats of our cars, is dotted by homes, so goddamned crowded even the rattlesnakes have slithered away from the place in search of more peaceful surroundings. But enough of my bellyaching! I hope this report gives you a clearer insight to the victim. No easy life, your Miss Ingress had. If you want me to nose around further, just let me know. It's a small favor for a man who saved my life in Nam. Best always, Victor.*

Bryce, smiling with fond memories of Victor Mc-

Kinney, laid the note aside and turned his attention to the report. Victor had organized the report in the sequence of the interviews with people who had known Hope Ingress.

The first was headed:

VIRGINIA HOWARD

Hope Ingress's homeroom high school teacher.

Hope was a bright child. Pretty, with grey eyes; they were sad, too, her eyes. She was tall for a girl; I remember she never wore high heels when the other girls started wearing them. She also wore hand-me-down clothes, her aunt's, I believe; they were too old for her and I think it embarrassed her. She was a loner. I recall she had only one friend. Marylou Stiles. And I don't think they were very close. Maybe that's why Hope applied herself to her studies with such fervor. Because she had no friends. I was not only her homeroom teacher; I taught typing and shorthand as well. She was the best pupil I ever had the good fortune to teach. We became as close friends as a teacher and pupil can become. She's never failed to remember me with a Christmas card and a note. I even received one this year; she must have mailed it shortly before that awful thing happened to her.

(A search through a hundred Christmas cards produced one from Hope Ingress. The following note was written hastily on the back.)

Dear Mrs. Howard,
   Yet another year has passed—and so quickly. I

hope this card finds you in good health and spirits. I am in both. Everything seems to be going right for me at last. I love my position as executive secretary with Multimedia and—you said it would happen—I'm in love with a man who loves me. Things can only get better. I'm looking forward to the happiest New Year ever. Your friend, Hope.

MARYLOU WARREN, nee STILES

Mrs. Warren says she was a friend of the subject, that Hope Ingress was in her classes and lived two houses away on the same street she had grown up on. She didn't know the subject was dead, but showed no particular emotion when she was told. (I don't feel Mrs. Warren was capable of any strong emotion. She is an obvious alcoholic and embittered over the way her life has turned out. She was, she boasted, voted The Girl Most Likely. That one always got me! Most likely to what?)

Hope was a bit uppity about boys. When I'd arrange a double date for us she'd look at me in that superior way of hers, as if I was some kind of Front Street tramp because I let the boys play around. Hell, I knew where it was at even then. Put out or get out! Out of the car, out of the fun times, out of life! I sowed my wild oats, and a good thing too. Now I'm married to a goddamned sawmiller. He's got sawdust in his veins instead of blood. And sawdust isn't hard, if you know what I mean. Hope, she was a priss. She thought it was a big sin to sleep with any man she didn't intend to marry. But it was all a lousy front, put on, I suppose, because of that Bible carrying uncle of hers and that psalm singing aunt. They took her in

238

when her parents were killed in a car accident. They taught her what they considered the most important things in life—they taught her about sin and burning in Hell and that you weren't supposed to have fun. Fun was for sinners. Righteous women just sat around with their legs crossed until a righteous man came along and chose her to birth his goddamned babies. Of course her uncle and aunt didn't have any kids of their own. I don't think they ever figured out how to do it.

But, like I said, Hope's righteousness was only a front. She must have shocked the holy shit out of her uncle and aunt when she turned up pregnant. I don't know what happened to the baby, whether she had it and adopted it out or had it aborted. She went away for six months, supposedly to stay with another aunt in Washington who was ill and needed her. Anyway, she came back trim and even more solemn and Uncle and Aunt Righteous went on holding their heads high at revival meetings and spouting the evils of lust and fun. Hope moved to Ashland that year and started college, got an apartment of her own. Me, I married Mr. Sawdust Dick and started having kids. We drifted apart and I never saw her much after that. When I did it was like talking to a stranger. She was even more solemn, still uppity, and, by the looks of her, damned lonely. And guilty. Probably because of the baby she'd given away or aborted.

GEORGETTA COX

(Hope Ingress's aunt)
(Mrs. Cox wouldn't let me use my notebook so I've

jotted down our conversation to the best of my memory.)

VM: Can you tell me anything about your niece that would shed some light on her personality?

GC: She wasn't a child of God.

VM: What do you mean by that, Mrs. Cox?

GC: She had the Devil in her, that girl. We did what we could for her, but the evil was too instilled in her by the time she came to us. We tried to drive it out of her, make her see His light. We dragged her to church and prayed over her, even beat her when it was needed, but she'd never humble herself. She had highfalutin ideas about herself and about life.

VM: What kind of ideas?

GC: Like she was special. She thought the books she brought home from that school were more important than His book. She'd fight to read them instead of joinin' us in our Bible readings. She was a dreamer, too, and dreams are the Devil's work! She'd sit for hours with that way off look in her eyes. I knew what was on her mind. It was men! Lustful thoughts! I'd make her get down on her knees and pray to God to forgive her.

VM: And did she pray with you?

GC: Of course she did. But there's praying and then there's praying. Even the Fallen Angel prayed, but there was mockery in his heart. Mockery in her heart, too. She brought shame on us, Peter and me. If it wasn't the Christian thing to do, I'd not have forgiven her.

240

VM: But you did forgive her? You remained friends?

GC: Sisters in God, that's what we were.

VM: What was the shame she brought on you and your husband? Was it her pregnancy?

GC: Who you been talkin' to?

VM: It doesn't matter. But I was told Hope went away to Washington to have a baby. Did you and your husband make those arrangements?

GC: Of course we did! We didn't want our neighbors to know her sin. It isn't everyone who has a Christian heart.

VM: What happened to the baby?

GC: A church agency took it, saw that it got a good Christian home.

VM: Is that what she wanted? To give her baby up?

GC: What does it matter what she wanted? It was the right thing to do. She had no husband. And what were we supposed to do? We took her in. Were we also supposed to take in her bastards?

VM: Did she resent having to give up her baby?

GC: She cried a lot. But we made her understand it was a cross she'd have to bear. You have to pay for your sins, if not in this life, then in the next.

VM: Did you know who the father of her child was?

GC: I ain't saying. Another sinner, like her. He had a mind full of lust and other evils. He wouldn't marry her. Couldn't. He was already married. The Commandments meant nothing to him.

VM: Did your niece keep in touch with you when she moved out of your house?

GC: She came once in a while while she was in college.

VM: And after she moved to San Francisco?

GC: She didn't come visit, if that's what you mean. She'd send a Christmas card on that holy day, send birthday cards to me and Peter before the Lord took him.

VM: But she didn't write you letters, tell you anything about her life away from Medford?

GC: No. But just as well. What could she write from that city of sin, that Gomorrah, that would be fit for my eyes? I prayed for her every night, that she'd let the Lord in, and I'll go on praying for her now that she's in limbo so the Lord will forgive her and keep her from Hell.

DOROTHY McKINNEY

That's my wife, Bryce. You'd like her if you could ever pull yourself away from San Francisco long enough to visit an old buddy. Dorothy's no great beauty, but she's about the kindest, most loving woman I've ever known—and there have been plenty, as you know.

I happened to mention to Dorothy that I was gathering some information for you on Hope Ingress. You could have knocked me out of my chair when she said she'd known Hope in college. They shared an apartment with another girl for two semesters. She said it was strange she couldn't remember much about the other roommate, but she remembered Hope well, says she was impressed by Hope because she was so devoted to her studies and ignored the boys who were

242

always hanging around the other roommate. They became fast friends during the time they shared the apartment.

But let me have Dorothy write down what information she remembers about the subject.

Dear Mr. Cochran,

Vic has asked me to write down what I can remember about Hope Ingress. I'm afraid it isn't anything startling, or that might help you with your case. We were juniors at the University of Oregon in Ashland when we met. Another girl whose name I can't remember had put a notice on the bulletin board of an apartment to share. Both Hope and I showed up. The To Share had been meant for one roommate, but it worked out that both Hope and I moved in. We shared a bedroom and split the cost of the apartment three ways. The unmemorable roomie had the master bedroom, a private bathroom and helped herself to all the food Hope and I stored in the refrigerator. She left her dirty dishes in the sink and her clothing scattered about the living room. I don't think Hope and I would have become friends at all if we hadn't banded together to prove to our landlady that she was not the Queen of Sheba and we her servants. We conspired to shame her into neatness, which worked for most of two semesters, when she returned to her old habits and the three of us parted.

Hope was an inward person. She seldom laughed and never volunteered information about herself unless pressed to do so. But I am inquisitive and, as Vic will tell you, could get the life story out of anyone. In less than a month, I had Hope talking, as if to a priest. Actually, I think a lot of her problem was caused by religion. She had been raised by an uncle and aunt who were religious fanatics. She had tried to live up to their demands—and their interpretation of God's demands—but she failed. She had met a married man who had seduced her by offering the love she had always felt denied her and had become pregnant. When she told him of her condition he dropped her as quickly as you would a potato hot from the oven. She had no recourse but to go to her aunt and uncle. They packed her away to Seattle where she had the baby and gave it over to adoption. I guess she almost went crazy then with guilt and loneliness and self-flagellation. She was filled with love, but told herself she was unlovable. Her parents hadn't loved her, her uncle and aunt hadn't loved her, the father of her child hadn't loved her, and the only person who could have loved her she had given up at birth.

Hope met several young men during our two semesters together. She would date (infrequently) but never the same man a second time. When I asked her about this, she said they just weren't the right men for her. When the right man came along she'd know it. "The Right Man" was almost an obsession for her.

I heard from Hope only on Christmases and my birthday. I read this year's card to Mrs. Howard and it's almost identical to mine. I do believe Hope thought she had found Mr. Right, or she would never have mentioned a man. On my birthday card (in late November) she had made mention of the man, saying he looked just as she told me he'd look, which, to the best of my recollection, is tall, dark, handsome—and not American. I don't know why, but Hope always said the man

244

she'd fall in love with and marry would be from a foreign country. She always mentioned this when describing his appearance, as if being foreign were a physical trait of its own as obvious as the color of one's eyes and hair. She also mentioned an obstacle on the birthday card, something standing between them. I don't know why, but I assumed by this that the man was married.

I hope my recollections of Hope have been of some help to you.

I would like to extend my own invitation for you to visit us. Vic has talked so much about you that I feel I already know you. You'll be welcomed in our home any time. Please come. It would mean so much to Vic—and to me. Yours truly, Dorothy McKinney.

Bryce closed the file on Hope Ingress from his old army buddy and lay it on the growing stack of folders accumulating on the case. It had told him much about Hope Ingress, but nothing that he could see that would be of assistance in finding her murderer.

He would continue as he had been. By shaking up the wives of the Multimedia executives, those included in the files he had found in Hope's bureau, and thereby shaking up the husbands through their wives.

He took the notebook from his breast pocket and crossed off Lizabeth Williams's name.

Next on the list was Joanna Wade.

Chapter
Twenty-Eight

ROSEMARY CLOSED THE door behind Joanna, turned, and started back to the drawing room when she was brought up short. The two Ming dynasty vases that stood on matching pedestals on either side of the drawing room doors had been removed. In their place someone had put the two marble statues from her upstairs getaway room. Not only was she upset by the change—the vases had picked up the color of the oriental carpet—but she was also upset to discover that someone had invaded her private retreat. Rosemary's anger rose. No maid would have taken the liberty. It had to be Patricia. She wanted to go, then and there, in search of the woman, but remembered all her guests had not gone.

Maureen seemed reluctant to leave, unusual since she was generally the first to dash off, anxious to get back to her Peninsula home and her children.

Controlling her anger, Rosemary continued on into the drawing room.

Maureen, whom she had left sitting on the sofa with a tepid cup of tea, had risen, helped herself to a cocktail, and was now standing in front of the fireplace staring into the flames. She looked older than her years, possibly because of her unkempt, graying hair and the drab dress she wore. She usually wore makeup, but not today; her lips were pale and her eyes appeared to float beneath lashless eyelids. She had remained silent during the meeting, scarcely speaking even when spoken to.

"The meeting was a farce," Rosemary said. She glanced at the bar, wanted a drink, but decided against it. She had cut down the number of pills she took to two a day, and her alcohol consumption to three cocktails, two before dinner and one before retiring, no minor feat in either case. She contented herself with warm tea. Maureen had not turned but continued to stand staring into the flames. "We scarcely discussed business," Rosemary went on. "No one seemed willing to get off the topic of that secretary's murder."

"You achieved one important thing," Maureen said without turning. "You challenged Lizabeth and withdrew your support for Chistopher Abbott. You know, you've never done that before, Rosemary. Come right out and accused anyone of trying to manipulate you. Of course you were right. That's exactly what Lizabeth was trying to do. She doesn't want Christopher Abbott promoted any more than I want Jake to move into that position. As to what her actual motives are, I couldn't say. But she has them. Lizabeth always has hidden motives." Maureen's voice was distant, as if the subject she discussed held very little interest for her. To accentuate this, she suddenly lowered herself to sit on the raised hearth, her shoulders stooped.

Rosemary sat forward in her chair with concern mirrored on her face. "What is it, Maureen? You're not yourself. Did it upset you, my challenging Lizabeth?"

"No. It was long overdue," Maureen said. She glanced at Rosemary then and her eyes held an expression of worry. "You know I've always been fond of the other wives," she said. "Especially you and Joanna. I've never felt like I really belonged to the group, but it's been the only thing in my life other than my family—and drinking." She raised the glass in a mock salute before draining the contents.

"Feeling you don't belong is nonsense," Rosemary told her. *But you do drink too much,* she wanted to add, but remained mute on that subject. "You're as important a member of our group as Joanna or Lizabeth or Vanessa or myself. Personally, I cherish your friendship. I think if there was one of the wives I could talk to about my innermost feelings it would be you."

"Do you really feel that way?" Maureen asked.

"Yes, I do," Rosemary assured her. She rose from her chair and went to the hearth to sit beside Maureen. "I've never seen you in such low spirits," she said. "Trouble with Jake, or the children?"

"Nothing out of the ordinary. Jake, Jr. is flunking his trigonometry, Moria is hysterical because she broke out in a rash the day before the Christmas dance. Robbie has a severe case of sibling rivalry, and Jake, Sr. is furious because I told him I didn't want him to take this promotion even if it was offered to him." She shrugged. "Nothing out of the ordinary," she repeated.

Rosemary laughed softly. "Sometimes I wish I had problems like those," she admitted.

"But something is bothering me," Maureen said. She set her empty glass on the hearth between them and folded her hands in her lap.

"Well, you can certainly tell me," Rosemary encouraged.

Maureen looked doubtful. "I want to," she murmured, "but I keep thinking I'll be betraying someone."

"One of our group?"

"Indirectly," Maureen answered. "Oh, hell, Rosemary! I have to tell someone!" She laced her fingers together, fidgeting. "I could hardly face Joanna at today's meeting."

Rosemary had discerned something different in Joanna, but had not determined the reason; Joanna had been almost as quiet as Maureen. "I'll take an oath of secrecy if you like."

Maureen rose from the hearth and returned to the sofa; resting her elbow on the sofa arm, she covered her eyes with her hand, her fingers massaging her forehead. "You know I drink a bit," she asked almost in a whisper. "It's something that could turn into a real problem unless I get it under control. But what the hell? Jake has his work and I have my cocktails. I never get falling-down drunk or have too much to take care of my responsibilities. I'm a good mother—and would be a good wife if Jake—" She let the sentence trail off. "I want Jake home more nights and weekends," she said. "That's one reason I don't want him to accept this promotion even if it's offered to him. He's home seldom enough now. If he takes on additional responsibilities for Multimedia, we'll never see him."

"Do you want me to have Keith speak to him?" Rosemary inquired when Maureen fell silent.

"No. It's something Jake and I have to settle on our own. Anyway, Jake was home last Sunday. We had an argument over just what I've told you, his being a weekend father and husband. He stormed into the spare bedroom we've made into his home office and locked the door. We were both acting like children. In fact, our children sometimes act more adult than their parents. The argument hurt us both. We usually discuss things without losing our tempers. But not Sunday. I wanted to apologize—I'm sure he did also—but neither one of us could bring ourselves to do so. The longer he stayed locked behind that door the more upset I became. Finally, in a flurry of hopelessness, I simply put on my coat and left the house. For a few minutes I had to forget about my responsibility to Jake and the children—I had to get off to myself. As Jake, Jr. is always saying, find my own space, until I cooled down.

"I got in the car and I drove. I had no particular destination in mind. It was sprinkling on the Peninsula, and I rolled down the window and let the rain blow in on my face. I drove up and down El Camino Avenue looking at the Christmas decorations. Then, as seems to be the case more and more lately, I badly needed a drink. I drove into the parking lot of a restaurant-bar. I sat there for half an hour fighting with myself not to have a drink, but I lost the battle. I went inside, perched on a bar stool like some Tenderloin frump, and ordered a double gin on the rocks.

"The bar was separated from the restaurant by a dark glass divider. The bar was dark, with only those candles burning in red bowls, so you could see out but not in. I sat there sipping my gin and staring at the diners on the other side of the glass. I'm a people watcher, always have been. I watch them and I make up stories about their lives. It's like writing your own novel in your head.

"I was on my second gin when the restaurant doors open and . . ."

"Go on," Rosemary urged.

"And in walks Justin Wade." Maureen turned and met Rosemary's gaze. "Justin wasn't alone. He was with Hope Ingress."

Rosemary started. Her hand, resting on the hearth,

moved involuntarily, struck the glass Maureen had abandoned and shattered it on the stones. "My God, Maureen, are you sure it was Hope Ingress?"

"Of course. I've met her several times. She was always so nice to me when I dropped into the offices. Distant, but nice."

"It was Sunday evening she was killed!"

Maureen nodded. "And Justin was with her. At least in the restaurant."

"How . . . how did they look?"

"If you mean, did they look like a boss and his secretary out for an innocent lunch, the answer is NO. God help Joanna, but they seemed to be having a lovers' quarrel."

Rosemary rose from the hearth and moved to the bar. She had cut her hand on the broken glass, and took a napkin from the bar to wrap around it. A drop of blood had fallen on her beige silk dress, but she didn't notice. She poured herself a shot of gin—*I'll have only one before dinner*—and downed it. "Justin and Hope Ingress," she murmured. And she had feared Keith had been involved in the secretary's death. "Poor Joanna. She almost idolizes Justin. Do you think that's why she was so unlike herself today? Because she suspects or knows? No, that's impossible. If she did, she wouldn't have showed up. She'd have called, made excuses, maybe . . ." Rosemary stopped in front of the sofa and confronted Maureen. "Have you told Jake?"

Maureen said she had not. "Things were still rather cool between us Sunday night, and then Monday when I heard the news I just couldn't bring myself to tell anyone."

"And an Inspector Cochran hasn't paid you a visit?"

"No."

"Well, he will," Rosemary said. "He's already called on Lizabeth and me."

"For heaven's sake, why?"

"To ask questions about Hope Ingress. At first I didn't consider there was anything unusual about his visit or the questions he asked. But later I reconsidered. I think he wanted to plant doubts in my mind, in all our minds, about our husbands, knowing we'd relate the details of his visits to them."

"I . . . I don't understand."

"The inspector thinks one of them is guilty, I'm sure of it," Rosemary said. "He's using us to put pressure on our husbands. He wants the murderer to squirm. What does it matter who makes him squirm? An inspector or a wife? Or both? If he squirms enough, feels enough pressure, he's apt to make a mistake and reveal himself."

"Oh, Rosemary, you sound like someone in one of those detective novels," Maureen cried.

"This isn't a novel, Maureen. It's happening to us." She dropped onto the sofa and sat staring into space. "Poor Joanna," she murmured. "Poor, poor Joanna." But it was relief she was feeling, because if Justin was guilty, then Keith was totally absolved.

Chapter
Twenty-Nine

WHEN JOANNA TURNED into the driveway of her Sausalito home she saw a green sedan blocking the garage door and a burly man standing on the porch; and her heart skipped a beat. Something about the man told her he was from the police department.

Her first instinct was to turn the sportscar around and drive quickly back down the hill. But that would only arouse suspicion. You can't run this time, she told herself. She parked her car to one side of the sedan, took a deep breath, and climbed out.

The man on the porch stood waiting for her as she climbed the stone steps. He had a sensitive face, understanding, but the smile on his lips was belied by the seriousness of his expression. "Mrs. Wade?"

Joanna forced herself to smile despite the nervous churning on her stomach. "Yes, Joanna Wade," she said. "You must be Inspector Cochran. Rosemary Marston told me to expect you."

"You wives have quite a grapevine," he said. "I wish communication in the department was half as efficient." He had been standing with one foot on the low ledge, his elbow resting on his raised knee. He straightened, still smiling. "May I have a few moments of your time?"

Joanna averted her gaze as she fumbled in her purse for the housekey. "A few moments only, Inspector," she said. "I'm trying to finish some canvases for a San Francisco showing." She inserted the key into the lock, struggling against the trembling of her hands and hoping he wouldn't notice. "Come in." She pushed the door open and he followed her into the entryway. She set her purse aside, removed her coat, and glanced at the grandfather clock. "My husband should be home soon," she said absently.

"It's about your husband that I came," Bryce told her. He did not bother to remove his coat because she did not offer to take it from him. He followed her into the living room and while she busied herself making a cocktail he stood staring from the glass doors at the dusk settling over the bay. Directly below, Christmas lights made a carnival of Sausalito. He waited until Joanna had settled herself on the sofa before turning. He knew she was nervous; she hid it well, but he sensed it. "Did your husband spend Sunday afternoon at home, Mrs. Wade?"

She had been expecting the question. It was scarcely out of his mouth before she answered, "Yes." A pause. "If I remember correctly, we had a quiet dinner. Then Justin watched television while I worked on a canvas." She sipped her cocktail. "I'm sorry. I would have offered you one, but since this is an official visit . . ."

Bryce waved away her apology. "Then neither of you went out on Sunday?"

Joanna tilted her head thoughtfully. "No, we didn't," she concluded. "Sunday's a lazy day for Justin. After a hectic six-day week at Multimedia . . . we sometimes have brunch at the Alta Mira, but last Sunday I was pressed for time . . . as I am today."

Bryce sat on the edge of an overstuffed chair. His

gray eyes met Joanna's, and held her gaze. "I apologize for interrupting your busy schedule," he said. "I understand you're a famous artist. I admire the arts. Unfortunately, I haven't seen your work. An oversight I'll correct. There's somewhat of an art to my profession also, Mrs. Wade. Not visually, you understand. It's a pity society needs my sort of art, but it does. I've also got a busy schedule, so I won't waste time for either of us. You say neither you nor your husband left the house on Sunday, but one of your neighbors distinctly remembers seeing both of you go out. Your husband early in the afternoon and you . . ." he opened his notebook and flipped through the pages . . . " 'her red sportscar went speeding from the drive in the late afternoon,' " he quoted. He snapped the notebook shut. "Now why would you lie to me?"

Joanna's eyes dropped. The cocktail in her hand was shaking so badly she was forced to set it aside.

"Unless you have something to hide?"

Joanna did not trust her voice to speak.

"Did you know Hope Ingress?" Bryce pressed.

Finally, she managed, "No."

"Not even by sight?"

"I . . . I saw her once. At Multimedia's annual party. I can't even remember anything about her except . . ."

"Except what?" Bryce asked patiently.

"Except that she continually stared at me."

Bryce could easily understand why anyone would want to stare at Joanna Wade. She was a beauty; slim, flaming red hair, pale blue eyes, good bone structure. "You must be accustomed to people staring at you," he said. "Even other women. What was so unusual about the way Hope Ingress stared at you?"

"I don't know. Maybe it was because she turned down several men who asked her to dance and just went on staring."

"And you found it disconcerting?"

"Very."

"Why? Why did you feel she was staring at you?"

"I don't know!" Joanna cried.

"Not even a flickering of feminine instinct as to her reason?"

"I told you I don't know!"

"Perhaps it had something to do with your husband? Did your husband ever mention his secretary to you?"

"Only that she was efficient," Joanna snapped.

"Ah, yes," Bryce murmured. "Everyone seems unanimous in appraising Miss Ingress's efficiency." Rising, he returned to the window and stood with his back to the room. He could see Joanna's reflection in the glass. "Do you have any reason to believe your husband was on more than friendly terms with Miss Ingress?"

Joanna sprang from the sofa. "You bastard!" she cried. "How dare you come in here with your insinuations and neighbors' gossip! Now, get out! Now!"

The redhead has a temper, he thought, amused. But he had what he had come for. Joanna Wade knew there was some connection between her husband and Hope Ingress. But what was that connection? Was Justin Wade her lover? Or a blackmail victim? Nodding, Bryce started for the door. "Good afternoon, Mrs. Wade. Thank you for your time."

Joanna, still standing before the sofa, did not speak. She watched him open the door and close it behind himself. Then she heard his car start, heard the motor as it faded away down the hillside. The quiet of the house settled about her. Her anger turned to hopeless fear. She fell onto the sofa and burst into tears.

When Justin entered the house it was in darkness. He knew Joanna was home because her sportscar was in the drive. He switched on the entryway lights and the switch that lit up the Christmas tree. The house was cold, as if it had stood empty all day without the furnace being turned on. He glanced up the stairs toward the studio and saw no light under the door. "Joanna?" He set the presents he carried beneath the Christmas tree, and called her name again. When there was no answer he went into the bedroom and flicked on the lamp to find the bed empty.

Returning to the living room, he felt the cold draft and noticed that the glass doors to the deck were open. There was a shape silhouetted against the lighter shade of the sky.

Joanna was sitting on the railing staring down toward the town. She was visible to him in profile; the glow of her cigarette cast an eerie light onto her face—it looked frozen, white marble turned golden by the cigarette's fire.

"Joanna?" he murmured uncertainly as he stepped into the open doorway. "You'll catch your death of cold out there. Come inside."

But she didn't respond, just went on smoking and staring down the hillside.

"Did you hear me, baby?" He moved across the deck until he was beside her. He saw that she wasn't staring at the lights of the town, but directly down off the deck. Below was the lower level of their house, a lawn no more than two yards wide, then the edge of the stone wall that kept the earth from sliding onto their back neighbors' stone terrace and filling their swimming pool. The pool lights were on, a strange blue shimmer through the fog, and Joanna was staring at them as if mesmerized. He went to touch her, but she shrugged his hand away.

"How far down do you think it is?" she asked in an odd, toneless voice.

"I don't know," he answered. "Come inside."

"It was further from Hope Ingress's balcony to the street, wouldn't you say?"

Justin stiffened.

"I wonder if she was unconscious when she struck the concrete."

"Joanna! God's Sake! Stop this! Come inside!" He reached for her, but again she shrugged his hand away.

She moved along the deck until there was a yard or so between them. Leaning on the railing, she flicked her cigarette into space, watching its descent until it disappeared into the fog. "Were you there when she went over the edge, Justin?"

Justin felt as if he had received a blow to the stomach. The breath went out of him with a startled gasp. He tried to swallow, but found his throat too constricted for that function.

She turned and looked at him then, her eyes no more than dark hollows in the paleness of her face.

"How . . . how did you find out about . . . about her?" he asked.

"It doesn't matter how," she said.

"She meant nothing to me! I swear it, Joanna! I . . . I don't even know how it started!" He felt the perspiration beading on his forehead despite the cold.

"It's the one fault I didn't suspect you of," she said quietly.

"I called it off with her. That day—I told her I'd seen her for the last time. I told her I loved you, only you, Joanna, and I couldn't go on . . ."

Joanna pulled herself up. As she walked past him she paused for only a moment, her expression telling him she did not believe his lie. She moved into the living room, went to the bar, and was pouring herself a strong shot of scotch when she heard him enter the room behind her and close the sliding doors. She drank the strong liquor before turning to face him.

Justin looked like a man defeated; his broad shoulders were slumped, his head tilted forward over his chest as if he no longer had the strength to support it. His arms hung limped to his sides.

Joanna felt a stirring in her chest at the sight of him.

"What will you do?" he asked.

"What can I do? You've made a sham of our entire life together with this shoddy affair. I gave up my friends for you. I changed my lifestyle, even stopped spending so much time with my painting to devote more time to you. I didn't object. I did it willingly. I'd never felt about a man the way I felt about you, Justin. I didn't think I was capable of the kind of love I felt for you. The combination of the man and the boy in you satisfied all my needs. I refused to listen to the things my friends said about you. They're wrong, I told myself, so wrong. They do him an injustice. But it appears I was the one who was wrong." She turned back to the bar, unable to look at him any longer without giving in to the tears that were beginning to brim in her eyes. "Oh, Christ, Justin! How many others were there beside this secretary? How many people have known and have laughed at me?"

Justin came up behind her. He laid his hands on her shoulders, but she refused to allow him to turn her around. "There were no others, Joanna," he whispered. "Believe me, she was the only one, and I don't even understand how it started. Afterward, I realized she had gone after me, but in the beginning . . . Joanna, please forgive me."

"I can't," she murmured. "Not now. Now I can only hate you for what you've done to me, to us."

"It can't have destroyed what we had. Not one

mistake. Let me make it up to you." He tried to turn her, tried to get her to look into his eyes.

"Stop!" she cried. "Stop touching me!" She let her head fall down on her arms on the bar. Burying her face in the crook of her elbow, she began to cry.

After a moment, Justin stepped away from her.

He was so silent she thought suddenly that he had left her and her head shot up from her arm. But he was there, standing beside the fireplace, watching her, that guilty little-boy expression on his face. Well, he hadn't been caught taking cookies from the cookie jar or change from his mother's purse this time. But she knew her anger was waning, and that alarmed her.

"The police were here asking questions," she told him.

And his guilty expression turned to one of terror. "What . . . what did you tell them?"

"Not that you were having an affair with your secretary," she answered. "Not that you aren't the perfect husband you've always pretended to be." She wiped her eyes with a paper napkin. "But he suspects you," she said. "He didn't say so directly, but I know he suspects you of killing her."

"Oh, dear God!" Justin mumbled and slumped onto the hearth. He ran his hands through his dark hair in a gesture of hopelessness.

It isn't only your world that's crumbling, she thought. She tried to mentally fan her anger, but the eye of the storm raging inside her had reached a calm. The scene she had planned since the inspector had left, the outrage and cries of betrayal, they would not surface; Max would be disappointed, she thought. Another potential scene worthy of Bette Davis and she was unable to see it through. So much for the dramatic career of Joanna Wade!

Justin was staring up at her. The tears were now in

his eyes. "I didn't love her, Joanna," he cried. "And I most certainly didn't kill her." His voice broke and he lowered his head into his hands.

Joanna couldn't hold back any longer. She went to him, sat beside him on the hearth, and pulled his head onto her shoulder.

Justin clung to her like a frightened little boy. Into her shoulder, he sobbed, "I didn't love her . . . I didn't kill her . . . you must believe me!"

"I do believe you," Joanna answered quietly. "I've given it a lot of thought, Justin," she said as she stroked his hair, "and I don't believe you're capable of loving anyone, Miss Ingress *or me*. It's as if something has been left out of you. As for killing her, I know you didn't do that. I know."

Chapter
Thirty

IT WAS A sunny day, Christmas Eve, and Bryce could think of a hundred places he would rather be than riding along in a funeral procession.

South of San Francisco, in a community where eighty percent of the real estate belonged to the dead, the procession turned off the highway and snaked its way along driveways flanked by white crosses. The crosses covered the slope of the hill and stretched down into the valley; they were very white, glaring in the sunlight against the green of the manicured grass.

The procession stopped near a covered mound of earth and mourners began to leave their automobiles. The wreaths of flowers came out of the hearse first, then the casket, the sun catching the brass handles. Bryce remained in the car until the others had grouped around the grave; then when he did approach, he hung back, feeling like an intruder.

". . . ashes to ashes . . ."

The group of mourners was small, mostly executives from Multimedia with their wives. Bryce noted how smartly the wives were dressed, all in black, with veiled hats, gloves, black leather purses. The husbands were in dark suits and ties, highly polished shoes with beads of moisture from the grass on the toes. Odd, but they reminded Bryce of a group of professional mourners whose attire had been meticulously selected by a costume rental agency.

". . . dust to dust . . ."

He had never seen such a dry-eyed group. He wondered why they had bothered to accompany Hope Ingress to her final resting place. None of them had been her friends; the wives had scarcely known her and the husbands admitted to no knowledge of her other than her extreme efficiency as a secretary.

Bryce gazed at each of the executives in turn. Keith Marston stood very erect, his gaze fixed straight ahead, his hands folded in front of him. Jake Sterne kept shifting his weight from one leg to the other. Mark Kirkman kept covering his mouth to conceal a yawn. Justin Wade stood with one arm around his wife as if she needed consoling. Merrill Williams tried to look sincere.

The wives' faces were hidden behind their veils—all except Joanna Wade's. She had turned her veil back over her hat. Her eyes were clear, the blue intensified by the sunlight. She was watching the minister as if memorizing the words. But her attention was easily drawn away to follow the flight of a screeching gull that passed overhead. A subtle increase of pressure from her husband's arm brought her attention back to the proceedings.

They had all noted Bryce's presence, but none acknowledged him. He, the intruder, the only one improperly dressed in his grey suit and brown shoes, could have been the gravedigger waiting to shovel the earth over the casket.

When the minister had finished and the casket was lowered, the mourners began walking to their cars. It was then that Keith Marston acknowledged Bryce with a slight nod.

Bryce stepped forward. He nodded a greeting to Rosemary Marston, and then spoke to Keith. "Will you be returning to the office today, Mr. Marston?"

"I hardly think so," the executive answered. "It's Christmas Eve and most of the staff left at noon. Why, Cochran? Is there something we can only discuss at the office?"

"No. Anywhere it's convenient will do nicely," Bryce answered.

"Then I'd suggest my home," Keith said. "That is, if it can't wait until after Christmas."

"I think not," Bryce said as he fell in step with the couple. They walked several steps in silence before he went on, "I notice Mr. Linquist didn't attend the funeral."

"Someone has to run the company," Keith said curtly. "His absence doesn't denote any lack of respect. Or guilt."

"None implied," Bryce murmured. "Actually, I was surprised to see so many representatives from Miss Ingress's company."

"No more surprised than we were to find no family or friends of the unfortunate woman," Keith countered.

"Well, she had only an aunt in Oregon. Apparently they didn't get along, some religious dispute. As for friends, I've never known a woman to live so private a life as your secretary."

"Some of us guard our privacy," Keith said.

"But not quite so closely as Miss Ingress," Bryce observed. They had reached the Marston limousine. "Then, may I have your permission to meet you at your home? No objections on your part, Mrs. Marston?"

Rosemary Marston opened her mouth to speak, but before the words could come out her husband said,

"We will expect you in half an hour, inspector. I trust this won't be a long interrogation. We have Christmas shopping to finish."

Bryce laughed quietly. "Interrogation is the wrong word. Discussion, I think would be more appropriate."

"As far as I'm concerned, there's little to discuss," Keith countered. "I've already told you all I know about Miss Ingress. I'm sorry I can't be of more assistance, but that's how it is. I knew very little about the woman personally." Reaching forward, Keith opened the door of the limousine and helped Rosemary in. He turned back to Bryce. "But if you insist . . ."

"It isn't Miss Ingress's private life I wish to discuss," Bryce told him. "It's the files found in her apartment."

The color drained from Keith's face. He glanced quickly inside the limousine at his wife, then back to Bryce. "All right," he said. "Half an hour."

Bryce returned to his car. He inserted the key in the ignition, but didn't turn it. He sat watching the others depart the cemetery. The automobiles were forced to make a U-turn and pass him going in the opposite direction. He sat window down, chin supported by his fingers, and stared into their cars as they passed. All of them were sitting very dignified, eyes fixed straight ahead—except for the Marston limousine, where Rosemary Marston seemed quite animated in a discussion with her husband. Or interrogation, he thought with mild amusement.

He waited until the cars had vanished onto the highway before starting the ignition and putting the sedan into gear. As he completed the U-turn and was driving away he saw the men approaching Hope Ingress's grave with shovels in hand.

Chapter
Thirty-One

ROSEMARY LIFTED THE veil from her face and turned to Keith. "You shouldn't have invited him to the house," she said. "Whatever has gotten into you? Everyone is going there now, and he'll only put a pall of gloom over the decorating of the Christmas tree."

Keith sat erect, hands folded in his lap, his eyes fixed on the back of the chauffeur's stout neck. "This is decidedly more important than the decoration of a tree," he said calmly. "Besides, you shouldn't have invited them without consulting me."

"I invited them to compensate for your having demanded they attend the funeral," she said stiffly. "You're not going to fool the inspector by forcing us to pretend to be mourners. It'll only confirm his opinion that one of the executives has something to hide."

Keith turned and looked at her with amusement. "Do you believe one of your friends' husbands *has* something to hide?" he asked.

"Yes, I do," she answered honestly.

"And on what do you base your opinion, my dear?"

Rosemary faltered; it would not do to tell Keith about Justin and the dead secretary, not yet. "Intuition," she said quietly.

"Ah, yes. Intuition. That great feminine catchall."

"You believe it also," she accused. "Otherwise you wouldn't be so nervous. The inspector may not have sensed your reaction to his presence, but I did. I could feel the tension in you."

"I've always known you were perceptive," he said blandly.

"Then you do believe it was one of them?"

"No! I believe Miss Ingress was killed by a lover, someone none of us know."

I know he's lying, Rosemary thought. *It's as obvious to me as his fear of the inspector.* She wondered if he suspected Justin. "What would you do if you knew it was one of the employees?" she asked.

"Accept his resignation first," Keith answered, "and then telephone the police. I wouldn't harbor a murderer at Multimedia. No more than you'd harbor one among your friends or in our home."

Rosemary flinched. Her gloved hands lay in her lap. Keith reached over and covered them with his own.

"How are you and Patricia getting on?" he asked, hoping to change the subject.

But Rosemary would not be swayed. "What were the files the inspector mentioned?" she asked.

After a moment's hesitation, Keith said, "It seems Miss Ingress had company files in her apartment. The inspector found them."

"What sort of files?" she pressed.

"Confidential files," he answered evasively.

"But as executive secretary all confidential files must have been available to her," Rosemary concluded. "She could have perused them to her heart's content at the office. So why should she carry them home?"

Keith went back to staring at the back of the chauffeur's neck. His expression was distant; he appeared not to have heard her question.

Rosemary turned in her seat and confronted him with sudden insight. "For someone else," she said. "For someone who couldn't read them in the office. That's it, isn't it?"

Keith said nothing.

"But why? For what purpose?"

"I don't know," he finally said.

"But you do know this makes a stronger case for the killer being from Multimedia?" she said. "She'd have no reason for taking confidential files home for a stranger to read."

"It could have been company espionage," Keith told her with a weary sigh. "There are any number of production companies that would pay handsomely to have the formats of our new shows for next season. For all we know Miss Ingress could have been involved with someone from a competing firm. She could have discovered he was using her without really caring and threatened to expose him. And now, my dear, if you don't mind, I'd like to discontinue this discussion. Bantering possibilities for Miss Ingress's murder puts as much a pall of gloom over me as you say the inspector's presence will over our guests."

Angered by his attitude, Rosemary sank into the leather cushions and sat staring at the passing scenery.

Keith handed Bryce a snifter of cognac, then seated himself in his favorite leather chair. He was uncomfortable and ill at ease, but managed to hide his feelings behind the mask of a smile. The study door was closed; down the hallway Rosemary and their guests were pretending to have the Christmas spirit as they decorated the tree. Keith knew their cheer was as shallow as the smile he wore.

He sipped the cognac, widened his smile, and said, "All right, inspector. What is it about the files?"

Bryce lit a cigarette before speaking. "Are you always so direct, Marston?"

"Generally. I don't mean to be rude, but we have guests and I'd like to join them as quickly as possible."

"Yes, of course. You know I've had time to read the files found in Miss Ingress's apartment."

Keith lowered his gaze and said nothing.

"Including the file on you," Bryce went on. He glanced up through a cloud of cigarette smoke and saw Keith Marston's face pale. "We needn't go into that."

"Oh, but I want to," Keith said. "That was a long time ago, inspector. I was only twenty-one at the time. Since then I've lived an exemplary life."

"Yes, I'm aware of that," Bryce assured him.

"And it wasn't as sordid as it must seem on paper." Keith set his cognac aside, rose, and began pacing about the study. He dropped the pretense of a smile. "I suppose most everyone has a skeleton in their closet," he said. "Something he wants to remain totally private." He looked at Bryce for confirmation, but when the inspector said nothing, just went on staring at him with his probing gray eyes, Keith sank back into his chair with a sigh. "I served one year in prison for rape," he said, and suddenly felt as he imagined an alcoholic would feel after admitting his affliction. "That is what's in the file, isn't it?"

Bryce nodded affirmatively.

"As I said, I was only twenty-one. Certainly old enough to be responsible, but . . . well, you'd have to understand my upbringing. My parents were strict, puritanical. My mother was Victorian. God, she even draped the piano legs because she said their nakedness offended her. My father was no better. I suppose he had a private life, a mistress or whores, but there was

269

no breath of it in our private discussions. We never had a man-to-man talk. He went along with my mother's demands for my upbringing. If it hadn't been for an understanding maid, I'd have been a virgin at the time of being charged with that woman's rape. I was twenty-one before I declared my independence and moved . . ."

"You needn't go into this," Bryce interrupted.

But Keith didn't seem to hear. "The young woman in question moved into the apartment building where I lived. She was . . . well, very experienced. I had the apartment next to hers and I saw the men coming and going at all hours. Things were nothing like they are now. Sex wasn't such an available commodity. At least if it was, I wasn't aware of it. I heard the neighbors whispering about the woman in question. She intrigued me and, I admit, excited me. The heater vent in my apartment was above the bed. At night I could hear the activities beyond the wall. The sounds made me remember the maid and reminded me of all I'd missed. I was as frustrated as I could get. One night when I had been drinking I knocked on the woman's door. I . . ."

"I said it wasn't necessary for you to go into this," Bryce repeated. "I'm not here as a Devil's advocate, or to judge."

"I realize that, inspector. I just wanted you to understand the circumstances." Keith drained the cognac in his snifter. Perspiration had beaded on his forehead; his brow was furrowed, his expression one of torment.

Bryce leaned forward in his chair. "Tell me, did your wife know about this skeleton in your closet?"

"Rosemary? Heavens, no! In many ways, Rosemary is as Victorian as my mother was."

"Then you have friends you've confided in?" Bryce pressed.

"No. I'm not the sort who feels driven to confession to purge my soul, inspector. Except for my first wife who managed to get the story out of me, there's no one in my later life who knows about the incident. Because she knew and threatened me with a subtle form of blackmail, I agreed to her outrageous demands when I divorced her." Keith rose and poured himself another cognac, noticed Bryce's glass was still full, and sat back down. "I suppose you're trying to determine where the information came from in that file," he said. "I can't imagine. It happened a long time ago and across the country. That was long before computers, and I doubt that the information could have been obtained easily."

"The important thing is not how the information came to be in a file on you, but why," Bryce said thoughtfully. "When I mentioned the files to you in your office you swore you were not being blackmailed. I ask you again, is that true? You're not the victim of a blackmailer?"

"Definitely not," Keith assured him. "If I had been, I most certainly would have paid handsomely. As my wife will tell you, I concern myself with appearances. And, in case it's crossing your mind, I can and would pay a blackmailer before restoring to murder. I'm a very wealthy man, inspector, and I'd use that wealth to protect my public image."

"Something I could easily discover from checking your personal accounts," Bryce told him. "The question remains of why these files exist and what Hope Ingress was doing with them."

"A question I can't answer. I suppose there's damning information on all the men in those files?"

"There is," Bryce admitted.

"And I don't suppose you'll let me see them?"

"You are correct in that assumption," Bryce said.

"Need I remind you they are my employees?"

"It doesn't matter," Bryce answered. "I wouldn't show their files to you any more than I'd show yours to one of them. If it's in my power they will not be made public."

"Thank God for that," Keith murmured with a sigh. "I would not like to have exposure hanging over . . ."

A knock on the door cut the sentence short.

The door opened and Rosemary stuck her head inside. Her gaze went from Keith to Bryce. "How much longer will you be?" she asked, her question directed to Bryce. "It's been a sort of tradition that my husband put the finishing touch on our Christmas tree," she said by way of explanation. In her hand, she held a crystal star that reflected the study lamps.

"I'll be there shortly," Keith said with veiled anger. When Rosemary had left them, he turned back to Bryce. "Is there anything else, inspector? If not, I'd like to join my wife and our guests."

"Only a few more questions," Bryce answered.

As Rosemary started back across the entryway, Joanna came from the drawing room and approached her. The artist had seemed distant and troubled all afternoon. Since arriving at the Marstons' she had uttered scarcely a dozen words.

"Rosemary, I have to talk to you," she said. "It's important. Is there someplace we can be alone without being interrupted?"

Rosemary nodded. "My room upstairs," she said. She suspected that Joanna had somehow learned about Justin's involvement with the dead secretary and needed to talk. She put the crystal tree ornament on the hall table and led Joanna up the spiral staircase.

As she opened her door, Rosemary stopped short so that Joanna, close behind, almost bumped into her. Sitting at Rosemary's vanity table, wearing Rosemary's gown and using her brush, was Patricia.

The younger woman was as startled as Rosemary. She sprang from the vanity stool and dropped the hairbrush. It clattered into a tray of bottles and when it settled it left a heavy silence.

Rosemary was speechless; she dared not vent her anger in front of Joanna, nor did she know what explanation to give for the woman's presence in her room. The moment that passed before she found her tongue seemed an eternity. She stepped forward, her smile belied by the cold anger in her eyes. "Patricia, darling, did you forget your hairbrush? Joanna, this is Patricia Eliott, our houseguest from New York. Patricia is Keith's son's fiancée."

The two women exchanged quick greetings; then Patricia excused herself and slipped from the room. Rosemary saw that Joanna was too preoccupied to question the odd meeting. Still trembling with anger, she led Joanna to the loveseat beneath the window and they sat down. She noticed that Joanna's eyes were ringed by dark circles beneath her makeup; she appeared to be on the verge of tears.

"It can't be all that bad," Rosemary told her.

"It couldn't be any worse," Joanna murmured. She rested her head against the back of the loveseat and closed her eyes. Now that she had gotten Rosemary alone she seemed reluctant to talk.

"Is it Justin?" Rosemary probed.

Joanna's blue eyes flickered open. "You know,

don't you, Rosemary? About Justin and Hope Ingress?"

Rosemary's silence confirmed her knowledge of the affair.

"I suppose you all know," Joanna murmured painfully. "That you've all been laughing at me."

Rosemary reached for Joanna's hand and held it. "You're overwrought," she said quietly. "All of us don't know, and if we did we certainly wouldn't laugh at you. Only Maureen and I know. Then only because Maureen saw them together the . . . the day Miss Ingress was killed."

Joanna flinched. "More damning evidence against Justin," she said scarcely above a whisper. "Poor Justin. He made a lousy adulterer." She pulled her hand gently from Rosemary's and covered her face. She appeared about to burst into tears, but then, as if swept by a sudden calm, she removed her hands and stared at Rosemary with dry eyes. "I dislike admitting it, but I guess he also made a lousy husband," she said. "I must have seen in Justin only what I wanted to see."

"You're putting everything in the past tense," Rosemary observed. "Does that mean . . ."

"I don't know what it means," Joanna said. "I haven't slept. I'm exhausted. The process of thinking is becoming more than I can cope with. I'd like to close my eyes right now and wake up to find this nightmare is finished."

"I can make excuses downstairs," Rosemary suggested. "I'll tell Justin and the others you have a migraine and will join us later in the . . ."

"No. He'd see through any excuse," Joanna told her. "He's terrified. I don't understand how none of you have noticed how he's trembling in his shoes. He's terrified of me, you see! It's not because I found out about his affair. It's because he thinks I'm going to tell that detective. I thought he was going to break into a run when the inspector showed up at the cemetery. I guess it was because of my exhaustion, but it was all I could do to keep from becoming hysterical. It crossed my mind that if I pushed him into running the inspector might shoot him and that would end . . . oh, Rosemary!" She fell into Rosemary's arms and the tears she had been holding back overflowed.

"There, there," Rosemary murmured. As she comforted Joanna, Rosemary realized that it was the first time in her life she had been called on to console another human being; she had always thought of herself as too weak—even when her mother had died it had been her father who had comforted her, not the other way around as it should have been. Holding Joanna and murmuring vague words of consolation, she suddenly felt as if she had stepped completely out of character.

When Joanna's tears stopped, Rosemary rose and went into the bedroom for a glass of the cognac Keith kept on the bed table.

The strong liquor revived Joanna somewhat. She straightened and dried her eyes. "The awful thing is that I let Justin be terrified of me," she said. "And for the wrong reason."

"I don't understand," Rosemary told her. "What do you mean?"

"If I tell the inspector about his affair with Hope Ingress and that he was with her the evening she was killed, he's terrified he'll be arrested for her murder," Joanna explained. "And because he's betrayed me, I've let him think there is such a possibility."

"I see," Rosemary said, but knew there was something she was missing in what Joanna was telling her.

"No. You don't really see," Joanna told her. "Do

you know why Justin was having an affair with her? Why he told me he was having an affair with her? Because she was helping him assure himself of the promotion."

"For heaven's sake, how?"

"By stealing Larry Linquist's confidential files and bringing them home for Justin to study. He took her to bed for that reason! For a damned promotion!"

"Those must be the files the inspector mentioned to Keith," Rosemary said. "But how could the files help him get the promotion?"

"They're files on all Larry's clients, backers, ad agency executives, station managers. Personal files giving their sexual preferences, weaknesses, that sort of thing."

"That's unethical!"

"That," Joanna said, "is business. At least, business as Larry sees it. It's no wonder he's been so successful since he took over Howard Barrett's position. Justin intended to use those files in the same manner. He was going to win over Larry's accounts before his replacement was decided upon and prove to Keith that he was the man for the promotion. And Hope Ingress was helping him."

Rosemary, who had remained standing since returning with the cognac, sank onto the loveseat beside Joanna.

"So," Joanna said in a quiet tone, "we wives were not the only ones trying to manipulate the promotion. My ambitious husband and his secretary were working at their own means of manipulation."

"Keith couldn't know such files exist," Rosemary said, more to herself than to Joanna. She wondered if that was what the inspector was telling him now in the study below. It would be bad enough for Keith when the truth about Justin came out, but the fact that an employee kept such files would make him feel a sense of betrayal as strong as Joanna's. She drew her attention back to Joanna.

". . . it's not the files that disgust me. It's not really even the knowledge that Justin was having an affair or that I was too naive to suspect him. It's not even finding out that I've been blind to him all this time. It's that I'm hiding the truth from him and letting him be terrified of my revenge!"

"It's only natural that you'd want revenge," Rosemary told her. Isn't that how she would feel if Keith's arrangement with Patricia ever saw fruition? "But what truth are you hiding from Justin?"

Joanna looked as if she were about to burst into tears again. Her lower lip trembled and her eyes were filling. "Justin was guilty of having an affair with Hope Ingress," she said, "but he isn't guilty of murdering her. I know! I was there!"

Rosemary and Joanna were descending the staircase when the study door opened and Keith and Bryce stepped into the entryway below. Both women stopped.

Joanna leaned toward Rosemary. "Thank you for being my friend," she whispered. "I needed someone to talk to, someone I trusted and who was strong enough to . . ."

"Ah, Rosemary," Keith said from below. "I've invited Mr. Cochran to join us in a Christmas drink."

"That's nice, dear," Rosemary said absently. As the two women continued their descent of the staircase, Rosemary said just loudly enough for Joanna to hear, "You know, Joanna, I think we wives have been wasting our time. Instead of mimicking our husbands' careers and trying to test our power over them, we should have spent our time together on ourselves. We let a silly, meddlesome game prevent us from becoming real friends."

As they reached the bottom of the staircase, Rosemary extended her hand grandly to the inspector and led him into the drawing room.

Chapter
Thirty-Two

KEITH WAS ALREADY in bed when Rosemary came in from her dressing room. He had on the dark-rimmed glasses which vanity made him discard for contact lenses when in public, and a book was open on his knees. The blue silk pajamas she had bought him at Sulka were open at the neck, revealing a tangle of grey hair on his chest.

Rosemary shed her dressing gown and crawled into bed beside him. She glanced at the digital clock and saw that it was a quarter past midnight. "Merry Christmas," she told him.

"Merry Christmas, darling." He glanced away from his book only long enough to accept her kiss.

She fluffed her pillows and reached for a magazine. An article on the great chefs of Europe began to blur before her eyes, and she discarded the magazine with a sigh. Her sleeping pills were in the top drawer of the bedside table; she considered taking one, and then decided against it. She had done well in the past few days, avoiding her customary drugs. She fussed with her pillows again, deliberately disturbing the bed, but Keith did not look up from his book. She turned and stared at him. He generally read in the study, sometimes coming to bed very early in the morning, and she wondered if receiving Bryce Cochran in that room had made him want to avoid it. He had said nothing since their guests had left, and she had not pressed him.

She raised herself to one elbow and said, "I wonder why the inspector was so interested in everyone's cigarette butts."

Keith scarcely glanced away from his book. "Was he? I didn't notice."

"Everyone else did," Rosemary told him. "The inspector isn't very subtle. But then, maybe that was his purpose. I thought Justin was going to faint when the inspector took one of his cigarette butts from the ashtray and slipped it into his pocket. Of course it could have been Joanna's cigarette butt. They both smoke those disgusting brown cigarettes with that foul sweet smell. Do you suppose Miss Ingress's murderer was so careless as to leave a cigarette butt in the ashtray?"

"I wouldn't know," Keith said quietly and without interest.

Rosemary saw that she was not going to draw his attention from his book. "There must be some sort of saliva test, do you think?"

"Having never been a mystery fan, I wouldn't know."

"You mean you don't like all those mystery shows you produce at Multimedia?" She laughed softly. When he didn't answer she lay back against the pillows and stared at the inside of the canopy top. The fabric color was a pale blue that reminded her of Joanna's eyes.

Poor Joanna . . .

"I know about the files," she said.

Keith did not look away from his book, but she felt his body stiffen beside her. After a moment of silence so heavy it could have been sliced by a knife, Keith closed his book and turned toward her. His face was pale and the muscles in his neck were throbbing and swollen. His voice was oddly pitched as he said, "What files?"

"The files the inspector mentioned to you at the cemetery," she said. "It was unethical of Larry to have compiled such files on company account executives and advertisers."

Keith visibly relaxed. "Oh, those files," he murmured.

"Did the inspector return the files?"

"No. But he'll attempt to keep them from becoming public."

"That must have been a relief to you."

"It is." He opened his book again and thumbed through the pages to locate his place.

"Of course you didn't know of their existence until the inspector informed you?" When he didn't answer, she said, "You won't do anything drastic? To Larry, I mean. After all, he's already decided to retire, and Janet's so worried about him as it is. If the files remain private there's no reason to seriously chastise Larry. Remember that, won't you, when you talk to him? They're our friends even if Larry will no longer be working at Multimedia. Keith, are you listening to me?"

"I'm listening," he said with veiled impatience.

"Then you won't go too hard on Larry, will you?"

"That, Rosemary, is a business matter."

"But I know you, Keith. I understand you must feel betrayed by what Larry has done by compiling those files. I agree it was unethical. I also agree you should speak to him. But not harshly. What purpose would it serve now except to alienate both Larry and Janet from us?"

"I don't wish to discuss it," he said sternly, using

the tone of voice that had always made her cower in the past.

But this time she didn't cower; she raised herself on one elbow again and stared directly into his eyes. "I know it makes you angry when you feel I'm meddling in your business," she said, "but there's something else I'd like to say, something that does not concern Larry or his files. I think this entire mess has come about because of the competition for Larry's position."

Keith had closed his book and was staring at her with a quizzical expression. "Do you know something you've not told me?" he asked. "Or have you wives been doing some second guessing during your meetings?"

"I've been doing some thinking, not second guessing," Rosemary said indignantly. "One conclusion I've come to is that this mess could get worse before it gets better. I think there's only one sensible thing you can do."

"And that is?" Keith murmured, his eyebrows arching.

"Announce that you're going to seek Larry Linquist's replacement from outside executive row," Rosemary told him. Rosemary had an impulse to hold her breath as she waited for his tirade at her interference.

But he only said rather blandly, "That's worth consideration." He opened his book again, but she saw that his eyes were no longer held by the pages he turned.

Rosemary lay back and pulled the sheets about her chin. She closed her eyes, but her mind was too filled by thoughts to allow sleep. The house was extremely quiet; there was the creaking of a floorboard in some distant corner, the raspy ticking of the antique clock

on the mantel, the occasional turning of the pages of
Keith's book—and outside, the foghorns from the bay,
a far-off siren, and for a moment the lonely sound of
heels clicking on the sidewalk out front. She considered taking a sleeping pill for a second time, but again
decided against it.

"Keith, do you love me?"

This sudden interruption when he must have
thought her asleep caused him to turn to her without
thinking. He smiled down at her. "What a strange
question," he said. "Of course I love you. That hasn't
changed."

Then why Patricia? she wanted to ask. Why the
arrangement? Why couldn't we have tried to work out
our problems without such an extreme measure? But
she could only say aloud, "Then make love to me.
Now." She pushed back the sheets and stretched her
hands behind his neck and pulled his head down to
her.

His lips were moist and yielding and she could taste
tobacco. For one terrible moment she thought he was
going to reject her by pulling away and she began to
panic. But his movements were only to free his arm
caught between them. His left hand wriggled beneath
her and he held her tightly. Their kiss continued and
his embrace became demanding. When their mouths
parted, Keith looked into her eyes and said in a
whisper, "Are you also going to become aggressive,
darling?"

She thought he was criticizing her and her panic
returned.

But he smiled and said, "I was always the one who
had to instigate anything that happened in bed. I like
this change in you."

"You're implying there are changes you don't ap-
prove of," she murmured. "If there are . . ."

"We'll discuss them later," he said, and brought his mouth back to hers to cut off her words.

His hands moved down her body and his touch made her tremble. She reached for his pajama top and began undoing the buttons; the top open, she found the pant cord and pulled. She reached inside, seeking the swollen flesh between his legs. It was unlike her, this aggression; she had always been passive during sex. She didn't know from what hidden chamber this self-assertiveness had emerged, but she did know that she was relishing it. And so was Keith. She could sense a desire, a lust inside him that she had forgotten had existed.

Chapter
Thirty-Three

IT WAS CHRISTMAS MORNING.

Although he had no search warrant, Bryce had no difficulty convincing the security guard at Multimedia in admitting him to the executive floor. Multimedia was run only by a skeleton staff; the executive floor was completely deserted.

There were only dim lights burning over the entrance door and a rear exit. Eerie glows were cast over the secretarial area occupying the center of the horse-shoe shaped offices. Bryce located a bank of switches near the door and flicked the buttons. Overhead lights flickered before bathing the room in bright light. Bryce remained just inside the door staring at the empty desks, the silent telephones and covered typewriters, and he was swept by a peculiar sense of having stumbled into a limbo where activity had been suddenly forbidden and he was defying the edict by his presence. He recalled his last visit to the offices and remembered the hive of activity that had greeted him on entering. He wished now he had asked Marston to meet him at the office, but that would have defeated his purpose.

He pushed away from the door and moved past the reception desk that stood sentinel over the quiet. His footsteps echoed on the tiles and he slowed his pace. Hope Ingress's desk was partitioned off from the other secretaries' by a chest-high wall of glass; it had no purpose he could see except to distinguish her position from the others. It certainly afforded her no greater privacy; he wondered if she had sometimes felt like a goldfish in a glass bowl.

He sat down in her chair and stared at the desktop. Everything was in meticulous order, a tribute no doubt by Miss Lynch to her predecessor; telephone books, steno pads, folders marked with the stenciled names of the five executives—all arranged by height and held snugly together by gray metal bookends. The typewriter cover as well as the machine beneath were also gray, as were the desk accessories. The blotter insert was new, bright blue, most likely chosen by Miss Lynch in a moment of rebellion against the drabness surrounding her. There was a paperweight, black onyx. Stamped across the top had been *H.I.*, but someone had scraped the periods away and it now read *HI*. A yellow sticker of a smiling line-drawing face had been pasted above the letters. A three-tier gray metal stand marked IN, OUT and FILE stood empty of papers and collecting holiday dust. The pencil holder was filled, the newly sharpened points facing upward. There was an intercom and a dictaphone, both covered, and a telephone, the disc in the middle of the dial reading *EXT. 100*.

Bryce opened the center drawer and saw the expected paperclips, erasers, and rubber bands all neatly separated into compartments. The back of the drawer was filled with containers of additional supplies. A telephone number had been written on the bottom of the drawer, but the ink had been smeared just enough to blur the last two digits. Unlike the image he had of Hope Ingress, but probably not important. The side drawers held paper and carbon and envelopes. There was a thesaurus and a copy of *20,000 WORDS* that looked unused. Nothing personal that could be connected to Miss Ingress or Miss Lynch.

It was while closing the last drawer that Bryce saw the small cardboard box shoved beneath the desk. He pulled it out and opened the lid. Here were the contents he had sought. A folding umbrella, fingernail file, a half-used tube of lipstick, a torn theater stub from the Curran, a carefully balanced bank statement, matchbooks from *Ernie's* and *The Shadows* (no matches torn out), a packet of Kleenex, sunglasses in a plastic case—except for the bank statement everything in the box could have belonged to a thousand secretaries. Miss Lynch had no doubt emptied the desk of Miss Ingress's belongings and had no idea what to do with them. Bryce picked up one item and then another and held them as if he were practicing psychometry. After a few moments he dropped everything back into the box and returned it to its place beneath the desk.

Behind the desk were three gray file cabinets. When he opened the first he heard the sound of metal against metal and dug down between the file folders to discover a ring of keys.

Careless of Miss Lynch, he thought. Miss Ingress, if she had been as efficient as everyone told him, would have selected a more secure hiding place. He counted the keys and found there were an even dozen. He sat staring at them for several minutes, and then rose and approached Marston's door. The third key he tried turned the lock. He stepped inside and looked around; then moved on to the next.

He didn't know why he was opening the office doors, didn't know why he had even bothered to come to the Multimedia offices on Christmas morning, except while he had been shaving that morning the thought had occurred to him. He hadn't really hoped to find anything.

Merrill Williams's office was as he remembered it; brown leather and highly polished wood and chocolate brown carpet, extremely masculine, the only splashes of color being the watercolors of sports scenes that hung on one wall. There was a portable bar, well stocked, and a shelf of crystal glasses. On his desk was a gold-framed photograph of his wife, taken aboard a yacht with the blue Pacific behind her; her blonde hair was wet and blowing in the breeze, her shapely figure emphasized by a scant bikini. She was laughing, happy, unlike the day Bryce had met her.

Justin Wade's office was similar to Williams's except that in place of the watercolors the walls were covered by oil paintings, all signed Joanna Wade or Joanna Carpenter. Bryce studied the paintings for several minutes, comparing them and deciding that Joanna Wade, nee Carpenter, had been a happier artist before her marriage. The subject matters of the earlier paintings had been simpler but the faces of the people had conveyed a sort of peacefulness that was missing in the later paintings.

Mark Kirkman's office was a duplicate of Wade's and Williams's except, again, for the wall hangings; it appeared that Multimedia's decorator allowed individuality only in the choice of wall hangings. On Kirkman's walls were prints of famous paintings.

Larry Linquist's office was new to Bryce. When he had met with Linquist it had been in the executives' lounge. There was a difference in decor here; the sofa and chairs were in a deep burgundy, old and in need of upholstering; the desk was cluttered, no photo of wife or children. There were no paintings or prints on the walls, only production schedules and a chart measur-

ing the popularity of Multimedia productions. Bryce
noticed the bar also was unlike those in the other
offices. The supply of liquor was limited and there
were only two glasses. He opened the lower doors and
was surprised to find a file cabinet. Why, with a file
room directly across the hallway, did the executive
need a private file cabinet? He bent and examined it,
noticing the scratch marks on the paint. He glanced at
the ring of keys in his hand, but realized none was
small enough to fit the lock. He pulled on the drawers
and they slid easily open. There was nothing inside.
He closed them and left Linquist's office.

Before returning the keys to where he had found
them he checked out the file room. It was enormous,
with row upon row of head-high metal cabinets. Some
were marked with an executive's name and *Confidential,* others were alphabetically initialed, still others
designated *Legal, Accounting, Production,* and so
forth from row to row. Even if the file cabinet keys had
been included on the ring he would not have known
into which cabinets to snoop, or even if the effort
would produce any information that would help him.
He locked the door and went back to Hope Ingress's
desk.

In some other part of the building there was a radio
playing. "Silent Night" was filtering up the elevator
shafts or stairwells.

Sighing, Bryce dropped the key ring back between
the file folders and slammed the drawer. He checked
to make certain he had left nothing out of place on the
desk; then, heels clicking back across the tiles, he
switched off the lights and let himself out.

The security guard was an old man, probably, Bryce
thought, an ex-cop who had taken the job after his
retirement to keep up with the escalating cost of living.
He nodded and touched the brim of his hat in farewell.

The streets were almost deserted. An occasional car passed the intersection of California Street, and the cable car bell clanged noisily as it began its descent of the steep hill. The early morning fog had burned off and the sun was shining brightly, glistening off the steel and glass front of the Multimedia building. The lamp posts and store windows were, of course, decorated for the Christmas season. As Bryce moved along the sidewalk, he thought the decorations somehow seemed depressing. But then tomorrow they would come down and be stored away until next year; as far as he was concerned, they might as well have not been put up at all—he had certainly had no Christmas spirit this year, nor for the past few years. Crime was at its highest during that season: robberies, suicides, murders, rapes.

At the corner of Market Street, he stopped and glanced at his wristwatch. It was still early. But no matter—it was going to be an unproductive day. Even he wouldn't feel right about barging into people's homes today, even though Vanessa Kirkman and Maureen Sterne were still on his list of Multimedia wives to visit. Tomorrow would suffice. This morning he had another call to make; then this afternoon he would spend time going over the information he had compiled on the Hope Ingress case.

He stopped on the corner of California Street and waited for the cable car. Fortunately, it was almost empty. He jumped on and rode through Chinatown, the only area of the city that seemed normal today. The cable car let him off in front of the Fairmont, and he walked down the hill toward Hope Ingress's apartment building.

Like so many San Franciscans, Bryce was offended by the modern steel and glass structure that stood wedged between the old Victorian houses. There was a time when builders had to have modern structures approved, but that had been before the numerous committees of aging residents had put down their banners and ceased marching against "progress." Only a few short years ago you could have driven to anywhere within one hundred miles of San Francisco, said you were going to The City, and everyone understood you meant San Francisco. Now they'd ask, *What city?* Times were changing rapidly—and the apartment building where Hope Ingress had lived was a symbol of those changing times.

The doorman could have been a clone of the security guard Bryce had met at Multimedia. He was in his late sixties with strands of white hair showing beneath his hat. His uniform was the same grey-blue, but instead of a shield on his shoulder he wore gold braid, instead of a pistol a ring of keys was slung from his waist. Watery blue eyes peered out from behind magnifying lenses. "Morning, Inspector Cochran."

Bryce searched through his memory and came up with the doorman's name. "Merry Christmas, Rubin. A lazy morning?"

"Just like Sundays," the doorman said. "I can sit for long spells without jumping up and down." He nodded toward the interior of the building. "Most of 'em hung over and sleepin' in. Will be until afternoon. Then the parties will start again."

Bryce laughed. Reaching into his breast pocket, he drew out an envelope and removed the photographs of several men: the five executives from Multimedia, a mug shot of a felon, a college snapshot of himself and two unknown actors. He handed them to Rubin. "Will you look at these pictures and tell me if you recognize the gentleman who visited Miss Ingress so frequently?"

Rubin adjusted his glasses and moved back into the

shade of the building to reduce the glare of sunlight. "Too young," he said, turning over Bryce's college snapshot. "Too mean-looking," he said of the felon. Of Keith Marston's photo, "Too old." Of one of the actor's, "Too prissy. Again, too old," he said of Larry Linquist.

He's in a real "too" mood today, Bryce thought. It discouraged him that the doorman was turning the photos so rapidly, scarcely taking time to examine them.

Rubin stopped at Mark Kirkman's photo and examined it more closely; then shrugging, he turned it over without comment.

"Ah! Here he is, inspector!" He handed Bryce one of the photographs. "And a good likeness, too."

Bryce found himself staring down at the smiling face of Justin Wade.

Chapter
Thirty-Four

LIZABETH TOOK THE telephone call in the breakfast room.

Merrill was still sleeping; he had told her before retiring that he had no intention of rising before noon. The maid had asked for and been granted the day off, although why Christmas should be a holiday to a Chinese atheist was beyond her. She had been forced to prepare her own breakfast, and since she was no cook the eggs were overdone and the toast burned. Even the coffee was bitter.

She was in a foul mood when she lifted the receiver and snapped, "Hello."

"Mrs. Williams?"

"Yes. Who's this?"

"Albert Coleman."

"Oh." Her voice changed instantly, the tone lowering to a near-whisper as she said, "You couldn't possibly have anything for me so soon, Mr. Coleman. Besides, it's Christmas. My husband is in the house."

"I do have the information you sought," Coleman told her. "Since I do business with Multimedia much of the information was already in my files. It was luck that brought you to me instead of another . . ."

"Luck had nothing to do with it," Lizabeth interrupted. "I was aware that you did business with Multimedia." She pushed strands of her blonde hair away from her face.

"If today isn't convenient . . ."

"No, wait! Where are you calling from, Mr. Coleman?"

"My office."

"Are you so overworked you can't afford holidays?"

"Quite the contrary," Coleman said seriously. "Should I telephone tomorrow?"

"No. I'll come to your office."

"When?"

"Now." Without saying goodbye or allowing him the opportunity to object, she returned the receiver to its cradle and rose from the table.

Upstairs, she peeked into the bedroom and saw that Merrill still slept soundly. She closed the door carefully, hurried back downstairs, and, grabbing her coat from the hall closet, left the house.

Market Street was nearly deserted. There was ample parking on the side streets, but still she parked in a tow-away zone in front of the pre-earthquake building. The building's foyer was empty and her footsteps echoed up the stairwell as she hurried to the ancient-looking elevator. She stepped inside and pressed a button; the gears groaned, the machine jerked and began rising slowly. On the fifth floor, Lizabeth stepped out into another empty hallway. The floors were dirty, entire sections of tiles missing, and the air smelled foul. She couldn't remember if Coleman's office was to the right or left; she went right, struck out, and retraced her steps until she saw the lettering on a frosted glass door: *Coleman Agency, Discretion is our Business.*

Albert Coleman was a small, untidy man in his early

fifties. He had removed his coat, and his shirt looked as if he had slept in it—for days. The cuffs were rolled back over hairy arms. His tie was spotted, the knot loosened and slipped down away from his Adam's apple. He looked up when the door opened and his thin lips parted in a smile. He rose, reached for his coat, decided against the formality, and came forward in his shirt sleeves, fat hand extended. "Merry Christmas, Mrs. Williams."

Lizabeth brushed by him with a nod and seated herself in the wooden chair opposite his desk. His office smelled worse than the hallway, stale cigarette smoke and male perspiration; she raised a gloved hand to her nostrils and inhaled the fragrance of her perfume. "I haven't much time, Mr. Coleman. Should we get directly to business?"

"Certainly, certainly!" He came back behind his desk and sat down. "I apologize for telephoning at an inopportune time, but I realized how anxious you were for this information." He reached for a manila folder, but instead of handing it across to her, rested it against his chest, and folded his arms in front of it as if protecting it from her. His thin lips had frozen into a smile and his dark, beady eyes studied her closely. "You said on the telephone that you were aware I did work for Multimedia. Would you mind telling me how you came by that information?"

"Does it matter?" Lizabeth said impatiently.

"Yes, it could," he told her. He leaned back in his chair and the manila folder slipped into his lap. "As the sign reads, discretion is our business."

"Mine also. Now, may I see the file?"

Ignoring her request, Coleman said, "Companies don't like it generally known that they do business with firms such as mine. Most employees aren't even aware of the extent firms go to to investigate them, especially those in responsible positions. Odd, isn't it, that the firms that report on people's credit have become accepted? They can tell you all sorts of things about a person in a matter of seconds. But a few years ago there were outraged cries against those firms. Cries of invasion of privacy, unjust reporting, secrecy. Now they command a position of respect in any community. You can't sign your name on a sales slip without having it punched into one of their computers. But with agencies like mine it's different."

"It sounds like you need a good P.R. firm," Lizabeth said sarcastically.

The expression in Albert Coleman's eyes didn't alter. "Multimedia is my most prestigious account. I've been with them since they established business in San Francisco. I wouldn't want to lose them because somebody was bandying our business relationship around. So, Mrs. Williams, would you mind answering my original question?"

Lizabeth saw she was going to get nowhere with the revolting little man without admitting, "I saw your agency's name on some personnel files my husband once brought home. When I found I needed the services you supply, I remembered it. It's that simple, Mr. Coleman. Now, if I may see the file on my husband?" She stretched out her gloved hand.

"First, there's a question of the balance due," Coleman said. "Not that I don't trust you, you understand, but I've known many a wife to read such a file, become hysterical, and run from my office in outrage. I'm left with an uncollectible bill."

"I can understand the outrage," Lizabeth said. She opened her purse and drew out an envelope containing the balance of Coleman's fee. She tossed it onto his desk. When she saw that he intended to count the bills before releasing the file, she said angrily, "I can understand the public's repugnance for agencies such as yours, Mr. Coleman. I only regret I had need of your services."

Coleman, seemingly unoffended, continued to count the money. When he had finished and was satisfied, he shoved the bills back into the envelope and deposited it in the top drawer of his desk. With a broadening smile, he extended the manila folder to Lizabeth. "The file on Merrill Williams, your husband," he said, and the smile turned into a smirk.

Lizabeth snatched the file away as she rose from the chair. She had an impulse to slap Coleman across the face with it, but instead, she turned for the door.

"Again, Merry Christmas," Coleman called as she opened the door. "It's been a pleasure serving you."

"Fuck you!" she said as she slammed the door behind her.

The elevator had returned to the first floor. She jabbed the button several times before the arrow above the door began to move.

Waiting, she opened the file and began to read.

The elevator arrived, the doors jerked noisily open—and then closed again.

Lizabeth, slumped against the opposite wall, looked as if she was about to faint.

Chapter
Thirty-Five

IT WAS THE day after Christmas.

Jake had gone eagerly back to work after the one-day holiday, but the children were on vacation for another eight days. Because the sun was shining, they were now in the back yard playing noisily in the pool despite the nip in the morning air. Their shouts and laughter drifted in through the kitchen window and mingled with the rock-and-roll music from the radio on the sill, both driving daggers through Maureen's head.

She sank onto a kitchen stool and stared at the kitchen mess. Last night, as a Christmas treat, Jake and the three children had consented to clean up after the dinner. Thoughtful of them, but they had doubled her work; dishes and pots and pans in the wrong cupboards, grease marks on the refrigerator and stove, distinct footprints on the tiles, leftovers uncovered and stacked haphazardly in the refrigerator. Even the scraps she had raked into a dish for the dog had been sandwiched in between the oddly colored yams and the turkey carcass.

She smiled wearily, lit a cigarette, and sat quietly with her eyes closed. God bless them, she thought. She'd have it no other way. Motherhood might get to her at times, but she wouldn't change places with

Rosemary or Joanna or Lizabeth or Vanessa. Although Vanessa had confessed to her at the Marstons' tree-decorating ceremony that she was pregnant, it was a big secret she was saving as a surprise for Mark on New Year's Eve. She was happy for Vanessa. Oh, to be back there again to when she had become pregnant with her first child! God, those had been happy days! She suddenly had a vision of Vanessa, ready to deliver, checking the baby's astrological charts, and then fighting to hold back delivery for better aspects in the stars and planets, and she burst into laughter.

"You gone crazy, Mom?" It was Moria. She had come quietly through the back door and stood dripping onto the floor.

Moria was at the awkward age, the difficult age. She had grown two inches in six months and was all legs. The tiny pimples of her breasts were scarcely visible beneath the top of her bathing suit. Her teeth were in braces—thank God for Robert Webb, that remarkable dentist who had charmed her into wearing them without protest. Her eyes were bright and intelligent like her father's. Unfortunately, she had inherited her mother's mousy-colored hair and high, sloping forehead—also her tendency to sometimes lapse into shyness.

Maureen looked at her daughter and thought, *Wet she looks like a starving kitten.* "No, I'm not crazy," she said. "I just thought of something amusing. It made me laugh."

Moria came on into the kitchen and slammed the door. "I don't care if you are crazy as long as you laugh," she said. "I like it when you laugh."

"Thank you so much. I prefer laughter to tears myself."

Moria tracked her way to the refrigerator. "No

cokes!" she complained. "I'm going to start hiding the cokes from them." She cast a disapproving glance through the kitchen window toward the pool where her brothers were cavorting.

"Since you're not supposed to have cokes anyway, I think you should be grateful." Maureen slid off the stool and began cleaning the counter. "They're bad for your complexion, among other things, and you know the scene we went through last week when your face broke out."

"That was because of the dance. I like cokes."

"Do you also like pimples?"

"Of course not."

"Then take your choice." She went on cleaning the counter, her back to her daughter, and did not see the sudden anger on the childish face.

Moria took the stool Maureen had vacated. "Booze isn't good for you, but you drink it anyway," she said quietly.

Maureen's hand, scrubbing at the white tiles, stopped. The words sent a sudden stab of pain to her chest. Don't show how much what she has said has affected you, she told herself. With forced cheerfulness, she said, "I'm past the pimple stage," and continued her scrubbing.

"But not the arguing stage," Moria said.

Maureen turned then. She was pale and struggled to control her trembling. Last night she had argued with Jake; he had brought up her drinking again. But it had been late, past midnight; they had thought the children had been sleeping.

"You woke me up," Moria said, her eyes cast down.

"I'm sorry," Maureen said quietly.

Moria glanced at her fleetingly; then away. "About the drinking? Or waking me?" she asked scarcely above a whisper.

Maureen caught her breath in a tormented gasp. She dropped the dishcloth, but didn't trust herself to stoop to pick it up. Her head was swimming, blood pounding at her temples. She had always deluded herself into thinking the children didn't notice her drinking. A closet drinker, that's what she considered herself.

"Mom, I'm sorry," Moria cried. She slid from the stool and dashed across the kitchen to fling her arms around her mother. She buried her face in Maureen's neck, clinging to her tightly. "Why . . . why do you do it?" she sobbed. "Is it because of Daddy? Does he make you unhappy?"

Maureen held her daughter, but didn't trust herself to speak.

Moria pulled back, eyes streaked with tears. "Is it us?" she whimpered. "Do you hate us? My girlfriend Peggy's mother drinks too. Peggy says she told her and her brother it was because . . . because they had stolen her youth away. Mama, I . . ."

"Hush, hush," Maureen murmured. She pulled her daughter back against her and held her. "It's not you. It's not your brothers," she said in a broken voice. "It's not even your father. I love all of you."

"Then why do you drink so much?" Moria asked, her voice muffled against Maureen's neck. "I heard Papa shout at you that you always drink too much when you go out or after we've gone to bed." She pulled back again, breaking their embrace, and looked up into her mother's face with the frank, demanding stare of a child.

Maureen wiped the strands of wet hair away from Moria's eyes. She took her arm and led her to the table, and they both sat down. Moria put her hands on the table, and Maureen covered them with her own. "Listen, sweetheart," she said, "I can't explain the reasons I drink too much. I could give you a lot of

excuses like I give myself . . . but most of them
wouldn't hold water. I will tell you that I thought I was
hiding the fact that I drink too much from you and your
brothers."

Moria averted her gaze.

"Oh, I see. The argument woke them up also?"
Maureen glanced through the window at her two sons;
beautiful sons, loving and intelligent, both very indi-
vidualistic. The stab of pain struck her chest again.
She felt her eyes filling.

"We all cried," Moria murmured. "I buried my face
in a pillow to keep you from hearing." She glanced up
sheepishly, saw the tears in her mother's eyes, and
began to cry herself.

Maureen dried her eyes and tried to stop the tears so
Moria would stop. She squeezed Moria's hands.
"Let's promise each other to stop crying," she murmured. "If we don't, the boys are going to hear us and
come in. We don't want a group cry-in, do we?"

Moria smiled through her tears and wiped the corners of her eyes. "Stop trying to be so with it, Mom,"
she said. "Cry-in, that's kid talk."

"Oh, my apologies. But I promise to stop crying if
you do, okay? I'll promise you something else also. I'll
cut down on my drinking. I may even stop entirely. I'll
be a model mom."

Moria looked at her uncertainly. "That's more than
you promised Daddy. Is that because you love us
more?"

"Not necessarily. Maybe it's because now that you
all know about my drinking I'm outnumbered."
There's certainly something to that, she thought. "I
can't disappoint all of you, the four most important
people in my life. I can't have you thinking I don't love
you when I love you all so very much."

"I love you, too, Mom. I'm sorry I made you cry."

"Ditto."

Maureen fought the impulse to pull Moria into her lap, to hold her as she had when she had been younger, but she understood that her daughter now thought of herself as too grown-up for such childish fondling. Would a child approach her mother about her drinking problem? She patted Moria's hands. "Why don't you get showered and dressed now?" she said. "Your big brother's promised to take you to the mall today to return that sweater you thought was such an ugly color."

"Didn't you think it was ugly? What was he thinking about buying me a sweater like that? Puce! Whoever heard of that color anyway?" She slipped from her chair, gave Maureen a quick peck on the cheek and hurried through the back door.

Maureen sat watching her children for several minutes. The pain in her chest had subsided, but she still felt weighted down. The silent tears welled up in her eyes again and overflowed. She wiped them away impatiently, rose and went to the living room.

The liquor bottles were still sitting on top of the bar. The quart of gin was half-empty. It had been full the day before and she had been too busy preparing Christmas dinner to have indulged until the children had gone to bed. Half a quart in less than two hours. Jake hated gin, so she knew he hadn't helped her consume the missing amount. Sighing, she returned the bottles to the inside of the bar and closed the door—out of sight, out of mind! No, that wasn't good enough.

I'll promise you something else also. I'll cut down on my drinking. I may even stop entirely. I'll be a model mom.

She wondered if she could stop drinking entirely. She had never considered it before, let alone planned a whole struggle. Ten years ago she didn't drink at all. When had she begun the cocktail routine? She couldn't remember. Now, having a few cocktails before dinner was a way of life. When had she started indulging after dinner? Before lunch? Before bedtime? Sometimes in the middle of the night? During the meetings with the other executive wives? She blamed Jake because he had changed their lives by transferring to San Francisco. They had left something behind that was important to her. Exactly what? No, she couldn't go on blaming Jake because he spent more hours at Multimedia than he did with his family. Maybe some change in her was the reason for his longer and longer hours.

Maureen, who had begun pacing about the living room while she had let her mind wander, stopped beside the telephone. She stared down at the instrument for several moments; then picked up the receiver and dialed.

Jake answered his private line almost immediately.

"Jake, it's Maureen." She felt somewhat guilty because she knew he disliked her calling during business hours unless it was an emergency, like the time she had had to rush Moria to the hospital with a burst appendix. Well, this was also an emergency!

"What is it, honey? What's wrong?"

"Jake, about last night . . ."

"Oh," he said, anticipating an apology. "It's all right, Maureen. We'll discuss it tonight."

"No! It's not all right, Jake. And I want to discuss it now. The children heard us."

"Oh, my God!"

"Jake, I had a talk with Moria," Maureen told him. "I think the three of them got together and she was elected to bring up the subject. She asked if I drank too much because I didn't love them. She . . . she . . ." she

304

paused to control her voice . . . "she asked if I hated them or you."

She waited for Jake to speak, but could only hear his breathing on the other end of the line.

"Jake, I have to do something! We have to do something!"

"I know," he said matter-of-factly. "I was going to talk to you tonight. We can't go on like this. If not for our own sake, for the children's."

"I'll call someone," Maureen mumbled. "A doctor. Or Alcoholics Anonymous. I'll call Rosemary. She'll know which is best, what doctor."

"No! Don't do that, Maureen! This is our problem. We'll handle it."

There was a moment of silence, and then Maureen said, "Thank you for saying 'our' problem, Jake." The tears were welling up again, but she held them back. She was surprised that her voice sounded remarkably controlled. "But you're going to have to do more than verbally accept it as a problem. I need more of your time, Jake. So do the children."

She expected his usual argument when she brought up the subject of his long hours at Multimedia, but instead, he said,

"You're going to have much more of me, honey. Probably more than you'll want. Keith announced this morning that he's going outside executive row for Larry's replacement."

"Oh!"

"I know you didn't want me to have that promotion," he said. "Oddly, once I knew it was going to an outsider, I wasn't disappointed. Something else, I've asked for time off until after New Year's. How about you and I and the kids driving down south for a few days?"

"Oh, Jake! I don't . . ."

"We can take them to Disneyland. Maybe we'll even find them a sitter and drive down to Old Mexico, just you and me. I've always wanted to see a bullfight and watch a jai alai game. It'll be the honeymoon we never had time to take."

"Oh, yes, Jake! Yes!"

"We'll leave in the morning." A long pause. "And when we come home we'll both see a doctor. If he advises A.A., we'll go together. They have a chapter for . . ." Jake heard the doorbell ringing on her end of the telephone. "Who's that?"

Maureen glanced impatiently toward the entryway. "Probably one of the children's friends," she said. In a raised voice, she shouted, "They're around at the pool!" She brought the mouthpiece back to her lips. "Jake, I love you."

"And I love you. I'm sorry if sometimes I fail to show it as I . . ."

The doorbell rang again, more persistently.

"All right, I'll let you go, honey," Jake told her. "I'll see you tonight. Goodbye. Oh, and, honey, I'm glad you reached the decision to do something without my trying to force you."

Jake hung up and the line went dead.

Maureen hurried into the entryway, her mood undaunted by the persistent doorbell.

But her smile faded when she opened the door.

"Oh," she mumbled. "Inspector Cochran, isn't it? Come in. I've been expecting you."

Chapter
Thirty-Six

LIZABETH ENTERED THE Multimedia offices and walked past the receptionist's desk without stopping.

Marge, the receptionist, rose from her cubicle to do battle for her job, but before she could shout out a protest, Miss Lynch, who was just returning from the file room, motioned for her to be silent.

"Mr. Williams's wife," she whispered.

Marge settled down, still upset at having her authority ignored, and Miss Lynch moved back to her desk and sat down to watch Lizabeth's determined stride along the executive hallway. She thought Lizabeth Williams looked like a jungle cat who had already decided upon its prey, had ignored the stalking and was charging ahead for the kill.

When Lizabeth reached Merrill's door it was standing open. She heard voices inside, but did not hesitate entering. Merrill was behind the desk; Mark Kirkman was standing behind his chair, studying a chart that had been spread out over the desk top. Lizabeth stopped just inside the door, watching them. She knew what a sight she must present with her no-fury-like-a-woman's-scorn expression. There were dark circles under her eyes because she had not slept since yesterday morning. She wore no makeup and her clothing was wrinkled; even the mink coat she had slung over her shoulders looked the worse for wear.

Merrill saw her out of the corner of his eye. Without looking up, he said, "Miss Lynch, would you . . ." and then he saw her.

She could not make out the expression that came to his face. Mostly, she decided, confusion. She walked across the office and dropped her purse into a leather chair. Without speaking, she went into the bar, poured herself a drink and then pushed it aside.

"Well," Mark said, "we'll go into this later. Good morning, Lizabeth."

Lizabeth nodded at him stiffly as he fled the office. She walked back to the door which he had left ajar, and slammed it.

"Lizabeth, where the hell have you been?" Merrill was on his feet now. He had decided on a particular emotion, and that was anger. His face was flushed and his stare intense. "Jesus Christ! When you weren't home by midnight I called the police and every hospital within a hundred miles. I was frantic with worry! You had no . . ."

Lizabeth silenced him with a wave of her hand. "I went for a long, long drive," she said coldly. "I got in that goddamned car and I drove north along the coast until I ran out of gas. Then I hitched a ride into Eureka and spent the night . . . oh, what the hell am I telling you for? I hope you were frantic. I hope you were so worried it shrank your goddamned prick into your groin!"

"Lizabeth! For Christ's sake, lower your voice! This is a place of business. Keith's office is right next door and the walls are . . ."

"Fuck Keith Marston!" Lizabeth shouted toward the wall.

Merrill, his face contorted with rage, started around

the desk, but Lizabeth's raised fist made him stop. "I've never seen you like this," he said. "What the hell has come over you? Have you gone mad?" If he hadn't been so befuddled by her anger, he would have found her small raised fist comical. If she had actually started to strike him, he could have brushed her aside with the smallest of effort. While she fumed silently, her fist still raised, he leaned against the side of his desk and folded his arms across his chest. "All right," he said. "Calm down and tell me what this is all about."

Lizabeth lowered her fist. Turning her back to him, she moved to the bar and took a swallow of the drink she had poured. The whiskey burned her throat and made her shudder. "Goddamn you, Merrill!" she said without turning. "Goddamn you to hell!" Some whiskey had spilled onto her chin and she wiped it away with the back of her hand. "You lousy fucking degenerate!" She spun to face him as she spat out the accusation. All night she had thought of the expression he would have on his face when she accused him. She had savored it—his shock, anger, guilt and anguish.

But only a flicker of emotion passed over his handsome face, and that he wiped away without effort. He pushed himself away from the desk and returned to his chair. Leaning back, hands folded in his lap, he contemplated her coolly. "Well, well," he said with remarkble composure. "At last the goose finds out the gander is also playing. Wipe that look of disgust off your face, Lizabeth, and sit down." When she continued to stand and glare at him, he shouted, "Sit down!"

He had never screamed at her before; they had argued, she had screamed—but not Merrill; it had often infuriated her that he never lost control during an argument. His sudden shouted command went through her like an electric current. Obediently, she crossed to the chair and sat down. She wanted suddenly to cry. But she knew she wouldn't; not her, not Lizabeth—it wasn't compatible with her image. She crossed her legs, pushed the mink from her shoulders, and continued to glare at him.

"You're a rotten bastard!" she said in a normal voice.

"And you're a whorish bitch," he said. "But we're not going to achieve anything by calling each other names."

"Queer! Hustler! Freak!"

"Are you quite finished?"

"Oh, God! The other names that passed through my mind all night! I even had time to arrange them so they'd rhyme. Do you know how many names there are for someone like you?"

"As many as there are for someone like you, I'm sure," he said. "If you'd like to continue with this childishness, we can each take paper and pencil and compile lists. The winner gets to kick the loser in the ass. How's that for a parlor game?"

"It's not enough!" Lizabeth cried.

"It'll have to do. Now, suppose you start at the brginning."

She stared at him without speaking. His composure was irritating the bejesus out of her. She had expected it to be completely different—for him to beg, plead for her mercy—and she would have driven the dagger of guilt into him up to the hilt. "I hate you," she said.

Merrill lifted his eyebrows in an expression of hopelessness. "From the beginning, Lizabeth? How did you discover this reason for hating me?"

"From a slimy detective agency."

"And what made you employ this slimy agency?"

Lizabeth told him about seeing him with Karl in the studio, seeing him with his arm about the young man's shoulders, his odd look of sexuality as they had entered the dressing room. "I should have suspected all along," she concluded. "What a laugh this will make. Me being married to a homosexual without suspecting."

"Did I give you reason to suspect?"

"Yes. In retrospect, you did," she answered. "All those nights when I couldn't coax you to have sex. That way of yours that I always took for sophistication."

"No one could satisfy you sexually, Lizabeth. No one man. As for that way of mine—I know you're trying to get at me—but there's nothing feminine about it. And as for homosexuality, that's not quite the right label. Bisexuality would be more accurate."

"Bastard!"

"We're not going back to name calling, are we? Should I get out the paper and pencils?" He leaned forward and folded his hands on the desk. "I know you're hurt, Lizabeth, but . . . "

"Hurt! What an ineffectual word! I discover you like the same sex I do, that you were nothing but a male whore, that you married me for my money—and you say you understand it's *hurt* me. You are a master of understatement!" Her voice had risen again. "Step right up, ladies and gentlemen! Meet my husband, the queer, whore, hustler! Oh, sorry! The bisexual, whore, hustler!"

Merrill, flushed again, brushed a hand through his hair; she saw the slight trembling, understood he was not as unrattled as he had been pretending, and felt a measure of satisfaction.

"What's going on in that mind of yours?" she demanded. "Inside, you're terrified, aren't you, my devious darling? You're asking yourself what I'm going to do when I've finished screaming my indignation."

She pushed forward until she was perched on the edge of her chair. "I'll tell you what I'm going to do. I'm going to make you squirm like a worm on the end of a hook. I'm going to take away all the toys I've given you."

"Take them." He managed to smile, almost convincingly.

"I'm going to see that everyone knows just what you are. I'm going to see that you lose this precious job, that you'll never work anywhere in this business again. Then I'm going to divorce you on the grounds of your infidelity with pretty boys." Her eyes had closed to mere slits. "But what I'd like to do is cut your goddamned heart right out of your chest!"

Rising, Merrill stared at her for several moments, a look bordering on pity in his eyes; then he turned, walked to the window, and stood staring out. "I know you'd like to do all those things, Lizabeth. I even believe you could be capable of cutting my heart out of my chest. In ancient cultures you would have made a perfect high priestess. That is, providing you needn't remain a virgin." He turned to her and this time his smile was genuine, if almost satanic. "But the truth of the matter is, my beloved, you will do nothing. Oh, you may take back your gifts. I'm tired of them anyway. But you'll tell no one, and you'll not divorce me. The facts are that simple."

Lizabeth laughed in a deep-throated tone. "If this is a prediction, you're a bad psychic. Just what do you think is going to stop me? Don't tell me you think I still love you after all I've found out about you?"

"You do," he said confidently. "But that isn't what will stop you. Any stones you cast would only become boomerangs. Because of your heritage, we're San Francisco society. Can you imagine what the social set would say if they were told your husband was . . ."

"Fuck San Francisco society!"

"You say it, but you don't mean it," Merrill told her. "You're one of the queens of the social set. Such a scandal would certainly dethrone you. If it didn't, they'd still look at you pityingly, and that would be even more intolerable for you."

"You think you know me so well."

"Yes, I do." Merrill sank back into his chair. "But in case I overestimate my understanding, there's the other side of the coin. There are all those rented apartments and hotel suites. All those young men who have been collected, used, paid, and discarded. *Our* Karl included. What a counter divorce claim I could file. We might even be sought after for interviews by Masters and Johnson. We could become the nineteen eighties Stanford White and Evelyn Nesbit. No, Lizabeth. You won't tell anyone what you've learned. You won't cost me my job, and you won't divorce me. The interesting part of the situation is that you and I are of one kind. We also . . . " Merrill was stopped by the buzzing of the intercom. He depressed the button angrily and said, "I'm not to be disturbed, Miss Lynch."

"But it's Mr. Marston," the secretary's voice stammered.

"Tell him I'll be with him when I'm free." He clicked off the intercom and turned back to Lizabeth.

She had become very still. The fury had gone from her face, her color had returned; still, her brown eyes stared at him unfalteringly. He understood that her screaming had relieved the explosive pressure of the turmoil inside her.

He kept his voice calm as he went on, "Besides, Lizabeth, as odd as it may seem to you, I love you in my own way. We are neither one of us very lovable people, but we love one another."

Lizabeth's eyes blinked several times in rapid succession; he wasn't certain, but he thought she was holding back tears. But then, falling back into the chair in a most unladylike way, she burst into peals of laughter.

Her laughter reverberated about the office and reached his ears with the force of a detonation. He glanced nervously toward the dividing walls separating him on one side from Keith Marston and the other from Justin Wade. If they had not heard her shouting obscenities and accusations, they most certainly heard her laughter. "Lizabeth, control yourself!" He sprang from his chair, rounded the desk, and pulling her to her feet, shook her.

Her laughter ceased long enough for her to say, "That commanding voice of yours worked once, but not a second time." Then her laughter continued, only lower and less etched by hysteria.

Merrill shook her again and was on the verge of slapping her when she pulled suddenly away from him and went to the bar to refill the glass she had left there. Her laughter turned to spasmodic choking sounds almost like sobs. She held her chest with one hand and poured a whiskey with the other, splashing it onto the countertop.

When she turned to him there were tears in her eyes—but not from sadness. A smile still lingered about her lips; only her eyes retained a hint of the fury from her arrival. "You're a smooth one, Merrill Williams. I give you that. You're as smooth as Vaseline on a stretched . . . "

"Lizabeth!"

"Oh, don't pretend I can still shock or offend you," she said. She held the glass of whiskey in front of her and knew he expected her to fling it in his face; he was prepared for it. Instead, she raised the glass in a mock salute before downing the contents. There was complete silence in the office and she could hear noises through the side walls. Her smile returned. "Do you suppose they heard us? Oh, well, you can tell them we've joined a little theater group and have been rehearsing *Who's Afraid of Virginia Woolf*. An updated version." She held the glass over the bar sink; instead of setting it down, she dropped it. It shattered against the steel. Walking back to her chair, she picked up the mink and draped it around her shoulders.

"Where are you going?" he asked, concern mirrored on his handsome face.

"To hell, eventually," she answered. "But for the time being I'm going out to find an occupant to fill one of those apartments or hotel suites. Tell me honestly, how long have you known about *my* hidden life?"

"From the beginning."

"That's certainly honest. Then your jealousy act was only a part of your role as the devoted husband?"

"Not entirely."

"Less honest," she said critically. She took up her purse and walked to the door, hesitating with her hand on the handle. Her expression had changed again; there was neither amusement nor fury in evidence. "You do know me well," she said. "My lust for vengeance died when I confronted you. I'd never expose you, for all the reasons you gave. Especially the last one. Despite everything, I do love you. I guess I always will."

"Then . . . then why the laughter?"

"Because, my darling, it crossed my mind that neither one of us really has any control over our destinies. It really doesn't much matter if I expose you or you me."

"I don't understand," Merrill told her.

"Well, darling, when I went to that slimy detective

agency used by Multimedia it took them less than forty-eight hours to come up with a complete dossier on you. Except for an afternoon tête-à-tête with a young man who must have been Karl at the queer bathhouse you frequent, the entire file was a xerox copy. Who, my beloved, ordered the original investigation? Who else has the power over you I'd never exercise?" Her lips parted in a broad smile, and he thought she was going to burst into another bout of laughter. She opened the door. "Have a pleasant afternoon," she said as she vanished around the frame.

Chapter
Thirty-Seven

WHEN KEITH RETURNED home in the late afternoon, Rosemary was not waiting for him in the drawing room, as was her custom. The house was remarkably quiet; even the cook's radio, often heard through the maze of doors, was silent.

He knew Rosemary was home; her car had been in the driveway and her mink in the closet when he had hung up his topcoat. He stopped outside the drawing room to give himself a quick glance in the gilt mirror. The day had been particularly trying, but he looked no worse for the wear. He brushed a hand through his greying hair, straightened the knot in his tie, and went in to the drawing room to make himself a drink. He made one for Rosemary also; then pulled the old-fashioned bell cord to summon the maid.

When the woman appeared he asked if his wife was in or was indisposed.

"No, sir. I think she's sleeping," the maid answered.

"Then wake her and tell her I'm home," he said, slightly perturbed. He had expected Rosemary to be waiting eagerly to question him; after all, it had been her suggestion that he announce he was going to the outside for Larry's replacement.

317

Merrill Williams had taken the announcement far worse than the others, although Justin had been overcome by a particularly dark, brooding mood, almost like a child, and had left the office early. Mark Kirkman had merely shrugged and gone on with his work, making it obvious he had not expected the promotion anyway. And Jake—odd how Jake had taken it—he had stared at Keith for several moments, and had then burst into unexplainable laughter.

But Merrill had seethed with anger, calling the decision an injustice to those on executive row—especially himself. He had voiced what objections he dared; he had even been on the point of offering his resignation, but had held himself back, knowing Keith would have accepted it.

It was not only the announcement that Keith had been eager to discuss with Rosemary. Since last night, since she had showed him a side of her that had become hidden, he felt different toward her. He didn't love her more—he couldn't love her more than he did—but all day he had thought of her and had felt like a youth in the throws of a first crush. It was time he made an important confession to her.

He carried his drink to the sofa and sat down.

He heard the maid descending the stairs; then Rosemary's slower, dignified steps.

She was wearing a deep blue suit, very tailored, that emphasized her good figure. About her throat, she wore a pale blue silk scarf. Her auburn hair had been brushed to an attractive sheen and was worn loose to frame her face. She was not smiling, and he knew from one quick glance at her eyes that she had been crying.

"Are you ill?" she asked with concern.

She shook her head.

For one dreadful moment he thought she had been drinking or had reverted to the "medications." No—

her eyes were not dilated, there wasn't that slight falter to her steps.

He rose and brought her a drink.

"No, thank you," she said quietly.

He waited for an explanation, but when he saw none was forthcoming he returned to the sofa and sat down facing her. "All right," he said. "Suppose you tell me what's wrong?"

She flinched slightly. "Am I so obvious?"

He said nothing.

"Very well, then," she said with a sigh. "You're going to be very angry with me." She looked at him then with that little-girl expression he found so objectionable.

What did she expect of him when she acted this way? Did she expect him to say, *Daddy won't punish you? It's all right, sweetheart? Nothing you could have done will make Daddy angry at you?* For Christ's sake, she had buried her father years ago! It was all he could do to refrain from screaming this last thought. It had been on his mind so many times in the past. He felt a sinking sensation. Rosemary had been so . . . different these past weeks. Was he going to see all his hopes crumble tonight? Aloud, he said, "Why would I be angry with you, Rosemary?"

But then a change came over her. She pulled herself erect in her chair and lifted her chin to a defiant tilt. The large, brown eyes that fixed themselves on him were cool and probing. "If you are angry, so be it," she said firmly. "There are certain things I will tolerate, and there are those I will not. Should you decide to follow through on your threat . . ."

"Threat? What are you talking about?"

"Patricia!" she said, spitting out the name. "I've thrown her out of the house!"

Keith stared at her; then, suddenly understanding

Jake Sterne's reaction that afternoon, burst into laughter. The irony of it was too much to let pass without enjoyment.

Rosemary's expression turned to one of puzzlement. "I . . . I fail to see . . ." She could not make herself heard over his laughter. She waited until his laughter had subsided before saying, "I couldn't bear the woman in my house any longer. Aside from the arrangement, which I've decided I could never go through with, she was making my life and the lives of the servants utterly miserable. She had taken over the running of everything! Today when she moved the furniture around again in my private room I could take no more. I'd warned her before that I would not tolerate . . ." She stopped suddenly, aware that Keith was smiling broadly. "I fail to see what you find so amusing! I expect you to come home and do battle with me, and you burst into laughter. Now you sit there smiling at me like the Cheshire Cat from *Alice in Wonderland!*"

"I was thinking you must have been magnificent with your anger aroused," he told her.

Rosemary paled with confusion.

"I'm glad you threw her out of the house," he said with a wink.

"You . . . You . . . oh, I see. You'd decided you didn't like your choice," she said. "You're glad I did the dirty work for you!" Her confusion was turning to anger. *Damn you,* she thought. *You'll see how magnificent I was this afternoon with that bitch!* She started to rise.

"No, no! You don't understand," Keith said. He set his drink aside and rose. Coming to her chair, he bent down beside her, taking her hands in his. "I hadn't planned to tell you like this, Rosemary, but . . ."

The ringing of the doorbell cut into his words.

"Dammit!" he said. "Are you expecting anyone?"

Rosemary told him she was not.

"Then let them go away."

But the maid had already hurried into the hall and was opening the door.

Keith and Rosemary heard Joanna's voice: "Is Mrs. Marston home?"

There was something in the tone of Joanna's voice that made Rosemary gently push Keith's hands aside and rise. She stepped to the door and motioned for the maid to admit the woman.

Joanna's desperation was mirrored on her face.

"Rosemary, can you come with me to the police station? Justin's been arrested for Hope Ingress's murder!"

Chapter
Thirty-Eight

BRYCE WAS WEARY beyond words.

It had been a sleepless week; he'd existed on no more than four hours sleep a night since the Ingress murder. When Justin Wade had been arrested, he had thought, *Sleep, at last!* He had even gone home, showered, and climbed into bed. But sleep had not come. Small details nagged him and finally loomed up so strongly that he had risen, dressed, and returned to the stationhouse. It had been his intention to go over the files again, even to question Justin Wade again— some piece of the puzzle was not falling into place.

But when he entered the stationhouse, Joanna Wade and the Marstons were just leaving. Keith Marston had insisted on talking to him, and he had reluctantly invited them into his office. Marston had been very much the executive, trying to take charge, making demands:

"A mistake," he had kept saying. "If you'll listen to what Joanna . . . Mrs. Wade has to say, you'll understand you've made a grave error in arresting her husband."

Bryce sighed wearily. Leaning back in his creaking desk chair, he fixed his gaze on Marston. "I would like nothing more than to hear what Mrs. Wade has to say," he said, "but I'm afraid it's difficult to speak over you."

Marston's lips closed firmly. With an angry wave of his hands, he turned and leaned his weight against the door frame. Bryce had a feeling he was upset about more than Justin Wade's arrest. Perhaps, he thought, he's afraid of his wife being here, afraid I'll mention the files and the damning account of his earlier mistake. Actually, he sympathized with Keith Marston. If he allowed himself, he could even like the man.

Joanna Wade had been in tears. She presented a far different image than the one she had given during his visit to her Sausalito home. She sat, shoulders humped over, and reminded Bryce more of the victim of a crime than the wife of a man arrested for committing one. Again, if he allowed himself, he could feel sympathy for her. She was beautiful, distressed, and, no matter how long he remained a cop, no matter how he hardened himself, he would always be susceptible to a beautiful woman in distress.

Rosemary Marston sat in the chair beside Joanna Wade, her arm protectively about the younger woman. If she had been older, she could have been mistaken for Joanna Wade's mother; the anger in her eyes said that she was ready to do battle to protect her charge. She met Bryce's gaze steadily. "My husband didn't mean to be rude, inspector," she said firmly. "Nor do I." But I will be if it's necessary, her tone conveyed. "But what Joanna has to tell you is important." She glanced at Joanna. "Since Joanna is too distraught, I'd like to tell you myself."

Keith, his eyebrows coming together to form the question on his mind, stepped away from the door frame. Joanna had told them nothing in the car except that she knew Justin was innocent. That meant that Rosemary had known all along—

"First," Rosemary said, "we'd like to know what evidence against Justin prompted his arrest."

Bryce, because of his exhaustion, felt his patience growing short.

"I realize this is out of the ordinary," Rosemary told him. "I assume you arrested Justin because you discovered his affair with Hope Ingress."

Keith's mouth fell open.

"Maureen Sterne must have told you," Rosemary went on. "I told her she must when you got around to your visit to her."

"Rosemary!"

Rosemary only glanced fleetingly at Keith. "I didn't withhold that evidence from you," she said quickly to Bryce. "I wasn't aware of the . . . the situation when you visited me."

Bryce smiled. "You seem to have withheld it from your husband," he said, noting Keith's astonishment.

"I was afraid my husband would fire Justin without consideration," she admitted.

"Consideration for whom?"

"For Joanna," Rosemary answered. "It wasn't until the night of the Christmas tree decorating that I discovered Joanna was also aware of Justin's indiscretion."

"But you still didn't inform your husband?"

Rosemary glanced apologetically at Keith. "No," she answered honestly. "My husband's chief concern was for the reputation of his company. I was afraid he would fire Justin immediately, and his dismissal would be paramount to an accusation."

"But if Mr. Wade was . . ."

"Oh, but Joanna knew Justin wasn't guilty," Rosemary interrupted. "She saw . . ."

Joanna straightened in her chair. "I can take over, Rosemary," she said, suddenly in control. "I know my husband didn't murder his mistress, inspector." She pushed her hair from her face with a trembling hand. "I . . . I was torturing him by not telling him I knew he was innocent. Oh, God! You must think me disgusting! But when I found out about his affair with that woman, I was . . . was so . . ."

"You needn't go into that," Rosemary told her. "You don't have to defend yourself." She glanced at Bryce for confirmation.

"If you'd just tell me how you know your husband is innocent," Bryce said patiently.

Joanna steadied herself. She opened her purse and took out a cigarette, one of the elegant brown cigarettes, specially ordered from a New York firm, that Bryce had found in Hope Ingress's ashtrays—cigarettes smoked by both Justin and Joanna Wade.

Bryce rose from behind his desk to light her cigarette, noting that she, like her husband, placed the cigarette between her lips straight from the packet without turning it, therefore lighting the end containing their name stamped in gold lettering.

Joanna inhaled deeply and turned to exhale the smoke away from Rosemary. The cigarette seemed to calm her frayed nerves, and Bryce allotted her several puffs before asking:

"Will you go on, Mrs. Wade?"

Joanna nodded. She told him in detail of coming to suspect Justin of seeing another woman, of promising her friend Max Whitely one of her paintings for his gallery to follow Justin on Sunday, of his confirming telephone call. "When you visited me, you mentioned that a neighbor had told you both my husband and I left our house on Sunday," she concluded. "That was true. I drove to the address Max gave me. I . . . I wanted to see Justin with the woman myself. I parked in the bus zone across from the building. I didn't know exactly what I was going to do. I thought of going inside, asking the doorman which apartment my husband had gone to, and going up to knock on the door. I wanted to confront them together. I . . . I didn't want Justin to be able to lie to me later so I'd . . ." she glanced at Keith and Rosemary with embarrassment . . . "so I'd believe him. I'm very gullible where Justin is concerned." She took another puff of her cigarette, leaned forward and crushed it out in Bryce's overflowing ashtray. "I guess that's because I love him so much," she murmured. "Anyway, I was still sitting in my car trying to work up the courage to enter the building when Justin came out. I suddenly felt so . . . so guilty and cheap for having followed him. It was like that with Justin and me. If I accused him of something, he had a way of putting me on the defensive and shaming me into believing in his innocence.

"When he came out of the building I slumped down in the car seat and opened a magazine, praying he wouldn't see me. If I had confronted him at that moment, I would have become hysterical and achieved nothing. When I looked up again, he was gone.

"I was still sitting there a few minutes later when . . . when I heard that dreadful scream and something . . . and Hope Ingress struck the sidewalk. Oh, God! The sound of that will never leave my . . ." Covering her face with her hands, Joanna again broke into tears.

Rosemary moved closer to comfort her.

"So you see, Cochran," Keith said, coming forward, "your arrest of Justin Wade was a mistake." But Keith's forcefulness had left him; the statement came out more like a question. "You will, of course, release him immediately."

Bryce, ignoring Keith, sat staring at the weeping Joanna. After several moments, he said, "I think not,

Mr. Marston." To Joanna, whose hands had come away from her face, he said, "I'm sorry, Mrs. Wade."

"But why not?" Rosemary demanded. "You've heard Joanna give him an alibi! Justin had left the building before Miss Ingress plunged to her death."

"What I heard," Bryce said slowly, "is that Mrs. Wade saw her husband come out of the building. Then, because she did not want to be discovered spying on him, she hid her face behind a magazine." He leaned forward, folding his hands on his desk top. "Who's to say he did not reenter the building, perhaps still angry over their fight, and return to her apartment to throw her from the balcony?"

Keith started to speak, but Bryce silenced him by raising a hand.

"Again, I'm sorry, Mrs. Wade," Bryce said, "but I can't release your husband. There's too much damning evidence against him."

"Are you referring to those files?" Keith asked; then, realizing what he had said, turned away to hide the expression he could not keep from his face.

"Justin told me about the files," Joanna said quickly. "Miss Ingress brought them home from the office so Justin could study them. He thought if he could learn about Larry's contacts, perhaps steal one away before Keith had decided on Larry's replacement, he would have an advantage."

"Contacts?" Bryce murmured with sudden interest.

"People Larry did business with," Joanna explained. "Station managers, ad agency executives, sponsors. Larry apparently kept a rather personal file on most of them."

Bryce and Keith exchanged glances.

And Rosemary took note of them.

Finally, Keith said, "When bail is set tomorrow, we'll be here, Cochran. And when your mistake is proven, you're going to be made to look like quite a fool."

Rosemary entered the house and, without waiting for Keith, climbed the stairs to their bedroom.

When he came upstairs she was sitting on the edge of the bed, still dressed. He removed his coat and placed it over the back of the metal valet. "Don't distress yourself," he said. "You begged her to come home with us, but she refused. Maybe she'll be more comfortable in her own house even if she is alone."

"I wasn't thinking about Joanna," Rosemary murmured. "Not entirely."

"Then why are you sitting there staring so thoughtfully into space?" he asked. "We'll have Justin out of there within twenty-four hours. He'll be back with Joanna until he's proven innocent. We have twelve of the best corporate lawyers in the country at our disposal. Certainly, with their contacts, they can bring in the best criminal lawyers for his defense."

Sighing, Rosemary rose from the bed and moved to her vanity table. She sat down and stared at her reflection—and Keith's behind her as he continued to undress. "I have a feeling Joanna won't take Justin back," she said quietly. "Innocent or guilty."

"Perhaps you're right," he said. "That's not our concern."

Rosemary watched him slip out of his underwear and into his pajamas. Then she turned on the stool to face him. "Why did you go back into the inspector's office to talk to him after we were in the lobby?" she asked.

Keith didn't answer immediately. He finished buttoning his pajama top before saying, "I merely wanted to tell him I'd see that Justin wouldn't be pushed around. Also that I wanted to prevent anything from getting into the newspapers that mentioned Multimedia."

"I almost believe you," she said.

"Almost?"

"It had something to do with the files, didn't it? I saw you and the inspector exchange glances when Joanna mentioned files on Larry's contacts. The inspector may be rather deadpan, but he displayed surprise when they were mentioned. I asked myself why. He brought up the question of the files at the cemetery. He also came here to discuss them with you that same evening."

Crawling into bed, Keith said, "You merely misjudged his expression, Rosemary."

"I think not," she said. Rising, she moved to the side of the bed and stood staring down at him. "There were other files, weren't there?" she insisted. "A second set?"

"No! Quit second guessing, and come to bed!"

"Keith, tell me one thing? Why did Larry retire? It wasn't voluntary, was it? You found out about the client files, and you forced him to retire or resign?"

"All right, yes!" he answered, exasperated. He angrily pulled the blankets about his chin and turned over in bed so that he faced away from her. "I'm tired. It's been one hell of a day! Come to bed."

Rosemary stared at the lump of blankets for several moments; then she switched off his lamp. "I can't sleep," she told him. "I'm going to read. Downstairs."

Chapter
Thirty-Nine

ROSEMARY GLANCED at the mantel clock. It was eight in the morning.

Upstairs, Keith was probably stirring, getting dressed for work. In the kitchen, she could hear the cook preparing breakfast; his radio was blaring and a loud, modern tune reached through the house whenever the maid opened or closed the kitchen door. The street traffic had grown heavier. The foghorns were blaring; she needn't rise and open the draperies to know what sort of day it was.

She had sat all night, not reading, as she had told Keith she wanted to do, but merely staring into space, thinking. In half an hour, Keith would come downstairs; he would be angry at her for staying up all night. She had practiced what she would say to him. She would tell him she felt responsible for Joanna's problem, for Justin's, even for that unfortunate secretary's fate, because she had meddled in the promotion. If it had not been for the promotion, things would be as they had been. But now that the time had almost come to confront Keith, she wanted to avoid the conversation. She knew he would not level with her; he did not want to burden her with realities.

But she had come to some conclusions on her own.

Rising suddenly, she slipped into the entryway and glanced toward the staircase, half expecting to see Keith descending. Before he could suddenly materialize, she took her coat from the closet and slipped out the door. The limousine was still in the driveway; she considered summoning the chauffeur, but decided against it. It was not far from Nob Hill to Russian Hill; she could walk. The fog was heavy; she could scarcely see the headlights of the cars on the street. She pulled the collar of her mink coat about her neck and hurried through the gate. Her heels made a dull clicking sound on the sidewalk. She had forgotten a scarf and the wet fog was taking the curl from her hair, but the dampness on her face revived her and drove away her need to sleep.

Larry and Janet Linquist lived in a three-story Victorian atop Russian Hill. The house's reconstruction, remodeling, and decorating had been Janet's major occupation during the past eight years.

As the familiar house emerged out of the fog, Rosemary's footsteps slowed. There was a light burning in an upstairs window but none below. Perhaps Larry was going to work late today—or not at all—and she wanted to see Janet alone. She chided herself for not having called, and was about to go in search of a telephone booth when she saw the automatic garage door opening, the interior light beaming out into the driveway. She stepped back until the fog swallowed her from sight, listening to the engine of Larry's car as it backed into the street and then crawled away down the hill.

Janet answered the door herself. "Rosemary!" Her surprise was evident. Still wearing a housecoat, she pulled the front together with a nervous hand.

"I'm sorry I didn't call first," Rosemary said as she stepped into the narrow entryway. "I hope you don't object to giving a friend a cup of coffee."

"No, of course not. It's still hot. Larry just left for work." She took Rosemary's coat and hung it in the hall closet.

"I saw him leaving," Rosemary said. She followed Janet down the hallway and into the kitchen.

The maid was there, cleaning up the breakfast dishes. At Janet's request, she got down cups and saucers, filled them, and then went silently back to her work.

"We can go into the living room," Janet murmured. In a near-whisper, she added, "Sally hates anyone in her kitchen, even me."

The living room was decorated with Victorian furniture; heavily carved pieces with dark, flocked upholstery fabric. The polished wood floors were covered in the center by a hooped rug. Coals glowed in the fireplace; *someone else had had a difficult night sleeping,* Rosemary thought. Because of the weather the room was in semi-darkness. Janet set down her coffee cup and moved around the room turning on lamps. When she sat down her hands trembled as she picked up her cup.

"Is there anything wrong, Rosemary?" she asked quietly. "Did you and Keith . . . ? No, that's a ridiculous question. I've never even known you and Keith to argue." She sipped her coffee, staring at Rosemary over the rim of the cup. She had not yet combed her hair; a grey wisp had straggled from under a clip and swayed about her face.

Rosemary had never seen Janet without makeup. It shocked her to see the age on the woman's face. "Justin Wade was arrested last night for Hope Ingress's murder," she said.

"Oh!" Janet, not trusting her hands to hold her coffee cup any longer, slipped it onto the coffee table. "That's dreadful," she said. "Poor Joanna!"

"Yes. Poor Joanna. And poor Justin."

Janet lowered her gaze. "I never knew Justin well," she said. "To me, he was always just Joanna's husband."

"I really don't think any of us knew one another well," Rosemary said. "Even we wives. We were too busy with our little game of aping our husbands' careers, testing our power. Of course, I was the most guilty, so busy playing *Mrs. President.*" She sat forward in her chair, legs crossed at the ankles, coffee cup and saucer balanced on her knee. "You haven't bothered with our meeting in some time, Janet."

"No. Well, with Larry retiring . . ." She opened a ceramic box on the table and took out a cigarette, although Rosemary had never known her to smoke.

"Even for several weeks before that," Rosemary murmured. "How far in advance did you know of Larry's decision?"

"Oh, only a few days. You know how secretive Larry is. He waited to tell me until just before informing Keith. It took me by complete surprise." She lit her cigarette, puffed without inhaling, and blew out the smoke. "But now that I've adjusted," she said more cheerfully, "I'm delighted. I've collected brochures from the travel agency and I'm planning an extended cruise. Larry needs to get away, so do I. San Francisco is so gloomy during the foggy season." She turned her head and glanced through the front windows. Head still turned, she asked, "How is Joanna taking it?"

"Not well," Rosemary answered. "She learned about his affair one day and a few days later he's taken away and booked for murder. But, of course, she knows he's innocent."

Janet's head snapped back.

"She was there outside Miss Ingress's apartment building when Justin came out," Rosemary explained. "Shortly after she heard Miss Ingress's screams and saw her hit the sidewalk."

"Oh! Then why hasn't she told that to the police?"

"She has. But they don't believe her. After all, she's a loving wife giving testimony to save her husband." Rosemary set her coffee cup on the table beside Janet's. "I think that's the one thing we wives all have in common," she said. "We all love our husbands dearly. Even Lizabeth, whom none of us ever understood."

"Yes, I suppose that's true," Janet agreed. "More coffee?"

"No, thank you. In the years we've known one another, we've never become intimate friends, Janet. I don't feel any of us have, not really."

"I'm sorry you feel that way."

"So am I," Rosemary murmured. "We all need close friends to talk to, to share things with. Like the last time you and Larry attended my dinner party. You suddenly unburdened yourself to me, remember? You were distraught because you said you didn't understand Larry's reason for early retirement. You thought maybe he was seriously ill and was hiding it from you."

"Yes. But now I know that isn't true."

"You wanted me to question Keith to see if Larry had given him a reason for retirement," Rosemary went on. "Why did you do that, Janet?"

"I . . . I don't understand." The cigarette trembled between her fingers.

"You knew then why Larry had retired," Rosemary

said bluntly. "You only wanted to know if I knew, if Keith had told me. I do know now, Janet. I know that Keith gave him the choice of retirement or dismissal."

Janet's eyes widened. "I . . . I didn't know," she mumbled weakly.

"I believe you did," Rosemary told her. "You knew about the files Larry kept. You always used to brag at our meetings that Larry told you everything."

"No, I told you Larry was a secretive man!"

"Secretive about his thinking, his feelings," Rosemary recalled, "but not about his business. You said he often bragged to you about his successes. Who else could he brag to? He couldn't brag to an associate about those disgusting files. He knew they were unethical and that a business associate would be offended by such a devious practice."

Anger flared in Janet's eyes, but, as if she could not sustain it, it died quickly. She slumped back in her chair, eyes watering, her cigarette hanging loosely from her fingers.

Rosemary wanted to stop, to rise and run from the house, but she knew that unless she continued now her purpose would be lost. "How did Larry discover that Hope Ingress was stealing his files to assist Justin in obtaining the promotion?" she asked.

Janet stared at her for several moments before answering weakly, "He didn't. Keith had demanded the files be destroyed, and they were. But apparently Miss Ingress found them before Larry had them shredded."

Rosemary took a deep breath before saying, "And the second set of files?"

Janet gave a little gasp and pushed herself erect in her chair. "Oh, God! You know about those also!"

Rosemary nodded, her gaze not faltering.

"But even Keith didn't know about *those* files!" Janet said. "Only Larry and . . . and that bitch!"

"Miss Ingress?"

Janet nodded. "The dossiers Larry had compiled on company employees were kept in his private file cabinet in his office. He was the only one with a key and . . ."

"Company employees?"

Janet looked up as if a jolt of current had suddenly passed through her body. "Damn you, Rosemary! You didn't know!"

"But I do now," Rosemary said with satisfaction. "That explains so much." She rose slowly. "That's why the inspector paid visits to all the wives. He thought Miss Ingress was blackmailing one of our husbands, perhaps all of them, and that one of them had killed her because of it." She stared down at Janet. "But why would Larry compile dossiers on Multimedia employees? He had the top position under Keith. What was his purpose?"

"Not blackmail," Janet said stiffly, reading the thought in Rosemary's mind.

"Then why?"

"Job security," Janet answered quietly. "He knew that sooner or later the younger men would be after his position. That they'd try to force him out. That's a sad fact of business and old age."

"And he'd use something in their files against them? But the mandatory retirement age? Larry only had a few years to . . ."

"Your husband was included in those files," Janet interrupted with a veiled smile. "You may criticize Larry and call him unethical and disgusting, but don't pride yourself on thinking your husband is a saint. There were things in his past, things Larry had intended to use when the time came that his retirement was called for. I daresay Keith would have contemplated a change in retirement policy."

"Then why didn't Larry use this information—if there really was anything—when Keith gave him a choice of retirement or dismissal?" Rosemary demanded.

"Because he had promised me not to," Janet answered. "After what happened to Howard Barrett, neither of us . . ." She broke off the sentence, realizing she had said more than she ought to.

"Howard!" Rosemary cried. "Oh, my God, Janet! You can't mean that Larry used something against Howard that drove him through that window!" Rosemary dropped back into her chair. "But why?"

Janet looked stricken. "For the same reason Larry expected the younger men to try to push him out eventually," she murmured. "For his position. Don't look so stunned, Rosemary. You're no naive girl. You've played *Mrs. President* long enough to understand the business world. It's *King of the Mountain*. It's not only getting there that counts, but staying there. God help him, but Larry got there. He hasn't had a day's peace since. Not only has he had to live with the guilt of Howard's suicide, but also with the threat that the younger men would one day do the same to him. He had those files compiled to protect himself. When Keith discovered the existence of the other files, those on ad executives and station managers, Larry contemplated using Keith's dossier against him . . ."

"And you don't call that blackmail?"

"He only contemplated it," Janet said strongly. "He had promised me when Howard threw himself through his window that he'd never use the dossiers again. Believe me, that's been something to live with. He didn't suspect Howard would do anything like that. I think Larry even forgot those dossiers were in his file cabinet until the other files were discovered. If only he had shredded them immediately, both sets of files . . ."

"Then Miss Ingress would be alive today," Rosemary finished.

A silence fell between them. Janet, unable to meet Rosemary's steady gaze, looked away. Outside, automobile tires squealed on the wet pavement. The maid was singing in the kitchen. A clock somewhere in the house was ticking noisily; floorboards creaked. Above all this, Rosemary heard the rapid beating of her own heart.

Quietly, she said, "And would you have stood silently by while Justin suffered for a crime he didn't commit?"

Janet looked up, but her expression was unfathomable.

"As you stood by when they all said Howard's suicide was caused by grief over his son's death?" Rosemary pressed.

"What good would it have done to confess?" Janet murmured. "Howard was dead. A confession wouldn't have brought him back."

"Justin isn't dead. You could save both him and Joanna a great amount of unpleasantness."

"You're assuming I know Justin isn't guilty," Janet said.

"I'm not assuming," Rosemary countered. "I know now he didn't kill her. The only thing I don't know is why it was necessary to kill Miss Ingress. Did she intend to use the files for the same purpose as Larry? To blackmail company employees? To blackmail Larry for having used the dossier against Howard?"

Janet, her composure suddenly crumbling, broke into sobs.

Rosemary went into the hallway and retrieved her coat. When she came back into the living room she stooped beside Janet's chair and took her hands. "I understand your wanting to protect your husband," she said quietly. "I can't tell you how sorry I am for Larry, and for you. But it's now out of your hands, Janet. If Larry doesn't come forward and confess . . ."

Janet's head shot up. She pushed Rosemary's hands away. "You still don't understand," she said in a broken voice. Rising, she moved to the fireplace, supported one hand on the mantel and stood staring into the coals. "Miss Ingress called the Saturday afternoon we attended your dinner party," she said distantly. "She asked to speak to Larry. I recognized her voice. I'd spoken to her often enough on the telephone, and I guess I'd made special note of it because of what Larry had told me. He didn't like Miss Ingress working for him, not because she wasn't efficient, but because he knew she had been close to Howard and Kathleen. Seeing her in his office, Howard's old office, awakened his guilt. I told her Larry wasn't available and I pressed for the reason for her call. I think I suspected the reason, because my heart was racing and my throat had gone dry.

"I was persistent. I could tell she was upset and I played on it. She finally told me. She was quite blunt. She had been bringing home Larry's files on ad executives and station managers and sponsors for Justin, her lover. He had promised her he would leave Joanna if he was promoted into Larry's position. I told her I thought she was a fool, that Justin Wade was using her, he'd never leave Joanna. Why should he? He had everything he wanted—Joanna's wealth and position, and her as a mistress.

"She became furious. I think she had been drinking. She called me some choice names and said I had no right to judge Justin when I had a husband whose vile business practices had murdered a good man like Howard Barrett.

"I must have cried out, because she started to laugh then. She told me she'd found those files also, that unless Larry came forward and recommended Justin to Keith for the promotion she'd see that it was made public that he drove Howard through the window. 'Murder!' she screamed. 'Your husband is a murderer!'

"I tried to reason with her then. I told her Larry's recommendation would mean nothing, but she insisted Keith would listen to him. I even offered to pay for her silence, but she laughed even louder. She said the only thing that would buy her silence was for Justin to be promoted so they could be together. If Larry didn't see to it, she'd destroy him.

"I concluded by promising to do what I could. I told her I would get back to her on Monday."

Janet turned away from the fireplace. Moving back to her chair, she sat down, leaned back, and closed her eyes.

"And that's why Keith and Larry were in the study so long after dinner?" Rosemary murmured. "You convinced Larry to support Justin?"

"No. I didn't even tell him about the phone call," Janet said. "He was upset enough about the forced retirement. He was trying to reason with Keith, to convince him to change his mind. But, of course, he failed. Your husband is very determined and stubborn. Have you ever seen a grown man cry, Rosemary? Well, Larry cried that night. It tore me apart, and I knew I couldn't tell him about Miss Ingress's threat. I couldn't add to his distress."

Rosemary, who had remained standing, suddenly felt her legs go weak. She moved quickly to a chair and sat down. "Then . . . then it was you . . . who . . ."

Almost in a monotone, Janet said, "I went to Miss Ingress's apartment late Sunday afternoon. I wanted to reason with her in person. The doorman was busy getting a taxi for a tenant and didn't see me go in. I got her apartment number from the mail box and took the elevator up. I was about to knock on her door when I heard the argument inside. I couldn't make out all the words, but I recognized Justin's voice. When I heard him coming toward the door I hurried down the hall and hid myself in a doorway. He didn't even glance in my direction. When the elevator door closed behind him I came out and went back to Miss Ingress's apartment. I was about to knock when I noticed Justin had left the door ajar. I simply stepped inside and closed the door. The apartment was dark except for a light coming from the bedroom. I don't know how long I stood there in the darkness. I saw her come out of the bedroom. She must have heard the sound of my foot striking the divider when I was shifting my weight, because she looked as if she expected someone—perhaps Justin—to be there. But she didn't see me. She went back into the bedroom and came out again with a cigarette. She sat smoking and I stood watching the glow of her cigarette in the darkness.

"I still don't understand why I didn't just step forward and confront her. I wasn't planning anything. Not until she stepped out onto the balcony. Then I thought how easy it would be to silence her forever and eliminate the threat to Larry."

Janet covered her face with her hands. Through splayed fingers, she sobbed, "It only took one shove. She lost her balance and tried to save herself by clutching at some potted plants, but they pulled out of the soil and . . .

"There were so many people running around outside the building and on the street that no one saw me leave. I remember staggering to the corner and climbing aboard a bus." Janet pulled her hands away from

341

her face. Her cheeks were streaked with tears. Sighing, she leaned forward toward Rosemary. "You may not believe this," she said, "but it's a relief having told you. I couldn't bring myself to tell Larry, although I've wanted to every moment since it happened."

"Janet, I . . . I . . ."

"It's not necessary to say anything," Janet told her. She rose and brushed away the tears with her fingers. "I know what I must do. I don't need you, as a friend or as *Mrs. President,* to tell me. I would appreciate it, as a friend, if you would accompany me downtown and . . . and if Keith would see that Larry isn't . . ."

The doorbell cut her off.

Both Janet and Rosemary were standing in the middle of the living room staring through the open doors into the hallway as the maid's heels clicked along the floorboards to answer the bell. They both heard:

"Is Mrs. Linquist in? My name is Inspector Cochran."

Rosemary slipped her arm around Janet to offer what support she could.

Epilogue

THE FOG HAD burned off and the afternoon sunlight was glistening off the bay. Outside Rosemary's drawing room windows, the shrubs were alive with chirping birds. Inside, there was a gloom the afternoon sun had not touched.

The wives had gathered to discuss Janet's arrest, but little had been said. Even Lizabeth, usually the first to offer an opinion or make an outrageous statement, was remarkably subdued. She sat cross-legged on the French sofa, holding a drink she had not touched and staring into the space of the room, lost in her own thoughts. Maureen was drinking soda water with a twist of lemon, also unusual, and Joanna, taking a sheet of paper and a pen from the desk, sat doodling.

Vanessa, since her arrival, had sat with her attention riveted to a book. "Ah, here it is!" she suddenly cried. "Mars in Taurus. That's what Janet is. A Taurus. A very bad aspect. Mars eclipsing . . ."

"Vanessa, please," Rosemary said with controlled impatience. "I don't think this is the time for an astrological chart." She turned away from the window where she had been standing watching the sailboats on the bay, and moved back to the sofa beside Lizabeth. She could not shake the image of Janet being led away by the police; she had appeared so old, so vulnerable.

"I was only trying to make Janet's . . . her action understandable," Vanessa said in an injured tone.

"I don't think you'll find understanding in astrology," Lizabeth said. "Not for Janet. Not for . . . not for any of us." She lifted her glass, forced a smile, and said, "L'chaim," and drained the contents.

"To life," Maureen echoed, sipping her soda. Despite the sad occasion, there was, Rosemary determined, a glow about Maureen. There was a sparkle in her eyes and she seemed less nervous, less preoccupied and eager to take her leave.

Joanna also joined the toast, only adding, "To art."

We've changed, Rosemary thought. We've all changed. With the possible exception of Vanessa, who still sought understanding of herself, her friends, of life in her astrology books.

Vanessa, as if aware of Rosemary's eyes on her, looked up from her book. "I'm glad it was Janet," she said.

For an instant they all looked shocked.

"Instead of one of us," Vanessa explained. She glanced at Joanna. "Or one of our husbands."

Rosemary felt a painful twinge.

Lizabeth laughed. "Leave it to Vanessa to express what we all feel," she said. Rising, she gathered up her purse. "It's true, isn't it? Admit it. We're a close-knit little group, and Janet was no longer one of us. Even if her Mars wasn't in Taurus, better Janet than one of us." All eyes on her, she started for the door. Hesitating, she turned, addressing no one in particular, "Have you considered what all of this has done to us?"

By *all of this* it was understood that Lizabeth meant more than just Janet's crime.

No one answered Lizabeth's question.

"We've learned something about ourselves," Lizabeth said. "As for myself, I feel I have new dimensions to explore. And us? Well, we no longer have to mimic our husbands. It was a foolish game anyway. If we continue these meetings, we can use them for a worthwhile purpose. To become genuine friends." Her gaze swept over the wives. "I'd like . . ." she faltered . . . "to be friends," she said.

Rosemary rose from the sofa and crossed to Lizabeth. She touched Lizabeth's arm with affection, leaned forward and brushed her lips against the blonde's cheek. "Friends," she said quietly.

Behind her, she heard the others echo almost simultaneously, "Friends."